SECOND SIGHT

SECOND SIGHT

A PAUL CHRISTOPHER NOVEL

Charles McCarry

A DUTTON BOOK

DUTTON
Published by the Penguin Group
Penguin Books USA Inc., 375 Hudson Street,
New York, New York 10014, U.S.A.
Penguin Books Ltd, 27 Wrights Lane,
London W8 5TZ, England
Penguin Books Australia Ltd, Ringwood,
Victoria, Australia
Penguin Books Canada Ltd, 2801 John Street,
Markham, Ontario, Canada L3R 1B4
Penguin Books (N.Z.) Ltd, 182-190 Wairau Road,
Auckland 10, New Zealand

Penguin Books Ltd, Registered Offices:
Harmondsworth, Middlesex, England

First published by Dutton, an imprint of New American Library,
a division of Penguin Books USA Inc.
Distributed in Canada by McClelland & Stewart Inc.

First Printing, July, 1991
10 9 8 7 6 5 4 3 2 1

 REGISTERED TRADEMARK—MARCA REGISTRADA

LIBRARY OF CONGRESS CATALOGING-IN-PUBLICATION DATA

McCarry, Charles.
  Second sight : a Christopher novel / Charles McCarry.
    p.   cm.
  ISBN 0-525-24985-0
  I. Title.
PS3563.C336S4   1991
813'.54—dc20
                                              90-25496
                                              CIP

Printed in the United States of America
Set in Times Roman
Designed by Julian Hamer

PUBLISHER'S NOTE

To Nancy and Pamela
(RUTH 1:16)

second sight

a supposed power by which occurrences in the future or things at a distance are perceived as though they were actually present.

Oxford English Dictionary

PROLOGUE

BEAUTIFUL DREAMERS

IT MADE NO DIFFERENCE TO DAVID PATCHEN, THE DIRECTOR OF THE Outfit, that his friend Paul Christopher had been out of the business of espionage for twenty years, or that he had spent more than half that time in a Chinese prison. He still told him secrets. Christopher did not want to hear them. He defended himself against them by pretending to listen to Patchen's revelations while in fact he thought about the past. Tonight, as Patchen sat in Christopher's peaceful garden in Georgetown, describing the kidnapping of an American agent in an Arab country, Christopher reconstructed a day from his childhood.

There wasn't much to it: On Easter Monday in 1928, when travel by automobile was still a novelty, he had driven with his parents in an open car over the Simplon Pass from Switzerland to Italy. The road had been opened by snowplows that morning, and deep winter drifts still lay on the mountainsides. The Christophers were bundled up against the cold in coats and mufflers, with a fuzzy red rug across their laps, and Paul, warmed by the heat of their bodies, sat between his mother and father under the heavy coverlet. It was a day of brilliant sunshine, and mountain people, whole families with the stunned faces of the rudely awakened, walked dreamily alongside the slowly moving car. They had been snowbound in their villages since October, and now they were bareheaded, with coats unbuttoned, as on a summer's day. Christopher's father tried to greet them, "*Grüß' Gott*! Good day!" But they did not answer. When the car approached the tunnel through the mountain on the Swiss-Italian frontier, the crowd, thirty or forty men, women, and children, stopped, turned around, and walked back the way they came. "Let's wait," Christopher's mother said. His father backed out of the tunnel, and they sat in the front seat eating a picnic lunch in the sunshine. Half an hour later the people reappeared, walking beside another car. They were very surprised to see the Christophers still sitting in their green Storch at the mouth of the tunnel, drinking cocoa from steaming cups. One of the men detached himself from the group, approached the car, squinted at them apprehensively, and pointed to the dark interior of the tunnel. *"Hierdurch Italien!"* he said in peculiar gargled German—this way to Italy.

In the garden in Washington more than fifty years later, Christopher chuckled at the memory.

"What's so funny?" Patchen asked.

"I remembered something from a long time ago," Christopher replied.

"Have you heard anything I've been telling you?"

Christopher shook his head. "Sorry. My mind wandered."

"Then I'll start over again."

"Don't bother on my account."

"I'm not worried about boring you. I want your help."

Patchen believed that Christopher had a gift for puzzles, that he saw solutions that were invisible to others. He also believed that Christopher, in spite of everything that had happened to him, still had a weakness for the Work, as the craft of intelligence was called by the few who practiced it.

"All right," Christopher said. "Let me put Lori to bed and I'll walk home with you."

Christopher's daughter had fallen asleep on his lap. He stood up, carefully, so as not to wake her, and carried her into the house.

To Patchen this was a strange and disorienting sight. He had known Christopher most of his life, but he had never imagined him as the father of a child. The women he had lived with in his youth, a wife who deserted him and a girl who died for his mistakes, had been too beautiful to play the role of mother. Then, in middle age, after Patchen rescued him from captivity in China, Christopher had married a younger woman, the daughter of a fellow spy, and she gave birth to this child. Christopher stayed home to care for the little girl while his wife pursued a career, going to an office every day, traveling to conferences, fighting off rivals, worrying about

10

money and her professional reputation. Patchen himself was child-less and mostly alone.

Christopher came back after a long absence inside the house.

"She woke up," he explained. "I had to read her a story."

Patchen said, "Her mother isn't here?"

"She's here, but it was my turn to read the story." Christopher's young wife was a feminist who insisted on the equitable division of domestic responsibility.

It was almost midnight by the time the two men set off together through the deserted streets of Georgetown. Four hundred people had been murdered in the city of Washington so far that year, and though only two or three members of the white bourgeoisie were among the victims, few went out on foot after dark. They passed Patchen's house, which lay a few blocks away from Christopher's, and entered the towpath of the C & O Canal. Patchen held the leash of a Doberman pinscher. The dog, and a heavy pistol he had carried for more than thirty years but never fired, were his only protection in an age in which men like himself were kidnapped or murdered by maniacs every day.

As they walked, Patchen described the work of a particular maniac.

"So far this fellow has kidnapped two of our people," Patchen said.

"Together?"

"No, a month apart, one in Jordan, one in Greece. He kept them over the weekend, then left them sitting in a car, alive and well, with a video tape recording what he or she—one of the victims was a woman—had spilled. Both were drugged—sound asleep when we found them."

"What kind of drugs?"

"From the symptoms, some kind of super tranquilizer, but masked with other drugs given before the victims, if that's the word, are released," Patchen said. "The lab hasn't been able to identify it precisely."

"Do you have a description of the kidnappers?"

"No. The tranquilizer takes care of that. They can't remember anything, except that it was the most pleasant experience of their lives. Apparently you could have your leg sawed off under the influence of this drug and not remember a thing."

"Do they remember being kidnapped before the drug was administered?"

"No. We've tried everything—our own drugs, hypnotism, something called 'enhanced debriefing.' "

"What's that?"

"It's similar to what the Chinese tried on you—hard-nosed moral suasion. No violence, no threats, just insistence on confession for your own good. No sleep, strange hours."

"Does it work?"

"Not very well. We're not as patient as the Chinese. Or as religious." Patchen believed that political conviction was the same thing as religious faith. "Anyway," he continued, "nothing really works. They just don't remember where they were or who they were with. Evidently they're injected in the first seconds and the stuff puts them under instantaneously. The woman was hit in a public toilet. The man was walking his dog, half a mile from his house. A spaniel, not a Doberman." Patchen smiled his gloomy smile. "All they remember after that is being happy and sleeping like tops. Evidently they're asleep most of the time. It takes days to wake them up completely, and when they do wake up, their minds are blank. We call the operation 'Beautiful Dreamer.' "

"What's on the tapes?"

"Everything the victims know. Everything. Not only about the Outfit, but about themselves. It's stream of consciousness; they go on and on, overjoyed at the opportunity to confess everything. You'd be amazed at the private lives some of our people have. Or maybe you wouldn't."

"The kidnappers don't ask for ransom?"

"They don't communicate with us in any way. They just take our people, flush out their brains, and give them back good as new. Like the Eskimo's wife."

Patchen let his dog off the leash and told it to run. It bounded away down the path for about twenty yards, turned around and ran back to Patchen, then repeated the circuit. The animal was never away from the man it had been trained to protect for more than a few seconds.

"We don't know who we're dealing with or why they're doing this," Patchen said. "What do they want? What's next?"

"Why should anything be next except another kidnapping?" Christopher asked. "Maybe all they want is information."

"That's what we thought in the beginning. But they don't seem to be *doing* anything with the information. They have the names of dozens of assets. Not one has been bothered. We're still running them, hoping these people will come after them so we can get one of *them* and give him a dose of their own medicine."

"Why do you say '*them*'?" Christopher asked. "Why should there be more than one person involved?"

Patchen was silent for a moment. Then he gripped Christopher's shoulder and squeezed. The pressure was painful: Patchen was partially paralyzed on the other side of his body as a result of war wounds, and his good hand was tremendously strong.

"I don't think there is more than one thinker involved," he said. "That's why I wanted to see what you thought."

"Oh?" Christopher said. "Why me?"

Patchen watched his dog galloping toward them in the darkness. There was an electronic device in its collar; when he pressed another device, about the size of a quarter, that he always carried in his pocket, the animal came. If he pressed it twice, it took up a protective stance. Three times and it attacked.

"Why you?" he said to Christopher. "I'll tell you why. Because when I read the files I thought you were back in business. Until this dream merchant came into view, I didn't think that anybody but you could think something like this up, let alone bring it off."

They stopped under a sputtering sodium light. Christopher smiled at his friend. "You can stop worrying," he said. "It isn't me."

"I know," Patchen replied. "It's worse than that. It's somebody just like you. And he's on the other side."

I

THE LOVE CHILD

ONE

1

CATHY CHRISTOPHER DISCOVERED THAT SHE WAS PREGNANT AFTER
she and her husband stopped living together. Although she had
taken lovers in the last months of the marriage, she was absolutely
sure that Paul Christopher was the father of her child. Against his
will, he had made love to her in a hospital bed in Rome while she
waited for the orderly to come and wheel her into the operating
room. She had been beaten nearly to death that morning by another man, an Italian film-maker she had slept with half a dozen
times without pleasure or emotion.

No one had ever hurt Cathy before. Her astonishing beauty had
always protected her from everything, and after the first blows fell,
her conscious mind left her body and floated upward, so that she
was looking down on herself being beaten while it was happening.
She felt the life going out of her and then coming back as her
attacker's fists thudded against her face and body. His eyes were
glazed by drugs. Grunting with every punch, he shouted insults in a
mixture of Italian and broken English—*American bitch! Pezzo di
merda! Stupid whore!* Other foreign women, friends of his, were
present, watching the beating while they drank *spumante* and smoked
marijuana.

Afterward, as she lay in the hospital, Cathy was overwhelmed by
the fear that she might die in surgery before Christopher ever made
love to her again. Her mind had never been as clear as it was at
that moment; she had never understood anything so well: he must
do this for her before she died and wipe out every trace of all the
other men with whom she had betrayed him. She had come to him

17

a virgin. He was the first man she had ever made love to. He was her husband, the only man who had ever had a right to her.

He was standing beside the bed, looking down at her. She slid her hand out from under the coarse hospital sheet and caressed him. He gasped and recoiled. She threw back the sheet. The shutters were closed but the dazzling afternoon sunlight came through the lattice, so that everything—her perfect legs, the white hospital gown, Christopher's bewildered face—were striped with light and shadow.

She struggled with him. Christopher said, "Cathy, no," and took hold of her wrists to restrain her. A crucifix hung on the whitewashed wall above the bed; nuns hovered just outside the door. Cathy's nose and the bones in her cheeks were smashed; the doctor said that her spleen was ruptured. He had given her injections, and billows of morphine bore her away from the worst pain she had ever felt. Nevertheless, she knew that it might come back at any moment. A kiss, a noise, anything, could start it up again.

She did not care. She fought Christopher, twisting her wrists out of his grasp. Sleeping with other men had taught her that her husband was utterly without vice, but she knew that he could not refuse her; he never had.

"Please, Paul, *please*," she said in a voice she did not recognize, "what if I never wake up?"

He stopped resisting. The pain-killer was so strong, and he was so gentle when at last he did as she wanted, that she hardly felt his weight upon her.

They took her into the operating room and asked her to count backward from twenty in Italian while they gave her another injection. As she was trying to remember the word for sixteen she lost consciousness.

Under the anesthesia she dreamed that Christopher, her one true love, was still with her, and she heard herself calling out to him. Much later, she believed that she already knew that she was pregnant.

I'm happy, Paul, she told him, *so happy.*

He never touched her again.

"MY GOD," SAID MARIA ROTHCHILD, MOMENTS AFTER CATHY LANDED in Geneva. "Who did this to you?"

She slammed on the brakes and steered the car off the airport road into a street lined with new houses.

"I was in an accident," Cathy said. The sudden stop had thrown her body forward, jarring her wounds; her voice was faint.

"An accident? With Paul?"

"No, not with Paul. There's no more Paul."

"No more Paul? What's that supposed to mean?"

Cathy removed the broad-brimmed hat and sunglasses that she had worn on the plane. More wounds became visible—the broken nose, the discolored flesh, the red puncture marks where the sutures had been removed. Maria's eyes widened. Behind them, a speeding Mercedes stopped with a shriek of tires and horn. The driver, a bald Swiss wearing new pigskin driving gloves, reversed and then pulled up beside them, shaking a bright yellow fist and shouting. Maria ignored him. She and Cathy had been at school together; she was demanding answers like the house captain she used to be.

"What kind of an accident?" she asked.

Cathy heard the question only faintly over the blare of the other car's horn.

"A motorbike," Cathy said.

"A motorbike? You were riding on a motorbike?"

"What difference does it make?" Cathy said. "It happened, that's all."

The Swiss in the Mercedes stopped blowing his horn and drove away. Through the windshield they could see huge airplanes lumbering into the sky, landing gear dangling over the pink tile rooftops of rows of identical new gray villas. Each little square house had a window box filled with geraniums and one juvenile linden tree planted in the raw earth of a tiny front yard. Maria waited for a Caravelle to climb out of earshot before she spoke again. Her voice was hostile, accusative.

"What did you mean when you said there's no more Paul?" she asked.

"It's over."

"You mean you've separated? In your condition?"

"It's not his fault."

"What difference does that make? Look at you. When did you and Paul separate?"

"This morning, just before I sent you the telegram," Cathy said. "Maria, please leave me alone."

Another plane took off, trailing vapor. The stench of burnt kerosene seeped into the car. Cathy realized that she had smelled this same odor in Rome as she turned away from Christopher for the last time and walked to her airplane. She felt tears on her cheeks.

Maria said, "Why did you come here—to us, of all people?"

"I can't let my parents or anyone see me like this. I needed a place to hide."

"Why here, why us? I don't understand. Did Paul suggest this?"

"No."

"Are you sure? Why don't you have any baggage?"

"I didn't want any," Cathy said. "And now I don't want to be here. Take me back to the airport."

Maria's expression, which had been cold and hard, changed. She plucked a tissue out of a box between the seats and handed it to Cathy.

"Sorry," she said. "Give me a minute to calm down."

Like Christopher, Maria was a spy. Or had been a spy—there had been some trouble, someone in Germany had been betrayed, killed before Christopher's eyes, and Christopher had found out that Maria and her husband, a disdainful White Russian years older than she was, were responsible somehow. The Rothchilds had lost their jobs; they had been forced to leave Paris. They blamed Christopher for these consequences.

Maria put the car in gear. "Never mind," she said. "I'm a worse bitch than usual these days. Living without money does that to you. Come on, I'll take you home. We'll get you fixed up. Otto's an expert on Swiss doctors."

She had the car in motion now, backing into a driveway, turning around, changing gears, dominating the machine. She was a superb driver.

"Are you and Paul really through?" she asked, eyes fixed on the rearview mirror as she accelerated into traffic on the main airport road.

"Yes," Cathy replied.

"And whatever happened to you is not Paul's fault?" Maria asked.

"No. Not any of it."

"Nothing ever is," Maria said. "Welcome to the world of basket cases."

3

NOT SO LONG AGO, IN PARIS, THE ROTHCHILDS HAD LIVED ON THE prow of the Ile Saint-Louis in a magnificent apartment filled with works of art. Their new place outside Geneva, a half-timbered farmhouse on a slope overlooking Lake Leman, was attached to a barn that was still used to store grain. On her first night, Cathy heard rats by the hundreds scampering across the plank flooring above her bedroom.

"That's why the farmer built himself a new house," Otto Rothchild told her the next morning. "He got married and his wife was afraid the rats would smell milk on her baby's breath and devour it in the night."

"God bless the rats," Maria said. "Nobody wants this place. The rent is only three hundred francs a month."

They were having breakfast in the garden. It did not go with the peasant house. It was quite large and strangely formal, with flower beds and shrubbery laid out between graveled walks, in the French style. Two little fountains, covered with moss, tinkled quietly. Otto had his tea in a glass; he placed a lump of sugar in his mouth and drank through the sugar, Russian style. His skin was the color of parchment, and he wore other shades of brown—a tweed jacket, a tan foulard ascot, suede shoes—to accentuate his complexion. Everything was freshly brushed, including his gray hair, which grew straight back from his sloping forehead.

Cathy knew that Maria had brushed his clothes and his hair, shaved him, and arranged him in his chair before she, Cathy, came downstairs. A couple of years before, the nerves along Otto's spine had been severed in an operation to control his alarmingly high blood pressure. Afterward he was able to do very little for himself.

Now Maria broke his orange into segments and arranged them prettily on his plate. His chair was placed so that he had the best view of the lake and the main range of the Alps beyond it. For

Cathy's benefit, he named the major peaks from left to right: Dents du Midi, Aiguille Vert, Dru, Aiguilles de Chamonix.

"Mont Blanc, the highest mountain in Europe, is just there, hidden in the mist, at two o'clock," Otto said. "Before the age of automobile exhaust you could see it quite clearly. Byron saw it every morning when he woke up and looked out the window in the summer of 1815. It was visible to W. Somerset Maugham a century later when he was an amateur agent for the British Secret Service in Geneva. But now it rarely appears through the smog. In three months in this house, we've seen it twice."

Cathy nodded to show her gratitude for this useless information. No fact was uninteresting to Otto; he memorized everything, an incurable habit that went with his former profession. While Cathy ate her bread and jam he recited the month and year of her birth, her parents' names and nicknames (Eleazer and Letitia, both called Lee; they were cousins from Kentucky who had the same surname, Kirkpatrick, even before they were married) and the name of a thoroughbred filly, Mean Irene, that the Kirkpatricks used to own. He had won a thousand French francs on her at Auteuil five years before.

"Mary Shelley wrote *Frankenstein* just up the lake, you know, when she and Shelley were cohabiting with Byron and Mary's stepsister, Claire Clairmont," Otto said. "Shelley adored communal sex—many poets do. Mary was the artist. Shelley was just another romantic pamphleteer. Propagandists never last. It's the Mary Shelleys, the simple storytellers, who live on. Everyone knows *Frankenstein,* but who remembers a line of *Queen Mab?*"

"I wonder if the Shelleys had rats," Maria said. "Imagine creeping from bed to bed and stepping on one."

When Maria was in the presence of her husband she strove to be intelligent and amusing. He smiled indulgently at her and finished his lecture. "Madame de Staël lived not far away from here," he said. "And much later, Jung, also. He is the most interesting of the psychiatric fortune-tellers because he actually *believed* in psychoanalysis. Freud was just a struggling young quack looking for a gimmick."

"Otto knew them both," Maria said.

"*Did* he?" Cathy said.

There was hardly anyone famous in Europe whom Otto did not know. The Klee hanging in the sitting room had been given to him by Klee; he dictated notes in sardonic French to André Malraux, sent clippings from German newspapers to Bertolt Brecht.

A small white paddle-wheel boat, followed by a flock of gulls, passed over the gray surface of the lake. Cathy watched it out of sight.

"Poor Cathy," Otto said. "Maria says you fell off a motorbike. Did you break any bones?"

"Only in my face," Cathy said. "And they took out my spleen." She removed her sunglasses and returned Otto's stare. "I've been dying to ask you—what does a spleen do? The doctors didn't tell me. All the way up on the plane I kept saying to myself, 'Otto will know.' "

"It filters the blood. Don't worry. You can easily live without it." He looked at Maria, resentfully. "You didn't tell me this detail."

"This is the first time I've heard it," Maria said. "How long ago did this accident happen?"

"I'm not sure, I've lost track of time," Cathy said. "About six weeks ago, I think."

Otto lifted a finger. Maria removed the cozy from the pot and poured him a second glass of tea. He placed another lump of sugar in his mouth and drank.

"Where was your husband while all this was happening?" he asked.

"With me."

"Even during the accident? Was he driving the motorcycle?"

"No. He came right afterward and took care of me."

"So Paul took care of you," Otto said, "but then, as soon as you were on your feet, he deserted you."

"He didn't desert me. We knew that everything was over between us long before I got hurt. He stayed with me anyway."

Maria said, "For old times' sake."

"Maria," Cathy said, "you really are a shit. You always were. Do you know that?"

Otto looked from one young woman to the other. "Please," he said. "Be pleasant. Maria, give Cathy some more coffee."

Cathy put her hand over her cup. "I think I'll take a walk in the garden," she said.

"Wait," Otto said. "You're welcome here, Cathy. I hope you'll stay a long time. But first I have to ask you about Paul. We have reason to be curious about him, too, you know, inasmuch as he ruined our lives. If we get this subject out of the way on the first morning, we'll never have to speak of it again. Otherwise we'll all be wondering and whispering and we'll never relax."

Cathy, still angry at Maria, averted her eyes for a long moment, gazing across the gray lake at the mountains.

"All right, Otto," she said at last. "What do you want to know?"

"Why did you separate? It can't be because you don't love him."

"That's right. Nobody can ever stop loving Paul. Not even you."

"Then why?"

"You want a simple answer? Because I hate secrets."

"Perhaps it was a mistake to marry a spy, then."

"Very few people know that until they marry one. That wasn't the problem. I could have gotten used to the absences, the phone ringing at midnight and Paul vanishing into Africa or Asia for weeks at a time. It was him, the way he is, the way God made him. He's *absent.* He won't let anyone know him. He might as well be from another planet, I used to tell him that. He doesn't know the meaning of jealousy."

"But you do."

"Oh, yes."

"You don't actually think that he was unfaithful to you?"

"Why not? He wasn't a virgin when we got married. Women adore him."

Otto frowned and waved a finger. "I can tell you categorically that adultery was impossible for Paul Christopher," he said.

"You can?" Cathy replied. "How do you know? Did you have him followed?"

"Sometimes."

"He'd know if he was followed."

"Yes, he would," Otto said. "But that's not what I mean. I've known him since childhood, you know."

"He never told me that."

Otto lifted his eyebrows. "I'm not sure he remembers," he said. "He had a remarkable mother, a German. He looks just like her. But morally, he's like his father—American, crazy virtuous, crazy brave. Dangerous."

Cathy started to ask a question: What is that supposed to mean? But Otto had closed his eyes and stopped talking. He was so perfectly still that she thought that he might have died. She gave Maria a questioning look.

"He's fallen asleep," Maria said. "He does that—drops off. It's a side effect of his surgery. I hope you'll stay. Otto really does like you, and we're expecting another guest—someone *you'll* like."

"Not a spy," Cathy said. "I don't want to know any more spies."

"Then you've come to the right place. They avoid us like the plague these days. No, she's something better—she can see into the future."

"You mean she's got second sight?"

"What's that?" Maria was often confused by Cathy's speech; at school she had such a Southern accent that she had to spell the numbers to the operator when she wanted to call home.

Cathy said, "It's Southern for clairvoyant. My Mammy had it, lots of black people do."

"I'm not talking about telling fortunes."

"Neither am I. Mammy could see into the past and the future, and when her son Harold was away in the Battle of the Bulge she saw him driving his truck without headlights. 'Slow down, Harold!' she'd cry while peeling potatoes or washing clothes. 'Turn on your headlights, y'hear?' You could hear her all over the house."

"Did he?"

"Harold said so when he came home. Anyway he didn't have a wreck and get killed like Mammy was afraid he would."

"And what did you call this gift she had?"

"Second sight."

"It sounds like a primitive form of what Lla Kahina has," Maria said. "But she's the real thing."

"So was Mammy," Cathy said. "Not like Freud and Jung and that crowd."

4

THE WOMAN WHO ARRIVED WITH MARIA FROM THE TRAIN STATION that afternoon was swathed in black—black dress, black stockings, a broad-brimmed black hat, and a great deal of gold jewelry: necklaces, earrings, bracelets, a beautiful filigree belt. The dress was elegant, obviously made in Paris, but she had sewn a row of purple tassels on its hem. She was small, less than five feet high, and very thin. Under the hat Cathy glimpsed a magnificent hooked nose and a mouth that was still sensual even though she must have been sixty years old.

Otto had been waiting impatiently for her arrival.

"Lla Kahina!" he cried when she appeared. "Come here and kiss me!"

"La Kahina?" Cathy said to Maria. "What is she, a soprano?"

"It's double 'l,' pronounced like 'Ella' without the 'E,' " Maria replied, whispering. "L-*LA* K*a*hee*na*. She's a Berber. It's a term of respect for women of rank, like 'Lady Kahina.' "

"Oh. She looks like that picture of Isak Dinesen on the back of *Winter's Tales*. But why does she wear all those purple tassels?"

"Ssshhh," Maria replied. She seemed to be overcome by respect; this was a side of Maria Cathy had never seen before.

Otto introduced them.

"Not a relation of Hubbard Christopher?" Lla Kahina said.

"I'm married to his son," Cathy said.

Lla Kahina looked at her closely. "Really?"

"No," Cathy said. "Not really. We're being divorced."

"That's too bad," Lla Kahina said. "He comes from a very good family."

"You know the family?"

"I did, years ago, when they were young."

"Oh? Where?"

"In Berlin. They were the happiest people I ever knew."

Lla Kahina smiled, showing even, white teeth. She was much fairer than Cathy would have expected someone from Africa to be. The creamy skin of her face had been tattooed with a small tear-drop beneath each eye.

"Maria, you and Cathy run along," Otto said. "I want to be alone with my friend."

Lla Kahina and Cathy shared the only guest bedroom. After spending the whole afternoon with Otto, Lla Kahina retired immediately after dinner. By the time Cathy came upstairs she was sound asleep in the other twin bed, her small body scarcely visible beneath the covers. Cathy herself fell asleep almost instantaneously, but woke after an hour or two, puzzled by the silence. She lay awake for a long time before she realized that the rats had stopped scampering over the plank floor upstairs.

26

SECOND SIGHT

All during the second day, Cathy was aware that Lla Kahina was looking at her. She would glance up from a book or turn away from a window and find her staring. The old woman had brilliantly intelligent, unwavering green eyes.

Finally Cathy said, in French, "Can I help you, Madame?"

Lla Kahina replied in English. "Thank you, I'm quite happy as I am."

Cathy took a novel into the garden. Cathy was soon absorbed by the story. When she closed the book hours later and looked up, she saw that Lla Kahina was sitting in another garden chair, still staring at her.

That night, when Cathy went upstairs, she found the old woman sitting at a table, playing solitaire by candlelight.

"Sit there, please," she said, pointing to a chair on the opposite side of the table.

"What for?"

"I am going to do a reading for you."

"You mean tell my fortune?"

"Switch off the lamp," Lla Kahina said. "Electricity is bad for the cards."

Cathy did as she was told. It was raining outside, and beyond Lla Kahina's shoulder the windowpane glistened in the candlelight.

"Do you do the past, too," Cathy asked, "or just the future? I knew someone when I was growing up who had second sight. She used tea leaves like you use cards. She called the past 'black and white' and the future 'color.' She'd say, 'Do you want black and white or color?' "

"Which did you choose?"

"Both, naturally."

"One is always stronger than the other. In your case, the future will be dominant."

"How can you tell before you even start?"

"But I have started," Lla Kahina said. "I've been seeing you in the cards for a long time. I just didn't know who you were."

She used ordinary playing cards, a garish French bridge deck. Following her instructions, Cathy shuffled the cards, then cut them into four stacks arranged in the shape of a diamond. Lla Kahina chose cards, three at a time, from the stacks.

"You grew up among horses," she said, looking at the first cards she drew.

Cathy nodded. Everybody knew that.

More cards. "You have been injured, badly, twice in your life—the wounds you have now, and when you fell off a black horse as a girl and broke a bone. A man, a relation but not an American, carried you home on his horse. He was a beautiful rider. You fell in love with him, but you were too young to do anything about it."

All this was true in every detail, but Cathy had often told this story; Maria probably knew it. She smiled. "All correct except the part about falling in love."

Lla Kahina looked at the cards. "It is quite clear that you fell in love with this man. Maybe you don't remember."

Cathy had had a crush on the man who carried her home when she broke her leg during a hunt on her thirteenth birthday—Don Jorge de Rodegas, a Spaniard who was a distant cousin of the Kirkpatricks.

"All right, I remember," Cathy said. "It was puppy love."

"You and this man are connected by a queen," Lla Kahina said, looking at new cards. "He has a picture of her in his house which looks like you, or which he says looks like you. Is that so?"

This was something the Rothchilds certainly did not know, unless Christopher had told them. Had he talked about her with these people? Lla Kahina gave Cathy a quizzical look.

"Is what I'm seeing about you the truth?" she asked. "You must help me or I won't be able to go on."

"I guess so," Cathy said. "We're connected through the Empress Eugénie, or so they say. Her mother was one of our cousins who married some ancestor of Don Jorge's. It's true about the painting, but I don't think I look a bit like Eugénie."

"Shuffle."

Lla Kahina then told Cathy things about herself that she had to admit were true—that she had never liked to study, that she could not remember things, that she had never had friends, that her worst fault was jealousy, that she had only loved once, and this had been an overpowering love that was destroyed by jealousy. Still, Cathy was not impressed. These facts were common knowledge; even Maria knew that much about her, or could have guessed. God knew what Otto might know. He spied on everyone, all the time.

Cathy's skepticism did not bother Lla Kahina. She asked Cathy to shuffle the cards over and over again. Sometimes nothing showed up.

Bored, Cathy said, "Does each card mean something?"

Lla Kahina looked up. "There is nothing in the cards them-selves," she replied. "I just use them to help me see."

"What *do* you see? Is it like the movies?"

"No."

Cathy cut the cards again and laid out the four piles. She could not get them even, and she tried to do it over again. Lla Kahina pounced, pressing the fingernail of her index finger into the back of Cathy's hand.

"No. Leave them. There's a reason why they're not equal."

Lla Kahina picked up three more cards.

"I see why you have been fighting me," she said. "You have secrets. Something very bad happened to you in a room where there were big pictures of you, photographs in which you look even more beautiful than you are."

This was true. Cathy had decorated her apartment in Rome, the place where the man had beaten her, with huge enlargements of photographs of herself. But no one knew that. The apartment was a secret, the place where she met lovers.

Cathy's hands trembled. Lla Kahina chose three more cards, then put them down.

"If you don't want me to see more we can stop," she said.

Cathy cleared her throat. "No. Go ahead."

Lla Kahina picked up the cards. "You were beaten by a man you let make love to you. This man hates you, not you yourself, but what you are. He is a political, so he is like an actor, always living somebody else's lie. He hates you because of his politics, because you are beautiful and American. But he went too far. You thought he was going to kill you. So did he. He could hardly stop himself in time. You were very close to death."

Cathy, shivering violently, got up and pulled a blanket off the bed. Lla Kahina stopped talking. Cathy wrapped herself in the blanket and sat down again.

"Does this disturb you?" Lla Kahina asked. "We can stop if you like."

"It doesn't matter," Cathy said. "Go on."

Lla Kahina looked at more cards. "Who is this other man—the one you love so much?" she asked.

"My husband," Cathy said.

"But he's not your husband any longer."

29

"No. Will he love me again?"

"No. Another woman is waiting for him already. He will love her, and no one else for the rest of his life."

The symptoms of jealousy—shortened breath, quickened heart-beat, mental images of Christopher talking to other women, looking at other women, touching other women—flooded into Cathy's breast.

"What woman?" she said. "What's her name? What does she look like? Why does he love her?"

"She is nothing to do with you, she would have come anyway," Lla Kahina said. "We should stop now."

"I want to go on."

Cathy raked in the cards, shuffled them rapidly, and cut the four piles. Her hands were steady and she was warmer now, wrapped in the blanket and heated by jealousy and anger.

Lla Kahina looked reluctantly at the cards, then put them down without speaking. She seemed to be very happy. Why?

"What do you see?" Cathy said. "Tell me."

"You are with child," Lla Kahina said.

5

CATHY LAY NAKED UNDER A SHEET IN THE GYNECOLOGIST'S OFFICE. The doctor wore a mirror on his forehead and a long white coat with his name, Docteur Jean-Henri Petitchou, embroidered above the pocket, like a garage mechanic in America. He had just discovered the half-healed incision made by the surgeon in Rome. There were just the two of them in the room; his nurse could be heard through the curtained glass door, talking on the telephone in the outer office. He looked down into Cathy's face, his hand in its rubber glove resting negligently on her rib cage, just beneath her left breast. Cathy could hear him breathing; his long face was slightly flushed. She knew his symptoms well.

"Your surgery is quite recent," he said. "What was it for?"

"I had an operation in Rome to remove my spleen."

"Why?"

"I was in an accident; they said it was ruptured."

"Italians! You'll have a scar."

"One expects to have a scar after surgery."

"In your case it is a pity. Wonders can be done nowadays. We have excellent plastic surgeons in Switzerland."

"I don't doubt it. May I get dressed now?"

The doctor took his hand away and left the room, stripping off his gloves as he went. Cathy stood up, an act that was still painful after her surgery. Her clothes were hanging on a rack, the same ones in which she had said goodbye to Christopher in Rome—a green Loden cape she had bought two winters before in Saint Anton, a tweed skirt and blazer, and a cashmere sweater. She had left everything else behind in Rome, wanting nothing from her former life.

The gynecologist was waiting for her behind his desk when she went into his office. He had taken off his mirror and his stethoscope.

"We will perform the usual tests," he said, "but there is no question as to your condition, Madame. You are well advanced into the second month of pregnancy. May I ask when exactly was your last menses?"

"Let me see your calendar," Cathy said. He handed it over, politely turning it so that the print was right side up. She flipped the pages, then pointed to a date. "That is the date of conception."

Acting again, the doctor raised his eyebrows. "You can be so sure?"

"There is no question. When will the child be born? I'm no good at arithmetic."

"Normally, mid-April. But you should consider this carefully."

"Consider what carefully?"

"Whether to go through with it."

"Go through with it? What choice do I have?"

The gynecologist smiled again, charmingly. "Pregnancy is not an irreversible condition," he said. "In Switzerland, provision is made for women in your circumstances."

"My circumstances? What circumstances are those?"

"This pregnancy could be—will be—quite dangerous for you and for the child."

"Dangerous? I don't understand. Is something wrong with the baby?"

"Madame, your spleen was removed almost, it would seem, at the same moment that your child was conceived. Recovery from such an operation is very taxing to the system."

"I was told I'd never miss it."

"Obviously your doctor did not realize your condition. The spleen is very important in pregnancy. It is the organ that discharges new blood cells into the system and filters out worn-out blood cells. The mother's blood is vital to her child, and to herself."

Cathy said, "What does my baby look like now?"

He shrugged. "Nothing. An embryo."

"Does it have fingers and toes? Can it move?"

"As I said, it is an embryo, a thing, not a person," the doctor replied. "You should not trouble yourself with such thoughts. I advise you to give up this thing, and then, after you are well again, to have another child." He leaned forward in his white coat and smiled yet again. "It's quite easy if you watch the calendar."

Cathy listened in silence. Then she said, "You're advising me to have an abortion. Is that what I am to understand?"

"We prefer to say therapeutic termination. But yes, that's what I am proposing."

"And you can arrange to do such a thing? I thought it was against the law."

"So it is, in your country and most others, even in France. But this procedure is provided for under Swiss law if the physical or mental health of the mother is threatened. In your case one could argue that both are in jeopardy."

"You think I'm mentally disturbed?"

"Certainly not. But as your condition progresses and your body tells you that it is not sufficiently healed from its injuries to manage a pregnancy, you will experience anxiety."

"I'm experiencing it already, just listening to you."

"There you are. The law requires that you consult another doctor who will confirm my diagnosis and concur in my recommendation for treatment." He put his hand on the telephone. "Shall I make an appointment?"

Cathy said nothing.

"It is a simple procedure, perfectly safe," Dr. Petitchou said. "You will come here one morning. An injection will be administered to help you relax. There will be only mild discomfort, nothing one could call pain, and then it will be over. You will rest for an hour, I will give you something to help you sleep when you go home, you will feel quite normal, and the next day. . . ."

He was already dialing the telephone.

"What about the next night?" Cathy said.

He gave her a look of surprise. "Madame?"

She placed a blue one-hundred franc note on his desk and rose to her feet.

The doctor cupped his hand over the mouthpiece. "If it is a question of religion, Madame," he said, "let me explain that no religious question exists. I am myself a Catholic, and I assure you that life has not yet begun."

"Does that cover your fee?" Cathy asked, pointing to the money.

"Two hundred-fifty, if you please," Dr. Petitchou said, hanging up the phone.

6

MARIA AND LLA KAHINA MET CATHY IN A CAFÉ IN THE PLACE DU Molard, just around the corner from the gynecologist's office. Maria had seen her coming across the square and ordered tea for her. As Cathy took her chair, the waiter set it down, a thick seamed glass in a metal holder equipped with a handle like a tea cup.

"You ought to get one of these rigs for Otto," Cathy said.

"He won't use them," Maria said. "Too crude. Where have you been?"

Cathy did not reply; she had said nothing to Maria about going to a gynecologist. She drank some tea. It was dark and terribly bitter. Cathy made a face and put the glass down. Lla Kahina, sitting opposite, tore open two fat packets of sugar and poured them into the cup.

Lla Kahina said, "Was I right?"

Swallowing, Cathy nodded.

"Right about what?" said Maria sharply.

Cathy said, "I think I'd like to buy some clothes. Do you know which stores to go to yet, Maria?"

Maria was not diverted. She said, "What was Lla Kahina right about?"

"Something she told me in the reading night before last."

Maria looked from one woman to the other. "You're pregnant," she said. "I knew it. You looked different when you got off the plane. I mean it wasn't just your face."

Cathy held Maria's stare for an instant, then picked up the bill and opened her purse.

"You *are,* aren't you?" Maria said.

Cathy separated a hundred franc note from a large wad of Swiss money she had bought for dollars at the airport bank. She always carried a lot of money with her; because she so often got lost even in familiar cities, she had a fear of being left alone and helpless in a foreign place. Money was the universal language.

Maria looked at the francs in disgust; she had always thought that Cathy had too much money, in addition to too much beauty. "Don't you have anything smaller?" she asked. "The waiter will complain."

Cathy gave the waiter her hundred franc note and smiled at him. He bowed and scurried off to find change.

"See?" Cathy said. "He didn't mind at all."

Maria was not finished with Cathy. "Let me understand this," she said. "Paul got you pregnant and then kicked you out?"

Cathy stood up and put on her cape. Across the room, a man watched her arched body as she swung the heavy garment around her shoulders.

7

THE NEXT MORNING AFTER BREAKFAST CATHY PLAYED FOR OTTO while Maria went shopping for groceries in the village. He had a small piano in his room, but it had a good tone. Sight-reading from a book of pieces she found inside the piano bench, she played the adagio from Schubert's Fantasia in C major. She played it very well. Music was, besides riding, Cathy's chief accomplishment.

Otto listened with his eyes closed. He was sitting up in bed against fresh pillows, wearing a silk polka-dot dressing gown and another of his ascot scarves. Otto's bedroom, formerly the salon, was a gallery of his acquisitions: his Klee, his Persian rug that was ancient not merely antique, his Rembrandt drawing, his millefleurs tapestry, his Louis XVI commode and desk, his many books bound in calfskin and signed by the famous and near-famous authors who had been his intimate acquaintances.

"I haven't heard that played in thirty years," Otto said. "Paul's mother used to play it in Berlin."

"Paul's mother played the piano?"

"Oh, yes. The Christophers always marry musical women."

There's a verse from *'Der Wanderer'* that goes with that piece Lori always recited it before she played:

Die Sonne dünkt mich hier so kalt,
die Blüthe welk, das Leben alt,
und was sie reden, leeren Schall,
ich bin ein Fremdling überalln."

"Translate," Cathy said.

"It means, approximately, 'The sun in this place seems to shine so coldly, the flowers fade, life is too long, what others say is empty words, I am a stranger wherever I go.' It sounds much better in German—sentimental nonsense always does. Schubert was a pederast, you know, what the Vienna police called a chicken hawk. He and his friends stole little boys from the poor quarter and abused them. That's why his music was hardly ever played in public in his lifetime. Decent Viennese wouldn't listen to his work. He was an outcast."

"Otto, how do you know these things? Why do you remember them?"

"I've lived as a foreigner in other people's countries since I was younger than you. It doesn't pay for an exile to forget anything." He coughed, then chose a small flask from his tray of medicines. "Here. Put six drops of this in a glass of water."

Cathy fixed the medicine and watched him drink it. She said, "Tell me about Paul's mother."

"She was highly intelligent," Otto said, "and beautiful in that unflawed German style. Also daring, for her time and class. Paul was conceived out of wedlock, you know."

"I didn't know."

"Maybe Paul doesn't know, though God knows Lori kept very little from him; he was treated as an equal even as an infant. That drawing he has of the nude girl—that's Lori, pregnant with him. The Gestapo arrested her before Paul's eyes on the day before the day the war began. Very traumatic. They grabbed her off a train at the French frontier and sent Hubbard and Paul across the border. Lori and Hubbard had been smuggling Jews out of Germany on their sailboat; it was insane, the risks they took. Lori was never

35

seen or heard from again. No one knows what happened to her. Hubbard never got over it. I don't suppose Paul did, either. But I'm telling you things you already know."

Cathy gazed at Otto for a long moment.

"No," she said, "you're not."

"He never told you?" Otto said. "How odd. But you should talk to Lla Kahina. She knew Lori better than anyone." He composed his lips in a smile. "Better, even, than Hubbard."

8

THAT AFTERNOON CATHY TOOK A NAP IN THE BEDROOM, BUT WAS awakened at about five o'clock by a hand on her face. The hand smelled of dishwater. She opened her eyes and saw Maria standing over her, wearing a white sweater with an exaggerated turtleneck that looked like an Elizabethan ruff.

"Let's go for a walk," Maria said. "I want to talk to you."

Wind and rain rattled the window. "Why can't we talk here?" Cathy asked.

"Outside is better."

Maria spoke in a low voice, almost a whisper. Cathy giggled. "You mean you think this place is bugged?" she said.

The paranoid drill of espionage—fear of microphones that did not exist, fear of being followed by enemies who were not there, the whole childish business of false names, passwords, and secret meetings—had always seemed ridiculous to her.

"It's raining outside," Cathy said. "Why can't we stay inside and whisper, instead?"

"Just get your cape," Maria said.

They walked down to the lake. Half a dozen swans bobbed up and down in the choppy water. The Alps were now obscured by a gray veil that was not quite fog, not quite cloud. Water and sky were the same shade of zinc. The wind blew steadily, creating a steady, nagging tone.

"The Bise, that's the name of this wind," Maria said in Otto's tone of voice, telling Cathy something that she was far too American to know. "It blows for days at a time, all winter long. The sun never comes out. The Genevese commit suicide in droves; it's worse than Budapest."

Cathy, bundled up in her Loden cape, turned her back to the storm. Maria seemed to enjoy the rain and wind in her face. Foul weather had never bothered her. She had been the captain of field hockey at Farmington, and Cathy's most vivid memories of her were ones in which Maria, plastered with mud and oozing blood from pink scrapes and scratches, sat around the locker room after a victory, leading the other girls in song.

"For the record," Maria said, ' 'I don't believe a word of that tale about falling off the motorbike."

"Is that why we're out here?" Cathy said. "To talk about what you don't believe?"

She turned to go, but Maria darted around her and spread her arms, blocking the path. "Wait," she said. "I want to tell you what Paul did to Otto and me."

The story Maria then told was so complicated that Cathy could scarcely follow it. A man in Russia, somebody Otto had known years before, had written a great novel. Otto and Maria had smuggled it out of Russia somehow, and one of the agents in the chain of couriers had been killed just after he handed the manuscript over to Christopher in Berlin.

"It was that, seeing a man die, actually die, that set Paul off," Maria said. "He has this American idea that things like that should never happen, that everybody, even the opposition, is made up of nice boys who went to Yale and Harvard and wouldn't hurt a fly."

"I thought Paul had seen plenty of people die."

"Really?" she said. "When did he see that?"

"In the war," Cathy replied. "He has bullet wounds all over his body."

"Oh, the war. That's something else altogether."

"Excuse me," Cathy said. "I didn't know that World War Two wasn't the real thing."

Maria went on as if Cathy had never interrupted her: Paul had not wanted to publish the book. Otto had insisted.

"Why did they disagree?" Cathy asked.

"Because it became obvious that publication might mean the end of the author."

"The end of him? You mean the Russians would have killed him?"

"Yes. Of course they would have killed him. But the author was prepared for that. It was Paul who objected to paying the necessary price."

"The necessary price? Who decides what that is?"

"Not Paul," Maria said. "It was none of Paul's business what this man did with his life. He was a great writer. He had been silent, imprisoned in the labor camps, for thirty years. This was his greatest work—in this novel he had captured Russia itself, Otto said. He sent it to Otto because Otto was the one person in the world he could trust to have the guts to get it into print no matter what. What did he care about death?"

"You mean Russians like to die?"

A smile of pleasure spread over Maria's wet face. "Paul should have talked to you," she said. "He might have understood things better if he had. The answer is yes, in certain circumstances, when there is no other way to assert one's humanity—yes, then they love death better than the alternative. That's exactly the point, the point that Paul could never understand."

"Oh, Maria," Cathy said, "what bullshit. You mean Paul found out you killed this man and turned you in."

Maria lifted her hands, fingers curved, then let them fall. "That's right, Cathy," she said. "Paul cracked the case—no one is better at that than Paul, as you have reason to know. He found out everything. And understood nothing."

Cathy shivered and shifted from foot to foot. "Are we close to the end of all this?" she asked. "I can't stay out here much longer."

"Paul made a case against us that Headquarters believed," Maria said. "They decided we were working for the other side, that Otto—*Otto!*—was working for the other side. Paul hounded us out of the Outfit. He turned everything Otto had ever done—done for Paul's precious America—to shit. So here we are, with no money, no pension, no honor."

"No wonder you were so glad to see me," Cathy said.

"That was before I knew about your souvenir," Maria said. "This *is* Paul's baby you're carrying?"

"Yes."

"There's no doubt about it?"

"None."

"Then for God's sake, Cathy, use your head for once," Maria said. "Get rid of it. Tomorrow. Don't bring another coldhearted bastard like its father into the world."

WHEN SHE GOT BACK TO THE HOUSE, CATHY WENT STRAIGHT TO BED. When she woke up Lla Kahina was playing cards by candlelight. It was four o'clock in the morning.

"You've been dreaming," Lla Kahina said.

"What about, do you know? I can never remember."

"It's not in the cards. You've been turning and talking."

"What *is* in the cards? Do you always play this way, day and night?"

"No. Something is trying to come through, but it can't. Something in this house is blocking it."

"That's a relief," Cathy said. "Everybody else in Switzerland wants to tell me something I don't want to hear."

Because the candle was between them, it shone on Lla Kahina's face, revealing it in a new way.

"I don't know why, Lla Kahina," Cathy said, "but I think I know you. I *recognize* you."

"Do you? That happens sometimes."

Cathy frowned, trying to remember. Lla Kahina was calm, patient. She waited for Cathy to speak again.

"I think I'll go to Paris tomorrow," Cathy said. "Do you want to come with me?"

She did not know why she asked the question. Lla Kahina was not in the least surprised by it.

"Of course," she said. "But we must take the train. No airplanes. You must not lose contact with the earth."

"That's fine with me," Cathy said.

T W O

1

CATHY SAW CHRISTOPHER FROM A LONG WAY OFF. HE WAS SITTING ON a bench in the Bois de Boulogne with his friend David Patchen. Cathy was cantering a borrowed chestnut mare along the bridle path near the Grande Cascade. He was looking straight at her. She slowed the mare to a trot, then to a walk, as she approached the bench.

Christopher stood up. Patchen rose, too, and turned around. He wore a black patch over one of his eyes. As soon as he saw Cathy, he limped away into the trees.

"You're riding again," Christopher said.

"Yes, almost every day. I'm all right again. Good genes."

This was a joke from the past. On being told that his daughter had married Christopher, her father had taken his new son-in-law aside and said, "You'll never have to worry about her health. The Kirkpatricks are never sick—good genes."

"Are you really all right?" Christopher said.

Cathy did not answer his question. "What about you?" she said. "This is kind of a cold morning to be sitting on a park bench."

"I guess so," Christopher said. "David likes to be outdoors."

"I remember."

Patchen was the man Christopher reported to in the Outfit. He came over to Paris five or six times a year, and Christopher went to Washington five or six times. The two of them walked all over both cities together, talking and talking, out of the reach of microphones.

"Where are you living?" Christopher asked.

"At my parents' place. For now. They won't be back until

40

spring." Cathy's mother and father came to Paris twice a year for the racing seasons at Auteuil and Longchamps.

"I saw your father in the bar of the Jockey Club just after you left Rome," Christopher said. "He asked about you. He invited me to dinner. He didn't seem to know what's happened to you and me."

"Who does? What did you say?"

"I said I hadn't seen you for a while. You haven't told them?"

Cathy shook her head. The mare fidgeted. Cathy's legs trembled slightly from the strain of keeping her under control; she was not really strong enough to ride yet. She felt dizzy, nauseated, feverish in her turtleneck sweater, her tweed jacket, her gloves. Would Christopher, who missed nothing, notice her condition? The baby showed very little, and she was wearing one of her mother's jackets that was a size or two too large for her.

Once again, frowning anxiously, Christopher said, "Are you all right?"

"Fine. My friend, here, doesn't want to stand still. And to tell the truth, I'm a little shaky, seeing you like this, all of a sudden."

"You too?"

Christopher took off his glove and held out his left hand. It trembled, something she had never seen before. He no longer wore his wedding band, but the impression it had made in the flesh of his finger was still clearly visible.

Christopher's presence silenced her. She had always been afraid, from the day she met him, that she was not smart enough for him, that she would say something that would drive him away from her. She made jokes for other men, but never for Christopher.

"It's hell, not knowing what to say like this," Cathy said. "Do you want to stick to the weather, or what?"

"We can talk about anything you want."

"Why don't you start?"

"I don't know what's left to say."

Cathy nodded, biting her lower lip again. "I was surprised when you cried that day," she said.

He had wept at the airport, saying goodbye to her.

"Before," Cathy said, "I was always the one who cried. I don't do that much anymore. I've seen the light."

Christopher reached out as if to touch her, remembered himself, and let his hand drop to his side.

"Oh, shit, Paul," she said. "What did I think I was doing?"

41

"I don't know, Cathy," he said.

She kicked the mare into a gallop and rode away. *Bastard,* she thought. *Bastard for not loving me enough to kill me for what I did to you.*

2

WHEN CATHY CAME BACK FROM THE BOIS DE BOULOGNE SHE WENT straight to her room, locked the door, and took a hot bath. During their marriage, because of Christopher's absences, she had fallen into the habit of talking to him when he was not there.

"God," she said to his invisible presence now, "how I wish I hadn't seen you today. How I wish that none of this had ever happened."

When they were married and he was always away, she used to imagine his return, imagine love in his glance, imagine the words he would speak; imagine his passion. In this make-believe homecoming, it was Christopher who longed for Cathy, Christopher who was half-mad with loneliness, Christopher who wept as they made love. The greatest surprise of her life was her love for him; she truly had not known that a woman could love a man more than he loved her. Nothing in her previous life, in which she had always been more beautiful than anyone else, always been the object of desire, had prepared her for this. She had supposed that the gift of her body would bring her, in return, absolute power over his heart. But had Christopher ever loved her? Had he always known, as Lla Kahina had told her, that the woman he would really love was waiting for him in the future? Who was this evil stranger? How could she be more beautiful than Cathy? What did she have that he wanted so desperately? He had never wanted anything when he was with Cathy; he had merely acquiesced in what she wanted. At the time she had mistaken that for love, but now she knew it for what it was—*politesse,* courtesy and consideration in which the heart played no part.

"All right, I understand," she said. "You're all through with politeness, Paul; it's time for love. I hope you find it."

For all Cathy knew, he had found it already. Why shouldn't he? Hadn't he earned it by living with her in a state of chivalry when what he really wanted was to love somebody more than she loved him? Cathy punched the water hard; a cupful flew across the room and splashed against the full-length mirror in which she had been watching herself.

"I hope the bitch dies on you," she said to the absent Christopher. She did not cry. "I'm all through crying," she said. "That's over. Lots of things are over."

She put on robe and slippers and went to the library. Lla Kahina was already having tea. Tea was her favorite meal; she often slept through lunch, the principal meal of the day, and consumed only liquids for dinner.

"Why?" Cathy had asked.

"I've never liked French food. My husband didn't like it either. He always ordered the same things in restaurants—oysters, clear soup, roast lamb, berries; things that didn't come in disguise."

"Is that what he called sauces? Disguises?"

"No. Paul's father called them that, in one of his novels. It was called *The Masked Ball*. It was all about people making themselves important."

"Are you in it?"

"Not in that one. He wrote it before we met."

Lla Kahina said no more on this subject. She said little about herself, and most of what Cathy knew about her she knew from Otto's stories or from her own observation. Lla Kahina seemed to have plenty of money; Cathy had seen her handing Maria Rothchild a huge wad of francs before they left Switzerland, and she was always telephoning shops for food and flowers for the apartment and for books for herself. She herself never went outside. She neither wrote nor received letters. She did not read the newspapers. She liked to listen in another room while Cathy played the piano. She seemed to practice no religion. This surprised Cathy; she had supposed that Moslems did their ablutions and prayed with their faces toward Mecca five times a day no matter where they found themselves. When Cathy asked questions, Lla Kahina answered them: she was separated from her husband, she had no children of her own, she came from a place in North Africa called the Idáren Dráren.

"Idáren Dráren," Cathy said. "That's beautiful. What does it mean in Berber?"

"The Mountains of Mountains."

"Is it beautiful there?"

"You will think so when you see it."

"I'm going to see it?"

"Oh, yes."

"The cards say so?"

"Yes."

Lla Kahina laid the deck on the table; Cathy cut and shuffled.

"Good, that's settled. What else do they say?"

"You saw your husband today," she said. "He was sitting on a bench with a man dressed in black. You ran your horse very fast afterward."

"You see all that in the six of hearts?"

"I saw some of it before."

"When?"

"In Switzerland."

"Why didn't you tell me before?"

"It wasn't clear in Switzerlad. In any case, what happened would still have happened."

"Then when is our next star-crossed meeting?"

All the cards had been turned over. Lla Kahina handed Cathy the deck to be shuffled. "He's gone forever," she said.

"Gone? You mean I'll never see him again?"

"Once more, perhaps. It isn't clear."

"How do you know? You're not even looking at the cards."

"No, but it was the first thing I ever saw about you, and I see it all the time; you know that."

"Then tell me something that I don't know; something nice."

Lla Kahina took back the shuffled deck and laid out three cards, then three more as if to check the result.

"There is a second child," she said.

Cathy thought immediately, with furious jealousy, of the woman in Christopher's future. Or were they together already? Had they already made love? The thought was unbearable.

"You mean somebody else is pregnant by Paul?"

"No. You're carrying twins."

Cathy swept the cards off the table. "I don't believe it," she said. "Enough is enough."

But when she went to the American Hospital for her next regular checkup, the doctor listened at her abdomen with a stethoscope for a long time, frowning in concentration. Finally he looked up and grinned.

"You know," he said, "I think Junior has company."

"What?"

"I get two heartbeats. Listen."

He handed her the instrument and held the bell in the right place. Cathy heard her own heart, and then a sound like that made by a stopwatch wrapped in a handkerchief.

"Hear it?" The doctor moved the bell downward; she heard the muffled ticking of a second stopwatch. "Hear that, honey? That's the other twin."

After that, Cathy had no doubts at all about Lla Kahina's power to know what was going to happen to her. But why was it happening? Why couldn't she just be happy?

3

FOR THE TWINS' SAKE, CATHY LIVED BY THE CLOCK. SHE WOKE UP AT eight, ate her breakfast at eight-thirty, and rode in the Bois de Boulogne from nine till ten-thirty. She was home by eleven, and bathed and dressed again by twelve. She read the inside pages of the *Herald-Tribune* until lunch at one o'clock, took an hour's nap, and spent two hours at the piano. In the late afternoon she went for a long walk, usually along the Seine. She wore her Loden cape with the hood up, so that she was as unrecognizable as a nun as she strode along the embankment beneath the bridges and up and down the steep stone stairs that connected the river and the streets.

In a used book stall on the Quai Voltaire, she found a battered portfolio containing Beethoven's last quartets, scored for the piano, and bought it for fifty francs. This music was beyond her ability as a pianist, but she decided to try to learn it anyway, as an aid to her program of forgetting. As she played, sight-reading from the yellowed pages of the score, she never knew what to expect. Tempo and tone shifted, the mood swung, texture changed without warning. The works were five long cries of abandonment and loneliness. They suited her mood.

This immensely complicated music did for Cathy what she had wanted it to do. It made it impossible to remember anything else. The effort of playing left her groggy and detached from her surroundings. Sometimes she would walk all the way to the Pont de la Concorde before her mind began to work normally again.

One afternoon in December, as she rose exhausted from the piano, she heard the telephone ringing. When she picked up the instrument an English-speaking male voice that she had heard before, but did not immediately recognize, said, "I'm trying to reach Catherine."

No one except teachers had ever called her Catherine. Cathy responded in French. "Who's calling?"

"A friend from college."

These words, delivered in a dry-throated, distant tone, brought her back to reality with a rush of anxiety. This was the recognition phrase that Christopher had set up so that she would know, if someone phoned while he was in the field, that the caller was a member of the Outfit with a message from him or news of him. She changed to English and gave the answering phrase.

"You're a long way from Philadelphia."

"Ah," said the caller. "I thought it was you, but you sound different in French."

It was David Patchen.

"Is something wrong?" she said.

"No, everything is all right," Patchen said. "I don't mean to upset you, but I'd like to talk to you."

Cathy nearly hung up the phone. Why should she want to talk to Patchen? "I'm not sure that's possible," she said.

"I'm afraid it has to be possible," Patchen replied.

Cathy took a deep breath, exhaled into the mouthpiece, and said, "All right."

"Good. Are you free for dinner tonight? I'm only in town for a limited time."

Patchen, like many people from the Outfit, seemed to prefer discussing secrets in expensive restaurants while surrounded by eavesdroppers. Cathy had never understood this.

"I don't go out at night," she said. "Why don't you come here for tea at five o'clock?"

"Tea," Patchen said, drawing out the word in a parody of enthusiasm. "That would be lovely."

David Patchen had been Christopher's best man, the only attendant, at Cathy's wedding. He and Christopher had been wounded in the same battle on Okinawa, Patchen far more seriously than Christopher. After the war they had been roommates in college, and now they were both members of the Outfit, the most exclusive fraternity in American history. Cathy felt sorry for Patchen because of his disfigured face and his withered limbs, but she did not like him.

Patchen realized this, and he wasted no time on polite greetings or expressions of regret. Because he had the full use of only one hand, he had trouble with the mechanics of afternoon tea. He took the cup that Cathy poured for him, but refused sandwiches and cakes.

"They're delicious," Cathy said, offering the plate.

"I'm sure they are," Patchen replied. "But no thank you."

"Paul always said you were an ascetic."

Cathy ate her usual egg and toast and fruit; she was scrupulous about her diet, and she had an appetite. She had walked all the way to the Pont Neuf that day, counting her steps in an attempt to keep from thinking about Patchen's phone call and what it might mean.

Patchen had no small talk even when it was appropriate, so he simply waited in silence while Cathy finished her food, holding his teacup in his good hand. He made no effort to conceal his interest in her new appearance. She had put on a full skirt, a loose blouse, and a blazer to conceal her slightly thickened abdomen, but he was completely uninterested in her clothes, or anything else except her damaged face.

Cathy wiped her unpainted lips with a napkin, and said, "Well, how do you like my face job?"

"You look a little different," Patchen said.

"Better or worse?"

"Less perfect."

"It's a great experience, having a new face."

Patchen smiled sardonically. "I know," he said.

His face had been shattered on Okinawa, along with his arm and leg. He had lost an eye.

"What did you look like, before?" Cathy asked; she had always wondered, and now she had the right to ask.

"Incredibly handsome," Patchen said.

He cleared his throat and said, "Can we talk about your condition for a moment?"

"My condition?"

Cathy's throat tightened. It was impossible to guess what he might know.

"I mean in regard to us," Patchen was saying, "now that you and Paul aren't together any more."

" 'Us'?"

"The Outfit."

"What does the Outfit have to do with it?"

"Divorces can be bitter," Patchen said. "I don't know how you feel about Paul at this point."

"You don't? Neither do I. How does Paul feel about me?"

Patchen went on as if she had not spoken. "Or how you feel about the Outfit," he said.

"That's easy. I think it's a joke."

Patchen was looking for a place to put the cup in which his tea had gone cold. Cathy reached across the table and took it from him. Patchen picked up the attaché case he had brought with him and opened the catches with a loud double snap. The case was black, like all of Patchen's accoutrements.

"Paperwork," he said. "I'm sorry to inflict this on you."

"Then why are you doing it?" Cathy said. "Why you? I thought you were too high-ranking to deal with abandoned wives."

He took a thick file of papers out of his case, closed the lid, and sighed.

"I'm here because I'm Paul's friend," he said, "and even though I don't expect you to believe me when I say this, I'm not your enemy. The Outfit has certain procedures when one of its officers parts from his wife, even when the circumstances are less dramatic than they are in this case."

"Why isn't Paul doing this himself?"

"Because he's one of the parties to the situation, and because he doesn't know everything that we know."

"What *do* you know?"

Patchen removed a thick file from his attaché case and handed it to Cathy. "More, frankly, than I wish we knew," he said.

Cathy had never seen an Outfit file before; she had imagined that they were stamped Top Secret and sealed with ribbons and wax inside impressive covers, but this one was just a plain manila folder filled with typed pages. There were no stamps, no labels, no titles, not even a name on the cover. It was absolutely sterile. It even smelled sterile, because of the faintly antiseptic odor of the fresh ink left by typewriter ribbons that were used only once, then burned.

"Am I supposed to read the whole thing?" Cathy said.

"You're not supposed to know it exists, but you can read it if you want to. Everything we know, officially, is in there. There are some things you don't know."

"That's an official warning?"

"I wouldn't call it that, but you should prepare yourself."

Cathy took the file to her father's desk, where the light was better. It took almost an hour to read it. Everything was there: her lovers' names; the dates and places on which she had seen them, transcripts of what they had said during the acts they had performed on her body and what she had said in reply; dry, neutral comments about her behavior and appearance by the anonymous people who had been watching her and listening to her with hidden microphones. As she read, a clot of nausea rose into her throat. Had these acts been photographed by secret cameras?

She handed the file back to Patchen.

"What? No photographs?" she said.

"I didn't bring them," Patchen said.

"But they exist?"

Patchen nodded. Cathy could barely breathe. What had been photographed? What exactly had Patchen seen? Had Paul seen her with her lovers? Had he ordered the pictures to be taken?

"Was it Paul who told these people to follow me?" she asked.

Insofar as Patchen was capable of registering shock, he registered it now.

"Of course not," he said. "A surveillance team was on your friend for other reasons. Moroni—the one who hit you. Is that the right name?"

He knew it was. Cathy refused to confirm information by so much as a nod.

"He's a parlor Stalinist, a useful idiot," Patchen said, "a believer, somebody who does favors for the other side; he was servicing interesting people. You just happened to walk into the picture."

"Were all the others enemy agents, too?"

"You mean your other . . . friends? No. Just Moroni. You were an object of interest because of the interest in him, so they surveilled you and everybody you came in contact with. That's the way it's done. They didn't even know who you were until they saw you with Paul."

"How could they not know that?"

"You weren't living at home. You rented your hideaway in a false name. You read the file: they didn't identify you until you went through a passport control, on your way to meet Paul in Spain."

"But Paul knew who I was, and after they told him what I was doing, he must have sat around discussing it with them. Wouldn't that be his duty?"

"That's not the way it was," Patchen said. "Paul was told because he needed to know, that's all. It turned out he knew already."

"Why did you think he needed to know?"

"Because the investigation of this man Moroni, the one who injured you, was connected to something Paul was working on."

"You mean Otto and Maria."

Patchen hesitated. "Yes, or so we thought at the time. Paul told you more than I thought."

"Don't worry. He didn't tell me anything I didn't need to know. I guarantee you."

Patchen was holding another paper in his hand. This one was a legal document, stapled into a blue backing.

"This is an agreement between you and us," he said, handing it over. "You agree never to reveal Paul's real occupation to anyone, and never to disclose any classified information that may have come to your knowledge as a result of your relationship with him. That includes the identity of other members of the Outfit you may have met."

"I'm making a contract with you to forget the whole thing. Is that it?"

Patchen nodded. "You could say that. It's the routine form."

"Give me your pen."

Cathy signed the document without reading it.

Patchen took it back and held it open, waiting for the ink to dry.

"If it isn't too late to ask," Cathy said, "what do I get out of this? When you pay blackmail you're supposed to get the incriminating evidence from the blackmailer, aren't you?"

"Moroni is in prison. He was caught smuggling opium into Turkey."

"Into Turkey? I thought that was where opium came from."

"Then I guess he was carrying coals to Newcastle."

"How long will he be in jail?"

"The sentence was twenty years."

"You-all paid him back. Not for me, but for what he did to Paul's wife. He damaged Outfit property. Was that it?"

Patchen did not argue with her. "To answer your earlier question," he said, "there is no quid pro quo for signing the agreement. However, the report you read is the only copy in existence. I'll burn it tonight," he said. "The original, which is identical, will remain in the files. But now that Moroni is out of the way, the case is closed. I'll send this file to the warehouse. It will be buried under tons of paper. Nobody will ever look for it there unless there's some compelling reason to do so."

"You can send it to the *Herald-Tribune* as far as I'm concerned."

A long time had passed since Patchen's arrival and he was beginning to show fatigue. His face was drawn and colorless. He closed his attaché case and twirled the combination locks. He stood up, painfully. He and Cathy looked dully at each other.

"There's one more thing I want to say to you, for old times' sake," Patchen said. "It would be a mistake to think that the people you visited in Switzerland are your friends."

"You mean Otto and Maria? I'll bear that in mind."

Patchen nodded, a brisk Germanic movement of his ruined head, and without uttering another sound, walked out of the room. He left the door open behind him. Cathy watched him hobble through the dimly lit salon on his way to the foyer, carrying his attaché case. Even from the back, he looked wasted, worn out. If he saw Lla Kahina in the shadows of the room, he gave no sign.

THREE

DAY BY DAY, CATHY TRIED TO CURE HERSELF OF CHRISTOPHER. IT was late March now, and her pregnancy was finally obvious. She was no longer able to ride comfortably, so she played the piano in the morning and took longer walks in the afternoon. She paid no attention to the weather, sometimes trudging through snow along the footpaths of the Bois de Boulogne, sometimes striding in a winter rain through miserable quarters of the Left Bank where she had never set foot before.

She always wore her Loden cape. Its thick wool kept out the water and the damp northern European cold that seeped through other garments. When it rained too hard, she went into a café and ordered a cup of tea and read whatever book she happened to have with her. She had her hair cut short, like Jean Seberg's in *A bout de souffle* and dyed it black. This, combined with the cape and its deep hood, made a good disguise. In her own neighborhood, people she knew walked by her with hardly a glance, mistaking her battered face inside the woolen cowl for that of someone who merely resembled her.

Every evening after tea, Lla Kahina told her fortune. The cards always said the same thing—Christopher would never come back.

All right, Cathy thought, walking along the Rue Saint-Sulpice on a day in March. *Go. Leave me in peace.* It was a bright, cold day, with light flashing from every glass surface. Cathy threw back the hood of her Loden cape and saw her own reflection in a shop window.

"Good God!" she said aloud. She looked like a nun with her cropped hair, her victim's face, and her enveloping cloak. Behind the glass, all kinds of religious objects were displayed, crucifixes and miters, chalices and wimples. She threw her head back and looked upward at the strip of pale sky above the narrow street.

"He works in mysterious ways," she said loudly, this time in clear French, and a woman passing by, noting her condition, smiled and responded, *"Vraiment, Madame!"*

Because of the sunshine that suffused their dreary city that day, the Parisians were in good humor. Cathy walked on between the shops filled with ecclesiastical apparatus until she came to the Rue Tournon. She turned right without thinking, and a moment later found herself looking at the Florentine mass of the Palace of Luxembourg.

How had she got here? She never went to the Luxembourg Gardens on her walks. It was a place where she had often met Christopher in the first days of their love. He had the use of an apartment, a safe house, only steps away in the Rue Bonaparte, and sometimes they would meet here, always by the puppet theater, and then go to the safe house and then to bed.

Cathy entered the gardens. The grass was still brown and the flower beds were muddy, but because of the bright weather, the gardens were crowded with mothers and children, students reading books and young couples walking under the leafless trees, kissing.

She walked along the broad curving path beside the fountain, picking her way among baby carriages and exchanging smiles with placid, sunbathing mothers. She turned toward the puppet theater. The first time she had met him here, Christopher had come up behind her and stood very close, not quite touching her body with his.

"Did you like Punch and Judy as a child?"

"No. It scared me."

"Maybe you didn't know enough about life."

I do now, Cathy thought.

She sat down on a bench with two mothers, who gave her resentful looks for invading their territory. A sharp little breeze was blowing, so she put up the hood of her cape.

"Look," one of the mothers said to the other. "She's in love."

Cathy looked. A girl about her own age was hurrying down the path. She was too spontaneous to be French, too happy to be American. She had long, very beautiful legs, and reddish hair that captured the sunlight. Her clothes were wrong, as if left over from school, but it made no difference what she wore. She looked like a woman who had made love that morning to someone she loved, and could not wait to meet him so that she could make love to him again in the afternoon. Whoever she was, the girl had found happiness; it was written all over her.

Just then she saw her lover, raised her hand, and began to walk more slowly, as if to prolong the moment. Cathy turned around to look at the man, and saw that it was Christopher. He was close enough so that Cathy heard the girl's name when he spoke it, "Molly."

The girl answered in what seemed to be an English accent, then touched the back of Christopher's hand with the tips of her fingers. It was a brief, almost furtive gesture. She did not kiss him or cling to him as Cathy would have done: Christopher hated to be embraced in public, and this girl already knew what Cathy had never been able to learn. How much more did she know in private?

Christopher seemed to have no idea that Cathy, wrapped up in her cloak, was watching them. He and Molly walked away together toward the Rue Bonaparte, still not touching, her titian head bobbing along beside his blond one, her lovely legs keeping step with his.

Cathy had always believed that Christopher could have any woman he wanted, and never doubted that he wanted other women. She was jealous of women who passed in the street, jealous of women's voices on the telephone, jealous of women in Asia and Africa who were flesh and blood to Christopher but invisible to her. In the last stages of her jealousy, before she decided to take real lovers to fight his imaginary ones, she became a detective. She examined his dirty clothes when he returned from the field for signs of infidelity, and while he was away, searched his car, collecting evidence—a long hair that was the wrong color to be Christopher's or her own, a cigarette butt smeared with lipstick, common pins, traces of mud that could only have come from shoes that had been walking in the woods, a clipped fingernail. When Cathy told him about her desperate plans to take lovers (for she had warned him before she did it), she wanted him to say, "If you let another man touch you, I'll kill you!" But he answered, instead, that her body belonged to her, that she could do with it as she pleased. She had done as he advised, and even in the first moment of her first adultery, she thought that she could never forgive him for letting her do what she was doing.

This Molly was the woman in the cards—the one who had been waiting for Christopher, the one he would really love for the rest of his life, the one whose existence she had never expected. The worst had happened; she knew the final secret, that he did not love her anymore, that he would never love her again, that he had never really loved her because he had been waiting for his true love all along, just as she had always suspected. Inside the cape, she put her hands on her children.

"I know you can hear me, Paul," she said, shouting.

The Frenchwomen on the bench shrank away from Cathy, staring.

She said, still shouting, "I swear that you'll never know that your children exist. They'll never know who their father is. From this moment you don't exist—not for me, not for your children. I'm going where you'll never find us."

In the distance, unhearing, Christopher kissed Molly.

2

LLA KAHINA SAT ON THE LEATHER LIBRARY SOFA, A GLASS OF MINT on the table beside her, a book in her hands. While listening to Cathy talk, she marked her place with a finger. The title of her book, written in what seemed to be, but could not be, the Hebrew alphabet, was printed on the back cover. Cathy did not know why she registered these details, except that she had been seeing and smelling everything with heightened intensity ever since witnessing Christopher's encounter with Molly.

"Do you mean what you say when you talk about my going home with you?" she asked.

"Of course I do," Lla Kahina replied.

"I don't mean for a visit. I mean to stay."

"The answer is the same."

"You'd better know why I'm asking," Cathy said. "I want to hide Paul's children from him, and to hide him from them. I don't want them to know who he is or him to know who they are. Ever."

Still wearing her cape, she paced back and forth across the carpet as she spoke. She had run home from the Luxembourg Garden through the balmy springlike air, and her face glistened with sweat. Her dampened hair stood up in peaks all over her head. She said, "Is it really as wild and lost where you come from as you say it is?"

"Yes, and as beautiful."

"Don't tell me any more than that. I don't want to know where I'm going, or where I am when I get there."

The next morning Cathy showed Lla Kahina a list of names, the people who knew about her pregnancy—the maid, the doctor, her banker, Otto and Maria Rothchild.

"The first three are easy," Cathy said. "But Otto and Maria are another matter."

"Paul will never see Otto again," Lla Kahina said.

Cathy gave her a sharp look. "What about Maria?"

"She has no power over a person like Paul."

A long silence ensued. For the twins' sake, Cathy ate the last of her breakfast—the milk for their bones, the eggs for their brains, the bread for their muscles. Finally she said, "I hope you're right about that."

She rang for the maid. The woman entered the breakfast room, holding her hands limply before her as though she had been forced against her will to touch something disgusting. She disliked working for a pregnant American woman who seemed to have no husband and no friends except a tattooed native who wore tassels on the hems of her garments.

"Blanche, I have something to tell you," Cathy said. "You can collect your things and go. I won't need you anymore."

"But why, madame?"

"I've decided to go back to America to have my child."

"On one day's notice?"

"That is my affair." Cathy was rude because she wanted the woman to remember what she had said about returning to America. "You will have six months' wages, one for every month you have been with us, and one as a bonus."

"Normally, madame—"

"I know what's normal in France."

Cathy took the money, in American dollars, out of her purse. She had miscalculated the exchange rate, as usual, and the amount she handed over was much more than six months' wages in francs. Blanche accepted the strange, drab, unFrench bills that had so much more value than was just and proper.

"You're very kind, madame," she said. "May I also have a reference? All this is so brusque that otherwise people may wonder."

Cathy handed her a letter, written in French on one side of the page and English on the other, saying that Blanche had shown herself to be an economical shopper and a good cook who had given satisfaction despite the hardship of working for foreigners.

Blanche left the soiled breakfast dishes on the table and departed without saying goodbye.

Outside the apartment, Cathy hailed a taxi, the first she had taken for months, and went to the American Hospital. She told the nurse that she had decided to have her babies in America.

"At this late date?" the nurse said. "Why?"

"They're Americans. They should be born in America. That way there'll never be any question about their citizenship."

"But the airlines won't let you fly after the seventh month," the nurse said. "You should talk to doctor before you do this. Really."

Cathy smiled a rich girl's smile: "I won't tell TWA if you won't. Just give me the records."

The nurse made her sign a form, and then handed over a manila envelope.

At D.&D. Laux & Co., she withdrew the entire balance of her account. The total, accumulated over the nearly two years when Christopher had paid most of her expenses, was more than fifty thousand dollars. Cathy asked for it in hundred-dollar bills.

"No traveler's checks, madam?"

"No, just money."

The man in the bank seemed quite young, no more than a year or two older than Cathy. He spoke excellent English with a child-like American accent, as if forming words he had recently heard for the first time.

"Did you happen to go to college in California?" Cathy asked. He was pleased by the question, the first personal one she had asked him in the three or four years she had been coming to him.

"Stanford. Where did you go?"

Cathy gave him the same smile she had given the nurse. "What an American question. Bryn Mawr, but I barely managed to graduate. I'll bet you got all A's."

"Sometimes a B, or even a C. There were many distractions at Stanford."

"That's why we go to college back home, for the distractions." Cathy leaned forward slightly. "Look, I'm going home to have my baby, and then we're going to travel, maybe for a long time. I'll cable or write when I want you to send me money."

"The deposits arrive from New York, normally, on the twentieth of each month."

Cathy's trust fund, set up by her maternal grandparents because, as they explained in their wills, Cathy's father was in the horse business and therefore liable to go broke at any moment, paid her between two and three thousand dollars a month, depending on how her stocks were doing. D.&D. Laux & Co. managed the trust and paid the taxes.

"There's one more favor," Cathy said to the banker. "I'd like to be able to send you letters for my parents. Can I just address them to you, and you can throw away the outer envelope and just give them the plain envelope inside?"

"With pleasure."

"Don't forget to throw away the postmarks. I don't want them coming to visit me for a while."

"You can be quite sure of my complete discretion."

Cathy picked up her money, five stacks of bills still in their paper bands marked with the name of the New York Federal Reserve Bank, and put them into her purse.

After leaving the bank she walked into the first travel agency she saw and bought two one-way airplane tickets to North Africa on the next day's flight. She paid cash.

That afternoon, as usual, Cathy ate the twins' tea and took her nap for them, but instead of going for her walk, she wrote a letter to her mother and father.

I haven't told you because I didn't know how to tell you, but Paul and I have separated. This happened late last summer, and it's all for the best. We just weren't meant for each other, although I had a very hard time believing that and Paul was too kind—or too something—to mention it, but he didn't argue when I finally figured it out for myself.

I've been staying here with a friend (a nice woman I met after the break-up, no one you know). My friend is kind of like a psychologist, and she's been a real help to me. I understand now what happened between Paul and me, and why it happened, and I accept it and am all right emotionally. Honest.

But I feel the need to be by myself, maybe for a long time, so

I've decided to travel for a while. And—this will be hard for you—I don't want anyone, not even you two, to know where I am. Please try to understand that this is absolutely necessary for me. I took all my money out of the bank, bought a ticket, and I leave tomorrow. I have no itinerary, no plan, no return date. I just want to go, and be alone, and think.

I don't know when I'll come back. I have enough money and enough sense to be all right wherever I am, so try not to worry. There's no getting back to the person I was before, but that may not be a bad thing, either. I'll write to you every month, or as often as I can, through the bank. Don't worry f I miss a month. I don't suppose you can trust the post office in some of the places I'll be.

Don't blame Paul for all this. That would be wrong and unjust. Just, please, don't try to see him. It's over and I want it to be over. He has somebody else now (this happened after we parted, so there's no need for Daddy to shoot him), and I hope that he'll be happy.

I love you both very, very much, and I hope that you can forgive me for not telling you all this before now. I just couldn't.

Cathy sealed the envelope and addressed it, then put it inside another envelope, and addressed that to the man at the bank. She knew, as surely as if Lla Kahina had seen it in the cards, that she would never see her parents, or anyone else she had known, ever again. Her old life was over. "Goodbye," she said aloud, shedding not one single tear, any more than she had done when she and Christopher parted.

3

CATHY LEFT PARIS, AS SHE HAD LEFT ROME, IN THE CLOTHES SHE wore, with only her large purse stuffed with money for luggage. After a long flight they approached the Idáren Dráren at sunset— snowy peaks and rust-colored crags silhouetted against a cloudless lavender sky. Just as Lla Kahina had predicted, the view was familiar, and Cathy felt a pang on seeing it through the scratched window of the airplane, as if she had been happy in this place a long time ago.

The heat on the ground was intense. After passing through

customs they took a taxi from the airport and drove through a city toward the mountains. Looking out the open window of the weaving car, Cathy had a blurry impression of narrow streets filled with children riding donkeys at the trot, men driving wagons pulled by emaciated horses, and veiled women carrying jugs and bundles balanced on their heads. The stink of many kinds of animal droppings came inside along with lungfuls of parched air stirred up by the passage of the car.

The taxi climbed into the foothills, leaving the paved road behind at the edge of town and following a bumpy dirt track for several miles until it, too, ended. The car stopped and they got out. Lla Kahina paid the driver, who unloaded their luggage, then turned his rattling Simca around and drove off without so much as a goodbye.

"The others are waiting for us a little higher up," Lla Kahina said, pointing in the direction of the mountains.

She set off along a steep path that ran beside a roaring brook. As they walked she pointed out the trees and wild flowers, naming them in Berber; Cathy nodded, not even knowing the names of American flora in English. As Lla Kahina had said so often, the landscape was the color of henna. Soil, rocks, the whole scene was composed of shades of red except for the trees, and even they looked red when viewed from a distance because they were coated with red dust. A deserted village, made of powdery henna bricks, was cemented somehow to the side of a dizzying cliff against a backdrop of rocky crags; its houses put out no smoke, nothing moved, she could see no path leading up from the valley.

"Who lives there?"

"Ghosts."

Cathy was short of breath, and stopped beside the path. She was surprised at how much strength the twins took out of her. This hadn't happened on her walks in the city.

"It's the altitude," Lla Kahina said. "Breathe deeply, go slowly. It's not far."

Soon they arrived at their destination. Around a turn in the trail, six men waited for them by a waterfall in a meadow. A small herd of animals—half a dozen sheep, a couple of kids, many donkeys, a dozen fine-boned Barbary horses—grazed on the other side of the stream. The men were all young—muscular, obvious horsemen, with handsome, clcan-shaven Semitic faces. They were dressed alike in white, with wide black sashes around their waists and large black turbans on their heads. All wore purple vests with many brass buttons and the inevitable purple tassels along the hem. They carried curved knives in ornate scabbards, and some had rifles slung over their backs.

Lla Kahina embraced them one by one, and then turned to Cathy. Each boy—now that she was closer, Cathy saw that most were barely out of their teens—shook hands with her, looking curiously into her face and talking loudly all the while in Berber, or what Cathy supposed was Berber. As a child, she had read, over and over again, a romantic book called *The Magnificent Barb,* about the fleet Moorish stallion that was bred to big-boned English mares to produce the Thoroughbred. This was like a scene from a book—bright rugs spread on the ground in front of low white tents turned pink by the dust, wisps of smoke rising from charcoal braziers.

"How long does it take to get where we're going?" she asked.

"Five days, usually," Lla Kahina said. "We'll start tomorrow morning."

4

RIDING UPHILL TAXES THE MUSCLES, BUT CATHY WAS IN NO GREAT discomfort. The twins were not due for another couple of weeks. Her belly was compact, and her muscles held the babies firmly even when she rode. The mountain trails were dizzying, but the horses never moved faster than a walk. The Ja'wabi stopped often to drink tea or wait for something to happen—Cathy never knew what; they would stop, listen, exchange opinions, and then, when whatever they had been expecting came to pass, always out of sight and hearing, they would repack, remount, and move on.

After they climbed above the tree line, the Ja'wabi fed the horses four times a day. This seemed excessive to Cathy.

"You don't want to ride a hungry horse along a trail with a thousand-foot drop at the edge of it," Lla Kahina explained. "What if he sees something to eat, a bunch of leaves, and reaches for it?"

It was cold now, with gusts of wind that smelled clean and damp instead of dusty and scorched. The Ja'wabi got out sheepskin coats. Cathy put on her Loden cape. On the fourth morning, after camping on a barren slope in a wind that drove grit through the walls of the tents, they rode along a path beside a deep river gorge. The trails were even narrower than before. Large pebbles, covering the track like the polished rocks in a stream bed, rolled under the animals' hooves. By noon they were only halfway across. They halted at a wider place, about the size of a large closet, that had been gouged out of the side of the cliff by the river millions of years before.

The boys lighted a fire to brew tea, then fed the donkeys and goats and left them standing on the trail, but tied the horses and sheep, which were too stupid to be trusted not to plunge over the edge, to outcroppings of rock.

Cathy drank her tea. It was highly sweetened; she had avoided sugar all her life and she did not really like it. But she knew she needed something to keep her going. She had eaten very little on the journey, only some bread and stewed vegetables. Despite her hunger, despite the wind, Cathy felt an overwhelming sense of well-being. She was warm, safe, and in the midst of a wildly beautiful and mysterious world. All morning, as they passed along the precipice, she had been talking to the twins in her thoughts, telling them that she would bring them back to this miraculous place as soon as they were old enough to ride, so that they could see it for themselves.

Suddenly she felt something warm, warmer than her skin, on the inside of her thigh. She handed Lla Kahina her half-empty glass of tea, turned her back to the boys, and touched her body. The legs of her woolen trousers were soaked with a sticky fluid.

"I think my water has broken," she said.

Lla Kahina reached inside Cathy's cape and felt with her own hand.

"The child is coming," she said.

"*Children*," Cathy said automatically. "There are two. Why do you always say 'child'?"

Just then Cathy felt the first contraction. It wasn't specially strong. The boys were putting up a tent. They worked in silence, holding on to the flapping canvas with difficulty. Sitting on a rock, she felt a second contraction, vague like the first, but more notice-able now that she was sure what it was. The boys finished what they were doing and left, driving the sheep and goats before them, leaving Cathy and Lla Kahina alone.

"God, what a wind," Cathy said. Her hood was down and she could hear it plainly, moaning through the rocks.

Lla Kahina led her inside the tent. Cathy followed obediently. The ground was covered with a rug, and in the middle of the rug, two large stones of equal size had been arranged side by side. Lla Kahina covered them with smaller rugs. A rope dangled from the ceiling. Cathy started to lie down on the floor.

"No. Sit on the stones," Lla Kahina said.

"The stones? What for?"

"It's better than lying down. Let me help you."

Passively, Cathy let Lla Kahina remove her dress. Her skin was dripping with sweat.

"It's all right," Lla Kahina said. "Sit down. That's it. Put one leg on one stone and the other on the other stone."

The position was uncomfortable. "I don't want to be like this," Cathy said. "I want to lie down."

"This is the bèst way," Lla Kahina said. "I know it seems strange to you, but believe me, it's better. Pull on the rope when you feel the pains."

Lit rosily from without by sunshine, the tent filled up with wind, collapsed, and then respired again, like a lung. After a while Lla Kahina put a baby into Cathy's arms and showed her how to feed it.

"Where is the other twin?" Cathy asked.

"Only one is alive," Lla Kahina said. She held a bundle in her arms.

"Show me," Cathy said.

Lla Kahina lifted the cloth. The face was peaceful, bronzed, with lidded eyes, like a death mask.

"Let me see the rest of him."

"It was a boy," Lla Kahina said, covering the tiny corpse as if she had not heard.

The living twin, a girl, was perfectly silent after its feed, sleeping. For some reason Lla Kahina had knotted a scarlet thread around her tiny wrist. Cathy was too tired to ask why; she fell asleep.

5

THE NEXT MORNING, WHEN CATHY WENT OUTSIDE INTO THE DAY-light, carrying the baby, no one was in sight except Lla Kahina, who stood over a charcoal brazier, stirring the breakfast pot. The boys had come back, and they squatted around the brazier in a circle, eating couscous with their fingers. Beyond the nearer peaks, gauzy cirrus clouds floated in a darkening sky. Cathy refused food, but drank several glasses of sugary mint tea. It made her more lightheaded than usual and everything—the gaudy landscape, the roaring fire, the dandelion sun coming up out of the Sahara on the other side of the mountains, the baby's surprisingly hot little body pressed against her chest, the odd, sweetish aroma of her own milk—took on a dreamy remoteness.

"You should eat," Lla Kahina said in a faraway voice. "The boys won't want to stop. It's going to snow."

Cathy ignored her words. "What did you do with the other baby?"

Lla Kahina paused with her fingers full of food. She put it back into her bowl and handed the bowl to one of the boys.

"Come," she said.

With Cathy following behind, she led the way to a cairn of round, bleached stones at the back of the campsite, up against the cliff. Other, older heaps of stones lay all around.

"He is here," Lla Kahina said, pointing.

"Underneath all those heavy stones?" Cathy said. "Without even a cross above his head?"

"It's better not to have a cross," Lla Kahina said. "Arabs hate Christian things; they would tear it down."

"Then I won't leave him here," Cathy said.

She fell to her knees and pried one of the stones out of the bottom of the cairn with her fingers. It was water-worn and smooth to the touch and wedged tightly in place by all the others, like a cobblestone. As soon as it came loose in her hand the whole layer to which it had belonged rattled to the ground and rolled away, forming a small avalanche that shot over the edge of the cliff, cannonading off the rock face of the chasm and setting up echoes.

Lla Kahina knelt beside Cathy and took her bleeding hands. "He isn't here," she said.

"He isn't here?" Cathy said. "Then where is he? What are you telling me?"

"His body is under the rocks, but he died a long time ago, in Paris," Lla Kahina said. "Daughter, listen. What is, is. You've had the child you were meant to have. Now come."

Obediently, Cathy followed Lla Kahina and mounted her horse.

The saddle was very uncomfortable, but she could not walk. After they had ridden a mile or two along the face of the cliff, Cathy standing up in the stirrups most of the way, snow began to descend in big sluggish flakes. It kept falling, covering people and animals with a thick white pelt, until just before sunset, when the Ja'wabi emerged from the rocks and the country opened up before them. A long way below, in a valley between two bosomlike hills, Cathy saw an expanse of grass and trees and cultivated fields, the first green things she had seen since leaving France. A silvery river threaded through it.

Lla Kahina rode up beside her.

"We're here," she said. "Hold up Zarah so she can see."

Who was Zarah? Lla Kahina held out her hands for the baby. Cathy took her out of her sling and handed her over. As before, she was wide awake but silent.

"Tifawt," Lla Kahina said, speaking directly to the infant as if she would recognize the name. She held the child up at arm's length, with its face toward the fortified village below. From this distance, it looked like a castle, walls and towers flashing like heliographs in the light of the descending sun.

"See how it glitters in the sun?" Lla Kahina said to the child, in English. "It was built with stones that are full of mica."

"What name did you call my baby by just now?" Cathy asked.

"Zarah," Lla Kahina said.

"That's not going to be her name."

"Then we'll only use it among ourselves, as her Ja'wabi name," Lla Kahina said.

Cathy looked into her daughter's face, and the child looked back at her out of Paul Christopher's unfathomable eyes.

INTERLUDE

BEAUTIFUL DREAMERS

EVEN AS A BOY, BEFORE HE WENT TO WAR, CHRISTOPHER HAD DISliked games because they were mere parodies of reality. Afterward, as a spy, he despised them, a peculiarity that set him apart from nearly everyone else in the Outfit, an organization populated in its early days by men who looked on the Cold War as a sort of Hasty Pudding Olympics between the combined track and field teams of Harvard, Princeton, and Yale and an awkward squad of European bookworms and Asiatic oafs.

"That was why you were so good—you didn't think like everybody else on our side," Patchen said. "Except maybe Wolkowicz, who was never really on our side. He thought you were a genius— did he ever tell you that?—because you were able to see the obvious while all around you were oblivious to reality. Nobody sees the obvious for us now. They depend on computers."

Christopher heard these words but did not register them. As he and his friend walked along the peopleless Mall with the floodlit and scaffolded Capitol dome rising up before them, he was thinking about a moment in Rome, years and years before, when he had woken in the night to find his lover Molly hanging a drawing of the dome of the church of San Pancrazio on a wall of their apartment. Thinking herself alone, she was working stark naked by the light of the lamps that lined the embankment of the Tiber beneath the living room windows. The drawing was a gift for Christopher, and he knew that she wanted him to see it in the morning and be surprised, so he did not reveal his presence. Lifting the framed picture onto its hook above her head, Molly rose on her toes with her long legs pressed modestly together and her round bottom

66

uplifted, and it seemed to Christopher then, as now, that she was, at that moment and in that brief attitude, the most innocently beautiful thing he had ever seen.

"It's been three weeks since the last Beautiful Dreamer was delivered to us," Patchen said. "The computer whizzes have gamed every possible combination of data—does the kidnapper strike when the moon is full, do his crimes coincide with the anniversaries of outrages against the Arab nation, is he trying to drive us crazy by running an operation that has no plan or purpose? Are you listening?"

"No," Christopher said.

"I thought not, when you let all those golden opinions go by without a peep."

"What golden opinions?"

"Never mind. There's something obvious in this situation, something hidden in plain sight that nobody has seen."

"Another purloined letter."

"That's right. Your specialty. Have you thought about this case at all since we last talked?"

A week had gone by since their last walk together.

Christopher said, "Yes, I've thought about it. What makes you think it will happen again?"

"If it stops now, what's the point of it?"

"If it doesn't stop, you'll have to shut up shop."

Patchen knew what Christopher meant. More important, he knew that he had his attention at last. So he said, "We will? Why?"

"You know why. Your whole stock-in-trade is secrets. But what happens to the market if you can't *keep* a secret, if you never know which one of your people is going to be grabbed next and given a shot of something that makes him want to tell everything he knows?"

"Go on."

Patchen was intense. Christopher was amused. "I can't, without expressing an opinion."

"Then express one," Patchen said.

"I think your kidnapper is doing the Lord's work. If he gave every member of the human race a shot of this stuff every day, he'd solve the problems of the world."

"That's right. There'd be a fresh corpse in every garage."

An ambulance sped by on Seventh Street in a deafening clamor of horns and sirens; hooting police cars converged from every direction on the scene of a crime.

"*Cinéma verité,*" Patchen said. It was an apt remark. Since midnight they had walked all the way from Georgetown, more than five miles, and at every step Patchen had repeated another of the known facts of the Beautiful Dreamers case, like a film director obsessively screening and rescreening the same rough cut in the hope of capturing some tiny detail, some fleeting image in the shadows of a single frame, some subversive wink of an actor's eye, that would explain why his own movie made no sense to him. "Okay, forgetting about a cure for original sin," Patchen said. "What do you really think?"

"David, I do not wish to think on behalf of the Outfit. I'm out."

"Then think like an outsider. What's going on here? Who are we dealing with? How does he do it?"

"What do you care about what, who, and how?" Christopher asked. "The only real question is 'Why?'"

"I agree," Patchen said. "But how do I answer it?"

Christopher shrugged. "That's obvious."

"It is? Explain it to me anyway."

A taxi approached. Christopher hailed it. As it pulled to the curb the Doberman tensed, ready to attack. It was trained to hurl itself through car windows in case of a threat to its master. Because Patchen was concentrating on Christopher, he neglected to give the animal a reassuring command; it bared its teeth and got ready to attack. "No thank *you,*" the taxi driver said, and sped away with squealing tires.

If Patchen noticed he gave no sign. "Come on," he said. "*What's* obvious?"

"Only the kidnapper knows the answer to your questions," Christopher said.

"So?"

Christopher signaled another taxi. "So kidnap the kidnapper," he said.

II

THE ONE-EYED MAN

ONE

1

FOR MORE THAN THIRTY YEARS DAVID PATCHEN SUSPECTED THAT HIS friend Paul Christopher had saved his life in battle. There was no eyewitness proof that this was so, only a few fragments of circumstantial evidence and memories he could not trust. Patchen never mentioned his suspicion to Christopher, though he often had the feeling that Christopher was waiting for him to do so. Christopher was his only friend, and before she was expelled from the Outfit, Maria Rothchild told Patchen that she believed that Christopher was his only link to human emotion. "You're like a disembodied spirit, following him around, watching him live, wondering what it would be like to have a body and a heart and *believe* in something," she said.

This was close to the truth. Even as a child Patchen had been an outcast, and after he was disfigured by his wounds, he might as well have been the last Neanderthal man, living in disguise among Cro-Magnons, for all the connection he felt to other human beings or they to him. The only exception to his loneliness was Christopher. Why? Late in their friendship, after Christopher was captured and imprisoned by the Chinese Communists, Patchen thought about this strange circumstance with new intensity, and came to the conclusion that it was because Christopher knew something about him that he himself did not know, and did not wish to know.

Whatever this was, it happened on Okinawa on the night of Thursday, May 24, 1945, when Patchen was blinded (or so he thought at the time) by a Japanese hand grenade. He was returning from a patrol along the Shuri Line when an enemy soldier leaped out of the darkness and grappled with him. It was like being

71

attacked by a lynx. The Japanese, who seemed to be naked, his skin smeared with some sort of grease, fought with the brainless fury of a cat, clinging to Patchen's back and raking him with a knife. He was small but almost unbelievably strong. He seized Patchen's helmet and jerked his head back, trying to cut his throat with the knife. Patchen dropped his rifle and seized the other man's wrist with both hands. The Japanese continued to pull on the helmet and Patchen heard himself gasping as the chin strap cut into his windpipe.

Patchen, nearly unconscious, whirled in the darkness, trying to dislodge his attacker. Finally he threw him to the ground. The enemy's knife flew out of his hand. He looked around desperately for his weapon, then scuttled away down the hillside, doubled over like a four-footed creature. He was wearing a white loincloth that bobbed in the darkness like a tail. Patchen drew his pistol and pursued him, bleeding and gasping. He found the Japanese crouching in a foxhole. He had wound a white rag around his head; his right arm, the one Patchen had seized, was broken. He cradled it with the other hand and shrieked in pain or terror in a weird feline voice. Roaring wordlessly in reply, Patchen lifted his pistol. The Japanese stood up and extended his left arm, stiffly. Patchen saw that he was holding a live grenade. For an instant his hand and the muzzle of Patchen's .45 almost touched. Patchen squeezed the trigger and felt the recoil a fraction of a second before the grenade went off in an eruption of fiery splinters.

Oddly, Patchen did not lose consciousness immediately, but this made him think that he was dead, because all his senses were extinguished by the explosion. He heard nothing except a soughing non-sound like the imitation of surf in a conch shell. His body was numb. He tasted nothing and smelled nothing even though the mud on which he lay was saturated with the feces and the rotting dead of two armies. He knew that his eyes were open, but he could see nothing, not even the residue of light captured by the pupils just before the lids closed. He stared, but saw only blackness; when he stared harder, the blackness deepened. Then his hand moved and he knew that he was alive. The hand touched his right eye, then his left, and sent a message to Patchen's brain that what it had encountered was formless slime. *"My God!"* he cried; these had been his eyes. He felt himself going under. The blackness deepened. He did not think or resist, but his mind, which had retained the last image his retina had captured, projected the grenade onto the screen of his memory, where it detonated again.

After a time Patchen woke up. At first he felt no pain, only a dreamy awareness of his injuries. Then, one by one, all his senses except sight returned. He could hear the stutter and pop of small arms fire and the muffled explosion of shells and the voices of Japanese soldiers shouting insults into the night. Patchen's throat was parched, but he did not dare reach for the canteen attached to his ammunition belt. What if a Japanese was watching him, bayonet at the ready, for some sign of life? Without warning, very close by, a wounded man screamed in a tremendous howling voice, so close to Patchen that he twitched in fear. He thought, *What if the Jap isn't dead?* What if his attacker was waking up, too? What if he was creeping toward him now with one hand blown away and a knife gripped in the other? Alone, defenseless, he waited, trying to feign death in case the Japanese stumbled on him. What if it wasn't a knife his enemy held in his remaining hand? What if it was another grenade?

The pain in Patchen's eyes was so intense that it made his body thrash. He could feel the involuntary reaction coming and he tried to control it, but in the end he was unable to do so. His face, his clothes, his whole sweaty body inside the thick cotton drill of his denims, were smeared with congealed blood. He groped under his clothes. To the touch his blood was sticky and scabby, like dried paste, and when he lifted his fingers to his nostrils it smelled like nothing Patchen had ever smelled before.

Each time he lost consciousness, he mistook what happened for death, only to wake up again to realize that it had not yet discovered him. When soldiers died in books they remembered moments of happiness, they saw beloved faces and heard their mother's voices. In Patchen's case, none of these things happened. He merely slept and woke and felt unbearable pain, and then slept again. He was awakened time after time by the screams of the wounded man who lay nearby. No matter how hard he listened, he could not tell if the voice belonged to an American or a Japanese.

Then he woke up and realized that he was being carried over the ground by another person. This rescuer, whoever he was, had slung Patchen across his shoulders and he was running in zig-zags over the blasted terrain. The man was very strong and swift. He seemed to be alone; there were no other voices, no other footsteps.

Patchen was wide awake now, but he existed in a bubble of quietude, floating inside the clamor of battle, in which all noises were distinct and separate. He heard his rescuer panting, he heard water sloshing in his canteen, he heard the thud of boots.

A mortar round detonated behind them and Patchen's rescuer dove forward, spilling Patchen onto the ground. He lost consciousness again. When he woke up, he was alone. His rescuer had vanished. Perhaps, Patchen thought, he had never actually existed; maybe he had imagined it all, maybe this was simply part of the process of dying. Was death itself a rescue? He drifted into unconsciousness again.

When he woke he felt himself being borne across the battlefield by the same running man. This time his rescuer was grunting out numbers in German as he rushed over the mud and slime, counting to four—*"Eins! Zwei! Drei! VIER! Eins! Zwei! Drei! VIER!"* over and over again. Who was this person?

Shells from American warships offshore moaned overhead and detonated on the Japanese positions. Mortar rounds burst all around them; the snicker of small-caliber Japanese bullets filled the air. Suddenly Patchen's rescuer grunted and fell to the ground with Patchen on top of him. Patchen reached out convulsively and gripped his leg just above the top of a Marine-issue boot. The man shouted in pain and pried Patchen's fingers loose.

"Don't do that again," he said in a low, barely audible tone, as if he might be overheard above the din. "Can you hear me?"

"Are you the corpsman?" Patchen asked.

"No. I was just passing by."

"Oh," Patchen said. "Was that German you were speaking?"

"Yes."

"Why?"

"Because German is the only language lions understand," the man replied.

"Lions?" Patchen said.

He lost consciousness again.

2

PATCHEN'S FRIENDSHIP WITH CHRISTOPHER BEGAN ON THE DAY HE discovered that he was not blind after all. He had spent a week in total darkness, with his entire head swathed in bandages, before a cheerful Navy physician unwound the gauze and let in the light. At first he thought that the indistinct glow filtering through the layers of gauze was an illusion, a trick of the mind, but then his remaining eye, the right one, was completely uncovered and it began registering images—a lamp, a row of surgical instruments laid out on a towel, a poster of a human head with the skin removed so that the muscles and eyeballs were exposed, and the round freckled face of a red-headed man wearing the undersize silver oak leaves of a Navy commander on the collar of his khaki shirt.

"My name is Dick Conaghan," the doctor said. "I'm a plastic surgeon—in the Navy. In civilian life I was a podiatrist, so I can only do one face. Everyone leaves here looking like Cary Grant. Okay?"

Patchen had not spoken since being evacuated from the battlefield, and he could not speak now. Conaghan shone a penlight in his eye, then examined the left side of his face.

He said, "Do you remember what happened?"

Patchen shook his head.

"That's okay. Hardly anyone does at first. You were wounded by a grenade. The damage is all on the left side of your body, so you must have reached for it before it went off, or something. It may all come back to you eventually, but then again, it may not. Don't worry about it."

Patchen listened in silence, waiting for darkness to descend again. He still believed that he was blind, that he was imagining, rather than actually seeing, the objects in the windowless room. Conaghan seemed to understand this. He gripped Patchen's unwounded biceps and squeezed it hard.

"Listen to me," he said. "You're not going to be blind. You've lost one eye, but the other one is going to be okay. I wouldn't bullshit anybody about a thing like this."

Patchen cleared his throat. "I believe you," he said. "I'm just surprised. I thought I was blind until you took the bandage off."

Conaghan cursed. "You mean nobody told you you still had one good eye?"

"No. What else is wrong with me?"

Without hesitation, Conaghan told him the details: he had taken the full force of the exploding grenade on the left side of his body. His face, his arm, his leg had been badly damaged. His left hand could be used as a claw, but he would never be able to write with it again.

Conaghan said, "Are you left-handed?"

"Yes."

"I thought so. You were lucky," he said. "They found you right away and got you to an aid station. Otherwise you would have bled to death."

Patchen remembered something about this, the sensation of being carried by another man. He closed his eye, trying to recapture the details. Conaghan misunderstood his reaction.

"We can fix you up," he said. "Not like new, but you should be able to live a normal life. What sports did you play in high school?"

"Football, baseball, basketball," Patchen said.

"What I want you to do is write to your mother and your girlfriend, using your right hand—you might as well get used to it—and ask them to send you all the photographs and snapshots of you that they have—all of them, plus your high school yearbook. Okay?"

Patchen nodded.

"Tell them why you need the pictures, so we can fix your face," Conaghan said. "Tell them what's happened to you. It's better that they know the truth right away. Have you *got* a girl?"

Patchen nodded.

"She'll be okay," Conaghan said. "Believe me, the ladies don't object to honorable wounds."

"Is that something else you wouldn't bullshit me about?" Patchen said.

"That's the last thing I'd bullshit you about," Conaghan replied.

He rebandaged Patchen's head, then clipped holes in the gauze for his eye and mouth. Patchen couldn't walk so Conaghan himself pushed him in a wheelchair. After a swift passage through a maze of corridors, they arrived in the ward. Patchen noticed immediately that he was the only patient whose head and face were completely covered by bandages. In the bed next to the one with his name on it, a blond man with his leg in a cast was reading a book.

"I lied to you," Conaghan said. "Not every patient ends up looking like Cary Grant. Sometimes I slip. Leftenant Christopher, here, came out looking like Alexander the Great. Paul Christopher, shake hands with David Patchen."

Christopher, smiling quietly, put down his book and leaned over and shook hands with Patchen. Under his Navy-issue bathrobe, his chest was heavily bandaged.

"Yeats?" Conaghan asked, craning to read the title on Christopher's book. "Slip me a stanza."

Christopher, smiling, read the first eight lines of *Sailing to Byzantium* aloud. His voice was pleasant, but barely audible. Conaghan held a hand behind his ear, like a deaf man; Christopher spoke in a murmur.

"Beautiful," Conaghan said. "Christopher's a mumbler, but he's the only other intellectual in the Marine Corps besides yourself. He even tells war stories in iambic pentameter. Gotta go."

After Conaghan left, Patchen said, "Did you really have plastic surgery?"

"No," Christopher replied. "He just noticed me reading poetry one day."

Patchen knew this faint voice. But how? He did not recognize Christopher's face or anything else about him. He asked another question.

"Were you on Okinawa?"

"Yes," Christopher said.

"What outfit?"

Christopher identified his unit. He spoke so softly that Patchen had to ask him to repeat what he said. They had belonged to adjoining battalions in the same regiment.

Without warning, Patchen began to weep. He did not know why this happened, but he was powerless to stop it. Tears welled up in his single blue eye, wetting the gauze that surrounded it; he uttered a series of brief, muffled sobs. Christopher did not avert his eyes or offer to help. After a few moments Patchen stopped crying.

"Do you play chess?" Christopher asked.

Patchen nodded. Despite the cast on his leg, Christopher swung himself out of bed, easily and smoothly, as if the movement was some sort of pleasurable gymnastic exercise, and sat in a chair facing Patchen's wheelchair. They played on a tiny portable chess set belonging to Christopher. He was an excellent player, but his moves were almost entirely defensive, as if the outcome did not matter to him.

"Why are you doing that?" Patchen said, after the second game.

"Doing what?"

"Letting me win."

Christopher smiled. "It won't happen again."

Those were his last words until lights out. He won six of the next ten games, but Patchen realized that he was still holding back, still was not playing as well as he knew how, as if his skill was a secret he was unwilling to share.

In the morning, Conaghan came by early to examine Patchen again. Christopher was already awake, reading again. He took the book out of his hand and looked at the title.

"*Wilhelm Meister* by Johann Wolfgang von Goethe?" he said. "*Lieber Gott*—enemy literature. Read something."

"It's in German."

"I know that. You can shout."

Most of the ward was still asleep. In the same murmur as before, Christopher read:

> "*Wer nie sein Brot mit Tränen ass*
> *Wer nie die kummervollen Nächte*
> *Auf seinem Bette weinend sass*
> *Der kennt euch nicht, ihr himmlischen Mächte.*"

"Gorgeous. What a genius, even if he was a Kraut," Conaghan said. "What does it mean?"

" 'He who never ate his bread with tears, who never sat on his bed weeping through the sad night, knows nothing of Heaven.' "

"See?" Conaghan said to Patchen. "I told you this guy was an intellectual. How about you, David—are you fluent in a foreign language?"

"I can count to four in German," Patchen replied.

Christopher gave him a look of interest, but said nothing.

"Great," Conaghan said. "You can be a sergeant in the other army if the Krauts win the war."

Although Patchen, at that moment, did not even know why he had said what he had said about being able to count in German—he spoke no German, did not remember the words of the man who had saved his life until months afterward—it was at this moment that he began the long process of remembering what had happened to him on Okinawa.

SOON AFTER THE FIRST OPERATION ON PATCHEN'S FACE, HE AND CHRISTOPHER and a few others were wheeled out to the hospital's parade ground to be decorated. Patchen received a medal for having wiped out an enemy position in hand-to-hand combat; he had no recollection whatever of the feats described in the citation.

Christopher was given the same medal for having rescued two wounded Marines under heavy fire, at night. According to the citation, read over the crackling loudspeaker system, he had carried the men home in relays, carrying or dragging one inert body twenty yards or so in the direction of the American lines, laying it down, going back for the other, and repeating this process until he brought both wounded men safely inside the perimeter. He had been wounded in the leg by Japanese small arms fire, and then shot in the chest by a U. S. Marine who fired on him when he rose out of the ground in front of the latter's foxhole with one of the rescued men in his arms.

This man saved Christopher's life, because most of the eight .30-caliber rounds fired by the panicky sentry struck his unconscious body instead of Christopher's. The citation did not mention the circumstances in which the chest wound was inflicted. It was Christopher who supplied this detail later on, in answer to Patchen's questions.

"Didn't you give the password?" Patchen asked.

"Yes," Christopher replied. "But I don't think he heard me. Nobody ever does."

"What happened to the guys you brought back?"

"The sentry killed the one I was carrying—he fired a whole clip at us. The other one lived."

"How do you know?"

"I brought him in first."

Christopher, limping along beside Patchen's wheelchair, unpinned the medal from his chest and put it into the pocket of his bathrobe.

Patchen said, "Why did you go out after those guys in the first place?"

"I didn't," Christopher said. "I was already out there, coming back from patrol, just like you were. I was carrying one of my own men back when I stumbled onto the other fellow."

"How did you find him in the dark?" Patchen asked.

"It wasn't difficult," Christopher said, giving Patchen a puzzled, sidelong look. "He was making a lot of noise."

"What kind of noise? The whole island was one big noise. How could you hear him?"

"He was screaming," Christopher said. "His wounds were pretty bad."

Something flickered in Patchen's memory.

"I think I heard him, too," he said.

4

PATCHEN UNDERWENT ELEVEN SEPARATE OPERATIONS TO RECON- struct the face that Conaghan saw in Patchen's high school year- book. When it was over, his left cheek remained paralyzed, but this was noticeable only when he smiled or displayed emotion. His left arm and leg, which had absorbed the main force of the exploding grenade, were stiff, and his left hand was useless.

Christopher remained in the hospital, in the bed next to Patchen's, for about a month after the medal ceremony. He made conversa- tion in the way he played chess. He volunteered no information about himself. He listened. He understood. He did not interrupt. He never argued or corrected, even when error was obvious. He behaved as if the lives of others were far more interesting than his own, and a better topic of conversation. In the sense that this reticent behavior concealed the facts of Christopher's life, even his beliefs, from everyone else, it was a subtle form of deception; Patchen understood this even then, but it only made the other man more interesting. He asked him few questions.

"When did you learn German?"

Looking up from a book: "As a child."

"Where?"

A smile. "In Germany."

"Are you German?"

"Half, on my mother's side. My father's American."

Christopher went back to his book; he seemed to live for books. He was always receiving them in the mail, and he read two or three a day; many were in German or French, and these he covered with brown wrapping paper to deflect curiosity. He gave away the ones in English, novels and poetry, as soon as he had finished them.

To distract Patchen from his pain after he came back from surgery, he read to him, not stories or poems, but facts. Holding a whole stack of books in his lap, he would read passages that informed Patchen that the amazing valor of the Japanese soldier had less to do with the code of Bushido than with the law of primogeniture, in which eldest sons inherited everything, and younger sons who had no hope of inheriting anything, or even marrying, went into the infantry. Or that Reichsführer SS Heinrich Himmler believed himself to be the reincarnation of Henry the Fowler, a tenth-century king of Germany. Or that Squanto, the Indian who taught the Pilgrims how to plant corn, had asked for a mug of ale, in English, on his first appearance in the Plymouth Colony; he had traveled to England aboard an English ship sometime before 1620 and developed a taste for the stuff.

Patchen remembered these odd facts for the rest of his life. Christopher's reluctance to talk made Patchen confessional. After Christopher told him about his mixed parentage, he revealed that he was only half American himself. His father was an Englishman, a pilot in the Royal Flying Corps who was shot down over the Western Front in 1918. His father and mother had met at a Nurses' and Officers' Ball on July 4, fallen immediately in love, and been married a week later. They had two weeks together in Paris, dining every night at Maxim's, before he went back to the Front and died.

Every year, on the anniversary of his death, Patchen's mother had shown him blurry photographs of his father standing beside his Sopwith Camel and documents and souvenirs relating to him—their marriage certificate, written in French in a copperplate hand, a Croix de Guerre with palm, and the letter written by the elder Patchen's commanding officer after he was killed. Patchen had memorized it. "My dear Mrs Patchen," it ran, "I am very sorry to tell you that your husband, Captain David Alan St. Clair Patchen, died on the 10th inst. whilst leading a patrol behind enemy lines. His flight was attacked by a larger German force and though he fought gallantly against overwhelming odds his machine was hit by enemy fire. Another officer who was by his side during the whole action reports that Captain Patchen's wound was instantaneously fatal and he did not suffer; there was no fire. You have my deepest sympathy in your great loss as well as that of every man who served with your husband who was a very gallant and much admired officer. Yours truly, [ILLEGIBLE]."

Patchen's mother had returned to Ohio to bear her child. He had never met his English relatives; the marriage had been secret.

Christopher's wounds healed long before Patchen's, and he left the hospital with orders to report to an infantry unit that was training for the invasion of Japan. Patchen learned this when he woke from an operation and found a goodbye note in Christopher's peculiar European handwriting. Everyone believed that more Americans would die in the invasion of Japan than had been killed in the whole war so far. Two weeks later the atom bomb exploded over Hiroshima. Patchen was relieved that Christopher would live, but he believed that he would vanish back into whatever world he had emerged from.

He was surprised, therefore, when he met him in Harvard Yard on a balmy Indian summer day a year later. Christopher was walking along by himself, reading a book. His gait was perfectly normal; so normal that he might never have been wounded. Patchen himself was still using a cane. He leaned his weight on it and spoke Christopher's name.

Christopher looked up from th book and said, "Hello, David."

He had never seen Patchen's original face, let alone the new one fabricated by Conaghan, because it had always been swathed in bandages.

"How did you know who I was?" Patchen asked.

"Who else could you possibly be?" Christopher asked, smiling.

5

PATCHEN HAD COME TO HARVARD BECAUSE HIS FIANCÉE WAS IN HER senior year at Radcliffe College. Her name was Martha Armstrong, and like Patchen she was a birthright Quaker; they came from the same town in Ohio. Patchen, who received a disability pension as well as a monthly allowance under the G. I. Bill of Rights, had plenty of money. Martha, who was at Radcliffe on a scholarship, had none, but she planned to get a job as a teacher as soon as she graduated and save half her salary, together with all of Patchen's pension, toward the cost of their honeymoon, which they had been planning ever since they decided to get married. "Unless," she said, "I hear the call. Or David does. If that happens we'll make other plans."

She meant, Patchen explained, a call from God to do His work. "She's a hell of a lot more likely to hear it than I am," he said to Christopher. "It was hard on her when I joined the Marines. But even after she saw this . . ." he pointed to his face, the only time Christopher ever saw him draw attention to his injuries . . . "she never reproached me. She's a good person, Paul." In any other man these words would have been meant as an apology for Martha's plainness, but Patchen was as oblivious to her lack of physical beauty as she seemed to be to his wounds. It was obvious that they loved each other. They went for a walk along the Charles together every morning before classes, studied together in the library every evening, and on Saturdays went into Boston to visit museums or go to a Red Sox game. Christopher often went with them, never taking a girl of his own because he felt that this would violate the couple's privacy. When the three of them were together, both Patchen and Martha were talkative, even gay; in the presence of strangers they were silent.

Patchen loved baseball. He said that he felt at home in Fenway Park because the Red Sox fans were like Cleveland Indians fans: loyal and passionate but childlike and ignorant. He had a theory that the players on both teams habitually lost the big games out of a subconscious need to punish their fans for their stupidity. "Imagine playing day after day in front of thousands of people who scream hysterically for pop-ups, sing a song that says Dominic DiMaggio is better than his brother Joe, and think that baseball was meant to be played without the bunt, the hit-and-run, or the stolen base, just boom, boom off a tin wall," he said. "Look at Ted Williams's face; he's playing in a state of hopeless disgust." Martha chided him when he spoke in this way. "Thee must not be so hurtful in your opinions," she would say. She studied at ballgames and cried in the movies, which were often, in those days just after the war, about sad misunderstandings between wounded veterans and the girls who loved them. She and Patchen seemed to have no misunderstandings. Christopher liked her tremendously, and while she was still in Cambridge she provided him and Patchen with an inexhaustible topic of conversation.

She graduated the following June. In September Patchen and Christopher became roommates; they had met too late the year before to move in together. Christopher's room contained a great many framed photographs and drawings. Most of these were pictures of the same pretty, fair-haired woman. She appeared in riding clothes, in a white tennis skirt, in a bathing suit, and many times in sailing clothes aboard the same boat.

"Your mother?" Patchen asked.

"Yes."

Oftentimes the woman held a child in her arms. It was obvious that the child was Christopher; his face resembled hers very closely. Patchen had become interested in art at Harvard, and he had encountered versions of the face Christopher shared with his mother in the engravings of Albrecht Dürer, especially the one called *Knight;* it was not that Christopher looked like Dürer's romanticized subject, but that some hint of the knight's features was present in his own still face. The effect was reinforced by a drawing in which a very young Christopher and his mother were idealized as Madonna and child after the style of the Italian Renaissance artists who had inspired Dürer. In another, larger drawing executed in pre-Raphaelite terms, she faced the artist serenely, feet together, arms hanging easily by her sides, nude and in an early stage of pregnancy. She was very young, with wide intelligent eyes, exquisite breasts, and graceful legs that were somewhat longer than they ought to have been in proportion to the rest of her body. She was smiling a deeply happy smile, as if she alone knew the secret of her condition. This astonishing picture, so perfectly drawn that it was more lifelike than a photograph, and the fact that it was displayed on Christopher's wall, made Patchen uncomfortable; he did not know what to say about it. Christopher clearly understood this; he even seemed to be amused by Patchen's embarrassment. But, as usual, he volunteered no explanatlons.

Patchen learned that Christopher's father was in Berlin, working for the military government, and that he had relatives named Hubbard who lived in New York City. That Thanksgiving Christopher invited Patchen to spend the holiday weekend in the country with his family.

"Won't I be in the way?" Patchen asked.

"No," Christopher said. "There's lots of room. My father is coming over. He may have someone with him, but there won't be many people. Two or three cousins."

The next night they took the midnight train from Boston to

Pittsfield, at the other end of Massachusetts, and after stopping at every station along the 150-mile line, arrived at dawn. Two raw-boned middle-aged men met them on the platform. From the train window they seemed to be twins, with the same long Yankee faces and the same gestures and voices. Patchen stood by, leaning on his cane, while they greeted Christopher. It was a joyous reunion, with the older men hugging him and ruffling his hair as if he were a boy coming home from school. After a moment they turned to Patchen and he saw that they were not identical: one was fair like Christopher but the other had darker hair. Both were very tall.

"My father, Hubbard Christopher," Christopher said, introducing the blond man, "and this is our cousin, Elliott Hubbard."

The Harbor, as the family's country house was called, lay in a valley between two steep, wooded mountains. There was nothing grand about it—it was an ordinary New England farmhouse, low and rambling, heated by wood stoves. No one else was awake when they arrived.

Elliott Hubbard led Patchen to his room over squeaking floors made of wide boards. "The Harbor was built by the first Aaron Hubbard in the early 1700s, soon after he married a widow named Fanny Christopher," Elliott said. "The two families have been marrying each other ever since. Hubbard's father and my mother were Christopher twins. So are Hubbard and I, for all intents and purposes, even though I'm a whole month older than he is."

Patchen said, "Paul doesn't resemble you."

"No," Elliott said. "He looks just like his mother."

"I know. Paul has a lot of pictures of her. Will Mrs. Christopher be here, too?"

The smile vanished from Elliott's face. "No, she won't," he said. "Didn't Paul tell you? Lori was arrested by the Gestapo in 1939. We haven't seen her since."

Patchen was unable to speak for a moment. Finally he said, "I'm sorry. I had no idea."

Elliott put a hand on his shoulder. "How could you know? I'm just glad you asked me instead of Hubbard. He thinks she's still alive."

"After all these years? What about Paul?"

"He may think so, too. Out of loyalty to his father. They were a very close family." He opened the door to a bedroom. "Here we are. The bathroom is right across the hall. Why don't you change into old clothes and come right down to breakfast? I'm on K.P."

By the time Patchen changed and found his way through the house to the kitchen, the other members of the house party were seated at the table. Christopher introduced them—Elliott's wife, Alice, and their son Horace, a lanky adolescent who looked like his father and Hubbard Christopher, and a squat, powerful man who obviously was not a member of the family.

"Barney Wolkowicz," the man said, lifting a hairy hand in greeting but not offering to shake hands.

"Barney works with my father in Berlin," Christopher said.

"*For* him," Wolkowicz said.

Breakfast, consisting of lumpy oatmeal porridge with maple sugar and cream, scorched pancakes with maple syrup, eggs and sausage, and thick slices of homemade bread toasted over an open stove lid, was cooked by Hubbard Christopher and Elliott Hubbard. While they worked they drank thirstily from large crockery mugs. It was not yet seven o'clock in the morning.

"Have some," Elliott said, pouring a glass for Patchen.

Patchen stared at the frothy liquid. "Is that beer?"

Hubbard Christopher lifted his mug. "Strong ale."

Alice Hubbard spoke up. She had an amused face, an amused voice. "The Hubbard idea is that everything you eat on Thanksgiving should be grown on your own land," she said. "Therefore, no coffee or tea. But if you want some you can have some. I'll smuggle it to you in a beer mug."

"Thank you. I'll try the ale."

Hubbard Christopher watched Patchen drink to make sure he liked it, then went back to frying pancakes. "All this stuff is storebought, of course," he said. "But all of it used to be grown here, even in my lifetime. Our grandfather made his own ale. The hops vine *his* grandfather planted is still alive out by the woodshed. About half the brew would explode all over the pantry walls, but what was left was potent."

Hubbard's friend Wolkowicz showed no interest in the stories. In complete silence, he loaded huge mouthfuls of egg, sausage, and pancake onto his fork and washed them down, apparently without chewing, with long drinks of ale.

At the end of the meal, Hubbard caught his eye. "Game for a treasure hunt, Barney?"

86

Wolkowicz mopped up his plate with a slab of toast. "What kind of a treasure hunt?"

"A real one. For real gold."

Hubbard produced a faded surveyor's map, much folded and mended at the creases with Scotch tape, and spread it out on the table. It had been ruled in pencil into squares, and inside each square a year had been written by different hands.

"This is the Harbor farm," he explained. "Each square is an acre. We search one square a year every Thanksgiving Day, trying to find a treasure that was buried somewhere on this map by our late cousin Eleazer Stickles. The treasure is buried underneath a wild apple tree that had been split by lightning, with the two parts bound together by a heavy chain, thirty-five paces straight north from a ledge on which the letter 'T' is carved."

" 'T' for 'treasure'?"

"Nobody knows."

"How do you know about the apple tree and all that?"

"Eleazer wrote it all down in his journal in cipher. Our fathers, Hubbard's and mine, cracked the code a hundred years later, when they were kids, and the treasure hunt has been on ever since."

"But only on Thanksgiving?"

Hubbard smiled. "Rules of the game."

He and Elliott led the party up a mountainside to a grove of enormous maple trees. To Patchen, raised in an Ohio village far from any real woods, the Berkshire forest seemed primeval: gnarled limbs etched against the bleached autumn sky; huge gray rocks, barnacled with fungus, rising out of the mat of soggy leaves.

Patchen still used a cane, and Christopher and Horace stayed by his side. Despite their slow progress they did not fall far behind the leaders, who stopped often to take compass sightings and consult the map.

Wolkowicz, apparently oblivious to nature, read a copy of *The Adventures of Tom Sawyer* as he sauntered along behind the group, but after the first half-hour he closed the book and plunged ahead on his own.

"Should I go after him?" Horace asked. "He doesn't know the woods."

Hubbard shook his head. "No need to worry about Wolkowicz," he said.

They watched him as he disappeared among the trees. Although everyone else was dressed for the woods in jeans and flannel shirts, Wolkowicz wore a Tyrolean hat and a peculiar dark suit that seemed to have been cut from an old Wehrmacht uniform: in the strong morning sunlight, the original gray-green color was still visible beneath the black dye.

A few minutes later, as the party crossed a clearing, he appeared on the ridgeline and whistled piercingly.

"I've found something," he said, when they reached him.

"Where?" Hubbard asked.

"Down there, on the other side of the brook."

Elliott consulted the treasure map. "If you crossed the brook you're in the wrong square," he said.

"The wrong square?" Wolkowicz said. "What's that supposed to mean?"

"It means you're outside this year's boundary on the map, Barney," Hubbard said. "We have to stay inside the square we're searching. Those are the rules."

"The rules," Wolkowicz said, tonelessly. "Okay, I call time out. Come on, kid."

He threw his arm around Horace's shoulder and led him away. The others followed them through a grove of paper birches and then down a defile beside a shallow brook. Finally they came to an immense uprooted maple. The tree had uplifted a disk of soil and moss perhaps twenty feet in diameter with it when it fell, and the big smooth prints of Wolkowicz's city shoes showed where he had walked on the moist earth. They led to a flat rock that lay in the middle of the circle.

Tell me something, Horace," he said. "Are you going to go to Yale like your old man and your uncles?"

"I hope so," Horace said.

"Then have a look under that rock," Wolkowicz said.

Horace slid the rock aside, revealing a round hole in the earth. There was some sort of cavity beneath.

"Reach inside," Wolkowicz said.

"Here comes the ball of drowsy black snakes," Hubbard said.

Horace lay down and reached inside the cavity. After a moment he sat up.

"It's full of bones," he said.

"Bones?" Elliott said. "What kind of bones?"

Wolkowicz fell to the ground beside Horace and thrust his own arm into the hole. He brought out a human skull, dangling from his forefinger by an eye socket.

"Here," he said to Patchen. "Hold this."

He flipped it through the air; Patchen trapped it against his chest with his good arm. Wolkowicz groped in the hole again and found another, smaller skull, and then what appeared to be a femur.

"That's enough," Elliott said.

Wolkowicz stood up, the femur in his hand. His suit was smeared with the manurish yellow soil. "Dry as chalk," he said. "These are old bones, maybe a hundred years old." He opened his hand and displayed a flint arrowhead. "This was in the hole, too. They must be Indians."

"Mahicans," Horace said. "It's a Mahican burial ground."

Wolkowicz took the larger skull out of Patchen's arm and handed it and the femur to Horace.

"Here, kid," he said. "Take these to Yale when you get there and add 'em to the collection at Skull and Bones. Maybe you'll make Reaper, like your Uncle Waddy."

He strode off through the woods.

Horace knelt by the burial place and replaced the skull and bones Wolkowicz had given him.

Elliott watched Wolkowicz's stocky figure as it disappeared among the trees. "Funny fellow," he said. "How did he know Waddy was Reaper in his year? How did he even know the word 'Reaper'?"

"Barney knows all about skeletons," Hubbard replied.

6

DURING THE LONG WALK DOWN THE MOUNTAIN, THE WIND GREW stronger. As they came to a place where they could see the Harbor in the valley below, Hubbard stopped and put his arm around his son's shoulders. The wind moaning among the trees produced a throaty animal-like sound, so that the mountain itself seemed to be growling.

"Lions," Hubbard said.

He and Christopher, grinning at each other, linked arms, faced the forest, and shouting in German at the top of their lungs, recited what seemed to be a poem.

They waited, listening intently. After a moment the wind

died. The pause was brief, but there was a noticeable interruption.

"It worked," Hubbard said. "It always works."

"What was it you were reciting?" Patchen asked.

"Scrambled Blake," Hubbard replied. "It means,

"Lion, lion, burning bright
In the forests of the night,
What immortal hand or eye
Dare frame thy fearful symmetry?

"It's nonsense in German, but it isn't the words that count, it's the language. German is the only language lions understand."

Patchen knew, even though he could not remember when or where, that he had heard this phrase before.

"What is that saying from?" he asked.

"What saying?"

" 'German is the only language lions understand.' "

"It's not from anything," Hubbard replied. "My wife made it up. When Paul was little, he thought the wind in the woods sounded like lions. Someone had told him there were lions in America, waiting to eat him up. One night when the wind was blowing like this, his mother brought him to this spot and told him to recite that verse in German. When he asked why, Paul was always asking why, that's what she told him."

T W O

1

HUBBARD CHRISTOPHER WAS KILLED THE FOLLOWING AUTUMN WHEN he was struck by a car in Berlin. In the family burial ground at the Harbor, Paul Christopher released a handful of his father's ashes into the wind on the hillside above the Harbor. The little company of mourners—members of the family and a few men from Washington—smiled faintly as they watched the puff of gray powder disperse in the limpid September air, as though an invisible Hubbard ambled from guest to guest, whispering jokes to relieve the solemnity of the moment.

Afterward, Patchen limped down the hill alone. One of the affable mourners, a pink-skinned, white-haired man in a dark suit and a homburg hat, slowed his pace to walk beside him.

"You must be David Patchen," he said.

"Yes."

He wore pince-nez with thick round lenses, and these reflected the autumn foliage and magnified his blue eyes. They twinkled: he looked like the kindly family doctor in a Norman Rockwell illustration.

"I don't know if you realize it," he said, "but Hubbard Christopher took a great shine to you."

"If that's so," Patchen said, "I'm very glad to hear it. We only met once."

"It's so, all right, or I wouldn't be telling you it is. Hubbard thought the world of you. Have you ever thought about getting a monocle?"

"A monocle? No."

"Hubbard thought it would be a good idea. He was going to

mention it to you next time you met. You might consider it. Once you learn to keep it screwed in it's a dandy thing to wear. Hypnotizes people—it's all they can look at, so they forget the rest of the appearance. 'What did he look like?' you ask. 'He had a monocle,' they say. Can't remember another blessed thing about the fellow. Hubbard's wife's uncle, old Paulus von Buecheler, had a monocle. Lost his eye in the First War, fighting the Russians. He got a monocle right away. In later years he fell off a jumping horse and kept the monocle in; fell off Hubbard's boat in a storm in the Baltic and swam ashore without losing it. Of course, he was a real old-fashioned Prussian, but there's no reason why a monocle wouldn't be a good solution for you."

"I'll consider it, sir."

"Will you, now? That would have pleased Hubbard. Well, if you decide to go ahead, ask Paul where his great-uncle Paulus got *his* monocles. He'll know the details. You've got to go to Germany to get the right kind."

"You knew the German side of the family?"

The man peered through his pince-nez as if the question was wholly unexpected but very welcome. "Yes, I did. Fine people, the old type of German. They weren't all thugs, you know; that was just a story the British started as propaganda in 1914. The Buechelers are all gone now, you know, except for Paulus's widow. Every one of their boys was killed in the First War, three of them. Then Paulus went back in as a general in the Second War at the age of sixty and was killed in Russia."

They reached the bottom of the hill. The others had gone inside the house. Cars were parked the whole length of the drive. A black Cadillac halfway down the line started its engine and rolled toward them, crunching gravel beneath its tires. The driver, a young man about Patchen's age, got out and came around the car to open the door.

"David Patchen, this is Tommy Dawson," he said. "You're a couple of ex-Marines. Tommy was in on Saipan and Iwo Jima, came out a major. We'll be going along—can't stay for lunch. You'd better get inside before they eat it all."

Patchen and Dawson shook hands. A grease-stained bag and a quart bottle of Hampden ale lay on the front seat.

"Ah," the man said. "You got the liverwurst sandwiches, Tommy?"

"Yes, sir. And the ale. Warm."

"Good." He turned to Patchen. "Elliott's cook makes wonderful liverwurst sandwiches, spreads Limburger cheese on one slice of rye bread, German mustard on the other. The local ale is good, smells like skunk the way ale should, but you have to drink it warm. Well, goodbye."

He held out his hand. His grip was powerful, not merely strong. He smiled, showing square, nicotine-stained teeth.

"You graduate in June?" he asked.

"February," Patchen replied.

"Do you now? Well, then, we'd better get busy. Any languages besides Japanese?"

"What?"

"Do you speak any other foreign languages besides Japanese?"

"I don't speak Japanese."

The other man gave him a look of keen interest.

"You don't? That's odd, somebody said you did," he said. "Not that it matters."

He got into the car. Patchen watched him open a briefcase, extract a desk diary, and study it. He rolled down the window.

"I'll be in Boston a week from Wednesday," he said. "Let's eat lunch together."

"All right."

He wrote in his book with the stub of a yellow pencil. "Twelve sharp." He gave Patchen the name of a club and its address on Beacon Street. "Just keep this to yourself for the time being, will you? Don't mention it to Paul just yet. Compartments!"

Patchen watched the black car go down the drive.

Compartments? he thought. *What are those*?

Patchen presented himself at the varnished black door of the club on Beacon Street at five minutes before noon on the appointed Wednesday. There was no sign or bell or knocker, only the house number. He lifted the latch and walked in. A porter in a threadbare jacket greeted him.

"Good day, sir."

Patchen said, "I'm meeting one of your members for lunch."

"Welcome, sir. May I ask which member?"

The man in the pince-nez had not told Patchen his name, and Patchen had asked no questions about him.

"I'll know him when I see him," he said.

If the porter saw anything strange in this reply, he gave no sign. "Very well, sir," he said.

The porter, a small elderly man with a deep convalescent's pallor, came out from behind his desk.

"Do you have to go to the bathroom?" he asked.

"No, thank you."

"Then follow me, if you please, sir. You can take a seat in the Strangers' Room. You'll be able to watch out for your gentleman from there."

He led him three steps across the foyer to a small anteroom furnished with Victorian sofas and chairs. Prints of Yankee clippers and portraits of old men in high collars and muttonchops hung on the wall. Patchen sat down on a horsehair sofa facing the door. Somewhere in the deeper precincts of the club a grandfather clock began to strike, and just as the chimes ended and the hour gong began, the man in the pince-nez came in. He looked quite different without his homburg hat, like an actor who has taken off his costume. His hat had flattened his white hair, which was parted in the middle to show a long straight line of pink scalp, and this slight dishevelment added to the transformation.

He was grinning with delight as he advanced toward Patchen with his hand outstretched, and Patchen could imagine what he must have looked like as a boy. "You found the place, I see," he said, crushing Patchen's hand. "Good. Do you have to go to the bathroom?"

"No, thanks. I've already been asked."

"Have you? Good. Graves is very conscientious about that; for some reason the younger porters don't like to ask. He says you wouldn't give my name."

"I don't know it, sir."

"You don't?"

"No. What shall I call you?"

The man in the pince-nez smiled and the boy showed through again. "I'll let you decide that," he said. He pulled a sheet of paper and a fountain pen out of the inside pocket of his jacket and, after uncapping the pen, handed both to Patchen. "Do you mind signing that here?" he asked. "We can't take papers upstairs."

Patchen looked at the paper. It was a form, a secrecy agreement under which the signer promised never to divulge to anyone any part of the conversation he was about to have on this date with the other person whose signature appeared below. Patchen signed it. The man in the pince-nez, leaning over a round parlor table covered with a fringed cloth, signed it too.

"Now for some food," he said.

In a dining room filled with members and waiters who were all white-haired or bald, the man in the pince-nez scribbled his name and the figure 2 on a chit and handed it to a waiter.

"And let us have a half-bottle of the good white, please."

They ate thick pea soup and cod cakes made from salted cod, followed by bread pudding. The "good white" turned out to be a 1929 Puligny-Montrachet, golden in the glass. Patchen had never tasted anything like it.

The man in the pince-nez, watching him take his first sip, said, "You like wine, do you?"

"I do now."

"Wine has been a good friend to man, especially when it's cod cakes for lunch."

While they ate the penitential food and drank the voluptuous wine, the man in the pince-nez talked about baseball. Patchen listened with interest as his host described having seen Tris Speaker, Napoleon Lajoie, Christy Mathewson, and Home Run Baker play during the era of the dead ball.

"I'm a great admirer of Babe Ruth and Ted Williams and modern fellows like that," the man in the pince-nez said, "but they changed the game when they introduced the rabbit ball. It became less of an imitation of life."

"How so?" Patchen asked.

"Taking a human lifetime as the equivalent of a season of baseball, nobody hits sixty home runs. Most hit one or two, or none, and think they've done all right. The most Home Run Baker managed in one year was ten, and look what they called *him*."

"Twelve," Patchen said. "In 1913."

The man in the pince-nez smiled with pleasure at the correction. "Absolutely correct," he said. "You know, mankind in all its thousands of years on earth has only invented two perfect systems, the English sonnet and the game of baseball. Each is governed by absolute rules which cannot be bent without destroying the form and therefore the result, and yet everything known to the human heart and mind, *everything,* can happen within them. Rules and imagination—that's the winning combination. Or don't you agree?"

"I agree," Patchen said.

"So did Hubbard Christopher," the man in the pince-nez said, wiping his lips on his napkin. "Most people think my idea about baseball and sonnets is hogwash. They're taught that everything is complicated, that rules get in the way and results don't matter. They think the game's the thing and never mind the consequences. Makes 'em feel they're pretty darn smart to get through the day uncaught. But they're wrong. Everything that really matters in this world is simple, and that's why it's so doggone hard to play the game. That's what I want to talk to you about. Let's go into the other room."

At a glass case by the entrance of a large sitting room, the man in the pince-nez selected two fat Havana cigars, clipped the ends himself, and handed one to Patchen.

"That's a whale oil lamp," he said, leaning over to light his cigar with the yellow flame.

They sat down together in facing armchairs in a far corner of the room. Other members wandered in, but did not come near.

"Well, let me put the question," the man in the pince-nez said. "Would you like to come to work for me?"

Patchen was not startled; nothing the man in the pince-nez said or did surprised him any longer. "What would I do?" he asked.

"That's not your worry. It's up to me to find out what you want to do and make it possible for you to do it. What do you *want* to do?"

"I want to live in privacy."

"That's all?"

"No."

"Then what? Tell me what's in your heart, son."

Patchen drew in a deep breath, and with it clouds of aromatic cigar smoke. He was unused to it and his eye watered.

"I want to work against war," he said.

"Work for peace?"

"No, none of that bullshit. I want to be an enemy of war."

The man in the pince-nez examined Patchen's wounds—it was impossible to look at him without doing so, but most people pretended not to see the damage. Then he leaned forward and squeezed his knee—not the wounded one, the whole one, knowing which was which.

"All right," he said. "When can you start?"

"Around the end of June," Patchen replied. "I'm getting married in April, but we'll be back by then."

"Back from where?"

"Paris."

"Good place for a honeymoon, Paris," the man in the pince-nez said. "But learn a little French before you go. Talk it to Paul, he's fluent. The French are bastards if you can't speak their language. Correct pronunciation is their idea of a system, but it ain't baseball. I'll send somebody up to see you with a contract. He'll mention that he's a friend of the O. G."

After supper that night, while he and Christopher were walking back to their room, Patchen asked a question. It was difficult because he did not want to remind Christopher of his father's death by using the wrong words.

He said, "That old fellow with the white hair who talked to me at the Harbor the other day . . . Do you know who I mean?"

"The one in the pinch-nose glasses?" Christopher said. "That's the O. G. He's the Director of the Outfit."

"The Outfit?"

"The U. S. intelligence service."

Patchen laughed, explosively, in astonishment. Only hours before, he had agreed to become a spy without realizing that he had done so.

"Is *that* who he is?" he said. "Why is he called the O. G.?"

"It stands for 'Old Gentleman.' It's a joke. Actually he's prematurely white—he's only a little older than my father."

"How did he know your father?"

"They worked together during the war," Christopher said. "Mr. Inside and Mr. Outside."

2

PATCHEN AND MARTHA HAD SEEN LITTLE OF EACH OTHER SINCE SHE graduated from Radcliffe. She had heard the call shortly after leaving Cambridge, and since then she had been in Guatemala, living with a tribe of Indians. They were all drunk all the time, from the age of puberty. They were peaceable drunks; they fermented alcohol from sugar cane to make a drink called *guaro* and consumed it for religious reasons, then lay about quietly in the drinking hut, which had been set aside for the purpose, waiting for visions. The cult had no priests or liturgy; drunkenness was all. Musicians took turns tapping out a mournful four-note tune on a marimba, day and night.

In their village, located in a clearing in the jungle near the overgrown ruins of Maya temples which looked like small green mountains, Martha had lived as the Indians lived in all respects except for the drinking. She slept on the ground in a leaky hut, weeded corn and cut cane with the women; she ate the tribal food, which consisted of unleavened corn bread, boiled beans with chili peppers, squash, a pear-shaped vegetable called *güisquil,* and potatoes. Martha spent much of her time treating the wounds the Indians inflicted on their own bodies: in their stupor they often fell down or ran into things, or cut or scalded themselves. One woman bled to death in front of Martha's eyes after she fell on her machete and severed a deep artery in her thigh. Martha, unable to locate the source of the bleeding, had been unable to save her life.

"The other women ran and got *guaro* for her, and she drank as she died," Martha told Patchen. "They said it would be a bad thing for her to go into the next world sober."

Martha was not a missionary in the usual sense of the term, and she made no attempt to convert the adult Indians, or even to turn them away from drink. She was a believer in the Inward Light, a form of Quakerism which emphasizes the Christ within each person while ignoring the Scriptures and the historical Jesus. As such, she confined herself to doing what she described as "the unasked," bandaging the Indians' wounds and sharing their work. Most died young, usually of liver disease and kidney failure, and their children, brain-damaged in the womb by alcohol, were born dull.

The children did not begin to drink until puberty, which came as early as ten in some of the girls, and Martha had concentrated on the younger children, teaching the girls how to sew and the boys how to repair an automobile; she had gone to night classes at a vocational school in Boston to learn these skills herself. With Patchen's help she had purchased a surplus Army Jeep which grease-smeared little boys took apart and put together again many times under her supervision. They enjoyed this work, and once they learned how to fit the parts together, were amazingly quick at it.

"It was always a wonderful moment when they stepped on the starter and the engine started after they'd put the Jeep back together," Martha said, "but they didn't really like noise made by a machine. After a minute or two they'd turn it off so they could hear the marimba."

Although the children were as clumsy as the adults—the girls pricked themselves with their needles, the boys suffered gashes and smashed fingers from wrenches and screwdrivers—Martha had hoped that embroidery and auto mechanics would prove to be means of escape from the village for some of her pupils. But as soon as pubic hair appeared on their bodies, the children were initiated into the cult by means of a ritual called *tragando el gato,* "swallowing the cat," so called because they were required to drink a whole cup of *guaro* without pausing for breath, and gulping that much raw alcohol for the first time was like letting a clawed animal with a long, twitching tail scramble down your throat. After initiation the children disappeared into the drinking hut. They did not seem to recognize Martha thereafter, but went about in the stupor that would last for the rest of their lives.

Martha investigated the origins of the cult and concluded from hazy stories the Indians told her that a Spanish deserter from the army of the conquistador Pedro de Alvarado, who subdued Guatemala in the sixteenth century, had taught them to ferment and drink alcohol. In the drinking hut, the largest building in the village, they kept a life-size effigy of the Spaniard, wearing his breastplate and helmet, seated on a throne. They called him Maximón.

A large unglazed pottery vessel, about a pint in capacity, hung from the effigy's neck, and the Indians filled this with *guaro* every morning; by nightfall the *guaro* was gone. The Indians said that Maximón drank it, but Martha thought that it vanished through evaporation. At evening they placed a lighted cigar between the effigy's lips, and it smoked this rapidly, down to the end, the tip glowing in the darkness and the acrid tobacco smoke drifting out of the hut.

"I think the Spanish deserter is their real god," Martha said, "but they're very secretive about him, except to say that he gave them a thousand children."

"How did he do that?" Patchen asked.

"By impregnating the women. I think he got them drunk, then did what he wanted to do."

"Then they're all related to God, who was a drunk."

Martha gave a little grunt, as if Patchen had implanted this blasphemous idea by injection instead of merely speaking it aloud; he was alway surprising her by seeing things that she could not see.

"Of course that's what they think," she said.

She began to weep.

"What's wrong?" Patchen asked.

"Thee just made me realize that there's no hope for my Indians in this world," she replied. She addressed Patchen with the Quaker "thee" when they were alone; it was a sign of love and belonging, and he liked it. Nevertheless, he called Martha "you"; he was a birthright Quaker himself, but a non-believer.

"*Your* Indians? How are they yours?"

"I am not speaking possessively. Thee will understand some day."

Martha did not believe in unbelief, only in the idea that people were sometimes mistaken about what they believed, or in Patchen's case, mistaken about what he thought he did not believe.

It was night, three days after Martha and Patchen had been married in Ohio. They stood together on the fantail of the liner *America,* watching the phosphorescent wake of the ship as it passed through the dingy waves of the North Atlantic. Martha had never been to sea before. She had never even seen the sea—she had traveled to her Indian village in her Jeep, driving alone through Mexico, navigating by compass and sleeping in the open—and she found its ceaseless motion soothing and mysterious.

"Maybe you've just got a taste for monotony," Patchen said after she had questioned him about the Pacific and he had told her that the two oceans were equally uninteresting.

"A taste for monotony? What does thee mean?"

"Well, the beat beat beat of the tom-tom in your village of drunks."

Her eyes filled with tears again. "Sometimes, David," she said. "I think thee has no heart at all."

Patchen said no more. He had practically no experience with women, apart from his mother, but he was beginning to understand, only two days out of New York, that it was far easier to make a joke to a good woman than to deal with the consequences.

BEFORE PATCHEN JOINED THE MARINES HE AND MARTHA PLANNED
their honeymoon in detail: they would sail to France on a luxury
liner, first class, using the money she had earned and saved for the
purpose. In Paris, but not before, they would consummate their
marriage. Because Martha had been called to Guatemala instead of
teaching school, she had been unable to save money for the wedding trip as she and Patchen had planned.

Fortunately, Patchen had already signed his contract with the
Outfit. The document, backed in blue like any other legal paper,
confused him when he read it. He and the courier who delivered it
to him met in the grill room of the Locke-Ober restaurant.

"I'm a friend of the O. G.'s," the courier said, smiling and
shaking hands. They were surrounded by lawyers and politicians
who all seemed to know each other and to remember each other's
stories; Patchen thought it was a strange place to do secret business, but the courier ordered oysters and ale to be followed by
stuffed lobster and a bottle of Pinot Gris as if the real purpose
of the meeting was to enjoy a good lunch surrounded by happy
strangers.

"This is not addressed to me," Patchen said. "It's in the name of
somebody called Percival D. Indagator."

"It's addressed to you, all right," the courier replied; he wore a
tweed jacket with leather patches on the elbows and smoked a
pipe, as if disguised for a sojourn among professors. "That's your
funny name, the name you'll go by on the inside. Actually, it's a
great compliment—the O. G. chose it himself. It means 'explorer'
or 'investigator' in Latin. There aren't very many Latin funny
names. Mine is Latvian, I think."

"Do I sign it Percival D. Indagator?"

"If you please. You'll get used to it. But don't get so used to it
that you sign checks with it. It's happened."

The courier uttered a soft, merry chuckle; as Patchen was to
learn, secret jokes, however small, were always more amusing to
Outfit bureaucrats than the ones outsiders were permitted to know.
The contract called for a starting salary of five thousand dollars a
year, nearly as much as Patchen's grandfather made as a judge in
Ohio. He signed it with his new pseudonym.

"I'll need a receipt for this, also signed with your funny name," the courier said, laying a plain manila envelope sealed with Scotch tape on the table. "Don't open it here. We'd like you to write us a letter every month to this address; it doesn't matter what you say in it, we just want to know you're alive and well."

He gave Patchen a file card with an improbable name, the Reverend S. Booth Conroy, D. D., and the number of a post office box in Washington, D. C., typed on it.

"Memorize the name and address, then burn it," the courier said. "The john's a good place to burn things if you don't have a fireplace. You can just flush the ashes down. Be sure to wipe the soot off the bowl and open the window to let the stink out." He handed Patchen another index card. "When you get back to the good old U. S. A.," he said, "please go to Washington and call this number at noon, twelve o'clock straight up, on August sixth. A man will answer by repeating the last four digits of the number in reverse order. You'll say, 'Hello, I'm a friend of Monsieur Georges.' The man will reply, 'Good Old Georges! Is he still wearing that green overcoat?' He'll suggest a meeting place and time. Do exactly as he says. When you meet he'll say, 'Do you have something for me?' Give him the keys you'll find in the envelope and say, 'Rue de Passy.' He'll respond, in French, with the house number, seventy-eight *bis*."

Patchen gazed steadily at the smiling courier, but made no reply.

"All understood?" the courier asked. "Remember, he'll answer with the last four digits of the number in reverse."

"I'll remember. What's the man's name?"

"They didn't tell me that—you must have a need to know, that's the rule. And I don't, in this case. Neither do you."

"But he knows who I am?"

"You can't be sure that he does. So don't tell him." The courier took his pipe out of his mouth and leaned across the table. "Compartments," he murmured. He left money on the table for the bill, rose to his feet, and walked rapidly out of the restaurant.

The manila envelope contained one thousand dollars in hundred-dollar bills, two round-trip first-class tickets to Le Havre aboard the *America,* the keys to an apartment in the rue de Passy, and a first edition of a nineteenth-century manual for suitors and bridegrooms entitled *What Every Young Man Ought to Know.*

"Be careful in Paris," the O. G. wrote in a typed, unsigned note. "The rue de Passy is full of White Russians; they all put a '*de*' in front of their names and try to borrow money from you. My best wishes to you and your bride."

Martha insisted, gently, that they adhere to their agreement to wait until they got to Paris to consummate the marriage. Patchen did not protest. Like most middle-class American males of his generation, he took it for granted that the female controlled sexual behavior. He had never thought of Martha in carnal terms. Before he left for his port of embarkation to the Pacific, Martha had shown him her breasts, but that was the closest he had ever come to a shared sexual experience. Martha, sitting in the front seat of his grandfather's Buick with her dress unbuttoned and her eyes closed, seemed to think that the sacrifice of her modesty was a gift that would carry him safely through battle—or if it did not, make dying more bearable.

Although his desires were as urgent as those of any man his age, he was remarkably clean-minded. Bawdy jokes had never amused him, and he was surprised when, in his senior year in college, Christopher told him that the lyrics of many popular songs had double meanings. It had never occurred to Patchen that "nothing could be finer than to be in Carolina in the mornin' " did not necessarily refer to the scenic beauty of a Southern state or "Making Whoopee" to dancing the Charleston and drinking whiskey from a hip flask.

On their wedding night, in a Pullman compartment, Patchen undressed in the cramped washroom and emerged in pajamas and bathrobe. Martha stood by the curtained window in her dark going-away suit with the corsage still pinned to the lapel; the scent of gardenias saturated the compartment.

"Thee remembers our promise about Paris?" she asked.

"Yes. Do we have to keep it?"

"Does thee want to become one person in a place like this?"

From Patchen's point of view, after half a lifetime of imagining sexual congress with a naked woman, anyplace would have done, but he had been cautioned that brides were sensitive to their surroundings. Only that morning his mother, who had never before mentioned sex to him, enjoined him to remember that he was responsible for Martha's pleasure, which came before his own because it made his pleasure possible. She had not used those plain words, but Patchen had understood her meaning.

Martha, tapping her foot, awaited his reply.

"I guess not," he said.

She shook a playful finger at him. "Then get thee into the upper berth."

Then, to his astonishment, Martha undressed before his eyes, removing her jacket and skirt and draping them on a hanger, then peeling off the rest of her many garments and folding them neatly. She kept her back turned to him all during this exciting process, but she was as unselfconscious as if she were all alone. Patchen had never seen her with her hair down, much less naked. When she turned around after loosening her hair and arranging it so that it covered her breasts, he gasped at the loveliness of what he saw. He had been raised in the belief that the female body was the most beautiful and desirable object in Creation, and his first glimpse of it—the small waist, the dimpled navel, the curve of the hip, the pink nipples shyly hiding beneath the curtain of hair with its rippling lights—made him understand that he had not been lied to.

"Please hold this for me," Martha said, handing him a mirror.

Holding one hand over her pubes, she brushed her hair with the other, fifty vigorous strokes on one side and fifty on the other. As she bent gracefully to the left, and then to the right, her breasts were fully exposed one after the other. Her hair crackled under the brush, and when, smiling mysteriously, she took the mirror back from Patchen, static electricity leaped between their fingers.

"Thank thee," Martha said.

Holding her body away from her bridegroom, like a young girl dancing with someone she does not like or does not know, she kissed him on the lips. Then, turning her back, she pulled a nightgown over her head and got into the lower berth. In a matter of minutes she was fast asleep, breathing regularly as the train rattled over the roadbed. Patchen fell asleep in a state of unbearable excitement and had a dream that relieved it almost immediately, although even in his sleep he felt a married man's twinge of guilt and tried, unsuccessfully, to stop his sleeping body from doing what it insisted on doing. Martha repeated the undressing ritual aboard ship on each of the nights they were at sea; after the first night on the train, Patchen managed to remain faithful to her in his sleep, but he looked forward eagerly to Paris.

Martha liked the borrowed apartment in the rue de Passy, which was equipped with everything needed for living, even food in the refrigerator. A stranger's clothes, two or three suits with London tailor's labels, and some shirts and ties, hung in the closet.

"Whose place is this?" she asked.

"It belongs to someone Paul knows," Patchen said. He had not yet told Martha what he was going to be doing in Washington, only that he had got a job in that city and the salary it paid, and his conscience told him that this was a deception even though he himself did not yet know what, exactly, his work would consist of.

On their first evening in Paris they went to Maxim's, as Martha had planned. Her only jewelry was her new wedding ring; she had refused a diamond engagement ring out of principle. She wore flat-heeled shoes and a dark dress—her mother had sewed her trousseau, which consisted of the same drab buttonless dresses and suits that Martha always wore—and on seeing her homemade clothes and Patchen's scarred face, the headwaiter pretended that he could not understand what Patchen was saying to him. As the O. G. had suggested, Patchen had learned a little conversational French from Christopher.

Patchen switched to English, but the headwaiter did not understand that language, either. When Martha tried Spanish, he turned his face away as if from a disagreeable odor. "If they pretend not to understand you," Christopher had advised concerning the French, "just give them some money." Patchen gave the headwaiter a thousand-franc note and they were shown to a table in a far corner of the dining room.

Patchen ordered two table d'hôte dinners, the cheapest meals on the menu, and half-bottles of Montrachet, Pommard, and Taittinger Champagne to go with the sole, lamb, and dessert. The sommelier nodded approvingly at each choice, and also, Patchen thought, at his frugality.

"Come on," Patchen said to Martha, standing up and offering his arm. Because her parents rejected music out of religious scruple, Martha had never learned to dance, but she followed him onto the floor. The orchestra, costumed in prewar tail suits and boiled shirts, was playing a Strauss medley, *Tales of the Vienna Woods, Wiener Blut,* and other waltzes that Patchen recognized but could not name. Midway through the second number, Martha caught on to the steps and the rhythm, and they whirled clumsily around the floor, Patchen limping on his bad leg, but as happy as he had ever been in his life, in this red-plush room filled with music and the smell of delicious food where his mother and father had danced on their wedding night.

The music stopped and they went back to their isolated table. The sommelier poured some white wine into Patchen's glass and he swirled it, inhaled it, and tasted it as he had seen the O. G. do in his club. The headwaiter himself served the fish, filets rolled up and decorated with tiny shrimp. Patchen took this gesture as some sort of apology, but then the man leaned over and whispered in his ear in English, a language he had been pretending not to understand only a few minutes before.

"I have been asked," he said, "to request that you and Madame will be so kind as not to dance any more."

After he went away Martha asked Patchen what he had said.

"Just telling us to enjoy the food. How do you like it?"

"It's not fishy at all," Martha said. "Thee was blushing so I wondered if he'd guessed we're on our honeymoon."

"Maybe he did at that," Patchen said.

That night Martha, a little giddy after drinking alcohol for the first time in her life, was very kind to him. He found, to his mortification, that he had some trouble making love because of the difficulty of turning over in bed when he only had the use of the muscles on one side of his body. Once he fell heavily on his bride, making her gasp. Martha, stroking his hair, found ways to accommodate to his disability. Wine quickened her responses and slowed Patchen's, so that they reached orgasm within moments of each other; Martha, astonished by the novelty, wanted another climax, and then another. Patchen provided what she asked. Finally, just before dawn, they fell asleep.

Patchen was awakened by the sound of the drapes being drawn. Martha, stark naked, stood in front of the filmy curtains, gazing out over the Trocadéro. The glass shivered slightly in sympathy with the traffic below. Seeing her in his first instant of consciousness, silhouetted against the gray foreign sky, Patchen was seized by an irrational fear that she was going to fall out of the window.

"Martha!" he cried.

She jumped in surprise and uttered a little shriek. The gesture and sound, and the sight of her body that had made him so happy, filled Patchen's heart to overpouring. He leaped out of bed and limped across the room, smiling.

He was naked, too. Martha had never seen him unclothed; they had made love in the dark, undressing each other under the covers. Now she saw his wounds for the first time, the mass of angry scar tissue that covered the left side of his chest, stomach, arm, and leg like a mass of congealed blood.

Martha had no time to think, no time to compose herself. Her eyes widened; she covered her mouth with both hands and staggered back against the window, wrapping herself in the curtain to hide the front of her body from Patchen, while she pressed her back, nude and still warm from their wedding bed, against the transparent glass.

4

ON THE APPOINTED DATE AND TIME, PATCHEN CALLED THE TELEPHONE number in Washington; as the courier had instructed, he identified himself as a friend of Monsieur Georges.

"Look," said the man who answered, "why don't we get together for breakfast and a chat about good old George?"

"Breakfast?" Patchen said. What about the green overcoat?

"It's the most important meal of the day—didn't your mommy tell you? I'll pick you up at seven sharp tomorrow morning on the northwest corner of 17th Street and Pennsylvania Avenue. Watch out for a small black Morris Minor. It's a British car. Have you ever seen one?"

"No."

"Then you'll recognize it. It doesn't resemble anything made in America."

The man repeated these simple instructions twice more before hanging up. To Patchen's surprise, he was effusively congratulated next morning by the driver of the Morris for having appeared on the right street corner at the right time.

"You'd be amazed how many graduates of our great Ivy League universities can't manage it," the man said. "Do you have something for me?"

Patchen, leaning over to look in the rolled-down window, gave him the keys to the apartment in Paris.

"Rue de Passy," he said.

"Soixante-dix-huit bis," the man replied, shaking hands through

the open window. "Hop in. You can call me Archie. I'm your instructor."

Archie's voice was different from the one Patchen had heard on the telephone. After he had fitted his tall, stiff body into the tiny front seat, Patchen mentioned this. Archie, a balding middle-aged man with the manners of a Jazz Age undergraduate, gave him a delighted sidelong look.

"You're right," he said. "We're all ventriloquists. We'll teach you how to change *your* voice. It's one of the first things we do."

Patchen had no idea why he had been summoned to Washington. While maneuvering his sluggish midget car through the sedate Washington rush-hour traffic, Archie explained.

"You're going to learn to be a spy," he said. "The course is called Tradecraft 101; I'm your dean of studies, spiritual adviser, and professor of philosophy. It's damn funny how much slower this car goes with two people in it."

Patchen underwent weeks of training and indoctrination in a safe house, a narrow brick residence on a quiet street near Washington Circle. Like the apartment in the rue de Passy, it was fitted out with clothes, books, phonograph records, opened letters and bills, toilet articles, food, and drink to create the illusion that the fictitious name in which it had been rented belonged to an actual person. Patchen spent the greater part of each day with Archie, chatting about his new world or watching training films in which obvious Americans met nervous Central Europeans in museums, cafés, and other public places. Usually the agents carried several objects—a wrapped package, a newspaper opened to a certain page, an umbrella—and gave the all clear signal by switching these objects from hand to hand or juggling them in some other way according to a prearranged sequence.

"If you know you're not being watched, why is an all clear signal necessary?" Patchen asked.

"Because you give no signal at all if you *are* being watched," Archie replied. "If you did, the people trailing you would see the signal and know it for what it was, and the cat would be out of the bag."

"I understand. But if you're *not* being watched, why not just walk up and say hello? Why transfer *Pravda* from your right hand to your left? Suppose there's an off-duty secret policeman in the museum and he sees you signaling?"

Archie feigned a look of thoughtful surprise. "Good point," he said. "I'll take it up with Dick Hannay."

Other instructors, all identified by first names only, dropped by to teach Patchen the rudiments of tradecraft, as the technique of espionage is called. He learned the elements of the Outfit's secret priestly vocabulary: dead-drops, cut-outs, brush contacts, sleepers, witting and unwitting assets, the difference between an agent and an asset, and much more. He learned how to detect people who were following him on foot or in automobiles and how to follow others without being detected, how to tell whether his telephone or room was bugged (always assume that it is), how to write in invisible ink made from cow's milk or his own urine and how to read it by holding the page over a gas burner, how to employ simple codes and ciphers, how to conduct a "seduction," as the recruitment of an agent was called (Archie advised him to read the relevant passage in Eric Ambler's *A Coffin for Dimitrios*), how to conduct a search and how to hide things so that they cannot be found. A sweaty man in a Madras jacket familiarized him with burglar tools—the man carried a complete set of jimmies in special pockets sewn into a canvas corset worn beneath his shirt—and taught him how to pick locks. "You'll never have to do this," the man said, while opening a couple of dozen locks he had brought along in a clinking satchel. "Just remember there's no such thing as a lock that can't be picked." Another technician showed him how to disguise himself with false beards, wigs, devices that slipped in between his teeth and his cheeks to change the shape of his face and the sound of his voice, and body pads that transformed him into a fat man with a thin neck. Most of these tricks seemed to Patchen to be superfluous, if not laughable.

"Isn't the spectacle of a grown man writing misspelled obscenities on a brick wall with a piece of chalk more likely to attract attention than otherwise?" he asked, after a street exercise on how to conduct meetings with agents that had required Patchen to chalk *'Fuk U!'* on a brick wall on L Street.

"You're right," Archie replied. "Most of this stuff is nonsense. We inherited it from the Brits, who adore it. So do the Russians, the Germans, and all the rest of them. But be careful what you say and who you say it to on this subject. Nobody laughs at the rigmarole; it's very bad form to laugh at it. Agents expect it; it's part of the forbidden atmosphere, like false whiskers and cyanide pills. Mumbo-jumbo makes the whole process seem more serious, more connected to some invisible power. Like the Freemasons. Mozart wrote a whole opera about it."

Patchen was an apt pupil. He quickly perceived that the world of espionage was a mirror image of the ordinary world, that tradecraft closely resembled the everyday behavior of people who live in small towns like the one he had grown up in and must hide their real selves from prying neighbors. His town's adulterers, embezzlers, wife-beaters, drunks, incestuous lovers, and many others employed lies, deceptions, clandestine relationships, code words, false identities, and the other tricks of the world of espionage as a matter of course.

Had his own mother really met and married an Englishman named Patchen who was killed in the war after he impregnated her on a star-crossed honeymoon between battles, or had she simply succumbed to some temporary officer and gentleman from New York or San Francisco (or even the suburbs of Paris) who gave her his Croix de Guerre in return for her favors? Was everything his mother had told him about his origins a cover story? Many suspected that Patchen's mother had never been married, that her son was a bastard conceived in a pasture in France, that she had made up the whole romantic story of her brief marriage. But no one dared say so to her face because no one in town knew the truth or possessed the resources to discover it.

"Suspicion is not proof," Archie explained. "It doesn't matter what the opposition thinks as long as it doesn't find out the real truth."

" 'The real truth'?" Patchen said. "You mean there are truths truths that aren't real?"

Archie beamed with avuncular pleasure, as he often did on hearing Patchen's questions. "Absolutely," he replied. "They're the whole basis of cover. Every truth about you is harmless, out in the open, and therefore beautifully misleading because, taken as a whole, they seem to explain everything about you. First, your wounds—they're the first thing anyone notices about you. You come from an all-American village in Ohio, from a good family, you're a Quaker who joined the Marines, choosing duty to country over your somewhat addlepated religion, got shot up on Okinawa and won the Silver Star, and then went to Harvard on the G. I. Bill of Rights. That's a hell of a lot of information, more than most people can deal with. It presses all the right buttons, which is one reason—your brain being the other—why the O. G. took such an interest in you. Who would ever think to ask if there's anything funny about you? How could there be, behind the smoke screen of all those credentials and honorable wounds?"

"*Is* there something funny about me?" Patchen asked.

"Of course there is. You're a spy. Espionage is a criminal activity. Therefore you've agreed to live the life of a criminal during business hours."

"I have? I didn't realize that."

"Please understand my meaning," Archie said. "I'm not suggesting that you really *are* a criminal, only that what you have agreed to do for your country will be regarded by its enemies as criminal. When a case officer recruits an agent, he suborns him to treason. That's a capital crime in every country in the world. Never forget that. Once you set foot on the territory of any country but your own, you're under sentence of death the minute suspicion of your true purposes turns into proof. So guard the evidence of your operations with every atom of your being. Never let anyone outside the Outfit—*anyone*—not your mother, not your wife, not your priest, not the deaf-mute who has been sentenced to life in solitary confinement, learn one single fact about your work, no matter how unimportant it seems. The tiniest crack is big enough to let disaster in."

"How about the President of the United States? Suppose he asks? Is it all right to tell him?"

"Results, yes. Methods, no," Archie replied. "But he won't ask. That's what an intelligence service is for—to do the things that Presidents want done but don't want to know about. That way, when they write their memoirs, they can say that God did their dirty work."

The safe house was well furnished with books of all kinds, from turgid texts on the nature of Soviet Communism by American professors to Olympia Press editions of the forbidden novels of Henry Miller and the poetry of e.e. cummings. Patchen, who found it difficult to fall asleep, stayed up most nights reading. For the first time since he was wounded he began to think about the future. He had no idea what his life as a spy would be like, but he felt instinctively that it would involve living through others. In a novel

about fifteenth-century Italy by W. Somerset Maugham, he found a
speech by Machiavelli that intrigued him:

> These painters with their colors and their brushes prate about the
> works of art they produce, but what are they in comparison with
> a work of art that is produced when your paints are living men
> and your brushes wit and cunning?

He copied down the words on the last page of his address book.

5

DURING HIS PERIOD OF TRAINING, PATCHEN WAS ALONE IN WASHING-
ton. After she and Patchen disembarked in New York, Martha had
taken the train back to Ohio. Aboard ship, he had explained that
he had been ordered to Washington in connection with his new job.

"What will thee be doing?" she asked.

"Working for the government," Patchen replied.

"Will thee be doing good works?"

"I hope so."

Martha asked no further questions about his occupation then or
for a long time afterward. She was not really interested in anything
that did not have to do with the Inward Light. What Patchen did
for a living was unimportant except that it put food on the table
and clothes on his back until he found the Christ within himself.
She mentioned to Patchen that many had discovered the Inward
Light under the most unlikely conditions—while in prison, or even
like the English sea captain who wrote the hymn "Amazing Grace"
after making a fortune as the master of a slave ship.

"Did this sea captain give all the money he'd made running
slaves to Negro Relief or did he just write the hymn and let it go at
that?" Patchen asked.

"The words tell how repentant the poor man was—'Amazing
grace, how sweet the sound, to save a wretch like me.' "

"He must have kept the money if his neighbors were willing to
swallow that. A poor man could never get away with such crap."

Martha was not sure that her husband, who had suffered such
awful injuries, would be able to overcome his bitterness and find
peace, but she did not discuss her doubts with him. They had been

very quiet with each other ever since she saw his scars for the first time; neither mentioned the incident after it took place, but they stopped making love.

Archie had provided Patchen with an accommodation address to which Martha could write, and one day toward the end of his training, he received a letter announcing that she was arriving at Union Station that same afternoon.

Archie said, "You'll have to stop her."

"How can I? She's on the train."

"Well, I guess there's no help for it. Do you want the bedroom cameras on or off?"

A female employee of the Outfit posing as Archie's wife kept Martha busy during the day with tours of the city. In the evening Martha heated up cans of Campbell's soup from the safe house's well-stocked cupboards and sometimes made bland casseroles by combining cream of tomato soup with peas and corn, cheese, and boiled rice. She was a vegetarian; one of the things she had liked best about her drunken Indians was their tasteless, odorless diet. After a week Patchen asked her to bring home a steak.

"It's not right," Martha said, "to kill and eat what God has made to keep thee and me company on earth."

"All these carrots and potatoes weren't alive before Campbell's chopped them up and made them into soup?"

"Thee makes a joke of everything."

"I just think that you should apply the same standards of judgment to everything."

"How? Good is good and evil is evil."

"Is it?" Patchen asked.

"I will not argue with thee."

Martha's face was flushed; her voice trembled. To her, Patchen realized, this mild exchange had seemed a quarrel. Since her arrival they had slept in the same bed, but they did not touch or kiss. That night Patchen stayed up late, reading; when he went to bed after undressing in the dark, he found Martha awaiting him between the sheets, naked. As before, she managed everything, but this time left all but the essential part of his body inside his buttoned pajamas. Next morning she woke him early and they made love again; Archie and his "wife" arrived downstairs in the middle of the act, at the moment when Martha uttered a long cry of pleasure.

"We are not alone," Patchen said.

"Then let them put beans in their ears," Martha said.

Her face glowed. Patchen laughed and drew her closer to him. Each time he saw her unclothed, or heard her crying out in pleasure, Patchen was amazed that such a pious girl should have been so perfectly made for sex.

"Does thee know what I am hoping?" she asked.

"No. What?"

"That the child we are making will look just like thee, not as the war made thee, but as God made thee."

Patchen turned away. Martha tried to make him look at her, but he resisted. She crawled over his body and knelt beside the bed until he opened his eye and looked into her uplifted face.

"If I could, I would unwound thee, but I can't," she said. "However, I *will* be a wife to thee."

THREE

1

THE OUTFIT HAD NO HEADQUARTERS. ITS EMPLOYEES, WHOSE NUM-bers, cost, and true identities were kept secret from everybody except the O. G., were scattered around Washington in gimcrack temporary government buildings left over from the First World War, or in offices with the names of fictitious organizations painted on the doors, or in private houses in discreet residential neighborhoods. This milieu, in which daring undertakings were planned and spacious ideas were discussed in mean little rooms by ardently ambitious men who were mostly very young, preserved a wartime atmosphere long after World War II was over. This was exactly what the O. G. wanted.

"Nooks and crannies, visibility zero—that's the ticket," he said. "The day we move into a big beautiful building with landscaped grounds and start hanging portraits of our founders is the day we begin to die."

The O. G. himself worked in a disused town house on a wooded knoll above the Potomac River. Until the last elderly member died during the latter days of the Franklin Roosevelt Administration, this had been the clubhouse of the Society of Euhemerus, made up of men directly descended in the male line from the original American colonists, and the ceilings were frescoed with scenes showing Bradfords, Oglethorpes, Newports, and other members of the nation's First Families in heroic postures. The watercolor on the O. G.'s ceiling depicted Squanto, a heap of dead mackerel at his feet, teaching Myles Standish and John Alden how to plant and fertilize corn.

"My Uncle Snowden called this picture 'the parable of the oafs

115

and the fishes,' " the O. G. told Patchen on his first day on the job. "He was the one who got the club to leave this place to the government. Do you know who Euhemerus was?"

"No, sir."

"He was a Greek who believed that the gods were originally human heroes. Hence the members of the Society were descendants of the American gods, who were, unfortunately, as yet undeified."

It was a humid August day, and the tall french windows were open, admitting a feeble river breeze. The O. G.'s office, a vaulted room with three exposures, was located at the top of the house. He stepped out onto a small balcony and gestured to Patchen to follow. The view from the balcony was famous: you could see the whole length of the Mall, from the Lincoln Memorial to the Capitol. Beyond this, the unroiled Potomac flowed between grassy banks.

"Washington," the O. G. said with a wave of the hand; he wore a gold ring with the seal of the Society of Euhemerus on his left little finger. "What do you think of it?"

"I like it," Patchen replied.

"Good for you. Not many people appreciate it."

Patchen was genuinely surprised to hear this. "Why not?"

"It's not fashionable—it's a backwater. You're just supposed to serve your time here with complaining while waiting to be sent to Paris or Vienna or London."

"I think it's beautiful. I feel at home here."

This was true. On arriving in Washington, although Patchen had never visited the place before, he had felt a puzzling sense of homecoming. He liked to walk at night along Constitution Avenue, past the massive city-within-a-city of silent, deserted Greco-Roman government buildings. At such times he felt like an archeologist transported by time machine to an Athens or Rome that had not yet been informed of the glories that awaited it. Washington was like the site for the capital of a world empire that had not yet come into existence; it was pregnant with the history of the future. Or so it seemed to Patchen on his lonely midnight walks; he did not confess these high-flown thoughts to the O. G., who had been chatting to him as his mind wandered.

"I've always liked this town, too, except for the climate," the O. G. was saying. "It's something like Weimar must have been in the time of Goethe. Big old houses filled with toadies and arrivistes, all wanting the same things—the ear of the prince, membership in the inner circle, decorations to wear to each other's fancy dress balls. There's no real conversation, just gossip, but there *are* good paintings in the museums, some pretty darn good chamber music, amateur theatricals—even, until Franklin Roosevelt passed away, a benevolent prince. But no Goethe. Anyway, I'm glad you like Washington, because this is where you're going to be for the rest of your career."

"No hope of Paris or London?"

"Nope. You're a born headquarters man."

The O. G. did not explain this statement. He was famous for his impulsive judgments. As Patchen himself would say years later, when he knew him better than anyone alive, the old man decided everything between his pelvis and his collarbone. He meant this as a compliment: any damn fool could be an intellectual.

"You're going to work for me, and only for me, right next door," he said. "Does that suit you?"

"Yes, sir," Patchen replied. "It does."

"I'll work you like a slave, but you'll be right at the hub of events, and if I'm right about you, you'll go up and up. Do you like that trade-off?"

"Sounds fine to me."

"Then let's get started."

He showed Patchen his new office, a musty cell lighted by a single horizontal aperture, like a cellar window, just below the ceiling. It adjoined the O. G.'s office, to which it was connected by a low door, plastered and set flush with the wall. The room was furnished with a battered metal desk, a straight chair, a gooseneck lamp, a wastebasket with the word BURN stenciled on the side, and a chipped Waterford crystal tumbler filled with sharpened yellow pencils. The dead air smelled of fresh pencil shavings. Enormous steel double doors led into a vault that was somewhat larger than the cubbyhole itself.

"This is where Uncle Snowden and his fellow Euhemerians used to hang their togas," the O. G. said. "Not much air or light, but it's got location."

He walked into the open vault. There were other safes within this safe, battered olive-drab file cabinets fitted with combination dials; these were stacked one on top of the other. After climbing a library ladder, the O. G. opened one, working the combination from memory, and rummaged in a drawer. He withdrew a stack of files stamped in carmine with the words TOP SECRET • EYES ONLY • NOFORN.

"Here," he said. "Read these and tell me whether you think these fellows have got any chance of bringing this operation off."

Patchen switched on the gooseneck lamp and began to read. It took him hours to work his way through the jumbled files, in which significant passages were sometimes separated by thirty or forty pages of seemingly irrelevant cables, dispatches, letters, and reports written in dense bureaucratic prose. The various parts had been contributed by many different people, some of them foreigners who had only begun to learn English, some of them Americans who had mastered the esoteric vocabulary of the inner government so thoroughly that their sentences were incomprehensible to anyone but another initiate. Neither human beings nor places went under their own names in these documents, but were identified instead by pseudonyms which sounded like real names, by cryptonyms which were gibberish, or sometimes by numbers or a combination of numbers and letters.

In the end Patchen understood, or thought he understood, that he had been reading the raw files of a plan to set up a network in Berlin, using the Russian-speaking daughters and widows of men who had been killed by the Communists to become the mistresses of high-ranking Soviet officers and entice them to reveal secrets. Many girls had already expressed interest in the scheme; it was thought that they would be both effective and reliable because they were motivated by hatred and revenge. Those who succeeded in trading sex for military secrets would be given new identities and allowed to emigrate to the United States.

"Well, what do you think?" the O. G. asked when Patchen knocked and entered the O. G.'s larger office.

"I think the idea is all right," Patchen replied. "But I think the operation itself is a recipe for disaster."

"Do you? Why's that?"

"We'll either get caught or get burned. The Russians must keep a close eye on their generals, and if two or three of them suddenly acquire good-looking young mistresses who all speak Russian, they may regard that as a suspicious circumstance."

"True. Anything else?"

"There's nothing in the files to suggest we've investigated the girls."

"That would be very difficult. They're all displaced persons from inside Russian-occupied Europe."

"You mean we picked them up on the streets and accepted their stories on faith?"

The O. G. nodded. "That's about the size of it."

"So all we really know about them is that they speak Russian and they're willing to sell their bodies in the cause of freedom."

"Yep."

"Then how do we know the Russians aren't sending these girls to us?"

"Why would they do that?"

"So that they can feed us false and misleading information through the girls. I think we should get rid of them and whoever introduced us to them, and then begin over again and concentrate."

The O. G. had been listening intently. "Concentrate on what?"

"New girls, just plain whores with no political motivation," Patchen said. "The targets should be younger Russians—captains, majors, lieutenant-colonels. Men young enough to think with their peckers. The girls should act like virgins, make the Russians fall in love with them. Then the girl says, 'Prove your love and I'll sleep with you. Bring me some little thing from your unit, a photograph of your tank, a telephone book, something written in Russian.' Then, when they're hooked, we move in and threaten to expose them unless they play ball. Some may know useful things right now. Others may be useful for the future."

The O. G. poured himself a glass of water from the thermos pitcher on his desk, and drank.

"Want some?" he asked, pointing to the pitcher.

Patchen nodded, poured himself a full glass, and drank thirstily; the O. G. watched him.

"The moral question doesn't trouble you?" he asked.

Patchen said, "What moral question?"

"Turning girls into whores. Blackmail."

"No. As you say, it's just a case of finding out what people want to do and making it possible for them to do it."

The O. G. gazed at him for several seconds in great seriousness. Then he threw back his head and laughed.

"I was right, by golly," he said. "I saw that you had your head

119

screwed on straight up in Boston, over the codfish cakes. Couldn't believe my luck."

"May I ask why, sir?"

"Because, Son, you're a skeptic and you say what you think. I've got all the enthusiasts I need around here."

Thereafter the O. G. and Patchen were together all day every working day from seven in the morning until whatever hour the O. G. went home. He met everyone the O. G. met, heard everything the O. G. heard, went with him to lunch every day. At the end of the day he rode with him to his house above Rock Creek Park, absorbing instructions that would require another two or three hours of work after he dropped the old man off.

The O. G. called Patchen "Son"; Patchen never called him anything but "Sir." Gradually, as his powers grew, Patchen became known and feared throughout the Outfit, but his duties and his position were never defined. Others thought that he operated outside the apparatus; in fact he was implanted so deeply within it as to be detached from its rules. At Harvard, Patchen had been a familiar but nameless figure; men in the Outfit who had been there at the same time remembered him because of his appearance, though few had ever known who he was. It was a puzzle to them why the O. G. preferred this grotesque outsider without background or connections to themselves.

As more and more prankish operations were disapproved before they could begin, many thought that Patchen was exercising a puritanical influence over the sunny nature of the O. G., that he was systematically robbing the Outfit of its schoolboy élan. One disappointed officer tried to saddle him with the nickame "Rasputin," but a cleverer rival gave him a crueler name, "The One-Eyed Man." It stuck.

Patchen did not object to the nickname because the proverb it came from—"In the country of the blind, the one-eyed man is king,"—expressed so aptly the situation in which he perceived himself to be from the first day he opened a secret operational file until his last day on duty.

2

ONLY DAYS AFTER HE STARTED HIS NEW JOB, PATCHEN CAME THROUGH the door and found Paul Christopher seated in front of the O. G.'s desk.

"I think you fellows know each other," the O. G. said. "Sit down next to your rescuer, Son."

Rescuer? Patchen did not understand the allusion. The O. G. went right on talking.

"Paul is going out to Indochina," he said, pausing to light his pipe. He gave Christopher a confiding nod. "David knows all about it."

This was true, in the sense that Patchen had studied the details of an operational plan that involved penetrating the Vietminh, as the guerrilla force fighting the French in Vietnam was called, in order to try to find out what its resources, tactics, and fighting spirit were. But the penetration agent had been identified by a pseudonym; Patchen had no idea that Christopher had also been recruited into the Outfit, much less that he was the agent in questlon. It was a very dangerous assignment; both the Vietminh and the French were likely to kill any American who got between them.

"I want you two to work with me on this," the O. G. said. "No desk officer—just the three of us."

"What about Waddy?" Christopher asked.

Wadsworth Jessup, Alice Hubbard's brother, was already in Hanoi, and the operational plan called for Christopher to report to him.

"Be kind to Waddy," the O. G. said. "Carry out his schemes with due regard for your own neck; observe the niceties. But Waddy's schemes aren't the reason for the trip."

The mechanism in a long-case clock standing against the wall whirred but did not strike; the O. G. kept it wound even though the chimes had been disconnected. The O. G. always ate his lunch at noon precisely, and now, as the clockwork clicked out the hour, they heard the rattle of china and glassware as a trolley from the kitchen approached his doors. So that the waiter would not see Christopher, he and Patchen went into Patchen's cell while the luncheon table was set up.

In Patchen's cell, he and Christopher exchanged amused smiles.

"I guess I'm not supposed to say this is a pleasant surprise," Patchen said.

"Or 'fancy meeting you here,' " Christopher replied. "How was Paris?"

"All right. Martha is here in Washington. We've just bought a house. Can you have supper with us tonight?"

"If I can bring a girl."

"Bring her. She and Martha can discuss the issues of the day."

They smiled again. Christopher's girls, invariably pretty, invariably earnest, invariably defenders of one political faith or another, had seldom warmed up to Patchen, or he to them.

The O. G. flung open the door to his office; a table was laid by the fireplace with a white cloth, dishes, and silver.

"There's a pretty nice rockfish out here," he said. "How about helping me eat it? I'll be Mother."

He fileted the grilled fish expertly, spooned asparagus and halved lemons onto the plates, and handed them around. Like the dented silver platters and the knives and forks, the china bore the seal of the Society of Euhemerus, a golden column surrounded by a wreath of Greek letters.

"Can you read the Greek, Paul?" the O. G. asked.

Christopher pushed his food aside with his knife and studied the seal. " 'Sacred scripture?' "

"Correct. That's how I want you fellows to communicate after Paul gets out there—in Greek cipher."

"I don't read Greek," Patchen said.

"No need to," the O. G. said. "All you have to do is learn the Greek alphabet—a morning's work. During the Indian Mutiny British officers sent hundreds of secret messages to each other through enemy country by writing plain English in the Greek alphabet. The code was never cracked."

The O. G. poured water into chipped crystal goblets. After their first lunch together Patchen never saw him drink wine again in daylight. The Montrachet he had ordered in Boston was meant to help him, Patchen, relax.

"The Brits all know about the Greek cipher," the O. G. said. "It was a jolly prank on the Wogs in addition to being useful. I knew a villain of a Brit who seduced the young wife of an American millionaire and used the Greek cipher to write her indecent letters describing their assignations. The husband found the letters, all tied up in a blue ribbon, got suspicious, and asked a Greek he knew to translate them. The Greek read every page, lingering here and there over an especially fine passage, then handed the letters back. 'This is a translation of *Alice in Wonderland*,' said the Greek, a fellow of some wisdom and experience. 'The letters are from your wife's teacher. She must be a remarkable woman—this is a most ingenious way to learn a foreign language.' The Greek dined out on the story for years afterward."

Before he spoke again the O. G. finished his lunch, working rapidly with his knife in his right hand and his fork in his left, bolting the food like a European. Then leaned back in his chair and lighted his pipe, studying his guests over the flare of the match.

"Ever heard of the Quoc Hoc School?" he asked.

The two younger men shook their heads.

"Famous high school in Hue, the imperial capital of Vietnam," the O. G. said. "Quoc Hoc is the womb of the revolution. Half the Vietminh went there—Ho Chi Minh among others. With darn few exceptions, every one of them came from a good bourgeois family. And thereby hangs a tale."

The O. G. taught by parable, and the tales he told often came out of his own experience. The moral was always the same: things done on impulse always turn out better than things done by calculation.

"During the war," the O. G. said, meaning the First World War, in which he had enlisted as an aviator while still in his teens and long before the United States became a belligerent, "I was posted to a French squadron for a while, flying Spads. Under the French system, every officer had a servant, and mine was this little Tonkinese fellow, no bigger than an American twelve-year-old and a lot less hairy. His name was Vo, and Vo was the worst servant in the squadron. He was always reading; another reason why he and Paul will get along. Vo would get lost in a book and forget to shine your boots or whatever. He'd had a hell of a time, fellows kicking him in the pants for lollygagging and so forth, but I thought he was all right. One morning I caught him reading Rousseau by the dawn's early light instead of heating up my shaving water, so I had to go up and search for the Red Baron without a shave. When I got back, he acted like he expected something pretty bad from me, but all I did was take him aside and talk to him about schedules. Had a hell of a time getting him to see my point."

The O. G. lived by his schedule, believing that it set him free; by using his time according to a predetermined plan, he enjoyed a hundred little moments of satisfaction in the course of every day, and also quarantined himself from bores. He was a good mimic. Now, speaking French with a flat American accent while acting the character that had been himself at age nineteen, and the same

123

language with a singsong intonation when playing the part of Vo, he reconstructed a conversation that took place thirty years before and three thousand miles away. He made himself large and earnest when he was the American, small and doubting when he was the Vietnamese. Finally Vo was convinced. The O. G. unstrapped his wristwatch, which Vo knew to be his most cherished possession because it had been given to him by his father, and gave it to the Vietnamese.

"Well, sir," the O. G. said, returning to real time and place, "Vo started living by a schedule the very next morning, and by George, he liked it! Changed his life. The first benefit came immediately: he was out of trouble for not doing his duty, because he had plenty of time to do whatever was required of him with plenty more left over to read to his heart's content. To make a long story short, Vo turned into a great scholar, which is the very highest and most respectable thing someone from his part of the world can be, and he went back to Hue and got a job teaching at Quoc Hoc School. He taught all those fellows that are out in the jungle now—taught 'em Rousseau, who begat the Vietminh. That's where it all began. How about some coffee?"

He poured muddy coffee, made according to the Euhemerian recipe by pouring boiling water into a bed of well-aged grounds to which a handful of fresh-ground coffee and an eggshell had been added. Cream poured into this liquid had no effect on its color, nor did sugar affect its taste. The O. G. drank a large cup of it, black, before he spoke again.

"Now this plan to penetrate the Vietminh is a good one," he said. "There's no telling what kind of information a smart young fellow might come back with, but information is funny stuff. In this game, there are lies, damn lies, and what you want to believe. What really counts is action, not words. Anyway, Vo's boys are going to beat the French, so what interests us is not the present, about which we can do nothing, but the future, where we might possibly have some influence. Paul should get in as deep as he can with these Communists and still walk back out. Remember, they're not simple peasants by a long shot. Keep eyes and ears open. Report all that stuff to Waddy. It's a nice diversion."

Eyes shining, the old man paused and looked from one young man to another.

"Diversion from what, sir?" Patchen asked.

"From Vo," the O. G. said. "That's Paul's real target. There was an inscription on the back of that watch I gave him. *'Sed fugit . . .inreparabile tempus*—time is flying, never to return.' Virgil. Look him up for me, Paul. Quote him the Virgil; he'll remember. He knows who and what I am now or I don't know Vo. If he doesn't turn you away from the door, get him to teach you Vietnamese. Become his student—that's the way to his heart. He must be thinking about the future, too. Find out what it is he wants to do, and let's see if we can make it possible for him to do it."

3

THE GIRL CHRISTOPHER BROUGHT TO DINNER AT THE PATCHENS', AN intense young woman named Maria Custer, was enthralled by Martha's adventure among the drunken Indians of Guatemala. She had just graduated from Vassar College.

"God, how I envy you," she said after hearing about the *guaro* cult. "How did you ever *find* these amazing people? You *are* going back, aren't you? You must be a legend to them. I mean, this white woman simply appearing out of the blue and binding up their wounds."

"I've thought of going back," Martha said, "but I have a husband now."

"What difference does that make? You *must* go back—I mean, they must be waiting for you. Look at the Aztecs. Cortés conquered them in no time because they thought he was the golden-bearded god they had been waiting for. What was his Aztec name, Paul?"

Patchen answered the question. "Quetzalcoatl."

"No, that's wrong; Quetzalcoatl is the plumed serpent," Maria said. "It starts with an 'M.' *Malinche!* That's it!"

"That was what Montezuma called Cortés, because that was the name of Doña Marina, Cortés interpreter, and the two of them were always together," Patchen said. "Quetzalcoatl had a long, dark beard."

"Did he? Maybe that explains the confusion over names," Maria said, smiling brightly as she waited for the interruption to end. She had very dark hair herself, set off dramatically by pale bluish skin. Her large, somewhat bulging eyes were placed very wide apart above high cheekbones. The hair was dyed, as Christopher realized when he encountered her a year or two later in Paris after it had gone back to its natural toast brown color.

"Anyway," Maria exclaimed to Martha, "you *must* go. Maybe you could adopt one of those pathetic children. Maybe you could get others to adopt them. Then when they grow up they can all go back and save the others."

"Maybe you can set something up with the Junior League," Patchen said. "Orphans by Peck and Peck."

Maria ignored him. "I'll bet plenty of American women would be willing to adopt a kid," she said to Martha. "I'm not talking about taking these children out of their way of life. I'm talking about raising them in such a way that they'd be able to go back and rescue their culture from the ghost of that Spanish drunk. The *symbolism* of it—him sitting there in his chair in his breastplate and helmet! How could you bear it? Can't you see our kids going back and heaving the bastard out the door, like Pizarro did with the Inca mummies? Do you know that story?"

Martha shook her head. Maria provided a detailed synopsis of W. H. Prescott's *The Conquest of Mexico* and *The Conquest of Peru,* books she had read for a political science course taught by a crypto-Marxist. It was her opinion that the effigy of Maximón in the drinking hut represented the specter of imperialism; although she was a Russian major, Maria had taken courses in psychology at Vassar, and she thought that the *guaro* cult itself was clearly an attempt by the Indians to escape from imperialism by entering into another state of consciousness.

"I mean it has to be entirely unconscious," she said. "But that only goes to show you how the masses have this deep need to have their natural disgust *explained* to them. I mean, teaching is all. In Poland, the schoolchildren sing this wonderful song, 'Long live Uncle Stalin, whose lips are sweeter than raspberries.' Now *that's* a work of genius, to turn the natural love of kids for the man who saved their country into poetry."

"Baloney," Patchen said. He was mildly drunk after consuming most of the bottle of Châteauneuf-du-Pape that Christopher had brought as a house gift.

"The same to you," Maria said. "In a just society, powerful men can love little children, and be loved by them, instead of proving their manhood by making war on women and children."

"You're saying that Stalin's Russia is a just society?"

"Not yet, not entirely, but it is consciously trying to become one. Do you read Russian?"

"No. Do you?"

"I majored in it. At least women are equal in the Soviet Union, eligible for anything, in contrast to the capitalist states, where they are regarded as the property of men and have no function except to breed and suffer."

"No kidding. Apart from childbirth, how do middle-class women suffer in America?"

"They suffer all right, and always have. Far more than men ever do."

Patchen poured himself another glass of wine. "Right," he said. "All those brave girls sleeping under the white crosses in war cemeteries all over the world. And who can forget the *Titanic*—the men sitting in the lifeboats in their fur coats with their jewel boxes on their laps while the band played 'Nearer My God to Thee' and the women went down with the ship."

Maria took Martha's hand and looked at her with deep sympathy. "You poor thing," she said.

A silence fell. Martha blushed. Maria turned a look of withering superiority on Patchen. She had exceptionally pretty breasts, quite large and widely separated like her eyes; her blouse clung to their contours, suggesting nipples without actually revealing them. For some reason this symmetry of eyes and breasts was acutely erotic. Patchen's good eye flickered from her face to her torso, and Maria's glare changed into a smile of scorn. She had possessed these extraordinary breasts since she was in the seventh grade, and she knew that no normal male could look at them without wanting to hold them in his hands and whimper. She inhaled, expelled the breath through her nostrils, turned to Martha, and started talking again.

By now they had finished the food, a watery casserole of potatoes, onions, and beets that Martha called "red flannel hash."

"Let's go outside," Patchen said.

On the screened porch, Patchen said, "Does she always spout that bullshit?"

"I don't know," Christopher said. "It's just small talk."

"Is she someone you're interested in?"

"No. I only have custody for the evening. She's job-hunting in Washington."

"*She's* not going to turn up in the O. G.'s office, is she?" Patchen asked.

"I don't know," Christopher replied. "But it was the O. G. who arranged this blind date. He says she speaks fluent Russian and has a first-class mind. He knew her uncle in the Navy."

"Good gravy."

The two friends smiled at each other. They were sitting on a tattered wicker sofa on the screened porch, which looked out onto an alley; the house itself was a flat-roofed wooden structure resembling a very large packing crate. It was sparsely furnished with canvas butterfly chairs and an uneven table made by laying an old door on sawhorses. The night was very hot, scarcely cooler than the feverish August day that had preceded it. Radios played on neighboring porches. A feeble breeze stirred the leaves of the old trees that had been planted to seclude these slave quarters from the big house to which they had formerly belonged.

Patchen asked a question. "What did the O. G. mean today when he called you my rescuer?"

In the spotty light from the streetlamp, Christopher shrugged. "Who can keep up with what the O. G. means?" he said.

"I thought he meant something different from what he was saying."

Christopher gave him a steady look. "What would that be?"

"I don't know," Patchen said. "That's what bothers me. Let me tell you something. Don't laugh."

"All right."

Patchen collected his thoughts before speaking. "I've always thought that I knew you before the hospital, that there's something about you that I don't remember. Sometimes I feel I'm on the verge of remembering it, whatever it is, but I never do."

Christopher made no reply.

"For example," Patchen said, "when you and your father recited that poem in German I thought I remembered it."

"The poem?"

"No, the part about German being the only language that lions understand. Had you ever told me that before?"

"It's possible," Christopher said. "It's a family saying."

128

4

THAT WINTER MARTHA RETURNED TO THE VILLAGE IN GUATEMALA. On her approach—she was still driving her surplus Army Jeep—the Indians fled from their village and hid in the jungle. Knowing their shy ways, Martha assumed that they did not realize that it was she who had come back to them, so she unpacked her belongings, moved back into the hut where she had formerly lived, and serenely awaited their return.

Several days passed; the Indians did not come back. It was, as she told Patchen when she returned to Washington the next spring, a mysterious experience.

"I don't know if thee can understand," she said, "but I felt there was some hidden or secret thing all about me in the air, trembling, as if the word of truth had been spoken in a powerful voice, but I was deaf and could not hear it."

Martha had known that the Indians were observing her, even though she could not see them. She thought it was possible that they thought she was someone else: with their golden skin and their straight black hair, they all looked alike to her; why shouldn't white people look alike to them? She would go outside from time to time and halloo, hoping that her friends would recognize her. She moved her hammock into the open and lay in it, feigning sleep, in case the Indians should tiptoe into camp and gaze into her face. They had taken with them the effigy of Maximón and the wooden tub they used to ferment *guaro,* along with the marimba. Each day, in the early morning, as Martha hoed and watered the village gardens, she noticed that corn had been plucked and beans and squash had been picked in the night.

Clearly her Indians were hidden somewhere in the jungle, gathered around Maximón, drinking. But why were they hiding? All day she heard the marimba playing in the distance, and finally she decided to walk toward the sound. But after she had sauntered under the trees for a few moments she realized that she could not locate the music accurately. She turned back, but even though she had traveled only a short distance into the forest she had trouble finding her way. Howler monkeys shrieked in the trees above her; she knew there were poisonous snakes and even jaguars in this place. Yet she felt no fear.

"None at all?" Patchen said. "That's amazing. Why not?"

"The Inward Light was very strong—it is strongest in the village compared to any other place in the world. And, of course, I knew that my Indians would save me if I became lost. They were watching over me every minute. I could feel them all around."

Finally she stumbled into a little clearing where a buried temple stood. For reasons of their own, the Indians had cleared a narrow path to the pinnacle, fifty or sixty feet above the ground, and Martha climbed up. The ground underfoot was free of stubble, in fact it was bare stone, and it was a pleasure to walk on a smooth surface. Nevertheless, it was a hard climb, and by the time she got to the top her body was running with sticky, thick sweat. From the summit, the deserted village was clearly visible. Martha took her bearings and regained it without difficulty.

A few days later the Indians came back. Martha woke up one morning to the notes of the marimba and found the village repopulated, Maximón back on his throne in the drinking hut, and the children playing their usual games. But as soon as she came outdoors, smiling in delight that the mistake over her identity had been corrected, the children ran away over the beaten earth between the huts, staring at the ground. This did not surprise her; the children had always stared at the ground in her presence. Even the adults were curiously shy about eye contact, preferring to stare downward or turn their backs when they conversed with her. Some even closed their eyes or covered them with their hands in her presence.

Martha did not pursue the children or try to coax them to come to her, but instead joined the women as they straggled toward the vegetable patch. They were all drunk, of course, and they staggered as they walked. About half of the women were with child; it was more difficult for drunks in the last stages of pregnancy to walk on the rough ground, and they often fell. Martha wanted to help them, but the other women kept her away by forming a screen with their bodies.

Otherwise they did not interfere with her. As before, they behaved as though she was not there. They did not speak to her, or reply when she spoke to them; she communicated with them, as she had formerly done with the children, in Spanish phrases that she was not sure they understood, and by working with them. The fact that they and she were making the same movements, performing the same tasks, seemed to soothe them; sometimes they even

130

smiled, shyly and secretly, as they stared down into the dirt. Martha had got so used to this way of being close to the Indians during her last visit that she had very nearly lost the need for speech, but it seemed strange to her now as she resumed her old behavior.

Every day Martha went outside and waited for the children to come back, but they did not do so. To entice them, she took the Jeep apart and put it back together again and sat on a chair in the sunlight, embroidering bright flowers on a blouse. These techniques had worked before, but they produced no results now. Evidently the children had satisfied their curiosity about her the year before and had no further interest in her or her ways. If she happened to come upon them, they would scatter. They were particularly shy if she happened to meet them after she had been working in the sun.

Returning one day from the cornfield, she broke a strap on one of her sandals and the other women got far ahead of her on the winding path. She took a shortcut through an isolated patch of jungle, and when she came to the other side, she saw the children waiting on the path. They had their backs turned, and as the women approached, smiling happily at the sight of the children, they did a puzzling thing: every one of them touched every one of the children on the crown of the head. As soon as they had done so, the children turned around and gazed upward, like normal boys and girls, straight into the eyes of the adults, who picked the smaller ones up in their arms and continued on into the village.

Martha let them go, and following stealthily by darting from hut to hut, managed to leap out and surprise the children at play. She touched one, then another, then a third on the hair, and then all the others, chasing them through the village giddily as if in a game of tag. As soon as she had touched their heads, they stopped running away and even looked into her eyes. But still they did not come to visit her and work with her.

She had brought a number of new things with her this time—a phonograph and records, a portable Singer sewing machine, and two bicycles. She played the phonograph in the evening. Somewhere the children were listening, because one morning as she woke she heard them singing the songs on the records: "Amazing Grace" and "Shall We Gather by the River" and "The Old Rugged Cross." Although they could not pronounce the English words, the children sang the music in voices of almost unbearable sweetness. Martha crept toward the sound and found them standing in rows like a choir, singing with their eyes closed. Watching from her hiding place and listening, she felt that the Inward Light was kindling in their tiny, glowing bodies.

The next morning she got out one of the bicycles and rode it through the village, looking neither to right nor left as she pumped up the gentle slopes and coasted down again with her hands clasped behind her head. This broke the spell, whatever it had been, and the children began coming to her hut again. But the Jeep no longer interested them, and they shunned the sewing machine after one of the girls sewed her index finger to a piece of material. She went about for several days with the cloth still stitched to her flesh until Martha coaxed her to let her snip the thread and sterilize the wound. They seldom sang the hymns; they did not really care about the phonograph; it interfered with the sound of the marimba. Weaving did not interest them; the Indians had their own looms and thought the one Martha had brought clumsy and inferior. Or so she thought: living in silence with her Indians, she had never learned even the rudiments of their language, and there was no possibility of learning it from anyone but them because no priest had ever been able to convert them and their speech had, consequently, never been written down.

What the children liked was the bicycles. They learned to ride with very little trouble. The village, with its clayey paths trampled smooth by generations of bare feet, was a good place to ride. Martha would line them up, stroke their hair, and send them off one by one. They rode as they had sung, like angels, bare feet on the pedals, arms outspread, inky bowl-cut hair flying, faces aglow; they could not get enough of it. At night she dreamed of them riding.

Early one morning, two of the larger boys borrowed the bicycles while Martha slept and carried them to the top of a buried temple. They tried to ride down it, pushing off from the site of the buried sacrificial altar, about sixty feet above ground level. One boy fell after only a few feet, but the other rider managed to stay upright until he was going fairly fast—fast enough so that when he went over the edge of a hidden rock shelf or step, his bicycle shot out into space. Along with all the children and the many adults who had gathered to witness the ride, Martha watched him fall. It was a beautiful sight in its way. His crown of lustrous black hair opened like some miraculous flower. This gave a breathtaking impression of liberation and elementary happiness; it really seemed to Martha that he could fly. And if she thought that, what must the Indians have been thinking?

Then, still clinging to the bicycle, the boy hit the ground and lay still. The Indians turned their backs to the child. He simply lay there in the wreckage of the bicycle, his marvelous skin seeping blood from a dozen scrapes and cuts. Martha ran to him and knelt down. He was conscious but in deep shock. His dark brown eyes looked directly into Martha's. She touched his hair and was surprised to find that it was soaked with sweat; but then she thought, *Of course it would be, thee has climbed up the pyramid in this heat.*

The boy's pulse was strong. Martha had studied advanced first aid during one of her extramural courses at college. She felt his bones and discovered that he had broken his arm, and maybe his collar bone. She rose to her feet and ran back to her hut for her first aid kit. The Indians, still utterly silent, still with their backs turned, did not interfere, but when she came back they were all gone, including the injured boy. Only the crumpled bicycle remained, and near the top of the buried temple where it had crashed, the debris of the second machine.

She tried to find the injured boy, but the Indians had taken him into the drinking hut, and when she followed and tried to go inside with her first aid kit, they formed a silent wall with their bodies, shutting her out. She could see over their heads quite easily. The boy was reclining at the feet of Maximón, happily drinking *guaro* from the effigy's own huge cup. She tried to tell them that his arm would be crooked if the broken bones were not set, but she could not make them understand. A month or two later she saw him again, walking through the village, drunk, with a deformed arm. When she tried to touch his hair, he ducked his head and ran away, limping.

In Washington, the O. G. had engaged dozens of men and women who were experts in arcane subjects. Their only duty was to know what they knew and keep abreast of their specialty, in case the knowledge was ever needed by the Outfit. Among these specialists was an anthropologist whose field was the Indians of tropical America. He had lived among them, studied them, written about them; his office was piled high with nearly every book and monograph ever published about them and some that were unpublishable. He knew their ways, their diets, their legends, their poisons, their systems of belief.

"There is," he told Patchen, explaining the importance of an open mind, "no such thing as superstition. A belief in snakes that fly and talk is inherently no more ridiculous than the account of Jesus turning water into wine at the wedding feast. Exactly the same critical faculties are suspended in both cases."

Patchen told him Martha's story. The anthropologist listened intently, asking many questions in a rumbling Central European accent and scribbling down Patchen's sketchy answers on large file cards that he retrieved from an inside pocket.

"What notes, exactly, do these Indians play on the marimba?" he asked.

"I don't know," Patchen replied. "My source doesn't read music."

"But one must! Otherwise what is the point? The skills must go with the field worker! They cannot be acquired *in situ!*"

"No doubt. But that was not the mission."

Patchen did not reveal that Martha was his wife, and the expert naturally assumed that she was an agent sent on some bizarre secret mission that had no intelligent purpose and was unlikely to produce any result that a sane person could regard as useful.

"Do you have an opinion about the Indians' behavior?" Patchen asked.

"Which aspect of it?"

"The shunning, the refusal to make eye contact, the vanishing act when they all left the village."

"It's quite obvious," the anthropologist said. "These people think your friend is possessed of the evil eye; that is why they touch the children on the scalp before they look at them to dispel its power. They think the evil eye, *his* evil eye, is causing all these accidents, these calamities, flags sewed to fingers, bicycle crashes, et cetera. Did that not occur to him?"

"It's a her," Patchen said. "Apparently not. Are they likely to harm her?"

"They harm *her?* That's a good one."

Patchen persisted. "Is she safe in that village?" he asked.

"As long as she stays out of the way of falling bicycles. But she should try to get a little education before she blunders into another situation."

Patchen did not repeat this advice to Martha, or tell her about the anthropologist's suggestion concerning the evil eye. She was incapable of believing such things.

"Thee will not be angry if I go back again?" she asked.

"No. But what's the point? They won't have anything to do with you."

"That is the point. If I stop now, the good that I was called to do may not be done."

"And if you go back what will happen?" Patchen asked.

"Perhaps I will be noticed."

"By whom? The Indians seem to know you're there."

She kissed him. They were in bed. "I'm not talking about the Indians," she said.

"Then who are you talking about?"

Her face was suffused with a smile of deep contentment; at that moment Patchen loved her with all his heart: her simplicity, her goodness, her obliviousness to the world as it really was and to the evidence before her eyes.

"Thee knows Who," she said.

5

PATCHEN'S MOTHER DIED, IN HER SLEEP, OF AN ANEURYSM, WHILE Martha was in Guatemala and Christopher was in Vietnam. His grandfather, the judge, had her body cremated before Patchen arrived in Ohio.

"It was her wish; nobody else in the family has ever done such a thing, but I suppose it had something to do with this," the judge said, handing Patchen a shoe box containing the photographs of his father in their silver frames, the wedding and birth certificates he had been invited to examine so many times, and his mother's wedding ring engraved with her initials and those of Captain David Alan St. Clair Patchen, R. F. C., engraved inside. As she had often explained, her husband had so many initials that there had been no room on the circlet for the date of their wedding, July 12, 1918. The judge inserted an oblong pasteboard envelope into the shoe box. "You may take anything else you want that belonged to your mother."

The oblong envelope contained an insurance policy on his mother's life for twenty thousand dollars. Patchen was the sole beneficiary; his mother had designated the American Red Cross as secondary beneficiary in case her son predeceased her—which, of course, he nearly had.

The room was very large and was fitted out as a boudoir, with the bed and dressers in one corner and a sofa and chairs in the other, arranged around a blue Belgian rug. It seemed forlorn without the shrine to Patchen's father, but he did not set up the photographs and framed decorations again. The drawn window shades glowed like parchment in the afternoon sun. He opened the closet; his mother's dresses, muted plaids and prints and polka dots, all in shades of gray and dark blue, hung on their padded hangers; her Red Cross shoes, laced and low-heeled, stood in a row; her white, long-skirted Red Cross nurse's uniform with its blue cape, lined in red, with the impressive enamel badge of her training hospital pinned to the collar, hung in a transparent plastic bag. The closet smelled of rose leaves; his mother had collected roses after they died, laid them in the sun to dry, plucked the dehydrated leaves, which retained their original brilliant colors and looked and rustled like dead insects, and sewn them into cheesecloth pouches for her closets and bureau drawers.

Holding the shoe box on his lap, he went through her souvenirs one by one, thinking that she might have left a letter for him, but there was no posthumous message. His curiosity about his father was overwhelming. Was there some piece of evidence concealed somewhere in this room? After all, his mother had died before she knew what was happening, so she would have had no time to conceal it. He paced the parquet floor, looking with a new and knowing eye at likely hiding places. If evidence existed, he knew that he could find it. The Outfit had trained him; he knew where to look and how to look. Had something been taped to the back of a dresser drawer? slipped between the rug and its pad? inserted into the pages of a book? sewn into a mattress? folded very small and jammed into the toe of a shoe? buried in the Chinese jar among the rose petals?

He started to open a dresser drawer, into which he had never looked, but closed it again before it had moved more than an inch on its guides. His mother had died in this room where she had spent twenty-five years recovering from her one night of love. He did not want to catch his mother in a lie now, any more than he had wished to do so when she was alive.

That evening he dined with his grandfather. Bunches of oak grapes decorated the table, the sideboard, the plate shelf that ran around the walls. The house was a vast red-brick Victorian structure, turreted and gingerbreaded, with every room trimmed in a different kind of polished wood, with furniture to match. His grandfather called the dining room the Oak Room, the parlor the Cherry Room, his study the Walnut Room. His grandfather had never treated him as a child, much less as a grandson: no rough rubbing of the head, no trips to Cleveland to see the Indians play, no quarters or half-dollars pressed into his small hand. Patchen called him "Judge"; he called Patchen "Young Fellow." The old man had treated Patchen courteously, even kindly, as if he were an uninvited guest who would sooner or later realize that it would be better to leave.

The judge was a Quaker, but in name only; he believed in the death penalty. It put him in a good mood to mete it out, and he always drank a glass of bourbon before dinner on days when he had sent someone to the electric chair; Patchen never smelled liquor on another man's breath without thinking about capital punishment, and he did not drink spirits himself until he was in his forties. The judge had approved of Patchen's joining the Marines, calling him into his study, which resembled a courtroom with its massive desk and somber woodwork and its rows of leatherbound books, and clapped him on the shoulder. "Good lad!" he said. "No matter what your mother may tell you, a man has to fight for his country or he's no damn good." The judge took up swearing—"damn" and "hell" and "little yellow bastards"—for the duration of the war, but gave it up as soon as the Japanese surrendered.

After finishing his plate of boiled beef and vegetables the judge said, "You know, your grandmother died of the same thing, aneurysm in the night. Hard to imagine a better death, but it's an old person's death. They were both young. Too young. It's something to think about if you believe in heredity."

He was a believer in eugenics, a popular theory that argued the superiority of some ethnic and racial groups over others and defended the necessity of maintaining such superiority by careful selection of mates from suitable breeding stock.

That night Patchen slept in his old room. Like the rest of the house it was kept absolutely free of dust by female inmates of the county jail who did the housework. Even the tissue-paper wings and fuselage of the model Sopwith Camel Patchen had made at age nine were spick and span. So were all his books: Zane Grey, James Oliver Curwood, William Allen White. As a boy Patchen had imagined himself a hunter and trapper, alone except for his horse and dog in the Rocky Mountains or on the frozen tundra above the Great Bear Lake in Canada. He had wanted to live among the Indians, with an Indian name and an Indian wife; before he went to sleep in these surroundings he realized why he understood Martha's passion for her Indians.

The funeral was a Quaker one, with no eulogist or minister. An urn containing the ashes of the deceased rested on the table. Because of the judge's high position, the funeral home was crowded. Finally the judge's old law partner, now a state senator, rose and spoke at length about the deceased, dwelling on her brave service in France and the tragic circumstances of her marriage. "Here lies one of our own, a heroine who fell in love with a hero and gave birth to a hero son!" the senator said. His words released some pent-up tension in the mourners. A collective sigh whispered through the room. Many looked at Patchen; women wept, men cleared their throats. Afterward many of them told him how much they had admired his mother. Looking into their remorseful faces, he realized that his wounds somehow made it impossible for anyone in town to doubt that his mother's story had been true.

The next morning Patchen packed his bag and went to the courthouse to say goodbye to his grandfather. The judge was trying a case of incest, and Patchen, leaving his suitcase in his chambers, took a seat in the courtroom and watched the proceeding. The defendant, an emigrant from Kentucky, was found guilty of having carnal knowledge of his fourteen-year-old daughter. Before sentence was passed, the man's wife, who was also the victim's mother, asked for permission to address the court. "She's *his,* Your Honor," she said. "She belongs to him. She knows that, I know that, *you* know that. The only reason she told the sheriff on him was because she was mad just because he drunk a few beers down to Pondi's and didn't have no money left to buy her this hat with Mickey Mouse ears she thought she had to have to wear to watch TV. That's all there was to it, Your Honor, spite. And that's the truth."

The judge sentenced the man to serve five to seven years in the state penitentiary and remanded the daughter into the custody of the county orphanage. Afterward, in his chambers, the old man said, "The trash just don't understand, David; it's in the blood, nothing can change the way they are."

"Well, Grandfather, goodbye," Patchen said.

"Goodbye, young fellow." His grandfather was still wearing his black judicial robes. "Got everything?"

"I think so," Patchen replied. "I took Mother's Chinese jar, the one with the rose petals in it. And her ashes."

"Did you now? I guess that's all right."

Patchen used the insurance money, a vast sum (the judge's house with its beautiful woodwork had cost four thousand dollars to build only forty years earlier), to paint his house and enlarge and paper the rooms. He had learned about antiques in order to monitor the overt business transactions of an antique shop the O. G. set up as a meeting place and dead drop for Balkan exiles, and he applied this knowledge to buy American versions of eighteenth-century English furniture, as well as some inexpensive still-life paintings by a forgotten American artist called Raphaelle Peale.

"How do you like the house?" he asked Martha when she came back from Guatemala the following spring.

"Thee has made it very worldly," she replied. "But I like the pictures of the fruit. It looks real enough to eat."

6

DURING HIS NIGHTTIME WALKS THROUGH THE CITY, PATCHEN OFTEN had the feeling that he was not alone. He had no evidence that this was so. Despite his training, he never detected anyone following him, and he certainly felt no fear. Postwar Washington was a law-abiding city almost to the point of farce: during the lunch hour, government workers stood on the curb along Pennsylvania Avenue, waiting for the WALK sign to flash even though no moving car was in sight for blocks in either direction. If someone jaywalked, the others would follow like sheep, but in the absence of a leader, they would wait patiently for the machine to tell them what to do. One day Patchen saw a herd of pedestrians being helped across the street by a policeman who held up his hand to stop invisible traffic, blew his whistle, and put them in motion with another hand signal: the WALK sign was broken, and they had waited obediently to be rescued.

This behavior interested Patchen, and he described it later to the O. G.. "Maybe we should get the psychologists to study pedestrian behavior in various foreign cities," he said.

Ordinarily the O. G. loved ideas of this kind; human eccentricities were his passion. But he didn't like this one.

"All mammals like to be in big groups with everybody heading in the same direction and eating the same kind of grass," he said. "Man is no exception. We already know that. We're not interested in the herd—that's politicians' business. Our animal is the maverick, God bless him."

"Do you remember what you said to me in Boston about the game of baseball and the English sonnet?" Patchen asked.

"About their being the only perfect systems ever devised by man?" the O. G. replied. "You bet. That's the Shakespearean *abab, cdcd, efef, gg* sonnet I was talking about, not all that other pap that doesn't rhyme."

"Is that what you're trying to create here, Sir? Do you want the Outfit to be the third such system?"

The O. G. jumped a little in his surprise, then threw back his head and laugh.

"By golly, Son," he said, "you're really something. I never thought of it that way, but I guess maybe that *is* what I'm trying to do around here. Let's just keep it between you and me."

His pince-nez flashed in the artificial light. The O. G. had come into Patchen's cell at the end of the day to return the files he had been working on to the vault. The stifling room was now brilliantly lit by buzzing fluorescent lights that covered the entire ceiling. In the glare from overhead, the O. G.'s skin lost its usual pink hue and his hair appeared to be several shades whiter than usual.

With his single eye, Patchen read hundreds of pages of reports, dispatches, and cables every day, then digested them for the O. G. Accomplishing this task by the light of the original gooseneck lamp had given him piercing headaches and nagging anxiety about his eye; despite the Navy surgeon's reassurances, he had never really believed that it would not eventually go blind. The appearance of the O. G., leached of most of his natural color, gave Patchen something else to think about: how he himself must look under this unnatural light. His visible wounds, and the impression they made on others, were never far from his mind.

"Meanwhile," the O. G. said, "come into the other room for a minute. I've got something to show you."

Patchen followed him through the door and saw Barney Wolkowicz standing in front of the fireplace, holding the leash of a large black and tan dog.

"Sorry to keep you, Barney," the O. G. said. "We got to talking baseball. You two know each other, I think."

"Yeah," Wolkowicz answered in his raspy voice, nodding to Patchen. "Patchen and me dug up some skulls and bones together once."

"Barney just flew in from Europe," the O. G. said.

Wolkowicz looked as if he had been traveling for days instead of hours. His shirt was smudged at the collar and the tail was out; he had not shaved; his Tyrolean hat, with its plume of pheasant tail feathers and horsehair, dangled from his free hand. In his other hand he held the leash; at the end of it the dog sat absolutely motionless, gazing into space like a bored soldier assigned to orderly duty.

"That's a beautiful dog," Patchen said.

"Glad you like him," Wolkowicz said.

"D'you recognize the breed?" the O. G. asked. He was fond of dogs, and sometimes brought his own elderly spaniel to work with him, where it slept peacefully in the kneehole of his desk.

Patchen said, "It's a Doberman pinscher, isn't it?"

"That's right," the O. G. said. "Good work. Not many people know about Dobermans outside of Germany. Best war dogs in the world. Incredible fighting spirit, amazing jaw strength. What's this one's name, Barney?"

"Faust."

"Crackerjack name. Think you can remember it, Son?"

"Me?" Patchen said.

"Yep." The O. G. was pleased with himself. "It's yours," he said. "Barney brought him from Berlin for you—I thought you'd appreciate company on your walks through the night."

7

OVER THE NEXT FEW NIGHTS WOLKOWICZ ACCOMPANIED PATCHEN ON his walks and taught him how to control the Doberman.

"He won't sit up or roll over," Wolkowicz explained. "He's only got one trick—homicide."

Otherwise the dog was perfectly trained: it would sit, heel, stay, come, or attack in instantaneous obedience to a command from its master. Patchen, who had never before owned an animal—his grandfather believed that unneeded food should be given to the poor, not to pets—was puzzled as to the reasons the O. G. had given him this one.

"Security reported you were wandering around by yourself at night," Wolkowicz said. "I guess it worried the O. G. He thinks you need protection."

"Why?"

"Because he's picked you to be the all-seeing eye of the Outfit. If the other side grabbed you, they'd know damn near as much as he knows."

"You think a dog would stop them?"

Wolkowicz looked him over. "*You* sure as hell wouldn't be able to. C'mere."

Wolkowicz stepped into the light of a streetlamp, gave the dog a command to prevent it from attacking, as it had been trained to do, at the sight of a firearm in the hand of anyone except the man holding its leash, and produced a Walther P-38 pistol.

"You know how to use this?" he asked.

"I know how to fire a pistol. This kind is new to me."

"The principle is the same as the forty-five automatic you carried in the Marines, except when you point this weapon at something, you hit it and it dies. The clip holds eight rounds of nine-millimeter Parabellum ammo plus one in the chamber. Forget safeties. It's double-action, like a revolver. To shoot, just squeeze the trigger. This one is fully loaded. See the pin sticking out of the slide? That's how you know." He shoved the pistol into a chamois-skin holster fitted with a spring-loaded clip designed to be slipped over the waistband of the wearer's trousers. "Here, take it," he said. "It's all yours."

Patchen took a half step backward. "No thanks."

Wolkowicz, stepping closer, continued to proffer the weapon. Patchen made no move to accept it.

"Look, kid," Wolkowicz said, "I know you're a Quaker and wouldn't hurt a fly and all that shit, but you either carry the gun and lead the dog when you're wandering around alone at night, or you get a baby-sitter. I'm the guy who picks the baby-sitters, so don't get me pissed off at you."

"Why?"

"Because that's the way it's going to be. Now take the fucking gun and put it on. Here's your permit."

Patchen examined the card, which bore his photograph and a false name signed in an imitation of his handwriting that was undetectable even to him. It identified him as a member of the United States Park Police.

"Is this I. D. phony, too?" he asked. He meant: Was it false-genuine, a real Park Police credential issued to an imaginary identity, or was it a simple forgery manufactured in one of the Outfit's print shops?

"Not so's anybody will notice it," Wolkowicz replied, telling him nothing. "If you want to shoot that thing off to get the feel of it, let me know and I'll call the firing range. You should be pretty good, using your right hand and your right eye. You've got no choice. I'm left-eyed and right-handed, so my nose gets in the way."

Patchen took the holstered pistol and slipped it over his belt.

"Get yourself some suspenders," Wolkowicz said. "The gun weighs a little over two pounds, loaded. You wouldn't want your pants to fall down and go boom."

Wolkowicz remained at Patchen's side for more than a week, picking him up at the office in the evening and dropping him off at home afterward, until he was sure that he could handle the Doberman. He seemed to have little else to do. Patchen remarked on this.

"I'm waiting for somebody," Wolkowicz said. Patchen did not ask who this might be. Wolkowicz mocked his curiosity anyway. "The key suspect," he said with an exaggerated wink.

He led Patchen to a car parked a few paces away on Constitution Avenue, then drove across the Potomac to Arlington National Cemetery, entering through a back road. They got out of the car and walked among the rows of white markers, the neon glow of the city providing enough light to find the way. Because the cemetery lay on a hill it was cooler there, and a whispering breeze stirred the trees and the many small American flags that had been thrust into the sod.

Finally Wolkowicz found a place to stand that was out of earshot for any possible eavesdropper, and began to talk.

"This is about Christopher," he said. "I know you're monitoring the op he's on in Indochina."

"You do?" Patchen replied.

"Yeah, I do. Let's cut the shit, okay? We're standing among the honored dead here, and I think we should tell each other the truth."

"All right. You first."

"His case officer is Waddy Jessup. Waddy was my commanding officer in Burma. Do you know about that?"

"I know what's in the files. I looked you both up."

"You ever met Waddy?"

Wolkowicz wore a look of crafty expectation; Patchen did not know why.

"No," he said.

"Wrong," Wolkowicz retorted. "He was your training officer—good old Archie. Remember *him?*"

Patchen snorted in surprise and amusement. He had never before put the two identities together.

"They say you've got total recall," Wolkowicz said. "I want you to visualize Archie, remember that accent, remind yourself of all the asshole things he said to you in that Yalie accent. Got the picture?"

"I remember Archie."

"Waddy. Let me tell you what's *not* in the file. He used up our whole unit—'Force Jessup,' Waddy called it—in a stupid attack on a fortified Jap position because he wanted an elephant to ride and the Japs had some elephants. Killed everybody except me. The other guys were Kachins, very good troops. Then he jumped on an elephant and ran away and left me to the Japs."

Wolkowicz lifted his hand to his mouth and spat two full dental plates into his palm. He held them out, perfect porcelain teeth glistening with spit, for Patchen's inspection.

"The Japs pried out all my teeth with the point of a bayonet," he said. "Waddy got away. When he got back to base, he put himself in for the D. S. C., and got it. I'm telling you all this for two reasons—first so you'll know I'm not exactly an unbiased observer, and second so you'll understand that I know what I'm talking about when I talk about Waddy."

Wolkowicz opened his toothless mouth wide and put his teeth back in, then wiped his palm on the seat of his pants.

"Now, down to business," he said. "I've got some sources in Vietnam, and they tell me that Waddy is going to get Christopher killed unless you get him out of there fast."

"Killed? How?"

"Waddy sent him out on a combat mission against the French with the fucking Vietminh. Then Waddy described the whole operation to a Vietnamese kid the French have planted on him."

Patchen felt a wave of nausea rising toward his throat.

"What Vietnamese kid?"

"A pretty little boy with a bottom like a peach," Wolkowicz said. "Christopher's still out in the jungle with the Communists. If they don't kill him because Waddy's told somebody *they've* got going down on him that he's an American spy, the French will."

He stepped closer, so that his face was only inches from Patchen's and whispered his next words: *"Get Christopher out of there."*

8

THE FLIMSY DOOR OF WADDY JESSUP'S APARTMENT IN HANOI WAS opened by a slender young barefoot Vietnamese who smiled contemptuously when he heard Patchen's French pronunciation. He showed him into the living room, where Waddy lay on a bamboo sofa, reading Stéphane Mallarmé's *Un coup de dés jamais n'abolira le hasard* and drinking some cloudy liquid out of a glass shaped like a tulip.

"My, this *is* a surprise," Waddy said, rising to his feet. "I guess the best thing for me to do is confess and get it over with. I lied to you. My name really isn't Archie."

They shook hands. Waddy was barefoot, too, and he was wearing a sarong; it was hotter in Hanoi than in Washington. "Would you like one of these?" he asked, holding his glass aloft. "It's Pernod poured over ice. *Ice.*"

"No, thanks. I was hoping you'd join me for dinner in a restaurant."

"Actually, Jean-Pierre was just making a cold supper when you arrived. I'm sure there'd be enough for two."

Waddy opened his eyes wide, drew a breath, and turned with a smile to the houseboy, who was hovering behind Patchen, as if to give an instruction.

"No, thank you," Patchen said. "I'd rather go out."

Lips already parted, Waddy paused for the briefest moment, then spoke at length to the servant in Vietnamese. The boy glowered and left them without uttering a word.

"I was just telling him you're a former student of mine who wants to treat me to dinner," Waddy said. "Changes in plans upset him. He's a moody fellow. He likes to be called Jean-Pierre, but his given name is Cu. That means 'penis' in Vietnamese. He had two older brothers who died in infancy. Naturally, when he was born his parents gave him an ugly, horrible name so the evil spirits wouldn't be envious and take him, too. The Vietnamese are *wonderful*, David. Be with you in a minute."

Joss sticks, burning in front of a collection of Jessup family photographs, filled the torpid air with sickly fumes. This arrangement suggested, while not quite imitating, the family shrine that was a fixture in every Buddhist home. The apartment, in fact, was furnished entirely in the Vietnamese style; Patchen supposed that the decor was designed as a statement of Waddy's sentiments in regard to the revolution. So, possibly, was the book of Mallarmé's poetry. He tried to read it while he waited, but the verses were written in such rudimentary French that he assumed there was some meaning beneath the banal surface which eluded him.

When Waddy emerged from his bedroom he was dressed in Ivy League clothes: white bucks, khaki pants, Brooks Brothers button-down shirt, "regimental" tie, seersucker jacket. He wore the small red, white, and blue enamel badge of the Distinguished Service Cross in his lapel, a touch he had not allowed himself when working under his alias in the safe house in Foggy Bottom.

The temperature was in the nineties. They dined in an open-air French restaurant on food invented in a cold and rainy country. Waddy discussed the wine list in voluble French with the listless wife of the owner-chef and despite the heat ordered a full bottle of Pouilly Fuissé and another of Vougeot. He drank most of the wine himself, but ate very little as he plied Patchen with questions about his village in Ohio, about Harvard, about Quakerism.

"Do you mind?" he said. "I've always wondered about George Fox and the Inner Light and all that. Do Quakers actually quake?"

"In*ward* Light," Patchen replied. "What church do you belong to?"

Waddy was chewing his asparagus. "Episcopalian," he said.

"Don't Episcopalians quake?"

"They barely twitch when they ejaculate," Waddy replied. "I don't mean to offend you. All I know about Ohio I learned from a classmate at Yale whose family made sheets and tubes in Youngstown."

"Weren't you in Burma with someone from Ohio?" Patchen asked.

Waddy's face did not flush on hearing this question, but Patchen had the impression that he prevented it by a conscious effort of the will.

"You've been talking to Barney," he replied after another reproving silence. "He had a good war, as the Brits say, whatever he may say about it now. Actually he's not a Buckeye at all, you khow. He's a *muzhik.*"

"What's that?"

"It's Russian for 'peasant.' He was born in Russia, carried out as a child on his father's back. Barney *père* walked two thousand miles through the Russian Civil War, cannons to the right of them, cannons to the left of them, corpses everywhere, and they both came out without a scratch. Amazing saga. Makes you wonder."

"About what?"

"I don't know," Waddy said with his bright smile. "Fate. *Un coup de dés*—a throw of the dice. Craps, as they say in Youngstown, Ohio."

After dinner they rode in rickshaws to one of the many lakes within the city limits. Speaking Vietnamese again, Waddy told the rickshaw boys, who were in fact emaciated gray-headed men, to wait for them. They walked along the shore beneath lanterns strung between trees.

"Your Vietnamese seems to be pretty good," Patchen said.

"Not really," Waddy replied. "You should hear Paul. He's the polyglot. Of course, all Vietnamese words have only one syllable, and he learned the language in bed from the most delicious little girl in Hanoi, but all the same he's a prodigy. He's like a musician with perfect pitch—amazing. Play it once and he repeats it with variations."

"Where is Paul?"

Waddy feigned surprise that the question should be asked by someone who was not, so far as he knew, authorized to know about Christopher's activities.

"He's out of town," he said.

"When will he be back?"

Waddy paused, to let Patchen know that he had gone far enough. "I really don't know," he said.

They had been moving through a thin crowd of Vietnamese, all

147

of whom were fanning themselves with cheap bamboo fans. Waddy had one, too. Patchen turned into a path that led away from the lake.

"Wrong way," Waddy said.

Patchen continued on without replying. Waddy hesitated, then followed. The three Vietnamese men who had been following them ever since they left Waddy's apartment drifted in and out of the lantern light at the end of the path, peering into the darkness after them.

When he reached Patchen, who had stopped in the middle of the path, Waddy put a hand on the small of his back.

"You don't remember your training very well, David," he said. "Those fellows who were following us now know, beyond the shadow of a doubt, that we know they're tailing us."

"I don't think the surprise will kill them," Patchen said.

"Maybe not, but there's such a thing as the niceties. I have to live and work here."

Patchen interrupted him. "Here," he said. "I have something for you." He handed him an envelope and a penlight.

"You want me to open this and read it here?" Waddy said.

"If you please."

Waddy tore open the envelope, turned on the little flashlight, and read, with his body hunched over the page to conceal it from the men at the end of the path. It was a letter from the O. G., in his own hand, informing Waddy of the death of his dear Aunt Judith and asking that he come home at once to deal with the estate. As he read, Waddy chewed his lower lip.

When he finished, Patchen handed him another envelope containing a ticket for the next day's flight to Paris.

"You'll be met at the customs barrier at Le Bourget by a man holding a sign that says 'Voyages Jean et Jeanne,' " Patchen said. "Someone else will approach him. Follow the two of them out of the terminal to the car."

" 'Voyages Jean et Jeanne'? Can't I just call the office?"

Patchen took back his penlight. "Those are the arrangements. I didn't make them."

"Who did? The Scarlet Pimpernel?"

"Do you want me to go through the details again?"

"I don't think so. How could anyone forget? When will I be back?"

"As soon as you settle Aunt Judith's estate, I guess. Meanwhile I need to know the time and place of your next contact with Paul, and the fallback."

All the possible meanings behind the letter he had just read, and the bizarre instructions he had just been given, were now flooding into Waddy's mind. No unit in the Outfit except Security would have made arrangements of this kind: they were like something out of a training film. Even in the dark, Patchen could sense his anxiety, but Waddy said nothing to betray it; he was already acting like a suspect.

"Paul and I have a date to play tennis at six-thirty in the morning next Tuesday."

This was three days ahead. Waddy gave the address of the tennis court.

"What's the fallback?"

"Same time the following Tuesday at the tomb of Thieu Tri in Hue."

"Why Hue?"

"Because it isn't Hanoi."

"And if he doesn't make that meeting?"

"Then I wait to hear from him. Except I won't be here."

"Who else would he contact?"

Waddy stood mute. He was very close to Patchen because they had been carrying on their conversation in whispers.

"Look," Patchen said. "I know what you've got him doing. How do you get a message to him if you have to?"

"Through friends of Cu's," Waddy said.

In the distance, the three Vietnamese were conferring, glancing in their direction. Rats gamboled on the path between them.

"Come closer," Patchen said. Waddy did so. Without warning, Patchen, whose undamaged arm and leg were very strong, gave him a powerful shove, knocking him off his feet.

"For Christ's sake!" Waddy said. "What was that for?"

"Cover," Patchen said. "You told me it should always be consistent with the character of the agent involved."

He stepped around Waddy's prostrate body and walked back to the rickshaws, telling his boy to take him to his hotel.

"What about the other one?" the boy asked.

"Monsieur a fait un jugement erroné," Patchen said in his awful French: the gentleman made an error in judgment.

149

The boys smiled; Waddy and his habits were well known in Hanoi.

9

CHRISTOPHER APPEARED ON SCHEDULE FOR HIS GAME OF TENNIS. THE courts, hidden among masses of bougainvillaea, were located at the rear of a large colonial villa in a French residential quarter that was strongly reminiscent of Passy. Patchen had arrived by car half an hour early for the meeting. This was a breach of security—clandestine meetings were supposed to be precisely timed to reduce the period of exposure—but Patchen did not see how the rules could possibly matter in this case: He had been followed by a team of Vietnamese ever since he first made contact with Waddy Jessup. On his way to the tennis court, however, the streets behind and ahead of him had been empty.

"There's no need for them to follow you here," Christopher explained, when Patchen mentioned this odd circumstance. "The courts belong to a Frenchman Waddy picked up at the Cercle Sportif in Saigon. He's in the colonial service, so the surveillance just gets here first on meeting days. A lip-reader watches through binoculars from the upstairs windows of the house."

"Waddy knew this?"

"He thinks it adds to the picture of innocence, as he calls it. Just two American pals, hitting at each other by the dawn's early light and talking about baseball. Besides, he says, it's flattering to have your own bilingual lip-reader. Where is Waddy?"

"The O. G. called him home." Patchen did not explain why; Christopher did not ask. "I've brought you a new friend," Patchen said, nodding in the direction of a young man on the other side of the net who was practicing his backhand by hitting a ball against the back wall of the court. "Not," Patchen said, "that you're going to need him. We want you to come home, too."

"Not yet," Christopher said.

His gaze, always intense, was now almost feverish. He looked as if he had just recovered from an attack of malaria—gaunt, weakened, pallid beneath a deeply tanned skin. No doubt he had; like many who fought in the Pacific, he was infected. He had been in the jungle with the Vietminh for exactly a month, a fact that

150

impressed Patchen—not the duration of the mission but the timing. The guerrillas had picked Christopher up in the middle of Hanoi and then dropped him off on a streetcorner as if they were running a bus service behind enemy lines. If they could do that, how much longer could this war last?

He said to Christopher, "What do you mean 'not yet'?"

"I've done what Waddy wanted. Now I'm going to do what I came here to do."

"That may not be as important now as it seemed before."

"After what I've just seen, I have to disagree."

Patchen made a noncommittal gesture. "We'll talk."

"We already have," Christopher said, straightening up.

As he talked, Christopher had kept his back turned to the house and leaned over as if to tie his shoelaces. He had arrived ready for the game, wearing tennis shoes, shorts, and a faded knit shirt. Now he walked onto the court, called out to the partner Patchen had provided, and hit a ball to him. Patchen sat down to watch. Christopher was a good player; so was the other man. They split two sets. Although this was a concrete court, Christopher's canvas shoes were spotted with grass stains and smudges of red clay. He never seemed to wear new clothes. Neither did the O. G. Neither, now, did Patchen, who was dressed in a seersucker suit and a black knit tie, the costume he would wear in summer for the remainder of his career.

At the end of the game, the players sat down side by side to cool off. When they got up they took each other's racquets, which were identical American models. Inside the hollow handle of Christopher's was his report on his journey with the Vietminh. Patchen read it later that afternoon in a safe house. It spoke in meticulous detail of night marches, tunnels, ambushes, political discussions, acts of atrocity. The writing was factual, neutral, stripped of opinion and emotion. Nevertheless, when he put it down, Patchen was convinced that Christopher had been changed in some fundamental way by his month with the Vietminh.

"Not changed, reminded," Christopher said later, when Patchen suggested this to him. "These people are killers. I saw them massacre whole villages. They call it Dâu Tô—'Struggle-Denunciation.' From their point of view they're not killing anything that has a right to live. Some of them talked to me about it. At first the work is disgusting, they said—the blood, the brains, the howls for mercy, shooting children or mutilating them. But you get used to it. It's done in the name of the cause, so it's virtuous. Everybody you know approves and sympathizes. The higher reasons are known to all. It gives you a moral glow. Heinrich Himmler said the same things about the Death's-head SS after watching them shoot Jewish children: 'Virtuous boys, to perform such unspeakable acts for the Reich.' "

"You're describing maniacs."

"Believers."

"According to your report they don't spend all their time massacring innocent people."

"No. They're good troops. As good as the Japanese."

"They seem to remind you of your enemies no matter how you look at them."

"Except that this bunch are going to win," Christopher said.

His voice, always difficult to hear, was practically inaudible over the scratchy music of a wind-up phonograph. They were drifting at night in a sampan on the River of Perfumes in Hue. It was very dark. The moving water splintered the yellow light from a lantern at the stern, where the boatman stood, bare toes gripping the deck as he sculled upriver, grunting a little each time he swiveled the oar. This was their first meeting since the tennis game.

The atmosphere in Hue, the imperial city of Vietnam, was less warlike than in Hanoi. All around them, other nearly identical sampans, each with an awning amidships and a lantern on the stern, were carried by the current. Plaintive songs from other phonographs drifted through the darkness. Pleasure sampans, these vessels were called, and in some of them, no doubt, guerrillas back from the scenes Christopher had described were being entertained by prostitutes. Vietnamese women were the most beautiful human beings Patchen had ever seen.

The record ended. Christopher said something in Vietnamese. The boatman went on sculling, winding up the machine with his foot and delicately placing the needle on the 78-rpm record with his toes.

Patchen said, "Tell me what you want to do and how long it will take."

"I don't know how long it will take. I've already met the schoolmaster."

He meant Vo, the O. G.'s friend from the First World War. Even though his voice was virtually drowned out by the tinny music issuing from the gramophone, even though Vo was one of the most common surnames in Vietnam, Christopher was careful not to pronounce it. By itself it would mean nothing to an eavesdropper. Even the full name, Vo Van Tho, would have been a feeble clue; "Van," the middle name of all Vietnamese males, means "civilized, literary," while "Tho," the given name, means longevity. The Vietnamese rarely tempt fate by using their given names among themselves, but are called by nicknames. Vo had a scraggly beard, like his classmate, Ho Chi Minh, and the nickname his students had given him was Rau, meaning "beard." That would have been a dangerous name to speak, because it would have identified him to anyone who happened to overhear or read Christopher's lips.

"How are you two getting along?" Patchen asked.

"All right, I think," Christopher said. "We talk about poetry."

"Yours or his?"

Vo Rau, under that name, was a well-known poet. Between the wars he had written verses in French, but after the Japanese vanquished the French and occupied Indochina, demonstrating that Asians could defeat Europeans, he had written only in Vietnamese, and only about restoring Vietnam to its own people. These patriotic works, disguised as love songs, were the foundation of his appeal to the young. As for Christopher, he had published a book of poems the year before. They, too, were about war and loss.

"We're exchanging favors," Christopher said. "He's helping me translate my stuff into Vietnamese, and I'm helping him with an English version of some of his poems."

"You think there's a market for the result?" Patchen asked.

"I think it's a way to talk about anything."

"Is he a believer?"

"I don't think so," Christopher said. "Just as his old friend said, he's a romantic. I think he's surprised at the effect of his poetry and his teaching. What has he done? He may not know the details of the Struggle-Denunciation, but I think he suspects the truth."

"Are you going to tell him his suspicions are correct?"

"In a poem, yes."

10

AFTER PATCHEN RETURNED TO WASHINGTON, CHRISTOPHER MOVED
to Hue and rented a small house near the Citadel. Hue was filled
with Christopher's fellow poets, many of whom were Communist
terrorists. The Annamese girl who had been sleeping with him in
Hanoi came with him and carried on with her work as a writer and
printer for an underground Communist newspaper. She was also
the Vietminh agent assigned to monitor Christopher and his activities.

Her revolutionary name was Phuoc, meaning "luck," but Christopher called her Lê, or "Tears," because like many people of deep
political conviction, she cried easily over trivial experiences. A
poem, a movie (even a French movie), a particularly lovely sunset
beyond Imperial Screen Mountain, a song, an orgasm, would cause
her soft brown eyes to glisten and overflow. She never sobbed,
never made a noise she did not intend to make.

"Lê is an unkind name to call me by," she told Christopher.

But she liked it because it was poetic, and because it acknowledged
her femininity. At heart she was a conventional girl in spite of the
bombings and assassinations she had carried out. She was an expert
rifle shot and maker of booby traps who had killed French soldiers
and other enemies of the cause. She had seduced Christopher in
the first place because she had been ordered to do so by the
apparatus, making the proposition herself when he failed to invite
her into bed in response to her signals.

She was surprised by her own ardor. He was her first white lover,
and she had not expected to feel passion for a body that was so
different from her own. As soon as they took off their clothes,
however, she discovered exciting similarities: a French bullet had
passed through the muscles of her arm and the tissue of her breast,
leaving puckered scars. Christopher had been wounded in Okinawa
in almost the same places: "Kissed by death before they kissed,"
as he wrote in a poem after she compared their wounds to love
bites. He made no attempt to teach her American-style lovemaking, if such a thing existed. Instead, he was content to discover Lê's
methods. She taught him the Vietnamese words for the sexual acts,
as for everything else. Sometimes, as she taught, she felt something
like amusement running through his body. She took strict precautions against pregnancy, knowing that any child they had would be
ugly and an outcast.

Although Lê was assigned to watch his every move, Christopher actually had a great deal of time to himself. Living the secret life in a country controlled by an intelligent enemy is time-consuming because of the elaborate precautions involved, and Lê's days and nights were consumed by writing, printing, and distributing her newspaper, her skin smelling of ink when she crawled into bed with him after a night at the print shop. She was required by the Party to attend innumerable Marxist-Leninist study, discussion, and self-criticism groups. Her schedule was as hectic, and as filled with snubs, slights, boredom, and dreams of marriage as that of a young American matron who has let herself become too deeply involved in community affairs. Christopher wrote no reports now, so he had nothing to hide. In Hanoi, he had composed them when she was out, in invisible ink in the Greek cipher, between the lines of the great epic poem *Kim Van Kieu,* which he was copying from a book as a means of perfecting his Vietnamese and getting the rhythms of classical Vietnamese verse into his head.

Lê came from a village about fifteen miles from Hue, and every Sunday she bicycled home to visit her parents after rising early to cook delicacies that she packed in a basket hung on the handlebars. Christopher never went with her. Her parents knew nothing of her politics and nothing about Christopher, or so she thought. They wanted her to marry one of the prosperous men of the village.

"As soon as the French are beaten I'll have to get married and stop being your *meo,"* she said to Christopher. *Meo,* "kitten," was the word for a married man's mistress.

"How can you be my *meo* if I'm not married?" he asked.

"You will be," she said. "In the next year of the rooster."

Lê often made confident predictions about Christopher's future. She had his horoscope drawn by the *cu si,* the Buddhist lay monk in charge of religious questions in her village. This man was not only an astrologer but also a geomancer, so she was in possession of a great deal of information about the three souls and the nine spirits that ruled Christopher's life. This knowledge was based on the hour, day, and place of his birth in the year of the rat. Christopher had given her the correct data when she asked for it, drawing a map to locate his birthplace, the island of Rügen in what was now the Soviet zone of Occupied Germany. Of course she reported these facts to the apparatus as well as the *cu si,* and for a long time afterward there was a school of opinion among Vietnamese Com-

155

munists that Christopher was in fact a German who had been tricked into revealing the truth about himself by his *meo*.

Some things about his fate Lê did not tell him. He was accompanied in life by a benevolent *con hoa*, the ghost of someone who had died by fire and wished to protect him from the same fate. Nevertheless, bad things lay ahead for him, but not until he was in his thirty-seventh year. The *cu si* was quite specific: In the year of the hare a woman would betray him, another woman would die for him, his enemies would put him in a cold place and separate him from his family. Lê did not warn Christopher of these misfortunes. It was useless: he could not change what was ordained by his stars even if he believed her (as few foreigners would), and besides, the years he was now living through were fortunate ones, dominated by *tien*, or good spirits, who had given him the gifts of intelligence, literary genius, and sexual grace and were protecting him for the time being from the wicked female spirits, the Ba Giang Ha, or Falling Goddesses, who were to cause such turmoil in his life later on.

Lê had no difficulty accommodating these beliefs, and many other superstitions, to the "scientific" Marxist-Leninism she studied so conscientiously and believed so blindly. Although this was never stated outright by any Vietnamese, she understood that Communism, like everything else that brought death and sorrow, was the product of the *yêu* and *tinh* and the other invisible demons that had always swarmed over Vietnam, catching at the legs of the Vietnamese and creating their mournful, inescapable history.

11

CHRISTOPHER AND VO RAU BECAME FRIENDS BY TALKING TO EACH other through their poems. They usually met in the cool of the evening in a sampan on the River of Perfumes, reading aloud in each other's language. The listener suggested refinements in the translation. Christopher's faint speaking voice was an asset to him in Hue, where Vietnamese was pronounced in refined, barely audible tones.

His friendship with Vo aroused curiosity, but no unusual suspicion. All but the most paranoid members of the Vietminh apparatus had lost interest in Christopher. In what way was he dangerous?

He was not French; he might even be German. It was also possible that he might be what he represented himself to be, a poet in search of experience who sometimes wrote articles about Vietnam for American and European magazines and newspapers. His journalism was scrupulously accurate and nonpolitical.

How can any man be nonpolitical? asked the apparatus. Why was he here in the midst of a colonial war that did not concern him or his country? When he went with the Vietminh in the jungle, though he refused to touch a weapon, they saw that he had been a soldier; maybe he still was.

The last thing they imagined was that an American might be patient enough to be interested in the future, that he was quiescent now in order to be the contrary in times to come.

Christopher never mentioned the O. G. to Vo, never gave him the slightest hint that he came from the Outfit. Vo did not need to know; he did not want to know. In time they came to understand each other completely.

When Vo was asked about his friendship with Christopher by one of his former students who was now Lê's control officer in Vietminh headquarters, he said, "He is a poet."

"A poet or somebody who wants us to think he's a poet?"

"See for yourself."

Vo showed the man a poem Christopher had written. It was about the fighters in the jungle, and if you understood how unsparingly truthful it was, it was very moving.

"You translated this for him?"

"No," Vo said. "He wrote it in Vietnamese. He can do the same in English and French, and I suppose German. He is gifted."

"Then why is he here?"

Vo sighed before he answered. "I think because he believes that Vietnam is the place where truth and lies will have their next great battle, and he wants to be present."

"On which side?"

"A poet is always on the side of truth," Vo said.

F O U R

1

A DECADE LATER, SOON AFTER CHRISTOPHER LIVED OUT THE PROPH-
ecies of Lê's fortune-teller and disappeared into China, Patchen
met Vo Rau on the River of Perfumes. They went out at midnight in
separate sampans rowed by agents of the Outfit—Khmer not Annamese
or Tonkinese or Cochinchinese—who lashed the hulls together so
that the two men could talk as they drifted with the current.

In the lantern light, Vo was white-bearded and emaciated, with
the weary eyes and benevolent air of the very old, but in fact he
was only sixty-four. Like his long-ago friend the O. G., he was
venerable before his time.

Patchen and Vo had never met.

"Do you know who I am?" Patchen asked. "Do you require
other proofs of identity?"

"No. He describes you in one of his poems. You couldn't be
anyone else."

"As you know, he has disappeared."

"And you think you will find him in Vietnam?"

"No. He's in China. I hope I can find out why in Vietnam."

" 'You will have your choice of explanations.' I am quoting poetry:

" 'When you ask the makers of the dead
to remember the reason why,
you will have your choice of explanations.' "

"That sounds like Paul."

"Yes. He wrote it ten years ago, here in Hue. Even then he was
curious about murderers. Too curious, too imaginative, too brave.
He was born under a very unpredictable star." The old man smiled.
"We Vietnamese are superstitious in these matters."

158

"Did he explain his theory to you?"

"That your American President had been killed in revenge for the murders of Ngo Dinh Diem and his two brothers? Yes."

"Do you believe that?"

"I thought it was a very dangerous idea. It suggested that the most powerful man in the world had been assassinated by the weak, and that he was in some way responsible for his own death. Whether it was true or not, the thought was intolerable."

"Did anyone in Vietnam besides yourself understand this?" Patchen asked.

"Everyone who heard it. We're weak, not stupid. But I think you're too late. There are no answers in Vietnam. Everyone here who wanted to harm Paul is dead. They were all killed *after* he was in China, and out of danger. That is rather strange."

"Yes," Patchen said, "it is."

Every one of Christopher's Vietnamese enemies had been murdered one after the other within twenty-four hours after the small plane he hired strayed off course and crash-landed on Chinese territory. This handful of deaths, occurring among so many others, had hardly been noticed.

Patchen said, "You say they were killed after he was out of danger. Is it your opinion that being in the hands of the Chinese Communists is the same as being out of danger?"

"No one can reach him in one of their prisons," Vo said. "Not Americans or Russians, and least of all Vietnamese."

"Especially if he is in a Chinese grave."

"Why would the Chinese kill him?" Vo asked. "They are glad to have him. A few years from now they can sell him to you for something they want. Then he will be free, they will be richer, and you will have paid your debt."

"You're happy he's a prisoner," Patchen said, truly surprised at his own thought.

"Of course I am," Vo said. "Otherwise he would be dead."

Patchen shifted his weight, and the movement of his stiff body made both sampans rock.

"Are you suggesting that all this was arranged as a *rescue?*" he asked.

"That would imply that a very, very clever person made the plan."

"Who?"

"Someone who loved our friend and wanted to save his life."

"You?"

Vo smiled benevolently. "I wish I could say yes. But no, this was someone with powerful friends, money, debts that he could call in for payment."

The two sampans bumped softly at the gunwales. Nothing else stirred. In the seamless Vietnamese night, sky and river were the same shade of black; water, air, and human skin the same degree of temperature. Patchen felt immersed in Vietnam, the subject of some biological process, like gestation or coma, that could only come to an end in its own natural time.

"Where will you look?" Vo asked.

"For what?" Patchen said.

"For the person who did this. For the explanation."

"Closer to home, if you're right in thinking that Paul's friends did this to him, instead of his enemies."

"And if I'm right and you decide what this person did was a good thing, what then?"

All the more reason to kill the bastard, Patchen thought. But he said, "I'm not sure motivation is the question. Everything is a matter of trust, in the end."

"Quite true," Vo said. "And now I think we should say goodnight."

Patchen reached into the other boat and shook hands. "You've been a great help," he said. "Thank you."

"It was a pleasure to see you at last after knowing you for such a long time in Paul's poem."

"The one you quoted?"

"No, another one. It's one of my favorites."

"What's it about?"

"It's about one soldier saving another's life in battle," Vo replied. "Both are wounded, but the rescued one is blinded. He thinks his rescuer may be Death. The rescuer can't see, either, because the night is so dark. He is struck by bullets. He wants to lie down beside the other man and die. He makes himself go on by imagining that he is carrying his wounded father toward a reunion with his mother, who has been lost for a long time. The battle sounds to him like the roaring of lions in a dream he had as a child. The last line was very difficult to render in Vietnamese: 'German is the only language that lions understand.' It would have been better, for the Vietnamese ear, to substitute 'Chinese' and 'tiger.' But when I translated it he insisted on a literal rendering. Paul was always on the side of the original meaning."

INTERLUDE

BEAUTIFUL DREAMERS

ON PATCHEN'S BIRTHDAY, A WEEK AFTER HIS WALK ALONG THE MALL with Christopher, the O. G. gave a supper for him. The only other guest was Christopher, and the three men sat down at ten o'clock, hours after the rest of Washington had dined. The food was cold, smoked trout accompanied by a sentimental bottle of Montrachet, followed by rare roast beef and raw vegetables and a decanted Bordeaux that had been breathing in a beaker for precisely one half-hour. The O. G. had converted the entire basement of his house into a wine cellar, refrigerated to a perpetual fifty-eight degrees Fahrenheit, and installed a heating and cooling system in the dining room that maintained a temperature suitable to the red wine being served.

Tonight the thermostat on the wall was set at sixty-six degrees. The O. G. filled Patchen's glass.

"All right," he said, and stepped back with an air of expectation.

Omitting the usual eucharistic flourishes of the wine taster, Patchen sniffed and sipped in a matter of two seconds. "Château Pétrus, 1961," he said.

"Hurrah," said the O. G., greatly pleased by the correct identification—after all, he had given Patchen his first glass of wine, all those years ago in Boston. "Happy birthday. I've only got six cases of this left—enough to get you through your sixties if you take care of your health."

Patchen was almost never stumped by a wine. He had an exceptionally keen sense of taste and, provided it was served at the correct temperature, which was almost never the case when he dined anywhere but at the O. G.'s, he could readily identify any French wine by region and château, and, in the case of great vintages, by year.

Patchen's beeper went off and he left the room to talk on the secure telephone in the O. G.'s library that was one of the perquisites of being a former Director. They both knew he was calling the duty officer on the ad hoc Beautiful Dreamers desk to check on developments.

The O. G. believed, though he had never mentioned this to Patchen, that the latter's extraordinary palate was a compensation for the loss of his left eye. He took advantage of his absence to pay him a compliment. "David tastes wine," he said, "like a blind man reads Braille."

Christopher smiled politely and said nothing in return; although he knew what the O. G. meant, he thought in his writerly way that this was a strange way of putting it. Did he taste it with his fingertips?

Usually the O. G. scrupulously avoided any talk about old times in Christopher's presence. Tonight, however, while Patchen lingered on the telephone, he departed from habit.

"I don't want to rouse painful memories," he said, "but David tells me you say that the important question about this Beautiful Dreamers business is not how or what or even who, but the everlasting 'why?'. It took me back."

"Took you back?" Christopher said. "Where to?"

"To your great days as a thorn in the side of the mighty. You said the same blessèd thing when the President was assassinated all those years ago—forget about puffs of smoke on the grassy knoll and all that folderol, just find out why. And look what *that* led to."

For a long moment Christopher watched the O. G.'s amiable, unreadable old face. Then he said, "What *did* it lead to?"

"I'm not sure I know. What's your opinion?"

"Nothing," Christopher said. "It led to nothing."

"I thought that might be the way you felt about it." The O. G. compressed his lips. "But it led to ten years in a Chinese jail for you and disgrace and death for Barney Wolkowicz. For the Outfit that was like losing Ruth and Gehrig in a train wreck. Most people would say all that adds up to more than zero."

The O. G. wasn't smiling. This was such a rare event that it changed the whole atmosphere. Christopher was surprised by the O. G.'s peevishness, and by the direction this conversation was taking. The O. G. had never before mentioned his imprisonment in China or the reasons behind it.

"All that came of asking the question, 'Why?'," the O. G. said. "I'm not saying the question shouldn't have been asked in that case, but most people sure as shooting didn't want it answered."

"As far as I know, it never was answered," Christopher said.

"No, by golly. But that wasn't for lack of trying on your part."

"Then maybe you should have given me the benefit of all this worldly wisdom at the time."

In fact the O. G. had made it plain that he did not want to know anything about Christopher's theory or his operations while they were going on; he let Patchen handle it.

"Sometimes I wish I had given you a talking to," the O. G. said. His frown lifted; his customary carefree twinkle returned. "But that's water under the bridge. Anyway, I know you: You wouldn't have listened; you were too busy romancing the eternal verities. And besides, I respected your instincts; they were the best instincts in the business, except, maybe, for Wolkowicz's. He must be burning in Hell, poor fellow . . . What's keeping David?"

The O. G. heaved himself out of his chair and fetched a bowl of walnuts and a silver tray holding a carafe of port wine and four glasses from the sideboard, where the dirty dishes were stacked. They were alone in the house, and the O. G. had buttled the supper himself.

Patchen returned, closing the door swiftly behind him so as not to let the heat in. "All quiet on the western front," he said, sitting down and spreading his napkin over his lap.

"No new victims?" the O. G. said.

"Not yet." Patchen looked his friends over. "Why the long faces?" he asked. "What have you been talking about?"

"Paul's ability to see things that others don't," the O. G. replied. "And the consequences thereof."

"No wonder you're glum."

"You used to believe in this gift of Paul's," the O. G. said. "Do you still think he's got second sight?"

"I wouldn't call it that," Patchen said.

"All right, then—blood wisdom."

" 'Fucking genius' is what Wolkowicz called it," Patchen said. "I don't think Paul has lost it, whatever it was. Although a hell of a lot good that does anybody since he won't use it."

"You don't mean it," the O. G. said. "Look what Paul's done already. Pointed the way."

"That's true," Patchen said, pouring himself a glass of port and sliding the bottle across the table to Christopher. "My apologies, Paul. You're a patriot after all."

"Well, then," the O. G. said, "we're unanimous, with Paul not voting. He's still able to say the sooth. He's asked the right question and made the right suggestion to clear up this Beautiful Dreamer business. So let's shake a leg and get going." He rubbed his hands together so briskly that the other two could hear the chafing of skin. He said, "Boy, this is going to be fun."

"What is?" Christopher said.

"Building a better mousetrap," the O. G. replied. "Catching this fellow by the tail, Paul, and asking him why he's been running up our pants leg. But how do we do it? What kind of cheese do we need? That's where you come in."

"Oh, no I don't," Christopher said.

The O. G. ignored Christopher's protest. "You've done it before, Paul—picture book stuff," he said. "Tell us how you'd do it again."

The O. G. radiated enthusiasm. He hadn't gotten to be the grand old man of dirty tricks by taking "no" for an answer from reluctant collaborators. Christopher shook his head in amused recognition; he had seen this virtuoso performance many times before.

Now, raising his eyebrows to summon forth Christopher's answer, the O. G. cracked a walnut, ate the meat to clear his tongue of the taste of the splendid Pomerol he had just finished drinking, and lifted his glass.

"To the next time," he said.

Christopher did not drink. "Uncle," he said, "I wouldn't do it again for all the rice in China."

"Then I guess you'll have to do it for some other reason," the O. G. replied, lifting his glass of port an inch higher. "Absent friends," he said.

They all drank. The O. G.'s eyes misted behind his pince-nez like a headmaster standing before his school's roll of old boys who had died in a war just ended. Then he recovered. "Now, Paul, David," he said. "Put on your thinking caps. How are we going to smear cold cream on this invisible man so we can see what he's up to?"

In spite of himself, out of some troublesome old code he had thought was foresworn and gone forever, Christopher answered the question.

"There you are!" the O. G. said. "Simple as pie, if you've got the mind for the Work."

III

PEOPLE
OF THE BOOK

ONE

1

ON THE MORNING AFTER THE MEETING WITH VO RAU, AS SOON AS IT was light, Patchen and Wolkowicz took off from Da Nang in an Outfit plane and headed out to sea. It was Wolkowicz's aircraft. In Outfit terms, Vietnam was Wolkowicz's country because he was in charge of operations there. Christopher had been kidnapped—if that was what had happened—in Vietnam, on Wolkowicz's territory: "On my watch," he had told Patchen, mocking the naval slang affected by some who had gone from the quarantine of Yale to the quarantine of Headquarters, bypassing what Wolkowicz regarded as real life.

Patchen looked out the window. Below the wings of the aircraft, in the South China Sea, junks and other unwieldy sailing vessels moved so slowly over the water that they left no wakes. Wolkowicz had told him that he wanted to talk about Christopher. What more was there to say? He was gone; he was beyond the Outfit's reach. There were some things Patchen was not prepared to say on this subject, especially to Wolkowicz. Patchen had never really believed Christopher's theory about the assassination of the President. It was too symmetrical. It was too much like Christopher himself: poetic, intelligent, subtle, logical. It was a morality tale in which the sin of pride is punished by a terrible act of vengeance. But these were not the only reasons why Patchen doubted the theory. He knew things Christopher had not known; he suspected people Christopher had trusted. He thought that someone had led Christopher in the direction of his strengths and virtues to a false but irresistible conclusion. There could be only one reason for such a dazzling act of intellectual jujitsu: to create a diversion, to lead investigators away from the true explanation, away from the real reason, away from the people truly responsible. Only someone who knew Christopher intimately, who understood the way his mind worked, could have deceived him in this way.

"We're here," Wolkowicz said. He knocked on the bulkhead, opened the cockpit door, and ordered the pilot to fly in circles.

From an inside pocket Wolkowicz produced a wad of paper and photographs, separated them, and handed them over to Patchen one by one: a marked aircraft map of the Chinese island of Hainan, a dozen black-and-white snapshots of a large villa surrounded by a wall, and a sheet of foolscap on which a floor plan had been drawn and labeled in Vietnamese. These documents were slightly damp with Wolkowicz's sweat.

Wolkowicz took the floor plan out of Patchen's hand and pressed his blunt finger onto the penciled square that represented a windowless storeroom off the villa's kitchen. "This is the room where Christopher is being held—for the moment," he said. "He'll be moved somewhere else in China tomorrow night."

Patchen lifted his eye to Wolkowicz's face. "What's the source of all this gossip?" he asked.

"We try to keep our eyes and ears open," Wolkowicz said.

They were whispering; it was more efficient than shouting, and the bulkhead between them and the pilot was very thin.

Patchen said, *"What is the source?"*

Wolkowicz opened his eyes wide. "If I didn't trust the source I wouldn't believe the report. But I do. Don't worry about it. I want to talk to you about Christopher."

"You're already doing that."

"Not yet I'm not. I want to go in and get him. Unmarked helicopters, shooters in civilian clothes." He pointed to the documents. "We know the exact location of the house. We know exactly where Christopher is inside the house. We know there are six guards on duty—one at the front door, one at the back, one on the roof, three on the gate. I've got a team on full alert. I've got two black helicopters standing by, no markings, extra fuel tanks. Hainan is close—two hundred miles from Da Nang. We can go in the dark, be in and out in fifteen minutes. We can bring him back alive. Tonight. Tomorrow is too late."

Listening to this, Patchen's expression did not change. "Let me understand this," he said. "You want to carry out a hostile military operation inside China."

"Correction. I want to carry out a clandestine operation to extract a captured agent."

"Christopher's not an agent."

"You're absolutely right—he's been off the payroll for three weeks. But what was he doing for fifteen years before that? Do you realize what he's going to spill?"

"I realize what the Chinese could do if they captured a U. S. assault team on their territory. No."

"No? You're saying no? Why not?"

"You know why not. What's the matter with you?"

Wolkowicz's face, already flushed, grew angrier. "You're asking me?" he said. "This guy is supposed to be your best friend."

"That's right. At least he's alive. You don't think one of those six guards is going to shoot him rather than give him back?"

"How do you know he's alive? How do you know there are six guards?"

"You say your information is correct. I'm being polite."

"Don't be. Just tell me your answer."

"No," Patchen replied. "The answer is no."

Wolkowicz gave him a look of deep contempt, but he did not argue. Then he pounded on the cockpit door.

"Home, James," he said.

The plane stopped circling and headed back for Saigon.

As if nothing had happened, Wolkowicz got drinks out of the cooler—mineral water for Patchen, another beer for himself.

"This is pretty goddamn funny when you think about it," he said.

Patchen did not ask what was so funny. He knew Wolkowicz's techniques too well.

"You know what I think?" Wolkowicz asked.

"No," Patchen said. "I don't."

They were still whispering.

"Then I'll tell you," Wolkowicz said. "I think you've got the idea that one of us put Christopher on ice."

Patchen regarded him with calm interest.

"One of us?" he said. "You mean somebody in the Outfit or somebody in this airplane?"

"Take your choice."

"Does that worry you, Barney?"

Wolkowicz grinned. "Me? Naw. Why should it? Whoever the villain is, he's safe as long as Christopher is locked up in China."

"Is he? How do you figure that?"

"Because whoever got him in can get him killed," Wolkowicz replied. "And we both love him too much to take a chance on that happening."

It was a confession; it was a threat. Or was it an accusation? Wolkowicz drank the last swallow of his beer and grinned again.

"What's the matter, kid?" he asked. "Airsick?"

2

WHEN HE RETURNED TO HEADQUARTERS FROM VIETNAM PATCHEN locked himself in his cell with the Outfit's complete files on Wolkowicz. These archives contained no arguments for or against Wolkowicz's guilt, no conclusions, no judgments, only the raw facts of his life and operations. If you believed what Patchen believed, if you could look behind the files and perceive what their bland surface concealed, the evidence of his treason was plain to see. But Patchen knew that nobody—not even Christopher if he came back—would see what he saw, believe what he believed. Wolkowicz was a hero who had bled for the Outfit and carried out some of its most famous operations. Patchen kept his own counsel, but for the next decade he had two fixations that were really a single, indivisible passion: the rescue of Christopher and the destruction of Wolkowicz. Nobody else was interested in either; Patchen was like the only sane man in an asylum; if he described what he knew he would destroy any chance he might have of being believed. Reality was poison. Too many people, over too many years, had failed to see the truth to be able to recognize it now.

In due course, Wolkowicz completed his tour in Saigon and came back to Washington for routine reassignment. He realized almost at once that Patchen was hunting him. The signs were unmistakable: he had nothing to do, and although no one could tell him why, he was treated at Headquarters with a cordiality that was subtly, almost unnoticeably, more intense. To Wolkowicz, the manners of the Ivy Leaguers who ran Headquarters had always been something like a shortwave broadcast: a wavering signal, obscured by static, emanating from a far-distant point. Now someone who understood the equipment had turned the dial a fraction of a millimeter to right or left and the announcer's voice was easier to hear.

"What the fuck is going on?" he asked Patchen, having surprised him and his Doberman pinscher by appearing on the deserted towpath beside the C & O Canal at one o'clock in the morning.

Wolkowicz fell to his knees to greet the Doberman. The dog licked his face and whined happily. It loved Wolkowicz.

Patchen said, "I'm not sure I understand the question." He was tired; he had left his cell only an hour before, at the end of a day that began at six-thirty in the morning.

"You're freezing me out. Why?"

"It isn't easy to find the right slot for a man of your experience and qualifications, Barney. You're a legend."

"You're right," Wolkowicz said. "And you're also pissed off at me. Ever since I came back from Saigon, ever since Christopher got his ass in a sling, I've been a leper." Wolkowicz stood up and rang an invisible bell. "Unclean! Unclean!"

"Oh. And why am I doing this to you, Barney?"

"Because I wanted to go in and get Christopher. In your book, that makes me a madman."

"You're not a madman," Patchen said. "Just a romantic."

"It would have worked. Two choppers, two squads of killers, in and out. We would have brought him home."

"With World War III as an encore."

"Ratshit. We would've brought him back alive and the Chinks would have swallowed it and kept their mouths shut. I've got to be honest with you, fella. I think you've got some deep, dark reason for wanting your best friend to be just exactly where he is."

Wolkowicz had waited until they were under a light to speak these words. He wanted to observe Patchen's reaction. Now, peering into his shadowy features, he saw the flash of surprise, the glint of anger that might be expected from an innocent man who has just been accused of a crime he did not commit. Wolkowicz saw something else also, and this was the thing he was looking for: a flicker of admiration. Patchen *knew*—knew beyond the shadow of a doubt that Wolkowicz had delivered Christopher to the Chinese. There was admiration in his expression because nobody but Wolkowicz would have been brilliant enough, or crude enough, or foolhardy enough, to drag Patchen's deepest suspicions into the open and fling them into his face, pretending that the suspect was the accuser and the accuser was the suspect.

"What's the matter?" Wolkowicz said. "Don't you like my theory?"

"I love it," Patchen said. He snorted in amusement, shook his head. "You have no shame, Barney, but nobody can say you haven't got balls."

"That's how I got to be such a fucking legend," Wolkowicz said. "But that's history. How about a job, Boss?"

Patchen was still shaking his head, trying not to laugh. He knew he had given himself away to Wolkowicz. Now what? The two of them were alone in the middle of an urban American woods, one of the most dangerous environments on earth. Wolkowicz was capable of anything. He knew how to murder another man in a dozen silent ways. He could kill Patchen and throw his body into the canal: "SPYMASTER SLAIN." Or carry it away: "OUTFIT CHIEF- TAIN VANISHES." Never to be found. Wolkowicz was fondling the dog again, baby-talking to it in German. Patchen laughed out loud.

"Have you ever killed a dog, Barney?"

Wolkowicz shook his head, staring fixedly into Patchen's face as if he wanted to avoid eye contact with the Doberman. "No," he said, "and if that's the kind of job you're going to offer me, forget it." He put a hand on Patchen's shoulder, the good one, and gave it a reassuring shake. "In fact," he said, "forget the whole fucking thing. We're just not meant for each other, kid, are we?"

"Well," Patchen said, "your ways are not my ways, Barney, but it's hard to argue with the results you get. In fact, I was going to ask you to have dinner with me tomorrow night to talk about your future."

Wolkowicz feigned astonishment, covering his mouth with his hand. "No shit? What an impatient fool I am. I hope I haven't spoiled everything."

"Far from it. You've saved me the price of a meal. How would you like to play Christopher for a while?"

Wolkowicz registered suspicion, not surprise. "What's that sup- posed to mean?"

"You're more like Christopher than you think. You know the work, you speak a lot of languages, you have a wide acquaintance among the misfits of the world. You'd be a singleton like him, under deep cover."

"What cover? I don't look like a poet."

"You'll think of something."

"The arrangement would be the same as the one he had? I'd be on my own in the field and drive everybody else crazy?"

"Yes."

"And I'd report to you, and only you?"

Patchen nodded. "To the Director, through me. What do you think?"

Wolkowicz laughed. He understood exactly what Patchen was doing: isolating him from everybody in the Outfit except himself, putting him out in the open where his every move could be observed, rendering him meaningless and friendless.

"Considering how Christopher ended up," Wolkowicz said, "I think it's fucking brilliant."

3

UNTIL WOLKOWICZ CALLED ON OTTO AND MARIA ROTHCHILD IN THEIR house on Lake Leman, he had not heard Cathy Christopher's name pronounced in more than ten years. Even then it came up by indirection when Maria chided Wolkowicz for neglecting his food. She had served poached trout, the Geneva delicacy, for lunch.

"You didn't eat the best part," Maria said. "The cheeks."

Wolkowicz picked up the skeleton of the fish by the tail and draped it over her plate. "Be my guest," he said.

Maria dug the tiny morsels of flesh from the head and ate them. "You're only the second person ever to make me a present of their trout cheeks, Barney," she said. "The other was Cathy Christopher. That was the only thing she ever gave anybody."

"She had her generous moments," Wolkowicz said. "What about all those Wops she banged in Rome when she was still married to her husband?"

Maria's face, slightly flushed by the wine she had drunk with her trout, lit up at the prospect of Outfit gossip, captured by hidden microphones, described by watchers in the shadows.

"How do you know about that?" she asked, as if she already knew all the details and was merely testing the extent of Wolkowicz's knowledge.

Wolkowicz went along. "I saw the pictures," he replied.

Maria drank more wine. "How did you get hold of *those?*"

"Patchen was handing them around."

"What a bastard. Did Paul see them?"

"I don't know. He might have felt better if he had. She didn't look like she was enjoying it very much."

173

"God, but that's awful," Maria said. "Patchen is such a shit."

"He stays in character," Wolkowicz said.

"So do we all," said Otto. "Look at poor Paul."

Although the weather was chilly, they were seated in the garden. Otto shivered and looked across the lake at the Môle, the snowy Alpine peak closest to Geneva and the only one visible today. He shivered again and fell asleep. Maria wrapped another blanket around him.

"Poor, poor Paul," he said.

Minutes before, Otto had received the news of Christopher's captivity with outward calm, but afterward his hands shook so badly that he was unable to use his knife and fork. After a brief outburst—sparkling eyes, a bark of laughter, a clap of the hands—Maria had mimicked his detachment, but she had been drinking wine recklessly ever since. After telling them about Christopher, Wolkowicz moved on to his real purpose. He had not come to Switzerland to discuss Christopher's fate, but to plant the idea in Otto Rothchild's mind that Patchen was responsible for it.

Otto could be counted on to spread the rumor throughout the half-world of people who worked secretly for the Americans. Even in disgrace he was in touch with dozens of the Outfit's assets in Europe, Africa, and Asia. They were his old friends, his circle. At one time, before he made them what they were today by plugging them in to easy American money and silly American secrets, he had been the shark and they had been his pilot fish. In a sense, they still were. Otto's disgrace, in the eyes of his friends, was the disgrace of the school prankster expelled by a slow-witted headmaster who detects the thousandth joke on himself and mistakes it for the first. They would all laugh about it at future reunions; they snickered about it now.

Maria opened a third bottle of Mont-sur-Rolle. It had been cooling in the running water of the mossy fountain, and the label came off with her hand when she set the bottle down.

"This is the only Swiss white Otto will allow in the house, even though he doesn't drink alcohol," Maria said. "We can't afford French wine, thanks to mutual friends. How many Italians did Cathy go to bed with, exactly? Is there an official Outfit count?"

"I don't remember. Half a dozen. One of them beat her up because she was such a lousy piece of ass."

"So *that* was it! She wouldn't tell me a thing."

"You saw her afterward?"

He was interested in this news. Maria, happier than she had been in a long time, leaned back in her chair and sipped her wine. She missed the Work tremendously.

"She *stayed* with us," she said. "That beautiful face was all smashed in. She wouldn't say who did it to her. I knew it couldn't be Paul."

"How do you figure that?"

"Paul would never have let her see he cared that much. He never left a mark on his victims. Look at Otto. Look at me. No, it wasn't Paul. I figured she must have decided to make Paul jealous and picked out a psychopath to have an affair with. It would have been just like her. She had the brains of a chicken."

Wolkowicz watched Maria pour herself more wine. "You sound like you didn't like her," he said. "I thought you two were old school chums. The Daisy Chain, all that crap."

"Cathy went to Bryn Mawr not Vassar," Maria said, annoyed at his mistake. "But if they had a daisy chain, Cathy would have been voted Queen of the May. How could anybody *like* somebody who looked like her and had all that money? She used to carry ten thousand dollars in cash around in her pocketbook."

"Do you think Christopher married her for her money?"

"No. That was hound dog lust. You could see it in his eyes."

Otto woke up and joined the conversation.

"That's not what Lla Kahina said," he said, clearing his throat. "Maria, water."

She came around the table and held the glass while he drank, then wiped his lips with his napkin.

"Lla Kahina?" Wolkowicz asked. "Who's that?"

"The Queen of the Berbers," Maria said.

Otto made a face of displeasure and pushed her away. *"In vino stupiditas,"* he said. "Lla Kahina is an old friend from North Africa who happened to be visiting when Cathy came."

"An amazing woman," Maria said. "She's a clairvoyant."

"She's a what?" Wolkowicz said.

"A clairvoyant," Otto said. "She sees into the future."

Maria said, "She said what happened between Christopher and Cathy was fate, that it had some hidden purpose."

"No shit?" Wolkowicz said. "What would that be?"

Rothchild made a weak gesture and cleared his throat again. Maria, still standing by, held the glass for him again and he drank.

"According to Lla Kahina," Otto said, "hound dog lust, as Maria calls it, is always a signal from the invisible powers that the two people who feel it for each other have been chosen to conceive an amazing child."

"The maculate conception," Maria said. "So to speak."

Otto ignored her again. "No matter how unsuited to each other the couple are in every other way, no matter how unhappy it makes them, they must do what is necessary to conceive the child."

"It is owed to the world from another life," Maria said.

"That was Lla Kahina's theory," Otto said.

Wolkowicz leaned back in his metal chair. "You go along with that?" he asked.

"Why not?" Otto said. "It certainly fits the case of Paul and Cathy. She said the same thing about Hubbard and Lori way back when, and look at the result. Paul."

"This clairvoyant was in Berlin in the twenties?"

Rothchild nodded. "Appeared from nowhere, this little golden girl from Africa with teardrops tattooed on her cheeks. Everyone, Barney, wanted to fuck her. Everyone."

"Did many succeed?"

"Nobody. She had ideas about racial purity."

"What was she, a Nazi?"

"No. She thought Aryans were inferior stock—it was the purity of her own tribe she was trying to preserve. The Ja'wabi, they were called. She wouldn't even consider other Berbers worthy of her favors. Ja'wabi or nothing was her motto."

Wolkowicz held out his glass for more wine. "The Ja'wabi, eh?" he said. "You've got quite a memory, Otto."

"She was a memorable female. She was called Meryem in those days. Hubbard quoted a charming poem about her in his novel *The Rose and the Lotus*. Maria, go fetch my copy."

Maria went into the house.

"Forgive my wife, she's a little drunk, we don't serve much wine in our circumstances," Otto said to Wolkowicz. "Brecht used to say Meryem came from the Mountains of the Moon. He was a great fornicator, you know, he bred half the heifers in Berlin, no conscience whatever, unlike poor Hubbard. Actually Meryem came from the Mountains of Mountains, the Idáren Dráren, as she called them. Ah!"

Maria returned with the book, already open to the right page. Otto read the lines in a dry, quavering voice:

" 'Meryem has no rival,
She is worth five hundred mares
She is worth five hundred she-camels.
Her saliva, I have tasted it,
It is the sugar of dried grapes.
How could I forget Meryem,
Meryem with her black lashes.' "

"Hubbard tasted her saliva?" Wolkowicz asked.

"Certainly not," Otto replied. "Hubbard tasted only one woman's saliva in his whole life, and I've told you about Meryem's principles. The poem's a translation from Arabic, something he found in a book by some French general who served in North Africa. Hubbard had no imagination. His novels are really just diaries. He just wrote down what happened every day."

"You mean it's non-fiction?"

"Not exactly," Otto said. "But it's not exactly fiction, either. It's Hubbard's version of the truth. Not because he was a liar—we both know he wasn't—but because he was an American. He didn't quite understand the world he was living in, but he thought he did, so he recorded his misconceptions. It gave his work a certain Dadaesque charm. Of course infantilism was all the rage in those days."

Wolkowicz listened without apparent interest. "Tell me more about this girlfriend of Christopher's mother," he said. "Was she like the Meryem in the poem?"

"She was exquisite. Zaentz—the man who made that nude drawing of Lori when she was pregnant with Paul—painted a sensational picture of her and Lori together. Here, look."

The frontispiece of Hubbard's novel was a tinted reproduction of a painting of two female heads, one fair, the other dark, gazing directly at the painter. The picture was as glossy and realistic as a photograph, but something was hidden in it.

Wolkowicz could not quite get it into focus. "There's something wrong with this," he said.

Otto was pleased by his confusion. "Do you see what it is?" he asked. "It's right there, in plain sight. Look again."

"I give up."

"Zaentz gave them each other's eyes. That's how close they were."

Wolkowicz looked again: the blonde had emerald eyes, the brunette enormous gray ones.

"In a way they were the same person," Maria said. "That's how Lla Kahina knew; that's why she came here."

"Knew what?" Wolkowicz said.

"That Cathy was pregnant with Paul Christopher's child."

Even Wolkowicz's natural cunning and long years of training were not strong enough to overcome the look of surprise that burst out on his broad face.

"Cathy was knocked up?" he said. "How did she know it was Paul's kid?"

"She knew," Maria said. "I advised her to get rid of it but she wouldn't do it. If it had belonged to some casual lover she would have gone straight to the abortionist."

"So where *did* she go?"

"With Lla Kahina," Otto said.

"Where to?" Wolkowicz said.

Otto shrugged. "Who knows?" he said. "They just vanished. Our letters came back. Even Cathy's parents don't know. It broke their hearts, as they say over there in Kentucky, across the water."

He smiled. So did Maria. Wolkowicz closed his eyes for a moment, then picked up Hubbard's novel and began to read.

4

WOLKOWICZ FOUND CATHY IN TIFAWT, LLA KAHINA'S VILLAGE HIGH in the Idáren Dráren. No roads led to this place, and the journey through the mountains by donkey had taken nearly a week. He arrived in the afternoon, and viewed from a distance in westerly sunlight, Tifawt glittered as if fragments of broken mirrors had been mortared by the thousands onto its walls and minarets. According to his French-Berber dictionary, which Wolkowicz consulted while sitting astride his donkey, the name meant "light."

Asking directions at the gate, Wolkowicz went directly to the house where Cathy lived. A servant opened the gate, admitting him to a courtyard.

Cathy found him kneeling beside the fountain, washing his face. He still smelled of donkey. His clothes, his hair, and his bushy black eyebrows were powdered with red dust.

"I'd forgotten how much you look like Beelzebub," she said.

"Well, you haven't seen me in a long time," said Wolkowicz.

178

"What are you doing here?"

"That's a rude question."

"Seeing you washing up in my fountain is a rude shock. I thought I was getting away from people like you. How did you find this place?"

"I heard this legend about a beautiful white goddess living in a city that sparkled like diamonds," Wolkowicz said. "So here I am. Can I come in? I bring news."

Cathy turned in a swirl of Berber skirts and led him inside, away from the midday sun. The house was very grand, with marble floors and magnificent gold-and-vermilion doors like pages from an illuminated manuscript. It was furnished in the Arab style, with carpets, low tables of hammered brass, and cushions on the floor, filigree screens instead of glass in the windows.

As they settled down on pillows to drink the tea that had been laid out on one of the tables, a muezzin called the noon prayer. The voice, an effortless bel canto baritone, came from quite nearby. Wolkowicz jerked his head in the direction of the sound and raised his eyebrows in inquiry.

"The minaret is right next door," Cathy said.

"How often does he come outside and warble?"

"Five times a day," Cathy said. "Sunrise, noon, afternoon, sunset, and bedtime. That's the *salat az-zuhr,* the noontime prayer. It's performed when the shadow of a stick driven vertically into the ground falls shortest. Next comes the afternoon prayer, *salat al-asr,* when the shadow is equal to the length of the stick, plus the length of the shadow at noon."

Wolkowicz swallowed a mouthful of very hot, very sweet mint tea. "What happens if you're at the North Pole?"

"Then you pray according to shadows at Mecca."

"How would you know?"

"Allah would provide."

"What are you, a convert?"

"No," Cathy said. "Who *did* tell you where I was?"

"Nobody. I just sort of figured it out."

"Tell me the truth."

"Okay," Wolkowicz said. "The truth is, Otto Rothchild told me you ran off with Lla Kahina. So all I had to do was find out where she was to know where you'd be."

"You know Lla Kahina?"

Wolkowicz shrugged. "Never had the pleasure. But we've got lots of mutual friends."

"Why did you want to know where I was? David Patchen told me I'd never see any of you people again."

"He lied. Look, I've got something to tell you."

Cathy rose to her feet. "If it's about Paul I don't want to hear it," she said.

"It's about Paul," Wolkowicz said. He told her where Christopher was now, leaving out none of the details. Her eyes widened and filled with tears.

"But how?" she said. "He was smarter than anybody else."

"In some ways, yes, he was," Wolkowicz said. "But he had a weakness for cripples."

Cathy had stopped crying. She said, "Cripples? Are you saying that David Patchen is responsible for this?"

"That's only my opinion. Don't be too hard on him. It's just his way of taking care of his friend."

"But good God," Cathy said. " 'Death with twenty years suspension of execution at solitary forced labor with observation of results?' What does a sentence like that *mean?*"

"It means they may or may not shoot him twenty years from now."

"Shoot who?" asked a voice.

A girl of about ten—Wolkowicz was not good at guessing the ages of children—had come into the room, unnoticed by Cathy, and listened to everything Wolkowicz had said. She was blond and slender, with steady gray eyes and the deeply calm demeanor of an exceptionally self-confident adult. There was no mistaking whose child she was.

"Your father," Wolkowicz said.

5

ZARAH CHRISTOPHER WAS NOT A FLAWLESS BEAUTY LIKE HER MOTHER, but Wolkowicz thought her the most ravishing child he had ever seen. Her comeliness lay not in the shape of her face and body, but in the calm intelligence that lit up her features. She had her father's gestures, his facial expressions, his faint voice, his quietude. It was strange to recognize these qualities in a child her age—not the promise of them, the fully realized qualities themselves—knowing that she had never met her father, had never even seen a photograph of him. All she knew about Christopher, until Wolkowicz arrived, was that she resembled him. As he later discovered, even this much knowledge was accidental. One day, standing outside a door, she had overheard Lla Kahina and her mother discussing the resemblance: *"How can she hold her head like that, how can she have that look in her eyes? She doesn't know he exists."*

"But Zarah doesn't really look like her father," Lla Kahina told Wolkowicz. "The likeness is deeper than that—both she and her father look like a third person."

"Who?" Wolkowicz asked.

"Her grandmother," Lla Kahina replied. "She's the image of Lori Christopher. Zarah should have been named for Lori, but she named herself."

"What do you mean, she named herself?"

"She was a twin. During labor she thrust her arm out of her mother's body, then drew it back inside. The midwife tied a scarlet thread around her wrist to show she was the firstborn."

"So?"

"So when she was born with the scarlet thread on her wrist we called her Zarah. The word means 'scarlet.' "

"Like Judah's harlot daughter-in-law."

"What?" Lla Kahina said.

Wolkowicz smiled merrily, pleased that he had surprised her. After Waddy Jessup abandoned him in Burma, he had spent two years in the jungle with no book to read but the Bible. He had virtually memorized it.

"The story of Judah and Tamar, in Genesis," he said. "Tamar was a widow. Her husband's brother, Onan, wouldn't give her a child, he spilled his seed on the ground to keep her from getting pregnant, so she veiled herself and posed as a prostitute when she saw her father-in-law coming to shear the sheep. Judah succumbed, and got her pregnant with twins. When they were born the same thing happened—one of the twins stuck its hand out and the midwife tied a red thread around it to show it was first out of the womb."

Lla Kahina gave him a deeply thoughtful look. "That's right. That child was named Zerah."

"So the kid's got a Hebrew name?"

Lla Kahina shrugged. She was in control of her expressions again. "A name from the Bible. So does her father. So do you."

That evening, by the running fountain in the courtyard, Wolkowicz pressed Cathy for more details about her life since she ran away from Christopher. Why had she come to this place? Why was she hiding Christopher's child from him?

"Why should I trust you?" she asked.

"You shouldn't trust anybody," Wolkowicz said. "But I already know your big secret. Maybe if you tell me a few little ones I'll understand what's going on in your head. I may even sympathize."

"You're offering me your friendship?"

"We've got a lot in common."

"We do? What?"

"What did the beauty and the beast have in common until they got to know each other?"

Wolkowicz grinned his crockery grin. Cathy smiled back in spite of herself. She had always sympathized with him, because of his grotesque physical being. Wolkowicz understood this. He had been inducing people to confess to him for most of his life. Gazing into Cathy's face, he thought that she was better looking now than before and much more interesting, like a portrait an artist had begun in youth and repainted in old age. The huge wisteria eyes, which used to be so empty and unfocused that she seemed to need glasses, were now filled with those distant cousins of intelligence, wariness and disdain.

"I'll tell you what," Wolkowicz said. "We're in the middle of nowhere out here. There are no witnesses. What say I tell you my biggest secret? Are you ready?"

Wolkowicz was clowning. Cathy nodded, amused in spite of herself.

"Okay," he said. "Here it is: I work for the Russians."

"You do *what?*"

"Surprise! I spy on the Outfit for the opposition. Always have. Patchen has figured it out, he thinks. He just can't prove it yet, but I'm sort of on the run."

"You're joking."

"No. If I lie to you, I blow the friendship. I'm an enemy agent. No shit."

Wolkowicz had Cathy's entire attention now. As she looked at him, a squat figure with black chest hair visible through the thin white fabric of his shirt, she began to smile. It was a slow smile that began in her eyes and spread gradually over her face. Wolkowicz knew that she believed him, that he had made the seduction.

"My God, but that's funny," she said. "Did Paul know?"

"He may have guessed. He was a great guesser. He never said anything."

"He never said anything about anything. But why?"

"I'm a Russian."

"You are? You mean you're one of those people they select in childhood and send to the States like time bombs? What are they called?"

"Sleepers. No. My father was an old Bolshevik, but a Trotskyist. When Stalin took over he had to leave Russia."

"What about your mother?"

"Dead, according to my father. I don't remember anything about her."

"Your father carried you all the way to China on his back, Paul told me."

"That's right."

"How old were you when all this took place?"

"Six, seven."

"Do you remember anything about it?"

"I remember riding on the old man's back, sleeping," Wolkowicz said. "We always traveled at night to avoid the soldiers. Stalin was trying to collectivize agriculture by shooting all the peasants. During the day guns were going off all over the place, villages were burning, people were yelling and screaming. There was no food, there was a big famine in Russia that winter. The peasants burned their crops and killed their horses and cows and sheep and pigs and chickens to keep Stalin from getting them. We ate dead animals. Millions of farm animals were rotting in the fields everywhere we went. The stink was unbelievable, but some of them froze. We'd find one that wasn't too bad, cut off a leg, and cook it. Tasted pretty good if you were hungry. Horses, cows, anything."

"Horses?" Cathy said, shuddering. "It doesn't make any sense," she said.

"What doesn't?" Wolkowicz said.

"The whole thing. That you're a Communist because you ate dead horses when you were six years old. What sense does that make?"

"What sense does anything make?" Wolkowicz asked. "Why did you decide to screw all those Wops when you were married to somebody like Christopher?"

"What do you know about that?"

He named her lovers, counting them off on his fingers. "Patchen showed me the pictures. Don't worry. Your husband never saw them."

"He's not my husband. Not anymore."

"He's not? That's good. Now it's your turn to tell me your secret. Why did you do this? Why is a girl like you hiding out with a bunch of natives in the middle of nowhere?"

"The reason is simple," she said. "Paul held out on me."

"Held out what?" Wolkowicz asked.

"Himself," she said. "He'd never let me see who he was. He never let me touch him, not the real Paul. I couldn't stand it."

"So now what have you got?"

"A part of him that he doesn't even know exists. That's pretty good revenge, don't you think?"

Cathy smiled triumphantly. Wolkowicz smiled back. He knew exactly what he was dealing with, exactly how to handle it.

6

CATHY'S DETERMINATION TO KEEP CHRISTOPHER AND EVERYTHING about him a secret from Zarah had only made him more real to the child. She had always known that her father must exist, and now Wolkowicz had confirmed it. She followed him everywhere, wanting to know more—her father's name, whether he resembled the father she had invented, whether he knew that she existed. Wolkowicz, however, was sworn to secrecy.

"Sorry," he told her when she asked questions. "I'm not allowed to talk about him."

"Why?"

"Because I promised I would never reveal his name or anything about him."

"Then tell me why he's in prison in China."

"How much did you hear the other day when I was talking to your mother?"

"Everything. I followed the two of you into the house."

"Good for you," Wolkowicz said. "He's in prison because a friend betrayed him."

"Why?"

"Because his friend was afraid that he'd be killed by enemies if he stayed outside. He thought he'd be safe if he was in prison."

"What enemies?"

"Everyone was his enemy."

"Why?"

"Because he knew the truth about them. Don't ask me what the truth was."

"But you said the Chinese might shoot him twenty years from now."

"Better twenty years from now than right away. At least that's what his friend thought."

"But he's in solitary confinement, all alone."

"That won't bother your father. He's always been alone."

"But he had my mother."

"For a while, yes. What I meant was, he's different from everybody else. He's one of a kind. Nobody ever understood him."

"Am I like him?"

"Yes, you are," Wolkowicz said. "In fact, the resemblance is amazing. If the two of you ever get together, he won't have to worry about being alone anymore. Neither will you."

Zarah asked the name of the friend who had betrayed her father.

"I've heard it was his best friend, the man he trusted most in the world," Wolkowicz said.

"What is his name?"

"David Patchen. But don't hold it against him. He thought he was doing the right thing."

"How could it be?"

"I don't know. Maybe you can ask Patchen when you grow up."

Zarah asked questions about the prison where her father was confined. Where was it?

"Nobody knows," Wolkowicz said. "Manchuria, probably. Very bleak, very cold."

"What is solitary forced labor?"

"Hard work, like chopping down trees or digging with a pick and shovel, all by yourself except for the guards. Do you want to read about it?"

Wolkowicz had brought a satchel full of books with him over the mountains. He brought it into the courtyard, where he and Zarah always met, and spilled them out onto the marble pavement. Some of the books were very valuable, and these were wrapped in cloth. In his new identity under deep cover, he was posing as a rare book dealer. He rummaged through the rest.

"Here it is," he said, handing Zarah a memoir written by a man who had served a sentence for political offenses in a Chinese prison. "Take this, too." The second book was a volume of Paul Christopher's poems. "Tell me what you think of the poems," he said, dropping volumes back into the canvas bag.

It never occurred to Wolkowicz to wonder whether Zarah would be able to understand the books he gave her or the things he told her. He knew that his words would lodge in her mind forever.

Cathy found the book of Christopher's poems in Zarah's room and confronted Wolkowicz with it.

"Just what the hell do you think you're doing?" she said, whispering.

"It's just a book," Wolkowicz said in his usual voice.

"Lower your voice. She's overheard enough."

"What are you so worried about? He's gone forever. She'll never lay eyes on him."

"You're sure of that? You know damn well they'll find each other if they know about each other. Nothing ever stopped Paul, and she's just like him."

"She could do worse."

"You're right. She could fall in love with him, and that's exactly what would happen the first moment she saw him. I don't want you giving her any more of your rotten clues."

"It won't do any good. If you didn't want her wondering about her father you should have told her he was dead."

"I've never lied to her."

"Then why are you so afraid of telling her the real truth?"

"There's a curse on the Christophers, that's why."

"That's horseshit. They've just had a little bad luck."

"Is that what you call disappearance and murder and prison generation after generation? I want Zarah to be happy, that's all. I want her to be free. I want her not to be a Christopher. Just keep your mouth shut about Paul. I don't know why you came here. I don't know why I don't throw you out."

"Why don't you?"

Cathy, who had been staring furiously into Wolkowicz's eyes until now, averted her gaze.

"Because then you *would* tell her."

"Okay, from now on I'll keep it impersonal," Wolkowicz said.

"But it won't do any good. She's already in love with him, thanks to you."

Wolkowicz kept his word, as he always did in unimportant matters, but it was impossible to keep Zarah off the subject that fascinated her. She spent as much time as possible with Wolkowicz, asking questions.

"Why is my father in prison?" she asked.

"I told you," Wolkowicz said. "His best friend did it."

"I don't mean that. What crime was he charged with?"

"Espionage."

"You mean he's a spy."

"That's what the Chinese think. But they're wrong."

"Then he was never a spy."

"I didn't say that."

"Then he was a spy at one time?"

"Let me tell you something," Wolkowicz said. "You're asking questions that nobody should ever ask and nobody would ever answer. People lie. You can't just ask for the truth and expect other people to tell it to you. It's too valuable. You have to watch, listen, read, remember, put things together. You have to keep quiet. For example, look at that old guy."

Wolkowicz and Zarah had gone for a walk in the village in the late afternoon. The narrow streets, barely wide enough for two people to walk abreast, were half in shadow, half suffused in the dusty light of the sinking sun. There were no wheeled vehicles of any kind in the village, only donkeys with loads lashed to pack saddles. The man Barney was talking about was an old Ja'wabi in a white caftan and turban who walked ahead of them through the sparse crowd.

"That's Suleyman," Zarah said. "He's going to the mosque."

"Let's follow him."

"We're already following him."

"I mean like spies. You go ahead, keep him in sight. I'll fall back, like I'm not with you. Count your steps. When you've taken two hundred steps, stop. Do something natural, like go into a shop for a minute. As soon as you stop, I'll take over and you'll fall back. I'll follow him for two hundred steps, then stop and do something natural. Then you take over and I fall back again. Got it?"

Zarah's solemn face broke into a smile. "It's like a game."

"That's right. Remember everything he does and says while you're on his tail—everything. No detail is too small. You're going to have to report. We'll go back to the house separately and meet in the courtyard. Go."

They followed old Suleyman for twenty minutes as he loitered through the streets, greeting friends, buying spices in a spice shop, and finally sauntering into the mosque just as the *salat al-maghrib*, the sunset prayer, was being called by the muezzin. Zarah was in the lead position, and although Wolkowicz had not instructed her to do so, she walked on, as if she were headed for some other place and had no interest in the man she was following.

"I think you're a natural, kid," Wolkowicz told her when they joined up later in the courtyard of her mother's house. "Give me your report."

Zarah recited detail after detail: the names of the spices Suleyman had bought and what he had paid for them, the words he had spoken, the identities of the men and women he had greeted.

"Okay," Wolkowicz said. "Was there anything he *didn't* do that he should have done?"

Zarah thought. She did this quietly, without changing the calm expression on her small face.

"I don't think so," she said.

"What about just before he went into the mosque?"

"He was just walking along."

"Right. Picture the mosque. As you walk toward it, what do you see?"

"The minaret, the square, the tree, the door."

"What's right beside the door?"

"The fountain."

"Now think again What did the old guy fail to do before he went into the mosque?"

Zarah remembered, but she was reluctant to say what she had missed.

"I know you know," Wolkowicz said. "Spit it out."

Zarah said, "He didn't wash."

"Right," Wolkowicz said. "Wasn't he supposed to wash his hands, face, and feet before going inside to pray? Isn't every good Moslem supposed to do that? What's it called?"

"*Wudu.*"

"Why didn't he do his *wudu?*"

Zarah's face flushed slightly but she did not answer.

"You're holding out on me," Wolkowicz said. "What's the big secret?"

Zarah did not answer. Was she embarrassed to have missed this detail? Wolkowicz didn't think so; he thought there was another reason for her silence. But he pressed on as if he suspected nothing.

"There were half a dozen other old men inside the mosque," he said, "but the ground around the fountain was dry. No splashes. I guess they didn't perform their *wudu* either. Isn't that kind of funny?"

Zarah made no reply at all, not even a shrug or a smile.

"I have to go now," she said.

"Keep thinking about it," Wolkowicz said. "Why didn't they wash? Don't tell anybody else what we found out. Tomorrow I'll show you how to write with invisible ink."

7

AT PRAYER TIMES FOR THE NEXT FEW DAYS WOLKOWICZ DROPPED BY the mosque to observe the worshippers as they went inside. Only old men seemed to attend, and like Suleyman most neglected to perform their ablutions before entering. Once inside, their prayers were too faint to be heard. In the cool of the morning he read the books he had brought with him—Hubbard Christopher's *The Rose and the Lotus;* histories of the Berbers in French and English; The Jerusalem Bible in plain English translated directly from the even plainer Hebrew of the Old Testament; the Koran.

One morning while Zarah was at her lessons he went next door to call on Lla Kahina.

"I've got something for you," he said. "Remember this?"

Wolkowicz produced the novel, open to the frontispiece.

Lla Kahina glanced at the picture of Lori and herself without surprise. "Zaentz's painting," she said.

"Otto told me about the eyes. I didn't see it at first."

"Nobody did, until they *saw* it. Then they saw nothing else. It caused a sensation—it's all there, in Hubbard's book. Zaentz was very clever."

"So was Hubbard. Did you know he was writing everything down like that?"

"He had our permission," she said.

"You mean the three of you faked the whole book?"

"No, lived it. Everyone thought we were a *ménage à trois,* so we played a joke on them. Hubbard called it 'the Experiment.' Everyone was experimenting in Berlin in those days. One day Lori was criticizing Hubbard because one of the characters in a story he was writing did something foolish or stupid. He defended himself by saying, 'My characters do whatever they like. I can't control them.' Lori was annoyed—she could be very Prussian, very exclamatory, especially about art, and she truly believed that Hubbard was an artist. She said, 'But you *must* control them! Otherwise there is no art!' Hubbard said, 'I can't, unless I lie about them.' Lori said, 'But they don't exist!' Hubbard said, 'They exist, all right. All I do is make them visible when they come into my head. Did Meryem exist for you, or you for her, until you met? Did you foresee what's happened because you did meet? Would either of you be what you are now if you hadn't met?' And Lori said, 'My God, you're right, you must write about us. We'll be your characters.' That's how the Experiment began."

"So what did you do then?"

"We went around Berlin as usual, seeing people, doing things, making conversation, and Hubbard watched and listened and wrote it all down."

"You mean he spied on you."

"With our permission. Anyway, all writers are spies."

"Did he tell you what to do?"

"He made suggestions, but we did as we liked. He said we were just like his other characters, rebellious. But he had more control than he thought. We soon became possessed by the Experiment, more like the beings he was writing about, less like ourselves. Lori said the book should have been called ¿*Which is Which?*"

"How did you know what he was writing about?"

"He read it to us every day. What he wrote was never exactly what had happened."

"Was it close?"

"Very close, but not stenography. He used our real names, but he didn't write what he already knew about us, only what we did and said, and what that revealed. He could improve on our speech, simplify it or make it more eloquent, as long as he respected the meaning. Those were the rules of the Experiment. He was scrupulous about the rules."

"There's nothing about Paul in the book."

"No. He wasn't part of the Experiment. But he was there."

"He must have been very small."

"Five or six."

"So there were Nazis already."

"The book is full of them. So was Berlin."

Wolkowicz said, "In the book you play the part of a Jew."

"That was Hubbard. Lori told him the Nazis would think what he wrote was the truth. He published it anyway."

Wolkowicz reclaimed the book from her hand. "What about this?" he asked, then read aloud from a marked page:

"An Aryan followed the girls down the Kurfürstendamm and into the Adlon Hotel. While they had their tea and the string quartet played a song written for saxophones on violins, he stared at them with eyes the color of rainwater from a table where he sat all alone. They thought he had fallen for Lori, like for like, but no he had exotic tastes and then he came over and bowed CLICK! CLICK! and asked Meryem to dance. Meryem? Meryem? he said, making her foxtrot, that's a Jew name but you look like a nigger and smell like one. Delicious! The Aryan looked like a boy who tortures cats. His breath smelled of Black Forest cake. Why do you wear purple tassels? he asked. Because Yahweh commanded us always to wear them, Numbers 15:37, Meryem said. Commanded who? Heydrich said, Jewesses? Yes, Meryem said, I confess I am from the Lost Tribe of Israel. Count for me, are you counting? I am the great great great great great great

       great great great great great great

       great great great great great great

       great great great great great

How many is that? Seventeen, the Aryan said. Meryem continued,

       great great great great great great

       great great great great great.

How many is that? Eleven more, twenty-eight altogether, the Aryan said. That's not enough, Meryem said, but this lovely song will be over if I go on, anyway we've been lost since Solomon was chosen by Yahweh to ascend the throne of Israel after the death of David, three thousand years ago more or less, *that's* how Jewish I am, I am a hundred times the granddaughter of Joab, the commander of the armies of Israel and Judah and the conscience of the king. And you don't have any eyebrows or eyelashes. *Wie heißen Sie?* what's *your* name, Aryan? Heydrich! the Aryan replied, and I am going to lick those tears off your face before I'm done, you delicious little nigger!"

Wolkowicz closed the book. "Did you really dance with Heydrich? Did you really say those things to him?"

"Yes, but he wasn't the real Heydrich at that time," Lla Kahina said, "There was no SS yet."

"How about afterward?"

"Afterward he knew about the Experiment."

"And then what?"

"Then he was the real Heydrich."

8

EVEN BEFORE HE FOUND CATHY AND ZARAH, WOLKOWICZ SENSED that he had stumbled onto some great secret about Lla Kahina and the Ja'wabi. Ordinarily he would have watched and waited as his suspicions matured, but he had very littie time to waste. He had been out of touch with the Outfit for almost two weeks, and if he did not report his whereabouts and account for his movements soon, he would have to invent explanations. This was always dangerous; in his circumstances it might be fatal.

In the few days left to him, he made a head-on assault on Lla Kahina, calling on her every morning. He approached her through *The Rose and the Lotus*. "What did you mean," he asked, "when you told Heydrich that you were one hundred times the granddaughter of Joab?"

The two of them sat together beside a fountain in the shade of a dusty olive tree.

"Heydrich?" Lla Kahina said.

"In Hubbard's book."

"Ah, we're back to the Experiment. Did I tell Heydrich that?"

"The Meryem in the book did."

"It sounds like something she'd say," Lla Kahina said. "So what is the topic for today?"

"Joab."

"Why Joab?"

"Because of what Meryem said to Heydrich. I don't want to repeat old questions, but why did you say that?"

"Who knows if I even said it?" Lla Kahina said. "Hubbard wrote what we told him, not what actually happened. He was fascinated by anything having to do with Jews, and that's why you should be careful what you believe when you read his books."

"Why Jews? He was a New England Yankee. What did he know about Jews?"

"He saw what was coming. He knew it wasn't the first time something like this had happened. Jews had been slaughtered before. He wanted to protect his friends, save them, defend them against slander."

"Lori felt the same?"

"Stronger."

"She was a Prussian."

"I don't know why she felt as she did; it's just the way she was. She hated stupidity and the Nazis were stupid. She loved intelligence and talent and Jews were the brightest people in Berlin."

Wolkowicz produced his copy of *The Rose and the Lotus* from the pocket of his rumpled jacket. "Listen," he said:

"When the violins started to play again the Aryan approached, smiling in time to the music, and bowed to Meryem. May I have the honor, *gnädige Fräulein?* Oh, dear, I'm sorry, no thank you, Meryem said. The Aryan said, What! are you going to hold a little joke against me? It isn't the joke that disgusts me when it's held against me, Meryem said, you are too susceptible to niggers; *that* is what offends me, that your mind and body go their own ways, the one so noble and anti-Semitic and the other so beastly. The Aryan said, On the contrary my mind and body are one and the same, everybody will be like that in the new Germany; we are going to kill all the gods other people have brought into Germany, the one the Jews gave us and the one the Christians gave us, both of which came from the Romans who had lost their original gods and therefore their reason for being. We are going to go back to our own German gods, back into the wonderful unified nature of our ancestors who lived in harmony with the German forest. Meryem said, Then you should go to the Grunewald since you are all tree worshipers and rub up against a tree, *gnädiger Herr,* good afternoon. The Aryan escorted her to the table. Smiling brilliantly and shouting *Herr Ober! Schaumwein!* the Aryan sat down at the table and said, If you will not dance with me then you must talk to me, it will be a strictly intellectual conversation: What do you think about killing gods? Meryem said, We Jews have a lot of experience with that: When Yahweh chose the Hebrews as his people he caused nations to fall before us but he always insisted that we destroy the gods of our enemies, showing no pity, he was very particular about that. The *Schaumwein* came. Gallantly lifting his glass filled with the sweet sparkling piss he had ordered the Aryan said, *Prosit!* Who is this Yahweh? I've never heard of any god by that name. Meryem said, You will if you go around trying to kill gods. That's his specialty. My tribe slew dozens for him. The Aryan said, Wonderful! The Berbers will be our shock troops. Lori said, Look, he behaves with the joyous conviction of the hopelessly insane; they all do."

"What tribe was Meryem talking about?" Wolkowicz asked. "The Jerawa?"

Lla Kahina laughed, genuinely surprised by his knowledge. "You know about the Jerawa?"

"I've been reading about them in Ibn Khaldūn. They were Jews, and they beat the Arab army on the Al Meskyana River in A. D. 688."

"Quite correct," Lla Kahina said.

"What interested me was the leader of the Jerawa," Wolkowicz said. "She was a woman, a prophetess who could see into the future. Her name was Kahina, just like you."

"It's a well-known story," Lla Kahina said. "Kahina called herself Queen of the Maghrib until the Arabs came back with a bigger army and defeated her. She was beheaded and the whole tribe converted to Islam."

"The whole tribe? I heard that some didn't convert, that they split off from the others and wandered away into the desert."

Outside the walls of the house, the village was quiet. Because of the absence of machines and outsiders and the Prophet Mohammed's supposed prohibition on the lute, the harp, and the flute, this was a deeply quiet place altogether, the quietest Wolkowicz had ever known except for the Burmese jungle.

He took an orange from the plate, slit the skin with his fingernail, and smelled it. "I've been wondering," he said. "Do you think any of the Berbers are *still* Jews who just pretend to be Moslems?"

Lla Kahina watched his eyes for a moment before replying. "Anything is possible," she said.

"I read an interesting fact in one of the books about the Berbers.

All through the desert of the Maghrib, from Tunisia to the Atlas Mountains, inscriptions have been found, all saying the same thing: *'Up to here, I, Joab, son of Zeruiah, pursued the Philistines.'* "

"What language are these inscriptions written in?"

"Hebrew. What if some of the Philistines escaped to Africa, and suppose that Joab, great soldier and Philistine killer that he was, raised an army of Jews and took out after them to finish them off?"

"How could he do that if Solomon had him assassinated?"

"He couldn't. But the first book of Kings doesn't say that Solomon actually saw the body. He relied on the word of the assassin, who happened to be one of Joab's officers. What if he *wasn't* assassinated? What if Yahweh saved him at the last minute for this African operation and didn't tell Solomon? What if the inscriptions in the desert are factual? What if 'Joab' and 'Ja'wab' are two ways of writing the same name in two different languages?"

Lla Kahina gave him a long look. "What if they are?" she asked.

"Then it's a hell of a story," Wolkowicz said. "Because if any of Queen Kahina's Jerawa still survive, hidden somewhere in these mountains under another name, like Ja'wabi, then God Almighty entrusted them, and them alone, with a secret that they've kept for three thousand years."

T W O

1

WHEN MERYEM WAS A CHILD, THE JA'WABI STILL SPENT SUMMERS IN the mountains with their flocks and winters with their camels in the Sahara. They believed that they were the first people to know the camel. It had never been a wild animal, they said, but had been created to assist them in crossing the desert in pursuit of the Philistines, whom Yahweh had commanded them to destroy. Although they did not eat its flesh as the Arabs did, the Ja'wabi esteemed the camel in every other way. In winter it drank only every eight or ten days and subsisted on the thorns and wild artichokes it found in the desert. Its urine sobered the drunken. Its hair had a multitude of uses: when reduced to ashes it stopped the worst hemorrhages, and in its natural state could be spun and woven into clothes, tents, rugs, and other useful and beautiful objects; its oil was good for the skin. Camel's milk was always drunk when dates were eaten to counteract the urgent effect of the latter. Although difficult individuals occurred among camels, their character on the whole was admirable. The gelded male worked without complaint. The female, after being covered by the *faâl,* or stud, invariably fell deeply in love with him and never wanted to be separated from him.

"Yahweh has never made anything better than the camel," the Ja'wabi said, but they also loved horses. They said:

> Horses for pleasure
> Camels for the desert
> Sheep for Yahweh

196

When in the desert the tribe lived in tents, traveling continually from pasturage to pasturage on a long, loop-shaped route until, in the early spring when the ewes and she-camels were ready to give birth, they arrived at the foot of the Idáren Dráren again. On the outward journey, twelve camels, never more or fewer, were loaded with two large panniers containing about 250 pounds of salt each. These camels were *zouzâls,* or geldings, chosen for their exceptional docility and obedience. Because the Ja'wabi traveled with about one hundred camels, the twelve plodding geldings carrying the salt were hardly noticeable as long as they showed no signs of temperament. Their good behavior was important, because the salt was the real reason for the winter journey of the Ja'wabi. Their destination was a pair of oases in the Azouâd Timétrine called Oën and Laşter. These oases, each containing a spring and date trees, were located one day's journey apart.

Each year, on arriving at the northernmost oasis, the main body of the Ja'wabi set up camp while twelve men mounted on camels set out for the second oasis, leading the *zouzâls* by long leather reins. On arrival, just before sunset, they unloaded the baskets of salt and left them beside the spring. Then they returned to camp in darkness, navigating by the stars. The next morning, when they returned, the salt was gone, and in its place they invariably found twelve small bars of gold, each stamped with a thumbless hand on which the twelve finger joints were clearly etched, and the twenty-four empty panniers (arranged in two groups of twelve each, one on either side of the spring) in which the salt had been transported the year before.

This silent trade had been going on for hundreds of years. The Ja'wabi had never seen the people who took the salt and left the gold. They knew only two things about them: that the number twelve was significant to them, and that they did not wish to be seen. If fewer or more than twelve camel loads of salt were deposited, or if fewer or more than twelve Ja'wabi brought the salt to the oasis, the other people left it undisturbed and went away, taking their gold with them. Once or twice, in the remote past, young Ja'wabi men had concealed themselves in the dunes overlooking the oasis, hoping to catch a glimpse of the owners of the gold. In those years the baskets of salt had been left untouched.

The twelve bars of gold were always carried back to the Idáren Dráren scattered among the pack saddles of the twelve *zouzâls*

197

which had carried the salt to the oasis. Over the centuries the Ja'wabi had laid up a large treasure of the small gold bars. This gold was the reason for the tribe's survival. With it they had purchased land and built their village of Tifawt in the mountains; with it they armed themselves, bribed their enemies, paid their taxes, and educated their children. The gold was communal property, and any Ja'wabi could ask for some of it, or its equivalent in currency or goods, for any good reason. Such requests were never refused, but they were rare, because the tribe owned nearly everything in common, and its members almost never needed cash.

The place where the gold was kept was known only to one man and one woman in each generation; they passed the secret on to another of their sex before they died. It had never happened that both had died violently before passing on their knowledge of the treasury's whereabouts, but of course this was a possibility.

While alone in the Sahara, the Ja'wabi lived according to their proverbs, without regard to the scrutiny of others, without calls to prayer, without the mask of alien customs and religion. Religious occasions were observed by animal sacrifices, with sprinkling of blood and the animals being burned in a fire to the accompaniment of prayers before their flesh was eaten.

Every year the exchange of salt for gold was the occasion for celebration. Sheep were slaughtered and eaten, wine was drunk, the camels were given extra rations of grain. The twelve camels which had carried the salt, and were now carrying the gold bars, were given dates.

It was during this celebration, in the year when Meryem was six, that she saw her first pictures of the future. While her mother was combing and braiding her hair in preparation for the celebration, Meryem, while wide awake, had a dream in which one of the gold-bearing *zouzâls* was led away into the desert by a rat. She and her mother were alone, inside the tent with the flaps closed. Meryem described what she was seeing as it happened in her dream. Her mother went on combing.

"What did the rat say to the camel?" she asked.

"Nothing," Meryem replied. "He had the rein his mouth."

"Was the rat stealing the gold?"

"No, he wanted salt."

That night a tethered *zouzâl* carrying a bar of gold in its saddle did escape, and when it was found the next day, miles away from camp among the dunes, the rat which had set it free by chewing through its leather tether was still tugging the obedient *zouzâl* toward the horizon. The boys who recaptured the camel had to kill the rat with stones because it would not let go of the rein; the leather was delicious to the little creature because it was permeated with the salt of human sweat.

After this first experience of clairvoyance, Meryem frequently saw pictures of the future. Usually these were small glimpses of homely details—the color of a stranger's coat, something spilled, the sex of an unborn child. If the people in the pictures spoke, she heard what they said. These visions occurred more frequently, and the details were more clearly observed, when she was in the desert. Inside the walls of the village her powers were much weaker, though even there she could determine the sex and sometimes the character of unborn babies and make other useful predictions. She knew when storms were coming and when the French were marching over the mountains to collect taxes.

As she approached puberty Meryem began to see and hear scenes from the past, also—people she recognized as ancestors of the Ja'wabi moving through a different, greener desert with thousands of camels and horses and other animals; men slaughtering and burning goats and lambs and heifers in roaring fires on a snowy mountaintop she recognized as Tinzár; a tremendous storm in which the sky suddenly turned aubergine from horizon to horizon and was rent by lightning while hailstones as large as dates pelted people and animals, drawing blood and causing the livestock to stampede.

She said nothing about this vision. By this time Meryem's family took her phantasma for granted. Although no one in the tribe had possessed the gift of prophecy for a long time, there had been other seers among the Ja'wabi, and these had almost always been females. The tribe recognized the reappearance of the gift in Meryem as they would have acknowledged an inherited physical characteristic, as something to be expected from generation to generation. Very often, they knew, these visions did not last beyond childhood.

Then, just before her twelfth birthday, Meryem dreamed, while wide awake as usual, of a woman with blue tears tattooed on her cheeks who smeared honey over her breasts and told two young men, one of them a Berber and the other an Arab captured in battle, to eat the honey as if they were children suckling at her bosom. "Those who are fed from the same mother's breasts become brothers," the woman said. This was a firm belief among the Ja'wabi, whose women nursed each other's babies as a matter of course, in the conviction that it bound them, and therefore the tribe, together for life. Later in the same dream Meryem heard the same woman, who now seemed to be older, tell the two young men that she had a vision in which she saw her own severed head being handed over to the enemy.

The appearance of the woman with blue tears in Meryem's dreams produced an entirely different effect on her family and the rest of the tribe, because the older Ja'wabi recognized what she had seen as true episodes from the life of Queen Kahina.

Meryem's dream was correct in all the essential details: After the battle on the Meskyana River Kahina had adopted a captured Arab warrior named Khaled, telling him, "You are the bravest and most handsome man I have ever seen." She had bonded her adopted son to her natural son by suckling them with honey (the Arabs said oil and barley flour) as in Meryem's dream. It was also known that five years later, on the eve of the battle in which Kahina's army was defeated by the Arabs, the queen had a vision of her own severed head being handed over to the victorious enemy. "Take care of the future," she told her sons, "for I am as good as dead." Khaled, the adopted son, urged her to flee into the desert without giving battle, but she refused; evidently she loved him too much to suspect (as the Ja'wabi had always believed) that he was still an Arab at heart, still a Moslem, and that he had betrayed her plans and given the order of battle to the enemy. As she had foreseen, she was killed and decapitated the next day at a place called Bir el Kahina, Kahina's Well. Her sons converted to Islam and were placed in command of twelve thousand horsemen charged with the duty of converting the Berbers by the sword.

After the death of Kahina the Ja'wabi had separated themselves from the Jerawa forever and begun to live apart from all other Berbers and Arabs. Although the existence of Kahina and the details of her battles with the Arab armies were recorded in Arab histories, the Ja'wabi regarded the person of Kahina and her deeds as belonging to their own secret lore.

Because Meryem was not yet twelve years and one day old, the age at which Ja'wabi girls became women according to law, and because the Ja'wabi were strictly forbidden to utter any detail of the tribe's history aloud, even to one another, except during secret coming-of-age ceremonies in which boys and girls were taken into the mountains or the desert by a single adult and told who and what they really were, it was impossible that she could have known about Kahina's existence before it was revealed to her in a vision.

2

WHEN MERYEM CAME OF AGE A FEW WEEKS AFTER HER DREAM ABOUT Kahina, an old woman called Ashbeah took her into the desert, and told her who the Ja'wabi were, and how Joab had led them out of Israel in pursuit of the Philistines. According to Ashbeah, Joab was King David's nephew, the son of David's older sister Zeruiah and the commander of the combined armies of Israel, which numbered eight hundred thousand men, and of Judah, numbering five hundred thousand.

Joab was David's right arm. All his life he had carried out the king's hidden wishes—arranging to let the enemy kill Uriah, Bathsheba's husband, so that he would not learn that his beautiful wife was pregnant by the king; assassinating Abner and Amasa, the commanders of the two armies, so that these armies, and therefore the Kingdoms of Israel and Judah, could be combined into one; killing the king's rebellious son Absalom by thrusting three darts into his heart with his own hand; and permitting David to deny to the world, with tears in his eyes, that he wanted these things to happen.

On returning to the city after the victory over Absalom's army, the soldiers found David inside his palace, weeping and crying, "My son Absalom! Oh, Absalom my son, my son!" With the dirt of battle still upon him, Joab went inside to the king and said, "Today you have made all your servants feel ashamed—today, when they have saved your life, the lives of your sons and daughters, the lives of your wives and of your concubines!—because you love those who hate you and hate those who love you. Today you have made it plain that commanders and soldiers mean nothing to you—for today I can see that you would be content if we were all dead, provided that Absalom was alive! Now get up, come out and reassure your soldiers; for if you do not come out, I swear by Yahweh, not one man will stay with you tonight; and this will be a worse misfortune for you than anything that has happened to you from your youth until now!" King David did as Joab said.

More than any other man, Joab knew the sins, weaknesses, and secrets of the king, because he had taken them upon himself. When David lay dying with the most beautiful girl in Israel beside him in his bed to keep him warm, he told his son Solomon, child of Bathsheba, that he must kill Joab if he wished to rule Israel and Judah without carrying the burden of Joab's sins. "You will be wise," David told Solomon, "not to let his gray head go down to Sheol [the grave] in peace."

So when he became king after his father's death, Solomon sent another famous champion, Benaiah of Kabzeel, son of Jehoiada, to kill Joab. Knowing Solomon's intentions, Joab had taken sanctuary in the Tent of Yahweh. Benaiah knew Joab well. He was a hero of the wars against the Philistines, and he had served as a member of the Thirty, King David's bodyguard, under the command of Joab's brother Abishai. Benaiah found Joab clinging to the horns of the altar. He refused to come outside away from the protection of Yahweh, saying, "Kill me here." But Benaiah, knowing of the great services Joab had rendered to Yahweh, was afraid to execute Solomon's death warrant.

But Solomon sent Benaiah back to the Tent of Yahweh, saying, "Strike him down and bury him, and so rid me and my family of the innocent blood which Joab has shed . . . without my father David's knowledge. May the blood come down on the head of Joab and his descendants forever, but may David, his descendants, his dynasty, his throne have peace forever from Yahweh."

Benaiah knew that he would be rewarded for killing Joab by being named commander of the army in his place. Yet he loved Joab because of his bravery, because of his obedience to Yahweh which had always been greater than his loyalty to David, and because he had forced the king to acknowledge his debt to the army.

Inside the Tent of Yahweh, Joab said to Benaiah who had been sent by Solomon to murder him, "The army knows the truth about David and Solomon, whose mother Bathsheba has put him on the throne, and if you kill me in the name of the king's lies, they will not follow you."

Benaiah knew that this was so. "Then what am I to do?" he asked.

"Ask Yahweh," Joab replied, handing him *urim* and *thummim*, the dice cast by the priests when prophesying.

Benaiah took the dice, saying, "Yahweh, God of Israel, if I am to kill Joab give *urim*, but if I am to let him go, give *thummim*."

Joab seized his hand before he could cast the dice and said, "I am telling you, Yahweh, that if you give *thummim*, I will pursue the Philistines who have sailed away in ships and kill them all and utterly destroy their temples, as you commanded Joshua to do and he failed to do. But I will kill them all and destroy their god. Now throw."

Benaiah threw, and it was *thummim*. Joab picked up the dice and placed them in his girdle. He carried them on his person for the remainder of his life.

To make the king think that Joab was dead as he had ordered, Benaiah wrapped him in a shroud stained with the blood of a goat and carried him to his home in the desert. But instead of burying him, as Benaiah reported to Solomon, he placed him at the head of an army composed entirely of men of the tribe of Judah, descendants of Joab's ancestor Caleb, whom Yahweh had sent with Joshua and ten others to spy out the land of Canaan, and who, alone among the twelve spies, had obeyed Yahweh completely, and to whom, in reward for his steadfastness, Yahweh afterward gave the land of Canaan.

Joab led this army with its camels, horses, flocks and herds, wives, children, and slaves (but no priests because there were no descendants of Aaron among them) into Sinai and then across Egypt and Libya, killing Philistines where he found them, until he reached the Idáren Dráren, where the Philistines had set up an altar on a hilltop to their god Baal and his companion the bull.

As the Ja'wabi attacked, a curtain of darkness came over the mountains and advanced across the plain with the Ja'wabi in sunshine on one side of the curtain and the Philistines in darkness on the other. The sky turned black, lightning flashed, and hailstones fell on the Philistines like missiles from a multitude of slingers. The horses and camels of the Philistines were terrified and ran away, but those of the Ja'wabi, basking in sunshine, were calm and steady. When the hail ceased to fall Joab and his army charged with spear and sword and destroyed the Philistines to the last man, woman, child, and animal. Then they demolished the temple of Baal as Yahweh had instructed Moses: "You must completely destroy all the places where the nations you dispossess have served their gods, on high mountains, on hills, under any spreading tree; you must tear down their altars, smash their sacred stones, burn their sacred poles, hack to bits the statues of their gods and obliterate their name from that place."

As they completed this work of destruction on behalf of Yahweh, the clouds rolled away from the mountaintops, revealing the snowy peak the Ja'wabi called Tinzár. Believing this mountain to be the highest place in the world, the Ja'wabi climbed to its summit and erected an altar to Yahweh, sacrificing and burning lambs, kids, and young bulls.

Joab's escape from Solomon and his destruction of the Philistines is not recorded in the Bible. Because Joab left Palestine, as the Ja'wabi believed, before the history of the Kings of Judah and Israel was written, the tribe knew what they knew about Saul and David and Solomon from the stories Joab himself had told them. As to the events described in Genesis, Exodus, Leviticus, Numbers, Deuteronomy, and Joshua, these were the life stories of the Ja'wabi's own families, as familiar to them as the gossip of their camps or their own genealogy, which they kept with great scrupulosity according to Yahweh's orders. They believed in the authenticity of what their ancestors had known before they left the Promised Land, and in nothing that had been recorded afterward: in their eyes, the Bible after the Book of Joshua was the work of priests relying on hearsay—or, worse, on King Solomon's version of events.

Even though they were far from Israel with many other gods between them and Yahweh, the Ja'wabi kept the main provisions of his law. They circumcised their male children on the eighth day, as Yahweh had commanded Abraham, offered animal sacrifices as he had instructed Moses, and in general followed the rules of sanitation and quarantine he had dictated to Moses. It was impossible for a people living in the desert as an army, as the Ja'wabi had done while pursuing the Philistines across North Africa and fighting other enemies for many generations afterward, to carry out Yahweh's wishes in every particular.

In his encounters with Moses after he led the Israelites out of Egypt, Yahweh had issued closely detailed instructions on almost every conceivable subject from the design of altars, sanctuaries, and priestly vestments to ecclesiastical law ("if a priest's daughter profanes herself by prostitution she . . . will be burnt alive") to common law ("if, when two men are fighting, the wife of one intervenes to protect her husband from the other's blows by reaching out and seizing the other by his private parts, you must cut off her hand and show no pity") to etiquette ("you will stand up in the presence of gray hair").

When Joab died, soon after his last victory of the Philistines, he bequeathed the dice to the Ja'wabi, instructing them to consult them whenever a question of life and death arose for the tribe. Thereafter they tested Yahweh's assent to all such decisions by casting the dice that Joab had taken from the Tent of Yahweh, calling out, "Yahweh, God of Israel, if you wish us to do thus, give *urim,* but if you wish us to do so, give *thummim."* They had found the oases where they traded salt and gold by casting dice: after they wandered away from the main body of Kahina's people after the defeat of her army, the dice told them which direction to take and which oasis to camp upon. The salt had been left behind by mistake, and when men went to fetch it after casting the dice, they found the gold in its place. The dice were ignored at the tribe's peril.

Apart from the influence he continued to exercise over the dice, the Ja'wabi had heard nothing from Yahweh for at least a hundred generations. This did not surprise them. He had ignored them for centuries in the past. It never crossed their minds that Joab himself might have seen Yahweh after he died: They had no concept of an afterlife in which God conversed with the spirits of the dead. They thought that Yahweh could not know what had happened unless the living told him what had happened; they thought it possible that he would never know, because he was so far away and there were so many other gods between them and him.

They had no idea that this moody god who had appeared from nowhere and chosen Israel as his people because all other peoples already had gods of their own could travel as far as they had traveled, much less that he was everywhere. Nor did they believe that they could return to Israel. How could they do so without revealing their secret? Joab himself had asked the dice if they might return to their own country after the victory over the Philistines and Yahweh had given *urim,* which always meant no.

205

THE JA'WABI SAID, "DOGS COLLECT TAXES, SHEEP PAY, WOLVES REFUSE."
They were wolves. Until the appearance of the French in the
Idáren Dráren in the late nineteenth century, they paid no taxes.
No other tribe of Berbers was ever strong enough to subdue them,
and neither the Romans after the destruction of Carthage nor the
Vandals after the fall of Rome ever penetrated the Idáren Dráren.
After the defeat of Kahina the Ja'wabi lived in such isolation, and
were thought to be so poor, that Arab tax collectors seldom ap-
proached them. When they tried to do so, they were attacked in
the passes. Few outsiders ever reached Tifawt. Those who did came
in peace and discovered what seemed on the surface to be a devout
Moslem community. As soon as visitors left, of course, the charade
ceased and the Ja'wabi went back to the practice of primitive
Judaism.

Their isolation ended in the early years of the twentieth century
when the French, who had already occupied Algeria and slaughtered or dispossessed most of the population of Casablanca, were
attempting to subdue the remainder of the Maghrib. Like the
Ja'wabi before them, and the Philistines before the Ja'wabi, they
recognized the strategic importance of Tifawt, which commanded
the marches to the only two passes through the high mountains.
Logic dictated that this objective must be taken.

The French surprised the Ja'wabi by approaching Tifawt through
the desert in winter, when most of the tribe was encamped far away
in the Sahara. The village was garrisoned by a force of fifty men, of
whom twenty were youths under eighteen. At the age of sixteen
every Ja'wabi male was given the single-shot rifle, sword, and
dagger he would carry on his person until he was sixty, and the
shock troops of the tribe, called Ibal Iden ("Another Spirit"), after
Yahweh's description of his faithful servant Caleb, were always
teenagers. Joab himself had laid down the rule that soldiers chosen
for the most dangerous missions must be nineteen or younger;
twenty was too old.

The French attacking force numbered 219 riflemen, or one somewhat understrength company of infantry, supported by a single
75mm. rapid-firing gun drawn by a team of four horses. To the
Ja'wabi, these odds of slightly more than four to one seemed
excellent. "If you live according to my laws," Yahweh had told

Moses on Mount Sinai, ". . . you will pursue your enemies and they will fall before your sword; five of you pursuing a hundred of them, one hundred pursuing ten thousand." Tifawt had been built as a fortress, with parapeted stone walls twenty feet high and two thick gates of oak with an iron portcullis gate in between. Tunnels running beneath the walls in all four directions made it possible for the defenders to pass beneath an attacking force and fall upon it from the rear. The minaret made an excellent observation post, commanding a view of the country for several miles around.

Although the Ja'wabi knew little about the French, it was evident that the French knew something about them. Immediately after their arrival they unlimbered their field gun and wheeled it into position with the muzzle pointing directly at the gates of Tifawt. To the sound of bugle calls, the infantry fixed bayonets and deployed into three sections. Because it was midafternoon and strangers were present, the muezzin called out the *salat al-asr* as a party of Frenchmen approached the walls under a white flag. Speaking to the Ja'wabi through an Arab interpreter, they demanded the immediate surrender of the town and its formal submission to French authority. One of the Ibal Iden shot the Arab through the heart as soon as the words were out of his mouth.

Without further warning, the French fired three rounds from the field gun, shattering the heavy timbers of the outer gate. They then launched a bayonet charge by one platoon of infantry while a second scaled the opposite wall with ropes and ladders. The Ja'wabi let the French advance through the wreckage of the main gate to the inner gate, then dropped the portcullis behind them. Snipers concealed on the parapet fired into this cage, methodically slaughtering the men trapped inside while other defenders on the opposite wall peppered the scaling party with rifle fire.

Meanwhile twenty Ibal Iden shock troops ran through a tunnel and emerged behind the French gun position. Rising up out of the ground, they overwhelmed the crew and turned the gun on the French reserve of about a hundred men, which was drawn up in two compact ranks a few hundred paces away. The entire Ja'wabi garrison thereupon went through the tunnels and surrounded the remnants of the French force, which had already suffered heavy losses as a result of being shelled by the captured field gun, and destroyed it in a withering crossfire. All 219 of the enemy died. The French officer in command, realizing the hopelessness of his situation, committed suicide where he stood. The Ja'wabi lost three men killed and five wounded.

Despite these favorable results, it was clear to the Ja'wabi that they had been fortunate to win the battle. The arms employed by the French—their powerful field gun and their 8mm. Lebel repeating rifles—were far superior to their own weapons or any others they had seen before. Clearly a people so well equipped for war had no other important purpose besides war. They would come back to fight again.

This happened in an unexpected way. Between the Idáren Dráren and the Sahara lies a range of low, barren mountains. The only way through this obstacle for 100 miles in either direction is a narrow pass that forms the knot in the noose-like route followed by the Ja'wabi on their annual trek into the desert. This gap in the rock is nowhere more than five paces wide, and in some places it is so narrow that its walls, made up of many-colored marbles, have been polished by the rubbing of pack saddles.

It was here, almost exactly one year after the massacre at Tifawt, that the French fought their second battle with the Ja'wabi. The tribe was traveling that year with about 500 camels, together with several thousand sheep and goats. Their own numbers were 554, of whom 300 were men of fighting age, including fifty Ibal Iden. The French were encamped on the other side of the gap with three companies of infantry, just under 750 men, and three field guns. Two of these were somewhat different in design from the gun they had used at Tifawt; it was difficult to tell because they were draped with canvas. These facts about the enemy were discovered by a party of Ibal Iden who were sent ahead of the main party to spy out the gap. The Ja'wabi had been attacked at this natural military position a number of times in their history, and they always sent a reconnaissance party ahead to make sure it was clear.

After hearing the report of the spies, the Ja'wabi consulted the dice, asking whether to attack the French or avoid battle by going around the end of the mountain range, a journey requiring six extra weeks. Yahweh's answer was *thummim*—attack. The Ja'wabi were not so confident in the protection of their absent god as to think that they could force the gap in the mountains when it was so heavily defended with such excellent weapons as those possessed by the French. They knew they would have to take it by surprise and subterfuge. Their plan of attack was simple: the Ibal Iden would climb over the mountains, infiltrate the camp, capture the guns and turn them on the French as before, driving the enemy toward the gap; the main body of Ja'wabi would ambush and slaughter the enemy there.

Leaving the rest of the tribe encamped in the desert, the Ja'wabi fighting men advanced at night toward the gap. The approach was overgrown with scrubby desert bushes, and during the day the Ja'wabi scattered, each man burying himself in the sand in the shade of one of these shrubs. They ate bread, dates, and curds, and drank a little water.

On the fourth night they climbed the mountain above the French camp. A hundred fires burned in the darkness below, silhouetting row on row of identical white military tents. There were no enemy lookouts on the mountaintop, and the French had no dogs to warn them of the approach of an enemy. Their camp was guarded instead by men who marched along its perimeter, shouting words of encouragement to each other in the darkness.

It was a moonless night. The Ibal Iden descended the mountain and crawled on their bellies into the sleeping camp. Their objective was the battery of guns, which they planned to capture and turn against the enemy as before. The remaining Ja'wabi, divided into two parties, approached in a pincer movement. At the explosion of the first round from the captured guns, they would hit the enemy from two sides, firing the captured rifles for their shock effect, then closing with sword and bayonet.

When the Ibal Iden reached the guns, they found that they were not guns at all but constructions of wood made to resemble guns. They immediately slashed the canvas of the nearest tents and found them empty. The French sentries had stopped shouting, and a peculiar silence enveloped the encampment. Realizing that they had walked into a trap, the Ibal Iden barked like dogs, the warning signal to the others, and prepared to die.

At this moment a tremendous fusillade erupted on two sides of them, and the last thing any of the lost boys of the Ibal Iden saw against the screen of the darkness was the flowery light created by the muzzle flashes of four hundred massed French rifles. Some of the older men on the other side of the mountain lived long enough to smell the dervishes of burnt cordite that swept across the desert floor, but none survived. The French troops who died to the last man before Tifawt had been members of this battalion.

4

APART FROM KILLING ALL BUT SIXTY OF THEIR MEN, DISARMING THE rest, and levying a fine of 500 camels and 3,000 sheep against the tribe, the French inflicted no further punishment on the Ja'wabi except for insisting that they pay taxes and learn French.

Without men and camels it was impossible to travel through the desert, so the silent trade of the twin oases ceased, and the tribe lived at Tifawt the whole year round. French officials, and later on journalists, anthropologists, and adventurous tourists began to visit the village. Because the Ja'wabi had made themselves interesting through their brilliant victory over a people that considered itself superior to all others not only in its modern inventions but also in its immemorial genes, they were closely questioned by nearly every French person who arrived among them. The Ja'wabi were unused to questions: there was little need for them within the tribe because they all knew the same things. Nevertheless they found a way to respond:

—*What is your creation myth? (God made the world.)*
—*How long have you lived in the desert? (Since God made the world.)*
—*Why do you love your camels so much? (Because God made them.)*
—*Why did you massacre the French so cruelly? (God sends us our enemies.)*
—*What will you do with so few men and so many women? (Make more men with God's help.)*

Outsiders never stayed more than a few days because the Ja'wabi offered them no hospitality, but they invariably went away satisfied and happy. More came in their place, asking the same questions, receiving the same answers, and departing with the same reassuring sense of having banality reconfirmed. The Ja'wabi never asked the French questions about themselves because everything interesting about them—their guns, their tribal pride, their amazing innocence—was obvious.

210

From the start, the French assumed that the Ja'wabi were devout servants of Allah. No other explanation occurred to them. Why would they have fought so fearlessly against such impossible odds if they did not expect to ascend immediately as martyrs into al-Jannah, the Garden of Delight, where they would enjoy, as the Holy Koran promises,

> Wide-eyed houris
> as the likeness of hidden pearls
> . . . Spotless virgins,
> chastely amorous.

As the Ja'wabi quickly discovered, this idea of post mortem sexual pleasure appealed deeply to the French, some of whom had acquired a theoretical knowledge of the Koran and Islamic religious practice that was far more detailed than that of any Ja'wabi—or, for that matter, of most genuine Moslems. The French seemed to think that it was possible to know everything by memorizing words. It was this lust for the superficial that made them, in the estimation of the Ja'wabi, so mad and so dangerous. Of the French, the Ja'wabi said, "They beat the camel to death in order to inhale the dust of its coat."

Before the French came, the muezzin sang in Tifawt only when there were strangers inside the gate. After the two massacres, the French removed the gates, making it impossible to know whether outsiders were present. Thereafter the Ja'wabi caused the call to prayer to be sung five times a day and assigned old men the duty of answering the muezzin's call so that the French would hear and see what they expected.

The Ja'wabi did not ask the dice if Yahweh approved of this subterfuge; it was clear for at least two reasons that the only possible answer was *thummim*. First, the French followed a policy of exaggerated respect for Moslem holy places. They had refused to fire on the minaret during the battle of Tifawt even when snipers concealed within it were killing French soldiers. After taking possession of the Ja'wabi stronghold they searched the mosque from top to bottom to make certain there were no arms concealed there, but never entered it again in the brief time, a little more than a century, that they controlled the Idáren Dráren. This bizarre *politesse* had the practical effect of giving the Ja'wabi (who would, of course, have razed every cathedral in France if the position had been reversed) an excellent safe house.

Second, it did not take the Ja'wabi long to realize that many of the Frenchmen they encountered loved Moslems because both hated Jews. They were always talking about a Jew called Dreyfus who had betrayed France. This man, an army officer, was an alien, they said; a danger to his comrades even if he had not turned out to be a spy: The Ja'wabi, of all people, would understand that.

The French learned Arab taunts: "Fleeing and even abandoning their women! Jews! Sons of Jews! May God curse them!" And Arab proverbs: "Only the Jewess surpasses Satan in malice"; "The Jew always comes into the house of the faithful with the money bag or the medicine bottle in his hand." When wishing to establish an atmosphere of camaraderie during their visits to Tifawt, they quoted these sayings.

The Ja'wabi listened with grave attention. They said, "Twist the horse's lip with a cord called hatred and he will not notice what is happening underneath his tail."

—*Has there ever been a traitor among the Ja'wabi? (God has spared us that.)*

THREE

1

SEBASTIAN LAUX APPEARED IN TIFAWT WHEN MERYEM WAS SIXTEEN years old. He was twenty, a small, neatly made young man with the curly head of a Botticelli cherub. Days before he arrived at the gates of the village, riding a pretty black mare and wearing a flat-brimmed U.S. Cavalry hat with a pointed crown, Meryem caught glimpses of him in her mind as he rode dreamily, all alone, among the snow-dusted russet crags and pied rocks of the Idáren Dráren, reciting verses in a language she could not understand. Because she knew exactly when he would arrive at the village gates, she was the first to see him in person.

Sebastian, still in the saddle, looked down into her solemn face and said, in French, "I had a feeling as I rode through your beautiful mountains these past few days that someone was watching me. I hope, Mademoiselle, that it was you." He smiled merrily and opened his clear brown eyes very wide, as if inviting her to read his thoughts. She fell in love with him on the spot.

"But he's French," her mother said, when Meryem told her of her feelings a few moments later.

"No," Meryem said. "He's from some other place, not France."

"What difference does that make? He's uncircumcised. He might as well be one of them—or even an Arab."

"No. I know him."

"From where?"

"From the past. We owe each other something, I don't know what. Perhaps he was killed before we could marry."

Dimya, Meryem's mother, did not like this kind of talk. She did not believe in ghosts; the dead were dead—for everybody except

Meryem. More and more, since the massacre of the Ja'wabi by the French, the girl encountered people in her dreams whom she thought she had known, or whom someone else in the tribe had known, in an earlier life. Nearly always they had unfinished business from their former existence—an unpaid debt, an uncompleted revenge, an unconceived child. But this was the first time Meryem had encountered a living person whom she thought she recognized as a wanderer from the distant past.

"Whatever he may have been before," her mother said, "remember what he is now."

"He's the same now as he was before, one of us. He knows it too."

She asked Sebastian to go riding with her the next morning. They rode into the desert, he on his tired black mare, Meryem on a nervous gray Barb, along the trail that led from Tifawt to the mountains. They started before dawn, and on their way, as the first red thread of dawn appeared behind them, they heard the muezzin calling the *salat as-subh*. Sebastian turned his mount toward the voice.

"Should we stop?" he asked.

"If you want to see the sunrise."

"You don't wish to pray?"

Meryem remained silent. After a moment the strip of ruby light along the flat eastern horizon was replaced by the blinding whiteness of the sun's rim, and then the entire orb catapulted out of the Sahara. It was the month of June; they felt the heat of it at once. The village lay below them, mica walls flashing, in a valley watered by a narrow river. In the other direction the snowy summit of Tinzár caught the light. Fruit trees and crops grew in bright red dirt on the terraced hillsides in between.

They ate their breakfast—fruit and a loaf of flat brown bread smeared with honey—under the broad fronds of a date palm.

"How did your people ever find such a wonderful place?" Sebastian asked.

"They found this date tree after a big battle, looked down and saw the river, so they stayed." Meryem replied.

"When was that?"

"Long ago."

"Where does the river come from?"

"You already know. You rode beside it coming down. Six rivers rise on Tinzár—the Dra'a, the Sús, the Um-er-Rabía, the Sebú, the Mulwíya, and the Ghír. All but this one flow into the desert and vanish in the sands."

"Then I chose the right one to follow."

"Why did you choose it?"

"I wanted to go to the strangest place on Earth."

Without being asked, he told her that he was an American, from New York, that he was studying at Yale College, that he had taken leave of absence for a term in order to be alone, in a strange place, to think. He had intended to ride across the steppes on a pony to Port Arthur and then take a ship home, but in Paris he had read a newspaper article about the Ja'wabi and changed his mind.

The look she gave him was like a kiss, or the memory of a kiss. He was overwhelmed by sexual desire. *My God,* he thought, *something irreversible is happening to my mind and body.*

"It was very odd," he said, "but when I saw the Idáren Dráren, I felt that I'd seen it before. It was red, like Mars, but very, very familiar. Now I think I've seen everything before. Even you. I think you *were* watching me in the mountains. Were you?"

"Were you shouting out poetry as you rode?"

"As a matter of fact, yes."

"Then I was the one. I didn't understand the words."

Sebastian smiled; he liked this sort of wordplay. "It was always the same poem," he said:

> "She lived unknown, and few could know
> When Lucy ceased to be;
> But she is in her grave, and, oh,
> The difference to me!"

Sebastian translated it into French. "It's Wordsworth," he said. The name meant nothing to Meryem, who had memorized long passages from Molière and Victor Hugo in school but had never heard of a poet who was not French.

"Riding through the mountains," Sebastian said, "I had this feeling that I, too, had loved a girl who died too soon. Silly, because I never did, but I would have sworn otherwise if anyone had come along and asked me."

They made no secret of their morning rendezvouses. Nevertheless the French tax collector, *sous-préfet,* and schoolteacher, who lived in French houses outside the walls of the village, knew all about them and were scandalized. They warned Sebastian that the Ja'wabi were still savages, that they guarded their women jealously, that Meryem was the most beautiful girl in the tribe.

"That I can easily believe," Sebastian said. "But we're doing no one any harm."

"It's dangerous, what you are doing," they said. "We tell you as fellow Christians: if you touch this girl, the Ja'wabi will cut your throat. First they will cut other things."

"Why would I touch her?" Sebastian asked. He was a virgin and so was Meryem; as he understood the world from the viewpoint of an American gentleman, only marriage could change that.

The French gave him knowing glances. If he chose to lie, how could they help him? In any other place they would not have bothered with him, he wore a ridiculous hat, he wasn't even French, but here, in the heart of Islam, they were obligated to him by religion and, loosely speaking, by race.

"Remember," the French said, each one of them in the same words but at different times, as if delivering a message from an all-wise higher authority, "you must ride back through the mountains alone. It can be very dangerous if you make enemies."

"I'll remember," Sebastian said.

In fact there was no one left among the Ja'wabi to be jealous of Meryem. In any other time, some young man of the tribe would have been in love with her, but there were few young men, and these knew little about jealousy. After the massacre of the Ja'wabi men by the French, females of childbearing age outnumbered potent males by more than four to one.

Because men could be kidnapped or even lost in the desert for years and still survive, and because there was no possibility of proving that a man who disappeared was dead because his corpse would invariably be devoured overnight by wild animals, no Ja'wabi woman regarded herself as a widow unless she had seen her husband's lifeless body. Most were in this position after the second battle with the French. Anxious to march to the Ja'wabi encampment and take the remainder of the tribe into military custody, the French left the enemy dead where they lay. Birds gathered at once for the feast, and at nightfall swarms of rodents, jackals, and hyenas, and even a few lions and leopards, descended on the killing ground. These creatures devoured the flesh of the fallen, scattering bones and skulls, which were dragged away by jackals or pulverized where they lay by hyenas for the marrow and brains they contained.

In these circumstances, no Ja'wabi widow could consider herself a widow. Because the threat to the tribe's survival was plain, the Ja'wabi submitted the question to the dice, saying, "If the women should remain widows, give *urim,* but if they should take other husbands, give *thummim.*" The answer was *thummim.* Concubinage was reintroduced after a lapse of several centuries, and within a short time most of the women had moved in with the surviving men as second and third wives, not because they required protection or food—the tribe would have provided these things in any case—but because they wanted children. The French, naturally, mistook the Ja'wabi practice of keeping multiple wives as another sign of Moslem orthodoxy.

"What do you do when you ride into the desert with this Gentile?" Dimya asked Meryem after Sebastian had been at Tifawt for a fortnight.

"We eat breakfast together under the date tree and talk."

"What do you *want* to do?"

"Make love."

"How badly?"

"Very badly."

"Him too?"

"Yes, but he never suggests it."

"Do you know what's going to happen?"

"I see myself alone. Then with him. Then alone."

"In the Idáren Dráren?"

"Not always. Sometimes I don't recognize the places where we're together."

2

SEBASTIAN RODE AWAY AT THE END OF SUMMER, THINKING THAT HE would never see Meryem again. On his first day in the Idáren Dráren, he watched a storm break around the summit of Tinzár. A line of clouds approached from the west and collided with the mountain. Blue-white lightning flickered among the crags, and then the rain fell in torrents.

Meryem had predicted this; she had seen it in a dream. Her

circumstantial descriptions of her daydreams seemed to him to be a charming kind of flirtation. Everything about her was charming—her small melancholy face, her great green eyes in which he saw her unmistakable love for him, her dark rippling hair which she uncovered and let fly when they were riding in the desert, her thrilling husky voice, her amazing intelligence. But he did not really believe that Meryem had seen him in her mind's eye as she said she did. How could he believe it? He was the descendant of five generations of bankers and Yale men who excelled in science and arithmetic; no one he knew or his family knew had ever had a vision. He could hardly believe that Meryem herself was real. Sometimes, after a gallop, he had seen her heart beating in her breast and heard his own heart thudding too. Nothing more than this had happened between them; it was inconceivable to Sebastian that it should; they had never so much as kissed.

Meryem had named his mare Tili, meaning "darkness" in Berber; she had called him Seba instead of Sebastian because she said Sebastian was not the name he had before. "What do you mean, 'before'?" he asked her. "The last time," she replied without further explanation—more chaste flirtation.

"What about after?"

"I will find you," she had said.

Now, half an hour after watching the cloudburst on Tinzár, Sebastian heard a distant wind accompanied by what sounded like the grinding of enormous teeth. He stopped his black mare in the middle of the stream to listen. The animal whinnied, bucked, and reared, hooves slithering over the stones in the stream bed. Although he was an excellent horseman, Sebastian could not hold her. She bolted out of the water and plunged up the bank. Once on dry ground she whirled and looked in the direction of the sound, ears pricked, hide shivering.

The sound grew progressively louder. Sebastian followed the mare's gaze and found himself staring at a narrow cleft in the rock through which the little river flowed. The windy sigh had changed into a roar; the grinding sound Sebastian had heard before now seemed to be enclosed within a louder din. Then a wall of water ten or twelve feet high appeared in the cleft. An instant later it burst through the fissure in a turbulent henna flood. As it swept by, whole trees gesticulated like the limbs of its writhing body, and

Sebastian could see the grinding teeth he had heard from afar—hundreds of tumbling rocks, some as big as human skulls.

When the flood passed, the stream was four or five times its former size. Astride his mare, having just missed being drowned, Sebastian shouted, "Meryem, I love you!" How inconsolable she would have been if he *had* perished! He imagined his riderless mare trotting toward Tifawt as the sun set beyond Tinzár and the jackals and hyenas sniffed the air and smelled the raw meat of his pulverized body. He imagined them trotting toward it, whimpering in anticipation.

As a parting gift Meryem had given him a magnificent embroidered black fleece coat. In return, on an impulse he hardly understood even now, he had given her the material object he loved best in the world, his key-wound watch, made for his grandfather by N. Eichler of Neuchâtel, which chimed the hours and half hours so that its owner could tell time in the dark before the invention of lucifer matches. He missed it now, in the silence of the mountains; always before, striking inside his breast pocket, it had kept him company and helped him to fall asleep. Now he would have to find some other way to make his eyes close.

He was wrapped in the fleece coat Meryem had given him; it smelled of the life of the animal from which it had been made, of dust and dung. Watching the moonlight on the snows of Tinzár, he worked out the arithmetic of the watch mechanism. How many chimes in a day? Forty-eight. In a year, 17,520. In sixty years (including fifteen leap years) 1,051,920. Meryem would remember him with every chime.

3

TWO YEARS LATER, WHEN SEBASTIAN EMERGED THROUGH THE VARnished oak doors of D. & D. Laux & Co.'s Paris office in the rue du Faubourg Saint-Honoré and found Meryem waiting for him, he noticed her pretty knees and the rows of heavy gold bracelets she wore on either arm, but he did not recognize her. She was dressed like a French girl in a short skirt, silk stockings, a peculiar fringed wrap, and a cloche that concealed her hair.

Then he saw her eyes.

"Meryem!" he cried, sweeping off his derby hat. "What in the world are you doing in Paris?"

"Finding you," she replied. "It's been very difficult."

"Difficult? Why?"

"All I saw, when I saw you, was this door. There are hundreds like it in Paris. It's taken a long time to find the right one."

Her visions again. Sebastian resumed the game as if they had never stopped playing it. He pointed to the brass nameplate on which the name of his family's private bank had been engraved in flowing script. He smiled. "You couldn't read the sign?"

"No. Besides, I didn't know that was your name."

Like everything else Meryem said, this was the truth. He had never told her his last name; it would have been rude to do so, as she did not have one of her own.

"Never mind," Sebastian said. "Now that we've found each other, let's make an evening of it. Are you free?"

She looked at him without smiling. "Here I am."

"Good," he said. "Splendid. What a surprise."

He could not quite believe that she was here, that the slender flapper inside the smart dress was the same wild superstitious girl he had fallen in love with in the Idáren Dráren. She did not belong in this place, in those clothes. Her elongated green eyes watched him calmly. Was she reading his thoughts? *Probably,* Sebastian thought.

He offered his arm and led her to a bright blue Studebaker phaeton parked at the curb. "Some friends are staying with me, you'll like them," he said, in the voice he would have used in speaking to a debutante from New York. "We can all have dinner together." He closed the car door behind her and looked westward, as if to study the horizon and prophesy the weather. It was a luminous evening in May and the crust-colored buildings absorbed the last of the sunshine as biscuits absorb cream. "Isn't it beautiful?" Sebastian said. "Shall we dine outdoors? Yes, I think we shall!"

Sebastian's friends, he explained, were Hubbard and Lori Christopher, from Berlin, and their small son, Paul; he wasn't quite sure how old the child was—three, perhaps; he walked, ate with a fork, drank without spilling, and talked quite plainly in both English and German.

"Paul has no French or Berber yet, I'm afraid," Sebastian said, "but his parents both talk French, Lori better than Hubbard. These German girls are educated to a fare thee well."

Speeding along the quais of the Seine toward his apartment on the Ile Saint-Louis, Sebastian chattered on about the Christophers: He and Hubbard had been at school together, then at Yale. During the summer of Sebastian's visit to the Idáren Dráren Hubbard had written a scandalous novel about his family, resigned from Yale, and moved to Berlin for no reason he could think of. There he had met Lori and married her. "Lori's a Prussian, a *von*—a *baronesse,* in fact, pretty as a picture, smart as a whip, charming as can be," Sebastian said. "Hubbard is crazy about her and their boy."

Meryem had no idea what a Prussian was; Sebastian's words did not register on her mind. While he talked and drove she watched the city stream by, Hôtel-Dieu on the right, Hôtel de Ville on the left, the Seine lined with fishermen in between. She was perfectly relaxed, a rare state of being for Sebastian's passengers. Taxicabs, practically the only other vehicles on the streets, honked wildly at him as he overtook them and cut them off. He swerved in front of a chauffeured Rolls-Royce, turned onto a bridge, bumped over the curb, and parked on the sidewalk.

"We're here," he said, pulling up the hand brake with a whirr of ratchet teeth. "Will you come upstairs? We'll be well chaperoned by the Christophers. You can't imagine how honorable Hubbard is."

Meryem asked, "Is he tall or short?"

"What do you predict?"

"I have no idea."

"You don't? That's amazing! He's enormous, like a Viking. Lori is about our size."

In the elevator, because it would have been bold to gaze into Meryem's eyes, Sebastian looked more closely at her gold bracelets. She also wore several gold necklaces and rings set with emeralds and rubies on every finger. He had been too busy driving to notice these until now. At first sight he had assumed that the bracelets were costume jewelry—how could they be anything else when there were so many of them?—but he was trained to recognize gems and precious metals, and he realized on closer inspection that everything she had on was quite genuine. Meryem was wearing enough wealth to buy the apartment building where he lived.

They were very close together in the rising cage. Despite her flapper's costume and the masses of gold jewelry, she smelled the same as she had smelled in the Idáren Dráren: musky, spiced, feral. The physical effect of her aroma was very powerful.

Meryem said, "Do you ever think of Tili?"

"Tili?" Sebastian said. "Oh—Tili! That nice little black mare. Yes, I do."

"I should hope so," Meryem said. "She saved your life. Didn't you hear the flood coming? Even after you saw the storm on Tinzár? Even after I warned you?"

The elevator came to a stop, bouncing on its cables. Sebastian did not open the gates: Meryem had his whole attention.

"Wait a minute," he said. "Are you telling me you saw the flood—saw *everything* that happened?"

"Perhaps not everything," Meryem said. "I saw Tili saving you, the water coming down, the stones inside the flood—and you, when you waved your hat and spoke to me."

"What else?"

Someone called the lift from below and it started down again. There was no stopping it.

"What did I say?" Sebastian asked.

"You said, 'Meryem, I love you,' " Meryem said. "Your watch had just chimed between my breasts."

Sebastian had never heard a woman refer to her own breasts. He found himself imagining them, brown like the rest of her, but with dark nipples like raisins. They reached the bottom of the elevator shaft. A middle-aged couple waited there with ill-concealed resentment that they had been inconvenienced. The woman was a hawk-faced blonde in a silk dress and fox furs who wore a single strand of pearls, as fashion dictated. She stared in disbelief at Meryem—what was this black girl clinking with bangles doing in her elevator?

"We're going back up, Monsieur-'Dame," Sebastian said. "We seem to be entrapped."

"Entrapped, Monsieur?"

"By fate," Sebastian said.

"We will wait until you are . . . finished," the woman said coldly.

As the lift rose again with a whine of its electric motor, Meryem pulled off her cloche. Her long black Oriental hair uncoiled and tumbled down. She put her beringed hands in it and shook it out, releasing scents of clove, ambergris, and the perfumed salts of perspiration. In this lightless space, she looked very dusky, very beckoning in her Paris frock and high-heeled pumps, as if dressed for a costume party on the other side of the world.

Now what am I going to do? Sebastian wondered.

4

AS SOON AS MERYEM SAW LORI AND HUBBARD CHRISTOPHER SHE realized that both their fathers, like her own, had been killed by their enemies. She waited until they were seated in the garden of a restaurant in the Bois de Boulogne before mentioning this.

"Yes, that's so," Lori said. "Mine was beaten to death by a mob of idealists in the Tiergarten; Hubbard's was shot, by mistake, as a spy by a firing squad of idealists in Mexico. Did Sebastian tell you all that?"

"No," Meryem said.

"Then how do you know?"

"My own father was killed by the French."

Lori looked with puzzlement into her unruffled face. "That seems to break the chain of idealists," she said.

Across the table, Sebastian was ordering dinner. "Clear soup, asparagus, grilled gray sole, saddle of lamb, wild strawberries for everyone," he said. "Ask the sommelier to choose a Chablis to drink with the fish; a Pauillac, the Château Pichon-Longueville 1919, with the meat; and a champagne with the strawberries—it doesn't matter what kind as long as it's *brut.*" He liked plain food. This was his spring and summer menu; between September and April he substituted oysters for the asparagus and cheese for the berries.

He turned to Lori. "Are you and Meryem having a nice chat?"

"We're discussing our murdered parents," Lori said. "It seems you're the only one at the table who is not yet unfathered."

She was smiling politely, but it was an effort: The death of her father, an army officer who had been kicked to death by a gang of Spartacists after surviving four years on the Western Front, was painful to her because the circumstances had been so stupid. She did not like being reminded of it by a stranger who had no right to know about it.

"I've offended you," Meryem said. She laid her brown hand over

Lori's white one on the tabletop. No one had touched Lori without her permission since infancy, but for reasons she never fully understood (she thought about her own gesture for the remainder of her life), she did not draw away. Instead, she turned her hand over and entwined her fingers with Meryem's.

"You haven't offended me," she said. "Just surprised me."

"What did she know?" Hubbard asked. His long face wore an expression of amused surprise. Why was Lori holding hands with this stranger?

"She knew that both our fathers had died violent deaths."

"Sebastian has been talking about us again."

"Not me," Sebastian said.

"Then who? Do we have somebody else in common?"

"The author of the universe," Sebastian said. "Meryem seems to be in touch with the Great Unknown."

Glancing from face to face, he told them about Meryem's visions of his escape from drowning in the Idáren Dráren.

Hubbard listened to the story with a cynical smile on his lips and his head tilted to one side. He had grown up in a family that believed in ghosts and second sight and mental telepathy, and he had made up his mind to live a life of complete rationality, in which nothing that could not be seen and touched was regarded as real.

"Forgive me, Meryem," he said. "But if you saw the thunderstorm on the mountaintop, and if you knew the river Sebastian had to cross rose on that mountain, and if you had seen such floods before, and knew horses, and knew Sebastian is the sort of fellow who'd wave his hat at a girl who isn't even there, then you could have deduced the whole scene."

"'Deduced'?" Sebastian said. "Really, Hubbard. She was miles away."

"Then how do you explain it?"

"It's obvious. Meryem is a clairvoyant."

"Oh. Sorry. I didn't realize." Hubbard, who towered over Sebastian and the rest of them even when sitting down, grinned merrily at Meryem as if they shared some delicious private joke. Meryem had never seen such friendly, guileless eyes as Hubbard's. "Do you see into the future as well as the past?" he asked. "My Aunt Lucy could do that. Out of the blue she'd say, 'Cousin Chloë died yesterday,' or 'Elliott is going to score the winning touchdown next Saturday.' And then, a couple of weeks later, we'd get a letter confirming the prophecy. Aunt Lucy said things just popped into her head—she'd be doing her embroidery and all of a sudden there was Chloë in her grave or Elliott running into the end zone to win the game for the Old Hundred. Is it the same with you, Meryem?"

Meryem did not answer. The fish arrived, glazed with butter. Butter was a new taste to Meryem. She did not like it.

"What you can do," Lori said to her, "is turn the fish over, then eat down to where the butter is."

Using two forks, she did this to the plump filets of sole the waiter had placed in front of her, then handed her plate to Meryem in exchange for her own.

"Thank you," Meryem said.

"If there's no such thing as clairvoyance," Lori said, "how did I know that Meryem doesn't like butter on her fish?"

Hubbard saw that Lori had decided to be Meryem's friend and dropped the banter. "How indeed?" he said between mouthfuls. "Very good food, Sebastian. A summer's night in Paris. Psychic girls. We're living in the land where dreams come true."

For the next several weeks Meryem and Lori spent every morning together. Except for Paul, who was always present, the two young women were alone from breakfast to luncheon: Hubbard was in another room, writing; Sebastian was at the bank; Sebastian's man-servant, a misogynist, went to the market every morning in order to avoid them.

They talked about Germany and the Idáren Dráren, discovering that Prussians and Ja'wabi had many things in common: for example, Lori's Uncle Paulus had cut off a Russian officer's arm in a sword fight at the Battle of Tannenberg and thrust the stump into a fire to cauterize it, and Meryem's grandfather had lopped off the limb of an Arab and stopped the bleeding with the ashes of camel's hair that every Ja'wabi carried into battle. They talked about horses, children, remedies for illness and injury, animal husbandry, land-scapes, weather, poetry, ancestors, music. Meryem sang plaintive Berber songs and Lori attempted to transcribe them on the piano, holding Paul on her lap while she did so.

Lori had never before had a friend of her own sex who did not talk about men to the exclusion of all other subjects. Sebastian was right about the systematic education of females in Germany: all the girls Lori knew in her own country had been taught to read Latin and Greek and speak French and English; they were acquainted with the most highly regarded works of literature and the main facts of history connected to all four of these languages as well as their own; they knew Greek and German mythology; they read music and could play the most popular works of the German composers from memory on at least one musical instrument. But when they were not in the presence of men, all this knowledge ceased to be interesting because it ceased to be useful in attracting, entertaining, outwitting, and manipulating men. So they talked about men—but with circumspection, as if there were spies in the room. And of course there always were; any one of them would go over to the enemy and betray them and their secrets at the first opportunity, and they all knew it.

Sebastian's apartment, where they met, was on the top floor of the house at the tip of the Ile Saint-Louis. Lori and Meryem spent their mornings on the balcony outside the salon. On days when there were wind and clouds it was like sailing through Paris while sitting on the prow of a ship, with Notre Dame off the port beam and the Church of Saint Gervais to starboard and the monotonous gray cliffs of Haussmann's Paris mercifully hidden beyond the horizon. Saint Gervais still bore marks of the damage done by a German shell from Big Bertha which had fallen on it on Good Friday, 1918, killing or wounding 200 poople who were, in some cases at least, in the act of praying for the death of all Germans.

The Christophers were amateur sailors. Hubbard had spent the small proceeds from the publication of his scandalous novel on a yawl; it was called *Mahican,* after a tribe of Red Indians. Lori described sailing with her husband and son over the gray waters of the Baltic to Denmark and Sweden and picnicking on the beaches. She had been sailing all her life.

"As a small child, in August, 1913, I sailed to Saint Petersburg with my father and my Uncle Paulus and my boy cousins," she said. "They were all on leave from the army. The sun shone from four in the morning until midnight. Saint Petersburg was like a city of doll houses, Venetian palaces way up north, made of stucco to resemble stone. When I asked what was inside, my cousin Bartholomäus said, 'Dolls. A czar doll, a czarina doll, a czarevich doll and thousands of other dolls all kissing their behinds.' "

"He's dead now," Meryem said.

"Yes, killed in the war," Lori said. "And both of his brothers, one in Russia, the other at Verdun. Everybody except Paulus and me—and my father, of course, until a German mob got him."

"And Paul."

Lori looked down at her blond child, who listened intently, as he seemed to listen to all adult conversations. "Paul is half American," she said, "so maybe he'll be half lucky."

"Is that why you married an American?" Meryem asked.

"Very likely. It's a well-known fact that the women of defeated nations are powerfully attracted to their conquerors."

"The Americans conquered Germany?" Meryem knew little of European history apart from the victories of France she had learned about in school; she had certainly never been told in a French classroom that the Americans played a part in the 1914-1918 War.

"They came just before the end on the side of the French and the English," Lori said. "Otherwise Germany might have won, although everybody I knew would have been dead just the same. They seemed very innocent to us. I guess I thought it would be a good thing to marry into a nation that was so ignorant of death. Besides, I couldn't wait to make love to him."

"You didn't see Paul when that happened?"

"See him? You mean imagine what he was going to be like before he was born?"

"Yes."

"I thought I did. But I had the wrong picture in my mind. I thought he would look like Hubbard, be sane like Hubbard—an American, safe from the lunatics of Europe. But from the moment he came into the world he looked just like my family. When they handed him to me I saw my father, my cousins. Regiments of the fallen."

Paul was gazing attentively into his mother's eyes.

"He's listening," Meryem said.

Lori kissed her son. "I hope so," she said.

5

"WE MUST GET MARRIED," SEBASTIAN SAID, SITTING BOLT UPRIGHT IN the bed he shared with Meryem. "But how? You're a Mohammedan and I'm a sort of Catholic. We'll have to go to the Mairie, have the civil ceremony, then work out the religious questions."

"Why should we get married?" Meryem asked.

"Why? Because of the child."

"What child?"

"The one we just conceived."

Sebastian, aged twenty-two, was under the impression that sexual union invariably resulted in pregnancy.

"There will be no child," Meryem said.

Sebastian looked down into her face with male knowingness. "Oh, no?" he said. "Let me tell you something, little nomad. There are more things in heaven and earth than are dreamed of in your clairvoyance."

"Then come closer."

It was eight o'clock on a Sunday morning. They had been making love since dawn, except for brief catnaps from which they awakened each other, and now they began again. A few steps away across the Pont Louis Philippe, the bells of Saint Gervais were pealing. To his great surprise Sebastian, committing fornication while church bells shook his bed, felt no guilt, only exhilaration over the amazing discoveries he had made about his body and Meryem's and the way in which they seemed to be connected to some mysterious bank vault in which the true pleasures of the flesh had been, until now, held in safekeeping for them.

Weeks had passed since their reunion, but this was the first time they had been alone together. They had spent the whole intervening time in the company of the Christophers, dining with them every night, going to the movies, the art galleries, and the theater, driving out to Versailles and Fontainebleau in Sebastian's Studebaker for picnics.

But the night before, Lori and Hubbard and Paul had taken the train to Berlin. Before boarding, while the men drank warm champagne in the Wagon-Lit compartment and talked over plans for a sailing voyage down the Volga, or perhaps a walking tour of Hungary, Lori took Meryem by the arm and strolled with her down the platform.

"You may already realize this," Lori said, "but if you want Sebastian you'll have to arrange it yourself. *He*'ll never ask the question. These well-brought-up Americans are unbelievably shy; they've been told that women are like flowers, too beautiful to pluck, and for some reason they believe it. If I were you, I'd get him into bed tonight."

"Tonight?"

"Yes. Otherwise you may never see him again. He avoids being alone with you. That must mean he can't trust himself. What more can you ask for?" Lori kissed Meryem on both cheeks, then, dryly, on the lips. "Come to Berlin," she said. "Don't write or telegram. Just come."

"I'll come."

"Remember what I said about tonight. Strike first, strike hard."

The train shuddered and then began to move. Hubbard shouted from the open door of the car. Lori, in high heels, sprinted after it, seized him by the hand, and swung aboard.

Sebastian stood on the platform, waving. "Good old Hubbard!" he said.

Meryem took his hand. He gave her an absent, tender look. The sentiment in his eyes had nothing to do with her—it was the residue of his goodbye to his friend.

"What now?" Meryem asked.

"Well," he said. "Meryem!"

They were alone for the first time. She looked like some glorious witch. She had drawn a black line along the edges of her eyelids; her long, electrified hair hung to her waist, she wore a silk shift that drew attention to the slender body moving within it. She had arranged her appearance in this way so that Sebastian would not take her to any of the usual places after the Christophers departed. Half a dozen times they had encountered people he knew, clients of the bank and acquaintances from New York, and he had presented her formally: "Mr. and Mrs. R. O. Schenck, of course you know Hubbard and Lori Christopher, but may I present our friend Mademoiselle Meryem." At such moments he conveyed the impression that Meryem was the daughter of an exotic client, an emir or a sultan, whom he was entertaining in line of duty. She knew that he was embarrassed by her—by her darkness, by her silence, by her long unfashionable hair, by her clear, unwavering eyes, by her great Asiatic nose, by her inability to smile at strangers, by her childlike frankness when she did speak, by the fortune in gold bangles she wore wherever she went.

One night, in the restaurant of the Ritz Hotel, Meryem dropped her purse; thousands of francs, a fortune in paper, spilled onto the floor. The waiter picked up the flimsy banknotes and handed them back to her. Sebastian was shocked. "Do you always carry so much money in your bag?" he asked. Meryem made no attempt to avoid any of his questions. "Not always," she replied. "I sold something today."

"*Sold* something?" Sebastian came from a world in which material objects, once acquired, were never sold: to do so would be to question one's own taste—or in the case of the Lauxes, to undermine confidence in D. & D. Laux & Co. by suggesting that its proprietors *needed* the money. "What did you sell?" Sebastian asked. "A bracelet," Meryem replied. Sebastian turned pink: what could this possibly mean? He waited for an explanation. Meryem offered none. Lori intervened. After looking to Meryem for permission to explain, she said, "That's why she *has* the gold, Sebastian. When she needs money, she sells a bracelet or a necklace." Hubbard put an arm around Sebastian and gave his friend's diminutive body a companionable shake. "You've fallen in love with a living, breathing, gloriously beautiful bank," he said. "Fate was the matchmaker—good title." Sebastian said, "Who says I'm in love?" But they all knew that he was.

Now, alone with Meryem on the empty platform of the Gare de l'Est, Sebastian said, "What next, indeed?"

"I'd like to go to a nightclub," Meryem said. "Lori says they're very amusing."

"In Berlin they are, because German politics are so comical. Here they're just indecent—Negresses wearing ostrich plumes and French girls singing awful songs about *l'amour.*"

"I won't be shocked, Sebastian. Lori has prepared me for anything."

Meryem looked solemn, expectant, resolute; different. Sebastian wondered if she knew something that he did not know about the evening ahead of them. He often had that feeling, that she was beside him in the here and now but somehow also waiting for him up ahead on the pathway of time. If time *was* a pathway; he was confused about such things as a result of falling in love with Meryem, who seemed to wander at will between the future and the past.

They went to a large nightclub on the Champs-Elysées where a nearly nude, very beautiful black woman sang love songs in a throaty voice that sounded tuneless to Sebastian but very pleasing to Meryem. They drank a good deal of champagne, and when Sebastian got the bill he said, "We may have to sell a bracelet to get out of here." Outside, a man gave them a card advertising a smaller nightclub in Montparnasse and they drove across the Pont de la Concorde, then sped through narrow streets until they found it, a smoke-filled cellar where men danced with men, women danced with women, and a singer with a clown's painted face whose nude body had also been painted white sat down in a fat man's lap. When she got up she left a huge chalky blotch on his black alpaca suit. One of the waiters handed her a whisk broom and she dusted the man's coat and trousers while she sang a song in argot that made the French people in the crowd roar with laughter. They stayed until the place closed.

Then Meryem took him by the hand and led him back to the Seine. They were not so very far from his apartment on the Ile Saint-Louis. She walked with him along the quais, keeping silent so as not to frighten him. He had drunk all but one glass from each of the three or four bottles of champagne he had ordered in the smoke-filled nightclub. Later in life he told himself that he was under an enchantment that night, but at the time he knew that he was drunk, and he may even have known what Meryem was up to.

In any case, he let her lead him to his doorway, where, to his surprise, she kissed him. They kissed again in the elevator, and again after they entered the darkened apartment. A moment later they were lying on the bed, kissing. Sebastian realized that he must stop. Pretending that he was tipsy, that it was all a joke, he rose to his feet and staggered into the bathroom. But he was not at all surprised to find Meryem in his bed when he came back. He lay down beside her. Then they were inside the cloud of her hair, back in the Idáren Dráren—or perhaps, as he thought a few moments afterward, even deeper in time than that.

In the morning, Meryem's jewelry lay in a strip of sunlight on the table across the room.

"Put on your gold, will you?" he said.

She got out of bed and did as he asked, then stepped naked into the light like a wild bride adorned with her dowry.

"My God," Sebastian said, knowing he was lost.

6

A WEEK LATER, BECAUSE D. & D. LAUX & CO. OBSERVED AMERICAN holidays and Sebastian was able to take the day off without attracting notice, he and Meryem were married in the Mairie of the

Fourth Arrondissement. The ceremony was quite patriotic, with the mayor wearing his tricolor sash of office and the Legion of Honor while delivering a homily about the Declaration of the Rights of Man and the duty of every Frenchwoman to replenish the ranks of France, mother of civic virtue.

Because of the religious question, it was a secret marriage.

"This will give us time to think, time to prepare our families for the formal wedding," Sebastian said.

"What is there to think about?" Meryem asked. "Everything has happened already."

"It will give you the legal rights of a wife anywhere in the world."

"What shall I do with them?"

"You may be glad to have them someday," Sebastian said. "Meanwhile we'll continue to have all the advantages of living in sin."

In the weeks that followed they saw no one except each other. The Parisians went away in a herd on their August migration to the countryside; Sebastian stopped accepting invitations from Americans, and his mantelshelf, formerly crowded with cards, was now empty. After lovemaking, that is to say half a dozen times a day, Sebastian told his bride about D. & D. Laux & Co. and tried to make her understand the romance of money.

"It has no physical reality," he said. "It's just worthless slips of paper with numbers and the picture of a hero printed on them. Yet people will exchange castles, land, great paintings, factories—anything—for it. Money is the universal mystery, the secret eucharist of the world, the one thing everyone believes in."

He loved D. & D. Laux & Co., loved sitting in a house full of money. He came home happy every night because there was more money in the bank at the end of the day than there had been at the beginning. Sebastian talked about the bank as if it had an intelligence of its own.

"The bank knows everything," he told Meryem. "It knew that the stock market was going to crash. Before that it knew that there was going to be a war."

"Who tells it these things?" Meryem asked.

Sebastian gathered her lovely body to his. "Money talks," he whispered.

They were hardly ever disturbed; Sebastian received all his mail at the bank, and letters played no role in Meryem's life. During the day, while Sebastian was at work, Meryem studied languages with tutors, English in the morning and German in the afternoon. As soon as she learned the elements of English she and Sebastian began speaking it together. She had a very good ear, and by the end of the summer she spoke it well, with a faint boarding school drawl like her husband's. She did not call him by that title or regard him as her husband in any formal sense because she did not recognize the right of the French Republic to legitimize their union.

Nevertheless she obeyed Sebastian. Because he wanted her to do so, she wore Berber clothes at home but French frocks when she went out. Sebastian kept his valuables in a wall safe in their bedroom, and now that she had a safe place to leave her gold she no longer wore it all the time. They ate dinner at home two or three nights a week, and on other evenings walked out to simple restaurants on the Left Bank, where Meryem was less noticeable and they were unlikely to meet customers of the bank. When they did run into people Sebastian knew there was just as much awkwardness as before. The older the acquaintances, the greater the difficulty. One evening in August, while they were walking together through the Place Vendôme, Sebastian was greeted by a snowy-haired American couple emerging from the Ritz Hotel. Meryem had been introduced to them once before but they did not acknowledge her. The old man took Sebastian by the arm.

"Can I have a word with you, my boy?" he said, speaking English. "Wild oats are fine, but you shouldn't sow them from the Eiffel Tower in broad daylight. The world doesn't care what you do as long as you do it with a decent regard for other people's feelings. I know you're young, I know what Paris is like. This girl of yours is a lovely little pickaninny. But think of the future. You're your father's only son. The bank will be yours someday. People will remember all this when they think about trusting you with their money. A word to the wise."

All through this speech, which caused a rush of blood to Sebastian's face, the old American and his wife smiled cordially at Meryem as if she were deaf. Their car had been waiting for them at the curb. They got into it and were driven away.

Sebastian stared after them. "Pompous ass," he said.

"Does he keep a lot of money in the bank?" Meryem asked.

"About five million."

"No wonder he doesn't like the look of me," Meryem said. "Maybe I should disguise myself a little better. I can cut my hair off. I can dye it yellow."

"Then what would I have to do to myself in order to fit in the Idáren Dráren?"

"Nothing. You already look like one of the Ja'wabi."

Sebastian gazed at himself in the window of Cartier: a wiry erect little man with an arched nose, olive skin, and umber eyes in which resentment still smoldered.

"By George, I think you're right," he said. "When did you first notice this?"

"A long time ago."

Sebastian was still examining his reflection. "But when, exactly?" he said. "We're talking about a historic moment."

Their eyes met in the glass. "You wouldn't remember," Meryem replied. "It was a *long* time ago."

Sebastian's father died at the end of September. The news came over the teletype at the bank. After receiving this message Sebastian spent twenty minutes alone, then called the staff of the Paris branch together, told them the news, and accepted their condolences. Then he sent for a tailor, who came to the bank and sewed a black mourning band onto the left sleeve of his coat. He sent a messenger to book passage for him on the *Normandie,* which sailed the next afternoon from Le Havre, and made certain other arrangements.

He went home at the usual hour. Meryem awaited him, as usual, on the balcony, where they always watched the sunset together.

"Please come inside," he said. She did so, and he bolted the french windows behind her. "My father is dead," he said, handing her the teletype message.

Until now he had been correct, controlled, firm of voice. But as soon as he uttered these words he began to weep.

"I want to thank you for not telling me that this was going to happen," he said. "Otherwise I would never have known happiness."

"I didn't know it was going to happen," Meryem said. This was true: since moving in with Sebastian her visions had ceased. There were surprises in her life for the first time. She needed no special powers to realize what this surprise meant.

Sebastian seemed not to hear her. "I have signed papers giving you a fifty-year lease to this apartment," he said.

"A fifty-year lease?" Meryem said. "What for?"

"It's a formality, a legal device, but my intention is that this apartment will always be yours."

"Why?"

"Because we have been so happy here."

"Are we no longer happy?"

"We will always be married," he said. "Mr. Wilbur Garrett, the manager of the Paris office, has been instructed to supply your need for money from my personal account. When you need cash, simply send Mr. Garrett a note with the amount required and your signature and he will send a messenger with the money. Please deal with him only; he is the only American on the staff."

"Where will you be?"

"I sail tomorrow on the *Normandie*. As head of the bank I will come to Paris every year. We'll be together then."

"But not in New York?"

He was shocked by her question. "How could we be?" he said. "How could I do that to my mother after the loss she has already suffered? Besides, as I just said, I will be head of the bank."

7

AFTER SEBASTIAN LEFT IN THE MORNING TO CATCH THE BOAT TRAIN, Meryem dismissed the manservant and gave him a note to Mr. Wilbur Garrett for two months' salary. She shuttered the apartment, put on her gold jewelry, packed a valise, and left.

Near the Gare de l'Est she went into a tattoo parlor and told the artist to draw a tear under each of her eyes.

"Tears, Mademoiselle?"

"Tears."

"I've never done tears," the man said. "There's no call for tears; no one wants them. What size? What color?"

"Natural size. The usual color."

"But water has no color, Mademoiselle."

"Violet, then."

"Do you wish to have a rivulet, a string of tears like pearls, or simply two individual tears?"

"Just the tears. About the size of lemon seeds."

"As you wish. Let me draw them first in ink, to see if you like them."

He worked for a few moments with a pen, spitting on his thumb to erase mistakes. When he was satisfied with the cartoon he handed Meryem a mirror and she looked at herself.

"Good. Do it," she said.

"You're completely sure?" the artist asked. "They won't come off, you know. There will be questions. The next man you fall in love with will wonder about his predecessor. He certainly won't like it."

"Begin, if you please. I am taking the train."

"Fifty francs in advance, please."

Meryem gave him the money. When the artist was finished he admired his own work. "I must say you were right," he said. "You were very pretty before, Mademoiselle. But now you're beautiful. The effect is truly pathetic. No one in the future will be able to forget you."

FOUR

1

"THOSE TEARS ARE WONDERFUL," LORI CHRISTOPHER SAID. "ARE THEY painted on?"

"Tattooed," Meryem said.

"Ah. What does Sebastian think of them?"

"He hasn't seen them." Meryem told her what had happened between her and her husband.

When she was finished Lori said, "Are you pregnant?"

"No."

"You're sure?"

"You sound like Sebastian," Meryem said. "I had proof on the train."

"You're quite sure you want to keep this marriage a secret?"

"Yes. Even from Hubbard."

Lori hesitated. "He already knows," she said. "Sebastian wrote to him."

They were seated together on a sofa in the Christophers' apartment in the neighborhood of Berlin known as Charlottenburg. Lori poured tea from a misshapen pottery vessel. "Our Dada teapot," she explained. "Hubbard loves it." The walls were covered with abstract paintings and gross caricatures of Berliners.

"Hubbard bought all these pictures on the advice of a White Russian before I met him," Lori said. "They were a great bargain. The teapot, too. And this apartment. He had American money at a time when you needed eighty billion marks to buy an egg. One U.S. dollar was worth two trillion Reichsmarks."

"How many eggs was that?"

"Who knows? Twenty-five? Twenty-five hundred? Two and a

half? That was the whole point of inflation. When the money collapsed, nobody was sure of anything. It was like God had died."

"You sound like Sebastian again."

Lori took her hand. "For a while everybody will sound like Sebastian to you," she said.

"What a fate," Hubbard said, overhearing Lori's words as he came in from the park with Paul on his shoulders.

"Who won?" Lori asked.

"Tie game," Hubbard said. "Two to two. Paul scored in the last second."

The knees of his trousers were covered with grass stains; when he and Paul played football, Hubbard played on his knees, to make the game fairer. He put Paul down, and the little boy shook hands with Meryem. Hubbard inspected the tea tray and spread butter and jam on a piece of black bread and gave it to Paul. He poured himself a cup of tea before sitting back on another sofa with his tremendous long legs spread out before him. Meryem thought, as she did every time she encountered Hubbard, that she had never seen such an untroubled, contented person, or such a large one.

"Those tears!" he said, smiling at Meryem. "Wait until Zaentz sees them."

"Who's Zaentz?" Meryem asked.

"A painter friend of ours. You'll meet him at dinner; he's usually here."

"Did he paint these?" Meryem indicated the revolutionary pictures on the wall.

"No. Zaentz is a gentle soul," Hubbard said, "something like Sebastian. How *is* your secret husband?"

"Gone to America," Meryem said. "His father died."

"No!" Hubbard said. "He dreaded the day this would happen. They'll put him in the vault—that's how he always described it. He'll never escape."

"Does he want to escape?"

Hubbard gave her a searching look. "Of course he does. Everyone does."

But he asked her no more questions.

2

THE CHRISTOPHERS KEPT OPEN HOUSE, A HOLDOVER FROM THE TIME of the great inflation ten years before when money meant nothing to Hubbard. Half a dozen people dressed in leather and corduroy straggled in as twilight began to fall, including Zaentz the artist, who came late, and Otto Rothchild, who was the first to arrive. Otto was accompanied by a blond young man who seemed to be very ill at ease.

Even then Otto was eager to teach, and when he saw Meryem's tears he said, "You know what God said about tattoos, don't you? He said, 'You will not tattoo yourselves.' "

"Where is that written?" Lori Christopher asked.

"In Leviticus, where God sends Moses down the mountain to tell the Israelites not to rend their clothes or gash their flesh when mourning the dead."

The blond young man laughed.

"Franz thinks I just told an anti-Semitic joke," Otto said. "All you have to do in Berlin to get a laugh these days is speak the word 'Jew.' "

Lori regarded Otto and his friend with undisguised loathing. She said, "I wish you wouldn't bring your Nazi friends here, Otto."

"I know," Otto replied, "but Hubbard needs them for his writing. Besides, Franz isn't a Nazi, are you, Franz?"

The young man shook his head. "Not at all," he said.

"Not yet," Lori said. "What are you in the meantime?"

"I believe in the revolution of youth," Franz said. "The values of our parents' generation are shit. They must be shoveled out and replaced with the clean new values of youth. Germany will be saved by discipline and willpower, not by the corrupt, vile system invented by the capitalist, anti-national force which is ruining the Fatherland."

"What capitalist, anti-national force is that, exactly?" Lori asked.

"You mustn't get the wrong idea," Otto said. "Franz is one of the *Wandervögel*. He and his friends are idealists. They sing the wonderful old German folk songs, go on hikes in *Lederhosen* through the German forest, rediscover the old German gods, make friends with the peasants, commune with the German soil. Quite harmless."

"It's good to have your reassurance about that, Otto," Lori said. "What is your family name, Franz?"

"Stutzer," Otto replied. "But Franz is not one of the real Stutzers. He's one of the new Germans."

At dinner Franz Stutzer ate in silence while the others talked. The main dish was spaghetti with tomato sauce; he was still bourgeois enough to watch the others to see how it should be eaten.

"You should like this dish even if it isn't German, Franz," Otto said, lifting a fork wrapped with strands of pasta. "It's Herr Hitler's favorite food. He always orders it in his favorite restaurant in Munich, and then cuts it up into little bits. That way it goes straight down into his stomach. He's far too busy thinking, of course, to be able to chew at the same time."

"I thought you said this fellow isn't a Nazi," Lori said.

"He isn't. But he admires Herr Hitler."

"Like so many others."

All this table talk was in German. At first Meryem had trouble following the staccato Berlin usage because she had only spoken the language with her teacher, a drawling Austrian. But as the evening wore on she found that she understood most of what was said. In the case of Lori, she often knew what the words would be before they were spoken.

Zaentz sat opposite her, a bearish man with a cropped white beard and oil paint smeared on his trousers. When he finished his spaghetti he wiped the plate with a slice of bread, then leaned across the table and said, "I'd like to paint you and Meryem together, Lori."

Hubbard was triumphant. "What did I tell you?"

"Why not just Meryem?" Lori said. "You've done me a dozen times."

"Yes, but there was always something missing."

"Wait a minute," Hubbard said. "What about the Madonna of Charlottenburg?" He meant the ethereal drawing Zaentz had made of Lori when she was pregnant.

"That turned out all right because Paul was hidden in the picture," Zaentz said. "But this will be better. These two are one. They complete each other."

"You mean you want to paint them as a single woman?" Hubbard said. "This is getting interesting."

"Possibly," Zaentz said. "I won't know until I start painting."

Otto interrupted. "How can you paint Meryem?" he said. "Islam forbids images. Isn't that so, Meryem?"

240

Meryem let him talk.

"On the Judgment Day, according to Moslem teaching, those who make images will be called upon to breathe life into them," Otto said. "If they can't do so they'll be punished."

"Then the risk is all mine," Zaentz said. He turned to Meryem. "Will you pose?"

"If Lori will."

Otto was talking again. "The teardrops are exquisite," he said. "Do they mean anything?"

"They're just teardrops," Meryem said.

"I wonder if they'd be considered an image on the Day of Judgment," Otto said. "If so you'll have those tears to answer for at the final trump, when, as the Holy Koran says, the world is rolled up like a scroll and the children's hair turns gray."

3

WHILE POSING FOR ZAENTZ'S PAINTING, MERYEM AND LORI SAT SIDE by side in identical costumes beneath a huge tilted window set into the roof of the artist's attic studio. Zaentz painted very slowly. He was capable of spending an entire morning working on one square inch of canvas. Because he had no interest in politics, he had not followed the Berlin fashion and become an abstractionist or a cartoonist. There was more light in his painting than in his studio: he painted as the young Velázquez might have painted if he had lived after the invention of electric light. His pictures were so naturalistic, so accurate in every detail, that they were sometimes mistaken for photographs. However, they did not lie, as photographs often do, by capturing a single isolated facial expression. Zaentz's subjects had faces in which many other faces were visible, depending on the light and the angle at which they were viewed: later in life Paul Christopher looked every day at a copy of the picture of Lori that his father called the Madonna of Charlottenburg and never saw the same person twice.

Every afternoon at about one o'clock, after he finished writing, Hubbard brought lunch in a picnic basket. In fair weather the four of them ate in Schiller Park, but when it rained, which was often in Berlin in autumn, they spread the food on a table beneath the big window. One day the rain was heavier than usual.

"You can't go out in this downpour," Zaentz said. "Let's play a game of whist."

Card games were unknown among the Ja'wabi, and Meryem had never handled cards. Hubbard explained their values and suits and the rules of the game. They began to play. As the cards were played, Meryem began to see pictures. There were so many of these at first—visions of the Ja'wabi in the desert, a scene in which Sebastian sat in a shadowy room with four silent women Meryem recognized as his mother and sisters, and indistinct images of people she did not know—that she could scarcely register them.

Lori held a very strong hand in diamonds, and as she played the ace and then the face cards, winning trick after trick, Meryem saw a sailing boat in a storm at sea. Lori, wearing a long sleeveless coat, was knocked overboard by the boom. She did not resist the water but sank helplessly to the bottom of the shallow sea, among large rocks bearded with seaweed. Paul, a much older Paul than the one she now knew, swam down to her, but was unable to save her because the long coat was holding her down.

Zaentz had been watching Meryem. When he saw the look in her eyes he threw down his hand and took her by the hand.

"Come over here and sit," he said, leading her toward the easel. "Don't change, don't speak, don't think of anything new."

4

HUBBARD'S NOVEL *THE ROSE AND THE LOTUS* WAS NEVER PUBLISHED in German, so he thought it was possible that Heydrich, who appeared in it under his own name, did not know of its existence. Heydrich knew about Zaentz's picture, however.

"I saw it before I saw you that day at the Adlon Hotel," he told Meryem. "After I danced with you, the amazing reality from which the picture came, I knew that I must have it, that I must know everything about it. I want you to come and see it."

"I've already seen it a thousand times," Meryem said.

"But not for a long while. You will be astonished by it. I've had it put into a beautiful gold frame with an electric light shining on it. It's the jewel of my collection. You *must* come see it."

"No, thank you."

"You can bring along your pretty baroness as chaperone. She too will be astonished by it."

Years had passed since Meryem first came to Berlin; she came every fall and stayed all winter. By now Adolf Hitler was in power, and despite his youth Heydrich was a Nazi notable, seen everywhere in Berlin in his SS uniform. He was wearing it now because he had leaped out of his staff car when he saw Meryem walking down the Prinz Albrechtstrasse, where his headquarters was located. According to Berlin gossip, as merchandised by Otto Rothchild, Heydrich had made his name as an imaginative killer in those very headquarters. He had led an assassination squad of five SS men who locked Gregor Strasser, one of Hitler's critics within the Nazi party, inside a cell. The condemned man was known for his wit and intelligence. While Strasser scrambled frantically from wall to wall, the SS men fired at him through the bars with pistols, laughing uproariously as they fired and shouting, "Tell us another one, Strasser!" When Strasser still showed signs of life even though he had been shot some forty times, Heydrich went inside the cell and finished him off by firing a bullet into the back of his neck.

"Will you come?" he said to Meryem. "Six o'clock. I'll send my car for you and your friend."

"I'm sorry," Meryem said, "it's impossible."

Heydrich gave her his brilliant smile; except for his broad, feminine hips, he was an ideal Aryan type—so perfectly blond and blue-eyed, in fact, that his chief, Heinrich Himmler, suspected that he must be concealing a Jewish ancestor inside this genetic disguise.

"You're maddening," Heydrich said, touching Meryem's chin with a gloved index finger. "I warn you, I will never give up." He smiled again, then lowered his voice to a stage whisper: "*You are in danger.*"

The next morning Meryem and Lori were arrested by the Gestapo after they returned to the stables after their ride in the Tiergarten. The arresting officers, two men in soft hats and long black leather coats, loaded them into a Mercedes, all four of them on the backseat with the secret policemen on the outside and the women in the middle. Their hips and legs were crushed together, but because of the leather coats the intimacy was reduced. "What is the meaning of this?" Lori asked. "Where are you taking us?"

The men did not answer. Lori leaned forward and turned her head to study their impassive faces. They stared straight ahead, avoiding eye contact.

"Seized by the Gestapo—it's like a Communist propaganda movie," Lori said. "Why didn't you see *this* in the cards, Meryem?"

The secret policemen seemed interested in this remark. Lori lifted her eyebrows and stopped talking. She was perfectly calm— even contemptuous. Although she was guilty many times over of crimes against the Reich, specifically of assisting Jews to escape from Germany, she was not frightened. Like every other member of her family, she had been raised to believe that fear was a bad habit that could be conquered like any other. Her father had been killed by a mob because he had conquered fear; her cousin Bartholomäus had saluted the American who sent him down in fiames because he had conquered it. She was teaching her son to conquer it.

The shades were drawn in the Mercedes. After a rapid passage through city streets and a lengthy ride along wooded roads, the car turned into a drive, tires crunching gravel, and stopped. The secret policemen, still silent, escorted them up the steps of a hunting lodge and showed them inside.

"What is this place?" Lori asked, gazing at the stuffed heads of stag and wild boar that crowded the walls.

No answer. It was still only seven-thirty in the morning, and the interior was chilly. The smell of coffee filled the air.

"I think I know," Meryem said.

A door painted with flowers opened and Heydrich appeared, wearing a silk dressing gown and a white aviator's scarf over the black riding breeches and gleaming black boots of his SS uniform.

"Dismissed!" he shouted.

The secret policemen clicked their heels, released their grip on the women's arms, and departed. Heydrich continued down the stairs.

"Good morning, dear ladies," he said. "I see that we are all dressed alike. Three people in breeches and boots, up early in the beautiful German morning. Smell that! Come, have some coffee with me."

"We prefer to leave," Lori said.

"Baronesse, please," Heydrich said, using the title by which the unmarried daughters of barons were addressed. "Surely you won't refuse a cup of coffee?"

"Please do not address me in that way. I am a married woman."

"Unlucky day! But I'm married too, you know, with two splendid children. My wife never comes here. Come. I've promised to show Fräulein Meryem something."

The painting was displayed on an easel. "I designed the frame myself," Heydrich said. "The lights are controlled by a rheostat. See?" He adjusted the lamp. "Bright, normal, dim at the touch of a finger. If only the artist were still in Germany I would have him redesign the picture. Alas, he was smuggled out of the country by enemies of the Reich."

"Redesign the picture?" Lori said.

"Yes, indeed. Wonderful as it is, it has a flaw. I've always thought the figures should be in a natural state."

" 'A natural state?' What do you mean by that?"

"Nude."

"And perhaps holding a pair of snow-white pigeons?"

"I hadn't thought of that," Heydrich said, "but you have a point. One dove could have green eyes, the other gray like the German sky, a mirror image of the girls. If we ever see Zaentz again I'll tell him about your idea. But I don't think we *will* see him, do you?"

"I shouldn't think so," Lori said.

"How reckless you are!" Heydrich said. "I admire that."

The Christophers had smuggled Zaentz to Denmark in the *Mahican* only a few weeks before because of a rumor that he was going to be arrested. They assumed that the police were after him because he was a Jew, but now Lori wondered if Heydrich had been behind it. Had he wanted to put him in a cage in order to watch him undress Meryem with his brushes?

"I'm surprised you're so interested in Zaentz's work," she said.

"I see your point, but of course he doesn't paint like a Jew," Heydrich said. "I defy anyone to look at this picture and identify it as the work of a Jew."

"Even the Führer?"

"I mean any ordinary person like you and me," Heydrich replied. "If Zaentz had chosen any other subject I would not have been interested, but this particular painting has me in its power. The easel is on casters, so I can take it with me from one room to another. I look up from my study desk late at night, or from one of my lonely suppers, or from my bed when I wake, and there it is."

"But how did you acquire it? I understood it had been sold to someone else."

"The picture was seized from a bankrupt Jew for unpaid taxes, and I was lucky enough to have the chance to purchase it at auction."

"You must have got a wonderful bargain," Lori said.

"Astonishing. I could hardly believe my luck, dear lady."

A male servant with a military haircut came into the room with a trolley.

"Ah, the coffee!" Heydrich said. "This is real Italian roasted coffee, straight from Rome. I always say there is no aroma like it."

He poured the coffee himself into gilded porcelain cups and offered one to Lori.

"No, thank you," she said.

"But you must have some," Heydrich said. "Also some of these delicious pastries. I won't let you go unless you have some."

He smiled yet again. "I really mean that."

Lori and Meryem each took a pastry.

Heydrich popped an eclair into his mouth. "It makes me so happy that you enjoy the same things I do," he said.

They rode back into Berlin in Heydrich's car. He sat between the women on the leather seat with his boots crossed at the ankles and propped up on the jump seat. He smelled of boot polish, brilliantine, and strong shaving lotion. Beyond a glass partition, the servant who had brought in the coffee sat in the front seat beside the driver. He now wore the uniform of an SS private, with a machine pistol slung across his chest. The Mercedes in which Lori and Meryem had been brought to the villa followed the staff car, and another, identical Mercedes led the way.

"You're well protected," Lori said. "You must be quite precious to your leader."

"The enemies of the Reich are everywhere and they tend to be cowardly—they specialize in ambushes with smuggled arms," Heydrich said. "Smuggling is a terrible problem. And you're right. The Führer himself is concerned about it. Which means that soon there will be no problem." He winked. "Smugglers should beware, dear lady."

They were approaching the Opera House, a few blocks away from the Christophers' apartment in Goethestrasse. Heydrich rapped on the glass partition and the car stopped. He picked up Lori's hand, then Meryem's, and kissed them one after the other.

"For the sake of your reputation I'll let you down here," he said. "Who would believe in our innocence if you got out of such a long motorcar as this one so early in the morning, right in front of your house? Your husband might be looking down from the windows and then what? What if he became suspicious? I tremble at the thought. After all, the pen is mightier than the sword."

He got out of the car and stood on the sidewalk with them.

Watery light filtered through a rank of linden trees planted along the street. "What a lovely neighborhood to live in," Heydrich said. "But now that you've seen my house perhaps I can persuade you to come again. I hope so!"

The three black cars sped away.

5

THE APARTMENT WAS QUIET. HUBBARD WAS WRITING; PAUL HAD GONE to the park.

"I think we won't mention this episode to Hubbard," Lori said.

"You think it will make him angry?"

"Possibly. But it will certanly make him write about it. I think he's written enough about Heydrich. The question is, what to do about you?"

"What about me?" Meryem said.

"That lunatic is obsessed by you. I think you should leave Germany."

"Where would I go?"

"What does it matter? This isn't the end of Heydrich. It's only the beginning. You can go to Paris, or to the Idáren Dráren, or even to America."

"Only if we all go. Sebastian will be in Paris next month."

Each June Sebastian came to Paris and Meryem went there to join him for a month. Then she returned to the Idáren Dráren for the summer.

"No," Lori said. "Hubbard can't be interrupted now."

"He can write anywhere."

Lori shook her head. "Not with these creatures in charge of Germany. I really must have a bath. Then we'll talk again. I think you should go at once. God knows what Heydrich might do the next time. Arrest you, declare you're a Jew, lock you in a room and keep you as a pet. He's mad."

"I know," Meryem said. "But, Lori, it isn't me he's obsessed by. I'm just the pretext. It's you."

THEREAFTER MERYEM AND LORI WERE ARRESTED ONCE OR TWICE A week by Heydrich's men. The pattern never varied. They would be seized in the Tiergarten at about seven o'clock in the morning, after their ride through the park. The same two secret policemen, wearing the same black fedoras and the same black leather coats, always made the arrest, showing their credentials and repeating the same words. Then came the ride across Berlin in the Mercedes, coffee and pastries in the hunting lodge with Heydrich, and the return to the city in his staff car.

They did not change their habits because it was obvious that Heydrich had the power to find them wherever they were. He knew all about their activities between arrests. Drinking coffee and munching on little frosted cakes and fruit tarts, he would say, "Did you enjoy your dinner party on Tuesday with the Hornbläser-Lottmanns? She's quite delightful, but *he's* a bit compulsive, don't you think? All that telephoning!" Or, "It's such a pity your son has no friends among German boys, Baronesse. They say he's a philo-Semite, and of course that makes him stand out, especially since he has an American father and the President of the United States is a Jew. Children are so cruel—but so honest and so just!" He always called Lori "baronesse," as if bestowing reinstated maidenhood upon her; she had given up correcting him.

These encounters took place while Hubbard was writing. Although Lori had never before kept a secret from her husband, he knew nothing about the arrests. While working, as he did every day from six in the morning until noon, Hubbard was oblivious to the world around him. By the time he emerged from his writing room the two women had returned, and the three of them had lunch together. After that Hubbard read aloud from his work in progress, and sometimes they had an outing—a drive through the Grunewald or a visit to an art gallery or a book store. Sometimes they sat in the park and talked.

On the advice of a friend in the American Embassy, the Christophers only discussed the Hitler government and the Nazi Party in the open air. "They've planted microphones everywhere, by golly!" their friend said. "I'd bet dollars to doughnuts your walls are full of them, considering who your friends are—or were."

The Christophers' noisy Bohemian dinners were a thing of the past; almost nobody came except Otto Rothchild, who still turned up once or twice a month. Most people they knew had left the country, many of them as clandestine passengers on the *Mahican* on one of its night sails to Denmark.

Most afternoons Hubbard and Paul played catch in the Schlossgarten. One evening they were an hour late coming home. Lori was not alarmed: father and son were not predictable—sometimes they went to the Kurfürstendamm for pastries, sometimes Hubbard took a model of the *Mahican* with him and he and Paul stopped to sail it in the Schlossgarten's ornamental lake.

When the doorbell rang at six o'clock she thought it was Hubbard, who often forgot his key. But when she opened the door, Heydrich stood in the corridor holding a silver bucket containing a bottle of champagne. He wore civilian clothes, a dark suit with a silk necktie. Two SS troopers stood behind him, their arms laden with white roses, boxes tied with ribbons, and a tray covered with a linen cloth.

"I thought it would be pleasant to spend the evening together," Heydrich said. "I've seen your picture in all lights, but the models in the flesh only in the morning."

"Spend the evening together?" Lori said. "That's completely impossible."

"Nothing is impossible when the will is strong enough," Heydrich replied. "We won't be interrupted until I give the word. Have no fear. Your husband and son were arrested in the Schlossgarten about an hour ago."

"Arrested?"

Heydrich waved a finger. He was wearing dove-gray gloves. "Their behavior was quite suspicious," he said. "They were sailing a model boat in the lake. For all I know there were toy Jews hidden in the hold. I have just assigned a new man to the island of Rügen, where you keep your wonderful sailboat, and he is anxious to talk to someone who knows about sailing small boats on the Baltic. So am I. Can you guess why?"

"No."

"Because I, too, have bought a house on an island in the Baltic. I'm an enthusiastic sailor, just like you. Who knows? Perhaps we'll meet on the water. Possibly we could have a picnic, all together."

Heydrich set the wine bucket down. His men arranged the flowers in a vase and laid out the things they had carried upstairs on trays.

"Nothing but the best," Heydrich said. "The SS has an excellent courier service: roses from Italy, Russian caviar from the Black Sea, goose liver from Strasbourg, and the champagne is Krug '09. And two beautiful hats from Paris. Please try them on, ladies. I can't wait to see you in them."

Lori and Meryem did so. Heydrich leaned back in his Savile Row suit and admired them. "How I would like to have a picture of that!" he said. "Alas, there is no camera." His servants passed a tray of champagne glasses and another of food.

"Go now," Heydrich told them. "Watch the door." He smiled at Lori. "I'm posting guards in case your husband escapes. But I don't think he will. I think you know the new man in Rügen—Franz Stutzer. He's very competent, one of my favorites. He came here to dinner as a boy with your husband's pushy Russian friend, the one who calls himself Rothchild. Do you remember Franz?"

"Yes."

"He'll be very pleased. He was absolutely dazzled by you."

Heydrich asked Lori to play the piano. "Sit beside her on the bench, please, Fräulein Meryem," he said.

Meryem said, "But I don't play."

"I know. It's the picture I want to see, the two of you side by side."

"What would you like to hear?" Lori asked.

"My tastes, as you know, are simple. I prefer Strauss. Perhaps 'The Merry Widow Waltz.' Do you know that one, Baronesse?"

"That's by Franz Lehár."

"Is it really? What a lot you know about everything! And I hope you'll teach me every bit of it."

After listening to the piano for an hour, sometimes beating time with his champagne glass, Heydrich turned to Meryem.

"Strange as it seems, Fräulein, we have never discussed the most famous thing about you."

"And what is that?"

"Your second sight. Such tales have we heard about your predictions! I don't think you realize how famous you are. Everybody in Berlin thinks you're infallible. Even the Führer has heard about you. He is, in a manner of speaking, a clairvoyant himself—albeit on a very, very high plane. Do you read palms?"

"No," Meryem said.

"Too bad. I've always wanted to have my palm read, but each

time I try the fortune-teller looks at it for a moment, then refuses to go on. Absolutely refuses! I can't tell you how often this has happened. If not palms, then what is your method?"

"Cards."

"Then we must have cards." Smiling again, he reached into his pocket and brought out a new deck, still in cellophane. "Let's begin at once. Is there a table?"

Meryem asked him to shuffle and cut. Heydrich divided the cards into four piles as instructed, holding a Havana cigar between the fingers of the hand that handled the cards.

"Do I ask questions?" he said.

Meryem had not yet picked up the cards. "What questions do you want to ask?"

"None. Whatever you tell me about the future I will believe absolutely."

Meryem picked up the cards and looked at them. She was very still. "There's nothing I can tell you," she said.

Heydrich banged his fist on the table in mock anger. "Again! But this time I'm in a position to insist. Tell me what you see."

"It's not clear," Meryem said. "Cut the cards again."

Heydrich did so. "If you see love, tell me at once," he said.

"I saw that before, but in the past," Meryem said. "You once loved a person with a birthmark."

Heydrich was staggered. "Dear God, yes!" he said. "What shape was the birthmark?"

"Like a petal."

"Like a tear—like your tattoo! Nobody knew about that. This is positively amazing. What do you see now?"

Meryem looked at the cards spread out on the table before her. She seemed reluctant to touch them.

"You will have a kingdom of your own and rule over it," she said.

"A kingdom! What kingdom? Where?"

"In the east," Meryem said.

"When?"

"Soon."

"What else?"

"That's all I can tell you now."

Heydrich was beaming. "No wonder the other fortune tellers wouldn't tell me the truth," he said. "A kingdom! Who would have

251

believed such a thing?" He swept the cards into a pile. "I'm going to keep these," he said, putting them back into his pocket. "No one else must use these cards."

The two SS men came upstairs at eleven o'clock and cleared away the bottle and glasses and the other things Heydrich had brought, even the hats and the roses. "You can keep these chez moi," he said. "We must be discreet. Next time you come to me you can put on the hats and my photographer will make pictures."

At the door he kissed their hands one after the other. "I must say goodnight," he said. "Duty calls. We'll meet again quite soon— and, remember, I hope you will both come to see me in my kingdom in the east."

Suddenly he saw something over Lori's shoulder. A lamp was burning in Hubbard's study and something inside caught his eye. He strode down the hallway and entered the room. Zaentz's nude study of Lori hung over the desk. He gasped as he looked at it.

"*Wunderschön!*" he cried.

After he was gone, Lori went into the bathroom and vomited. When she came back to the sitting room, pale and haggard, she found Meryem sitting on the sofa with her legs drawn up beneath her. Lori opened all the windows and stood in front of one for several moments, breathing deeply. Then she sat down beside Meryem.

"What did you really see in the cards?" she asked.

"What I said—Heydrich ruling over a kingdom."

"God knows anything is possible. But you didn't tell him everything. I saw it in your face. What else did you see?"

"Death."

"A war?"

"Worse than war. I don't know what it was."

"What else?"

"Heydrich, dying. He dies first, before the others."

"Not soon enough."

"No," Meryem said. "Not soon enough. Lori, get Paul away from him."

Lori rose to her feet and went to the open window. In the street below, Hubbard and Paul were alighting from a large black automobile.

"I wonder what he'll want in return?" she said. "You know, Meryem, it's very odd, but even before he was born I thought Paul was in danger. I've known this day would come. But how? I'm not you. How could I possibly have known?"

Hubbard's key turned in the lock and he and Paul came into the room.

"Well, you two," Lori said, smiling brightly. "It's about time."

7

AFTER PAUL WENT TO BED, HUBBARD RECOUNTED THE DETAILS OF their encounter with the secret police. "There wasn't much to it, he said. "We were arrested by two men in leather coats in the Schlossgarten and taken to Gestapo headquarters. There the Dandy awaited us."

The Christophers called Heydrich's man Franz Stutzer "the Dandy" because that was what his surname meant in English and because he was always dressed entirely in black, like an actor playing Death in an arty movie—black Gestapo leather coat, black fedora, black kid gloves, black jacket, black breeches, black riding boots, black tie.

"What did he want?" Lori asked.

"It was very odd," Hubbard replied. "I expected a lot of questions about night sails to Denmark with forbidden cargo. But all he wanted to talk about was Paul's passport."

"What about it?"

"He said that Paul's American passport had no validity under German law. He kept repeating the same phrase over and over: 'This child was born in Germany of a German mother, therefore he is a German citizen who must have German papers.' "

"And what did you say in reply?"

"I asked him how anybody who was half American could be a German under the racial laws."

"Oh? And what did he say to that?"

"He said that was a dangerous question because the racial laws applied to Jews. It made him wonder if there was Jewish blood on the American side. 'That would explain a great deal,' he said. Really, it was a comedy—the windowless room, the bright light on the desk shining in our eyes, Stutzer lurking in the shadows, the guard outside the door, the pointless questions. He kept saying the same things over and over again, as if he was killing time."

"Maybe he was. What else did he say about Paul?"

"I told you. He only had one thing to say: His American passport is not valid in the eyes of the government of the Reich."

Lori went to the open window and looked down into the street. Because it was very late, there was no noise at all, nothing for the ear to apprehend. Lamplight glowed through the linden trees, casting dappled shadows that created the illusion that they were living in an underwater city. Goethestrasse seemed to be empty. But was it? It was impossible to be sure.

"I think we should go out to dinner tomorrow night," Lori said.

Because hardly anyone went there at night, they dined at the Swedischer Pavillon, in the Grunewald, with Paul and Hubbard's friend from the American Embassy. He was another classmate of Hubbard's—they seemed to be everywhere—and he knew Lori well. Though he was no relation, Paul called him "Uncle." This had been the man's idea. "Uncle What?" Paul had asked. "Just 'Uncle,' " the older man said, "I'm the only one you've got, so there's no need for formality."

Hubbard repeated the story of his arrest.

"Have you done something to annoy this man Stutzer?" the American asked.

"Lori smacked him in the face a while ago in front of fifty people," Hubbard said. "That may have upset him."

"Did she, by George? Draw any blood?"

"A little, from the nose," Hubbard said. He told the story—how the old drunk, a shell-shocked veteran everyone knew and tolerated, drank cream from the little pitcher that came with Stutzer's coffee at the outdoor table, how Stutzer had swung his boot, how Lori slapped him so hard that his black hat flew off, how they had taken the victim to the hospital.

"That would be enough," the American said. "In the eyes of American law, this man is wrong about Paul's citizenship. The fact that he was born abroad to a foreign mother means nothing. He's a full-fledged American citizen. If the Germans claim him too, he could be subject to German military service. And obviously there could be other inconveniences."

Lori said, "You're saying you couldn't protect him?"

"It could be difficult. Even if his citizenship was undisputed, he's subject to German law like anyone else as long as he lives in Germany no matter what his parentage may be."

"German law?" Lori said. "What's that? These people do whatever they like."

"True," the American said. "This is no country to live in if you want to go around slapping the Gestapo in the face."

"What's done is done," Lori said.

"True again." The American patted her hand. "I'll tell you what," he said. "I'm sailing to New York next Monday. I'd be glad to have Paul's company."

"I'll cable Elliott," Hubbard said.

The American smiled his casual smile. "Why don't you let me do that from the Embassy?" he said. "Nosey Parker is the postmaster here. I'll book Paul's passage, too."

Paul was sitting on his mother's right. He took her hand under the table. It was almost identical to his own, with long tapered fingers and limber bones. Because Lori had been playing the piano every day since childhood, her hands were very strong. She laced her fingers into his and wove their two hands into a single fist. Her eyes smiled when she looked at him. Squeezing Paul's hand until the skin turned white, she drew in a long shuddering breath and shook her head, as if to rid herself of a bad memory. Aboard ship, and for years afterward, Paul wondered what the memory might have been, if memory it was.

8

IN TIFAWT, A QUARTER OF A CENTURY LATER, WOLKOWICZ SAID, "SO what's the rest of the story?"

"You know the rest," Lla Kahina replied. "Lori disappeared."

"Not for another two years. What happened in the meantime?"

"Heydrich got worse. It was like a game of dolls—sit here, wear that, say this, eat some more pastries. Sometimes he'd ask me to read the cards."

"What did you see?"

"I always told him he was going to rule over a kingdom in the east. That was what he wanted to hear."

"You were right. Hitler made him Protector of Bohemia and Moravia. To all intents and purposes he was king of Czechoslovakia."

"That was after my time in Germany. Lori and Hubbard got me out of the country in 1939—took me to Denmark on the *Mahican*."

"How could they get away with that without Heydrich knowing it? He ran the whole Nazi secret police operation."

"I think he did know. He had that man Stutzer in Rügen to watch the Christophers, but Stutzer never tried to prevent them from sailing. He'd search the boat after they got back and make accusations, but that was all. I think Heydrich *wanted* them to commit these crimes. It gave him power over Lori. If she didn't do as he wanted he could put Hubbard in prison—kill him, even. He had the power of life and death over everyone in Germany."

"Did he really think *you* were a Jew?"

"What did it matter? I was just part of the decor. It was Lori who fascinated him because she was so far above him. He was hypnotized by that nude drawing that Zaentz made of her when she was pregnant with Paul. He'd come and look at it when Hubbard wasn't there. One day he came in disguise when Hubbard *was* there."

"In disguise?"

"Gray wig, beard, even a false nose. He said he was the Reich Inspector of Paintings. He made a terrible scene, shouting at Hubbard. 'Why do you have all these Jewish paintings?' he said. 'Look, you let a Jew draw a picture of your wife in the nude! All this shit will be confiscated and burned!' But he loved the picture. 'I must have it!' he'd say to Lori. 'If I took it your husband would find out about us. But if I *confiscate* it . . .' "

"Hubbard never suspected any of this?"

"Why should he? They loved each other."

"But she let this happen."

"What was she supposed to do about it? Hubbard and Paul were Heydrich's hostages."

"There was more to it than that."

"That's possible," Lla Kahina said.

Twilight was falling. Next door, the muezzin called the *salat al-maghrib*.

"The only thing the Christophers took with them besides their clothes when they finally tried to get out of Germany was that drawing of Lori," Lla Kahina said. "The Gestapo confiscated it when they arrested Lori. It was never seen again. Neither was she."

Lla Kahina saw someone behind Wolkowicz and smiled. She opened her arms in a gesture of love. Zarah Christopher came into the courtyard and kissed the old woman on the cheeks. Lla Kahina took her onto her lap and stroked her thick blond hair.

"Who, Nanna?" Zarah asked.

"*La belle dame sans peur,*" Lla Kahina said. "The beautiful lady who wasn't afraid of anything."

9

WOLKOWICZ DEPARTED THE NEXT DAY AT DAWN. NERVOUSLY, CATHY gave her permission for Zarah to ride with him toward the mountains as far as the Ja'wabi date tree.

"Just remember your promise," Cathy said to Wolkowicz. "Not a word about Paul and the rest of them."

"Okay," Wolkowicz replied. "But I don't know what you're so worried about. He's gone, sweetheart. The kid will never lay eyes on him."

"You're sure of that? They'd find each other if they knew about each other. Nothing ever stopped Paul, and she's just like him."

"What if they did? They're father and daughter. Are you jealous of your own kid?"

"I want her to be happy, that's all. I want her to be free. There's a curse on the Christophers."

"Okay. I'll keep it impersonal."

Until now Wolkowicz had not mentioned Christopher's name to Zarah. It was not necessary. Wolkowicz was the one who had informed her, in the first words he spoke in her presence, that her father existed. Thereafter, as he confided the details to Cathy and Lla Kahina he relied on the child's ingenuity.

Just after dawn they dismounted—Zarah from her mare, Wolkowicz from his donkey—and ate their breakfast beneath the date tree. The village lay below them, mica walls scattering the rays of the early morning sun. In the other direction the snowy peaks of the Idáren Dráren caught the same horizontal light. If Wolkowicz appreciated this unique spectacle, he gave no sign.

"I think you should learn Chinese," he said.

"Chinese? What for?"

"You may have to go to China someday."

"Why?"

"Who knows? To visit relatives, maybe."

Zarah was peeling an orange, turning it against the knife so as to make a long continuous spiral of the skin. She finished what she was doing, divided the orange in two, and shared it with Wolkowicz. He ate it slowly, section by section, then took the child's hands in his.

"Time to say goodbye," he said. "Before I leave I want you to know that I came here to see you, nobody else. I did it because I knew I could trust you to remember something. I'm your father's friend. Whatever you may hear in the future, whatever other people may try to tell you, that's the truth. Remember that. When you see him, and I know you're going to find him someday, tell him what I told you."

He released her hands. "Open the book I gave you to page one hundred," he said. Zarah did so and found a brand-new American hundred dollar bill. Wolkowicz said, "Tear it in half." Without hesitation Zarah folded the crisp banknote in half, creased it, and tore it neatly along the seam. "Keep half and give me the other half," Wolkowicz said. Once again Zarah obeyed.

"Don't lose your half," Wolkowicz said. "Someday somebody may give you the other half. If it matches, you'll know that whoever gives it to you is your father's friend, just like I am, and that I told that person something I want you to know—something that's important to your father. Even if I'm dead, whatever the person with the other half of the hundred tells you comes straight from me. Got it?"

Zarah nodded.

"Good," Wolkowicz said. He gave her a boost onto her horse, and when she looked down from the saddle into his broad homely face, he grinned at her.

"Don't forget," he said. "I'm counting on you."

INTERLUDE

BEAUTIFUL DREAMERS

"THE O.G. LIVES IN THE FUTURE," PATCHEN SAID. "ALL GREAT PRAC-tical jokers do. He can't wait for Sis to find the frog in her bed or the pan of water balanced on the door to spill on Cousin Oscar's head. That's why he likes your idea—it's a terrific prank."

"But you don't like it," Christopher said.

"I didn't say that," Patchen replied. "But it doesn't answer what you say is the important question: 'Why?' "

"No. All it does is put you in a position to ask the question of somebody who knows the answer."

They were walking home together after Patchen's birthday supper. They had stayed late at the O. G.'s, trapped by his enthusiasm for Christopher's idea.

The O. G., who had always insisted that all good ideas can be expressed in a single sentence, was captivated by the simplicity of the plan: get the kidnapper out in the open by isolating him on a single target. "That's the stuff!" he had cried. "Tie up the goat in the moonlight, climb the tree, wait for the tiger to come."

Now, walking past the hushed mansions of the O. G.'s hidden neighborhood, Patchen discussed the proposal more calmly. "How, exactly, do we lead the enemy to the target of our choice?" he asked.

"By removing every target except the one you want him to hit," Christopher replied.

"I understand the principle," Patchen said. "But you're talking about a lot of people. We have stations, bases, and deep-cover operations in every country in the world. Tell me more details."

Christopher did so, tersely: clear the embassies of Outfit people, break contact with every agent in the world, explain nothing, create unbearable curiosity. Then put somebody out in the open—one in

259

each danger zone, the Middle East, Europe, Washington—and wait for the kidnappers to strike.

"You mean bait the trap with real Outfitters who know real secrets?"

"They'd have to be genuine to stand up under the drug. But they don't have to be in on the details. You'd falsify them—give them something to confess that they believed was true, some-thing" . . . he spoke the next words in an imitation of the O. G.'s ardent tones . . . "that would keep the tiger's attention on the goat until Jim Corbett got in his shot."

Patchen was not amused. "You mean lie to our own people, set them up?"

Christopher did not bother to smile. "If you want them to lie effectively under this drug," he said, "they will have to believe that they're telling the truth."

"The voice of experience," Patchen said.

"What do you mean by that?"

"Wasn't that what happened in China? Didn't you hold out under their interrogation till the end by telling nothing but the truth, as you knew it?"

Christopher stopped in his tracks. "Yes," he said. "I never thought of it in quite that way. But that's what I was doing. Otherwise there would have been no hope."

"No hope?"

"I thought I was never going to get out," Christopher said. "If I had lied to please the people who had me in their power, what would I have had left?"

They were in a dense man-made forest in which every grand, sepulchral house stood in a clearing, hidden from its neighbors and disjoined from the life of the city; the silence was eerie—deeper, even, than the silence of Manchuria, where Christopher in his prison cell had always heard the wind blowing or the rain falling or a guard hawking and spitting outside the bars.

After a short pause, only a step or two, Patchen broke the tension with his own little joke about the O. G. and his mordant opinion, which they both shared, of the double-tongued courtesans of Washington.

"*Circumspice,*" he said in the old man's fractured Latin. "Look around you."

IV

BYGONES

ONE

1

TEN YEARS AFTER PAUL CHRISTOPHER WAS ARRESTED AND IMPRIS-
oned by the Chinese Communists, David Patchen met in Tokyo
with a man named Yeho Stern. Patchen had become Director of
the Outfit only two weeks before, and this was his first meeting
with the head of a foreign intelligence service since his appointment. Yeho Stern did not congratulate Patchen on his promotion.
He had no manners in the usual sense of the word; he had stripped
his personality and appearance of all bourgeois traits as a matter of
ethnic pride and did not want to be mistaken for anything but what
he was, a Jew who had, by a miracle, escaped with his life from
Christendom and now had the means to defend himself and others
against its murderous delusions. To Yeho, courtesy was strictly
utilitarian, and its only rule could be expressed in a single sentence:
Never do anything that might compromise secrecy. Yeho regarded
this encounter, which had been arranged without explanation on
short notice, as a breach of etiquette. In more than twenty years of
clandestine meetings, he and Patchen had never before met outdoors, let alone in a foreign country inhabited by a different race of
people. Even among their own kind they were a noticeable pair:
Yeho was a stout but very short man, almost a midget, while
Patchen stood over six feet high and looked even taller because he
was so gaunt.

Now they stood side by side on the Full-Moon Bridge of the
Korakuen Garden in central Tokyo. It was very early in the morning on a cold, smoggy day, but the park was already full of Japanese. Tame carp hung in the murky water beneath the bridge,
waiting to be fed. Yeho did not look down at the gold and silver

fishes, some of them older than the oldest living human being; they were irrelevant. Sound carried over still water. That was relevant.

"Why did you choose this place for a meeting?" he asked, looking around him in all directions before he spoke and then barely voicing the words.

"I wanted to talk to you before you left for China tomorrow," Patchen said.

Despite the clammy archipelagic weather, Yeho wore his Jerusalem clothes: a short-sleeved shirt that exposed his stubby, muscular arms, rumpled cotton trousers, sandals, no necktie. He always wore sandals; he did not own a necktie, and it was said that he did not even know how to tie one. He was called Yeho by his equals, never Stern, which wasn't his name in any case, but the shortened form of the name his family had been given in 1787 when Austria passed a law requiring all Jews living within its borders to adopt Germanized surnames. Prosperous families were named for jewels (Rubin) or flowers (Rosen) or for admirable traits such as honesty (Ehrlich). Most ordinary people, who could not pay bribes, were given one of four utilitarian names derived from their appearance: Schwarz (black), Weiss (white), Klein (little), Gross (big). The wretched were saddled with jokes as names. Yeho's ancestor, a tanner who reeked of puer, the solution of hot water and dog dung in which animal hides were steeped after being treated with lime, had been entered on the rolls as Hundsstern, or "dog star."

On arrival in Palestine Yeho shortened it to Stern, a resonant name in the story of the creation of the Jewish state. In his own organization, and within the Outfit, where Yeho had many admirers but few acquaintances, he was called the Memuneh, the Big Boss. This did not offend his otherwise invincible modesty.

In order to look into Patchen's face without straining his neck, Yeho had to stand several steps away. He had large translucent ears, and because he was standing with his back to the morning sun, they glowed bright pink.

"So," he said. "Speak."

Patchen said, "I want to do the Chinese a favor."

Yeho clucked his tongue. "Another one?"

In China, where Americans had been forbidden to tread for more than twenty years, Yeho was welcome as an honest broker. In addition to the business he carried out in the name of his own service, he had also done many favors on Patchen's behalf. These had usually taken the form of small but valuable gifts that were useful to the Chinese in their operations against their archenemy, Soviet Russia—a piece of hardware, a scrap of information that completed a puzzle, a timely warning. Yeho had never asked for anything in return for these benefices, but after delivering them he always inquired, discreetly, about the American prisoner, Paul Christopher, so that the Chinese would understand where the favor really came from.

So far they had shown no sign that they would ever let Christopher go; in their penal methods, the Chinese placed great emphasis on remorse, confession, and reform, but Christopher refused to admit his crimes against China. Unless he confessed and apologized, they explained, he was doomed.

On the Full-Moon Bridge in Tokyo, Patchen looked into Yeho Stern's upturned face and said, "I want to give them Butterfly."

"Give them *Butterfly?*"

Yeho threw up his stubby arms in disbelief and turned his back.

Butterfly was the cryptonym by which Patchen and Yeho, and two or three others, knew an operative of the Russian intelligence service—they called it that, or the RIS, never "the Soviet intelligence service" or "the KGB," because in their opinion there was no such thing as the Soviet Union, only the Russian empire operating under an assumed name.

For the past year and a half Yeho and Patchen and a very small group of people from their two organizations had been paying close attention to Butterfly. He came to their attention after he managed the assassination or kidnapping of half a dozen agents of the People's Republic of China in Europe and Africa. On the surface, these were senseless operations. The victims were doing the Russians no harm, and even if the opposite had been true, it is seldom good practice for an intelligence service to kill an enemy it knows, because the victim will only be replaced by one that it does not know and must therefore identify and neutralize at great expense in time, manpower, and money.

It was the very pointlessness of these operations that aroused Patchen's curiosity: if there was no apparent purpose to an act, it followed that there must be a hidden purpose. In order to discover what the RIS's secret motive was, he set up a team to watch Butterfly, putting Horace Hubbard, Paul Christopher's younger cousin, in charge of this operation. Patchen trusted Horace absolutely on the basis of his bloodlines, but he was qualified in other ways, too: after leading a Marine rifle platoon in Korea he had concentrated in Chinese at Yale and later learned Arabic while working for the Outfit in the Middle East. He had worked for Barney Wolkowicz in Vietnam, where he mastered Vietnamese and was the last American known to have seen Christopher before he vanished into China. Horace had a flair for dangerous operations, and because he spoke so many Oriental languages he was credited with understanding the Eastern mind. He put together a group that included several American Chinese, with a sprinkling of Chinese refugees from Vietnam, and with the help of an Outfit computer expert, targeted the Chinese missions in Europe whose intelligence officers were most likely to be hit next.

The computer expert, a spinster whose specialty was the laws of probability, predicted that the next killing would take place in a neutral country—possibly Austria, but more probably Switzerland because it provided a larger number of escape routes. Within a month another Chinese was shot to death as he waited in the Parc Mon Repos in Geneva for a contact. As in all previous cases, the assassins used a silenced Czech-made 7.65mm Skorpion machine pistol, firing all twenty rounds from the magazine into the target's back from a range of about one meter.

Horace's agents, posing as tourists from the Far East, were witnesses to the assassination. Using a video camera concealed in a baby carriage, they recorded the killing on tape, then followed the murderers home to a safe house across the French frontier in Annemasse. This led the American team to the terrorists' support group, and, in due course, to Butterfly himself.

From Outfit file data the computer expert established that Butterfly's false-true RIS name—that is, the one he used inside his own headquarters in Moscow—was Gherman Wolyinski. He spoke fluent Arabic and English and was an expert in small arms, explosives, and small-scale guerrilla operations.

"The strange thing about this operation," Horace reported, "is that all of Butterfly's shooters and all the supporting cast are Palestinian Arabs or bourgeois European leftists—romantic females, in about half the cases—who sympathize with the Palestinian cause. The question is, Why would they want to use Arabs to kill Chinese Communists?"

"I don't know," Patchen replied. "But since it involves Arabs I think we'd better ask the Memuneh."

Patchen flew to Tel Aviv and told Yeho Stern everything the Outfit knew about Butterfly. Yeho listened intently—far more intently than Patchen, or the chief of any other secret service in the world would have done. Yeho's country, Israel, was alone in the world, surrounded by enemies. His mother and father and every other member of his family except himself had perished in the Nazi death camps, and before that his ancestors had been murdered by Crusaders, burned at the stake by Inquisitors, raped and slaughtered by Cossacks, and torn apart by pious mobs whose members believed that Jews drank the blood of Christian babies. There was not the slightest doubt in Yeho's mind that Israel's enemies wanted to kill every Jew that Hitler had left alive, together with all their children and grandchildren down to the last infant who was suspected of having a single drop of Jewish blood in its veins. It did not take him long to form an opinion about the true purposes of Butterfly's operations against the Chinese. Soon enough, Butterfly's terrorists would start killing Jews—Yeho was sure of it. Making the killers wait to do their real work, to achieve their real reward, was just an exercise in control and discipline.

"He's training Palestinians?" Yeho said. "Then all this is nothing but a rehearsal. This Russian is blooding his dogs. Next comes the *real* operation—against Israel, against the U. S."

"But why kill so many Chinese?" Patchen asked. "Why not target Jews from the start, or even Americans?"

"Because he wants privacy," Yeho replied. "Of all the people on earth, the Chinese are the most isolated, the least likely to tell the Western press what's happening to them and who's responsible. Not that the media, or even Western governments, would care. They're only interested in what happens to white people."

A troop of Japanese tourists, stunted homely people like Yeho in cheap foreign clothes, marched onto the Full-Moon Bridge behind a girl wearing a smart blue uniform and white gloves. They paused, listening obediently, while the guide described the bridge and the lake. Then they stepped to the rail one by one and fed rice balls to the carp, which had now schooled in such large numbers just beneath the surface that they resembled a rusty carnival mechanism that had fallen into the murky water.

"Give Butterfly to the Chinese?" Yeho said. "No, absolutely not."

"Yeho, listen," Patchen said.

"Why should I listen? Never. That's all."

Knowing who Butterfly was, watching him, identifying and monitoring his assets, had become Yeho's most important operation because it could prevent the spilling of Jewish blood. If Butterfly was replaced by another Russian, it might take years to identify the newcomer. In the meantime Yeho would not know where the next assassination, the next bombing, the next kidnapping, the next enemy from among the millions who surrounded Israel, was going to come from. There was no question that Israel's innumerable enemies would attack, one at a time or in concert. But when? where? using what weapons? Yeho would go to any lengths to discover the answers to these questions.

The Japanese tour group fell back into formation and marched away. Patchen handed Yeho a sheet of paper. Yeho accepted it reluctantly. It was a surveillance report filed by Horace's team. Butterfly had left Moscow the day before, flying to Stockholm as a member of a Soviet sports delegation. There he had changed passports and traveled by ferry to Denmark and by train to Milan as a Canadian professor of social anthropology on sabbatical from his post at Carleton University in Ottawa. He was now registered under this false Canadian identity at a small hotel near Pesaro.

The Italian tourist season was over; the Germans who thronged the Adriatic beaches in summer had gone home. Butterfly was virtually alone in his hotel; he took long walks on the deserted beach, inhaling the salt air, while he waited for whoever he was waiting for. When he went out, he absent-mindedly left a well-worn Samsonite briefcase containing his false Canadian passport, his half-used round-trip ticket to Ottawa, his wallet with driver's license, checkbook, credit cards, and family photographs, behind in his room. Also a knapsack full of scholarly journals and books and the typed manuscript of an article on marriage customs among the Greenland Inuit.

"How old is this report?" Yeho asked.

"Twenty-six hours."

"All right," Yeho said. "Tell me why you want to do this insane thing."

"We think Butterfly is going to turn his networks loose."

"What do you mean, turn them loose?"

Patchen handed over a large brown envelope. Yeho peeked inside, examining the contents without removing them. The envelope contained an eight-by-ten-inch X-ray print of a full-length silhouette of an adult male. Black images of hundreds of small rectangles were scattered all over the torso and legs.

"Who took this?" Yeho asked.

"We did, in Milan, while he was waiting for his bags. Those are two-ounce gold ingots, two hundred and twenty of them, sewn into his coat and pants. The photo-analysts think he's also carrying a lot of cash in that money belt and in false bottoms—more than a million dollars."

"And you think he's going to give all this loot to somebody?"

"To his Arabs. And then he's going to wish them luck and say goodbye."

"Why?"

"Think about it."

Yeho saw Patchen's point. Butterfly's mission had been to create an asylum full of lunatics, and then unlock the doors and let them go. He was going to give them twenty-eight pounds of gold and a million dollars in currency, tell them they could kill anyone they wanted to kill, and say goodbye. Butterfly and the RIS had never had any intention of controlling the monster they had created. They *wanted* these terrorists out of control, acting according to no discernible plan—and, above all, disconnected from themselves. When the slaughter began, they would deny that they knew anything about the terrorists.

Yeho gave Patchen back his documents. "Okay," he said. "Tell me the scenario."

2

HORACE HUBBARD ARRIVED IN TOKYO FROM MILAN THAT NIGHT. YEHO Stern and Patchen met him at two o'clock in the morning in the Bubble, as the soundproof, Plexiglas room in the basement of the American Embassy was called. Yeho was much more comfortable here, where no listening devices, not even the Outfit's, could possibly exist. He put his elbows on the transparent tabletop and studied Horace's long, equine face. It was unshaven and pale, but the merry eyes showed not even the smallest sign of fatigue after a twelve-hour flight over the Arctic.

"You look like your uncle," Yeho said.

"More like my father, actually—I inherited his dark hair," Horace replied. "You knew my uncle?"

"A long time ago. He was a benefactor to me and many others."

Horace nodded, unsurprised, and let Yeho's reply go at that; he was used to meeting people who had some reason to remember Hubbard Christopher with gratitude; very often they were Jews. It was astonishing how many of these unhappy people the Christophers—Paul, too, after his parents were gone; he had inherited the weakness—had rescued or befriended.

Knowing that Yeho had a sweet tooth, Horace had brought a large sack of jelly doughnuts with him, and he opened the bag, releasing the smell of baked goods, and offered them around. Yeho selected one and took a bite. He did not touch the weak American coffee furnished by the Embassy.

"So, Horace," Yeho said. "You're the head kidnapper. What's this stuff inside the doughnut?"

"Red bean paste," Horace replied. "They put it in everything sweet."

"It could be poisoned."

"I suppose so, but I picked out these doughnuts myself."

"You speak Japanese?"

"Enough to get the doughnuts I want."

"Are you personally also picking out everything for this operation?" Yeho asked. "The right men, the right plan, the right equipment?"

"Keep the equipment to a minimum," Patchen said. "No fancy stuff. This is just a plain old-fashioned kidnapping."

"The voice of Headquarters," Yeho said.

His own weakness for the gadgetry of espionage was well known. He equipped his agents with invisible ink, with luggage with secret compartments, with miniature radios, with code books that destroyed themselves when ampules of acid concealed in their spines were crushed in the instant before capture. In his day Yeho had been a great field agent, a master smuggler. During the British mandate in Palestine, when he was a young operative in the Jewish Underground, he had carried a pistol through many check points by taking it apart and taping the disassembled pieces to various parts of his body with flesh-colored tape to which he had glued body hair plucked from the thick mats of black fur on his chest and back. Even when the British stripped him naked they did not discover the pistol. He used it to kill three people—two Arabs and a Sephardic Jew from London whom he suspected of being an agent of the RIS, which was already, even then, trying to penetrate the future secret service of the unborn Jewish state.

"Tell me, young man," he said to Horace. "Do you know about the fuse on the bomb that was supposed to kill Adolf Hitler on July 20, 1944?"

Horace knew all about the bomb and the plot by German aristocrats to kill Hitler and end the war, but he shook his head no. He wanted to listen to this man, no matter what the subject, in the same way that a young physicist would want to listen to Einstein.

"This particular bomb had to be a time bomb, to allow the assassin time to get away," Yeho said. "But it had to be silent, no ticking clock, because everything was very hushed in the presence of the Führer. A special trigger was invented—a wire inside a glass capsule submerged in acid, inside a metal tube. When you crushed the tube with a pair of pliers, the glass capsule broke and the acid ate through the wire in a stated number of minutes, tripping the detonator. The technology was amazing for 1944. It made the conspirators feel very good. 'Look how much smarter we are than Hitler to have such a bomb,' they said to themselves. They were aristocrats, the flower of the German nobility, all *von*s and *zu*s. The assassin, Colonel Count Klaus von Stauffenberg, smuggled the bomb into Hitler's presence in his briefcase. First, in the toilet, he broke the tube with his pliers, which wasn't easy because he only had one arm and one eye as a result of war wounds—no offense, David. He placed the briefcase at the target's feet, under the conference table, and left the room. Another man who knew nothing, suspected nothing, pushed the briefcase six inches across the floor because it was in his way. Because he did this, the briefcase with the bomb and its wonderful silent trigger was now in a different position—the leg of the table stood between Hitler and the bomb, so when it went off most of the force of the explosion was absorbed by the table leg. All that happened to Hitler was that his eardrums were broken and he suffered a little concussion. He thought that the Teuton gods had saved him so that he could carry out his great destiny. His secret police tortured the bluebloods who had tried to kill him, then wrapped piano wire around their necks and hung them on meat hooks. His photographers made movies of them as they died, quite slowly, and Hitler watched these movies while maybe five million extra people, Jews mostly, died because he was still in charge and the war didn't end for another eleven months . . . What is the moral of the story, Horace?"

Horace looked across the table. "Leave nothing to chance," he said.

"Right," Yeho said. "When most people hear that story, they say there was something wrong with Stauffenberg's bomb. But there was nothing wrong with the bomb. It functioned perfectly. There was something wrong with the assassin. He was very brave, very daring. But he was a snob and he could not stop being a snob even to rid the world of a monster. He armed the bomb and excused himself. Not because he was afraid to die, but because Stauffenbergs don't die in the same room with scum like Adolf Hitler; it simply isn't done."

Horace did not argue with Yeho's conclusions about the attempt on Hitler's life. Instead, speaking without notes, he described, step by step, the plan to kidnap Butterfly. The actual abduction would be handled by a team of five Outfit employees, all highly trained commandos. They would seize the Russian on the beach, give him an injection, throw him into an inflatable Zodiac boat equipped with a high-speed outboard motor, ferry him to a larger boat waiting offshore, interrogate him on board, then bring him ashore somewhere else and give him to the Chinese.

"How long has this team trained together?" Yeho asked.

"More than a year," Horace said.

"Too long," Yeho said. "They'll be so pent up they'll kill everybody. What's their age?"

"Late twenties, early thirties."

"Too old. You have to get them when they're nineteen for this kind of work, while they're still enthusiastic. Twenty is too old."

"They'll be all right," Horace said. "We recruited most of them when they *were* nineteen."

"And they've been rehearsing ever since for the real thing? How do you know they won't just kill everybody when you turn them loose?"

"That's why they rehearse, so they won't act on impulse."

"You guarantee results, is that what you're telling me?"

"No. But there's no Stauffenberg factor."

Yeho peppered him with questions designed to detect some hidden flaw, some possible failure, in every aspect of the operation.

"When you go ashore you will go to a safe house," he said. "Does this safe house have a secret room?" he asked.

"In a manner of speaking, yes," Horace replied.

He would have said more, but Yeho interrupted him. "Good. This is extremely important. The entrance must be perfectly concealed. Inside, in the secret room behind the wall, you must put everything you might conceivably need—water in sealed bottles, food in cans, weapons, a transceiver radio with earphones, and two containers that can be tightly sealed, for body slops. Also some lime, to deodorize the slops. Your enemies have five senses, remember."

Yeho, as a boy, had hidden from the Nazis in just such a secret room as he described. Even the family of Viennese who took over the aparment after his parents went to their deaths at Auschwitz never suspected that the room existed, or that he was inside it, waiting. He lived with them like a mouse for three years, slipping out at night to steal food and water and dispose of his bodily wastes.

Horace knew this; it was a famous story in the secret world. "We're going to keep the prisoner in a box," he said.

"A box? What box?"

"Actually it's a portable cell, disguised to look like one of those crates they load onto ships."

"What's inside?"

"Besides Butterfly? A chair, bolted to the box, and the straps binding him to the chair so that he won't rattle around."

"What about piss and shit?"

"All the conveniences you mentioned will be provided."

Yeho plunged on. "How do you protect the box?"

"With two men inside it with the prisoner—it's quite a large box—and six outside. He'll stay inside until we hand him over to the Chinese."

"Box and all?"

"Yes. After we've asked our questions—and whatever questions you want us to ask on your behalf."

"You expect the prisoner to volunteer his answers?"

"No. We'll use drugs."

273

"That's all you'll use?"

"We think that will be enough."

Yeho peered at Horace, looking for the slightest trace of a smile. He saw none. Horace's eyes were friendly, interested, and utterly free of scorn and contempt, like Hubbard Christopher's eyes.

"What if the Chinese are delayed?" Yeho asked. "What if the opposition finds out you have him and where he is? How will you hide him?"

"In the first case, we'll move the box," Horace said. "In the second, we'll shoot him."

"Don't be saucy," Yeho said; his English idioms, learned from a prewar grammar for Austrian schoolchildren, sometimes surprised native English-speakers. "There's one thing you haven't explained to me," he continued. "What happens if Butterfly ever gets traded back to the Russians and he tells them what the Outfit did to him?"

"First he'd have to know the Outfit did it," Horace said. "He won't. Every member of my team is Chinese; he won't see anybody who is not Chinese. He doesn't speak the language. He'll be full of sodium pentothal and other good things. Do you think he'll know the difference between Chinese-Americans and Vietnamese Chinese and the Chinese-Chinese he meets in China?"

"Maybe, maybe not," Yeho said.

But he was beginning to respect Horace. An all-Chinese team? He seemed to have a natural gift for work in which there were very few naturals. He stood up, yawned, and stretched.

"Are you in?" Patchen asked.

"Now he asks me," Yeho said.

3

"WHAT DID BUTTERFLY SPILL?" YEHO ASKED ON HIS RETURN FROM China. By that time Butterfly had been in Horace's possession for a week. "Are you sure you got everything?"

"Everything that time permitted," Horace said.

He and Yeho faced each other across a table in the captain's cabin of a rusty freighter bound for Haifa, where the crate containing Butterfly would be off-loaded, then transferred to a Chinese ship that had been diverted from Oran.

"What about my cousin?" Horace asked.

"They agreed to release him soon after we deliver Butterfly."

"*How* soon?"

"As soon as the politicals say 'yes.' The CIS has no power to let him go on their own. Face is involved. If your cousin would just acknowledge his guilt there'd be no problem, but even after ten years he won't unbend. They talk to him every day, trying to persuade him, and every day he refuses to confess."

"Then they'd do well to give up. He's not guilty; he'll never say that he is."

"You can tell them that when you get there, but it's very difficult for them. They've had so many missionaries, first the Christians and then the Communists; they believe in redemption."

"To answer your question about the interrogation of Butterfly," Horace said, "the whole interrogation is on video tape. We have an unedited copy for you. In brief, we confirmed all the names and faces of Butterfly's network. Also details of the network's organization and training."

"Confirmed?" Yeho said. "That means we already knew all that. What else?"

"More confirmation. Butterfly did in fact come to Italy to turn these maniacs loose. Moscow doesn't *want* to know what they're going to do. From now on there'll be no Russian handlers, no cutouts, no communications, no further support. They're cut off, on their own."

"On their own?" Yeho said. "How can they be on their own when Russians are involved?"

"The Russians want total deniability. There's no telling who these people might kill."

"There is no list of targets?"

"No list; only categories. They simply swear an oath to kill Jews and all those who help Jews to disinherit and oppress the Palestinian Arabs."

"But there must be a hit list of individuals," Yeho said. "Otherwise how do they make choices?"

"That occurred to us, too," Horace said. "But Butterfly insists that no such list exists. The whole operation was designed to be random, uncontrolled, unpredictable, with no two actions resembling each other."

"Then why did they always use the same methods against the Chinese?"

"The method in those cases was dictated by the target. The Chinese are very regular in their habits."

"True," Yeho said. "And why? Because their service was founded on the principles of the RIS—leave nothing to chance, never depart from procedure, control every detail. And now you're telling me the rules don't apply to these Frankenstein monsters they've created?"

There was something wrong here. Yeho did not trust the results of interrogations carried out by the Americans. They were too fastidious in their methods. They worried about their own immortal souls and the Bill of Rights. They relied on drugs and the polygraph apparatus and the witchcraft of psychology. They were too easily satisfied with the paltry results yielded by these superficial methods. They never went all the way to the bottom of the prisoner's mind because in their hearts they did not believe that any enemy was truly dangerous to them. America was too big, too rich, too young, too strong and healthy to imagine that any adversary could do it permanent, let alone fatal harm. Therefore the intentions of their enemies did not really matter to them. If worse came to worst, the Americans would go to war, win, and convert their defeated enemies into replicas of themselves.

To Yeho, the servant of an isolated and terrorized nation, the enemy's intentions were a matter of life and death. He looked across the table at Horace Hubbard and said, "I would like to ask this Russian a few simple questions before you give him to his new owners. Without drugs."

Horace turned his enormous hands palm upward in a gesture of generosity. "Be my guest," he said.

4

WHEN YEHO FOLLOWED HORACE DOWN INTO THE HOLD OF THE LITtle ship and saw the arrangements that had been made for the interrogation of Butterfly, he could not believe his eyes. The box in which the prisoner was confined was wired for closed-circuit television and sound. Horace sat Yeho down in front of a row of monitors and switched it on. Butterfly's face, familiar to Yeho because, courtesy of Horace Hubbard, he had seen so many photographs of it, appeared immediately in fall color. The eyes were dull, the face slack. He was seated in a metal chair, his wrists and ankles secured by heavy straps.

"Is he drugged?" Yeho asked.

"He's hung over from drugs, but the primary effects have worn off," Horace replied. "He may be a little disoriented. After all, he's a Russian and he's in the hands of the Mongols."

"Does he remember being drugged?"

"Yes, of course. But in theory he doesn't remember what he said to us while under the influence."

"Then he doesn't know that you know that Jews are the real target?"

"No. He thinks the Chinese have grabbed him for what he did to them."

"Why does he think that?"

"Because all he sees when he's conscious is angry yellow faces. And all he hears is angry questions about the Chinese murders."

Horace threw another switch. The features of one of his young Chinese operatives appeared, wearing a headset like an airplane pilot's, with earphones and microphone. This man was inside the box with Butterfly. He had a Chinese haircut and a Chinese wristwatch; he held a Chinese version of the Soviet 9mm Makarova pistol in his hand. He was dressed in blue overalls made in China and laundered with Chinese soap; he had been eating Chinese food for several weeks so that he smelled like a Chinese. A photograph of Chairman Mao and a poster quoting him hung on the wall ("WE CAN LEARN WHAT WE DO NOT KNOW. WE ARE NOT ONLY GOOD AT DESTROYING THE OLD WORLD, WE ARE ALSO GOOD AT BUILDING THE NEW.").

"Just like the movies," Horace said. He put on a headset and handed another to Yeho. Then he spoke into the microphone in English, a series of codewords that were gibberish to Yeho. The man inside answered in Mandarin. Horace responded in the same tongue; it was obvious that he was explaining Yeho's presence and giving instructions. Finally he turned to Yeho. "Just ask your questions. Wong will repeat them to Butterfly in Russian and you'll hear the answers over the headset."

"That's it?"

"What do you mean, Memuneh?"

"This is as close as I get?"

"Unless you can turn yourself into a Chinese, I'm afraid it is. I'll leave you to it." Horace got up to leave. Looking down on Yeho, who now wore a headset clamped to his large, fuzzy head, his eyes danced with amusement. "Memuneh?" he said.

"What?"

"No loud noises, please."

"Very funny," Yeho said. "Out!"

Horace departed, grinning at his own joke. Thirty years before, in time of war, as the youthful chief of an irregular intelligence unit, Yeho made a practice of questioning enemy prisoners in pairs consisting of one man who knew something of value (or was suspected of knowing something of value) and a second man who was known to have no useful information whatsoever. This second man could be anybody—an Arab culled from a POW stockade or even captured specially for the occasion—but he was indispensable to the success of the interrogation. He and the man who knew something would be locked in the same cell for several hours or several days, depending on the time available.

After they had gotten to know each other, Yeho would have the two men brought to him, always at night, at some remote and secret place in the desert. They would find him sitting in a tent behind a bare desk with two empty chairs in front of it. After the prisoners' ankles had been shackled to the chairs Yeho would order the guards to untie their hands and remove their blindfolds. He would offer them cigarettes and sweetened tea. As they smoked and drank together in this parody of hospitality, he would chat with them in fluent Palestinian Arabic, a dialect in which he knew several dozen dirty jokes and many amusing anecdotes. Yeho was an excellent storyteller, and he could usually break through the prisoners' natural wall of suspicion and fear in a matter of fifteen or twenty minutes. By that time they would actually be laughing at his jokes; because they were afraid, they laughed very hard.

At this point he would tell his best joke, and while they were still laughing at it Yeho would produce a .455-caliber Webley revolver from the drawer of his desk and, without the slightest warning or change of demeanor, shoot the extra prisoner, the one who knew nothing, between the eyes. The Webley, which made a deafening noise when it went off, delivered a soft lead bullet with enough force to lift the target into the air and fling him a considerable distance backward, chair and all.

The victim's skull was, of course, shattered by the impact, and the survivor, sitting right next to him, was drenched by a shower of brains, blood, and splintered bone. Yeho would give him no opportunity to recover from the shock. Instead, he would cock the Webley by thumbing back the hammer, point it directly at the survivor's head and say, in the same genial tone of voice in which he had been telling jokes only a moment before, "Now, my friend, there are a few simple questions I would like to ask you."

The Outfit's technology was no substitute for this sort of intimate contact and direct action, and an RIS man who had been promised—personally, by Yeho—to the Chinese intelligence service was not the same as an Arab captured in Samaria. But Yeho had no choice but to accommodate to the situation as he found it. Besides, he was no more anxious to be seen by Butterfly than Horace was to have him seen. He switched on his microphone.

"Hello, Wong," he said. "To make things simple, I'm going to speak Russian. Is that all right? Touch your chin for yes, touch your cheek for no. I don't understand Chinese." Wong touched his chin. Yeho said, "Do you have to go to the toilet?" Wong touched his cheek. "Good," Yeho said, "because this may take a long time." In the other monitor, he watched Butterfly, who was paying close attention to Wong's signals; although he was strapped into a chair like a murderer (which, of course, he was) awaiting electrocution, the man was alert, he was watchful, he hadn't given up. "Good," Yeho said again. "Let's begin."

After a lifetime of inducing confessions from people like Butterfly, Yeho held certain basic principles. All spies are liars, it is their métier, and like ordinary liars they live in a panic, knowing that the truth about themselves may be discovered at any moment—or worse, is already known by people who are too disgusted, or too clever, to confront them with it. A spy under questioning by the enemy is in a state surpassing dread because he knows that he must sooner or later tell the truth. His captors will use any means to get it out of him, and sooner or later he will spill what he knows because he cannot stand the pain, or because he is so exhausted that he will do anything for sleep, or because he *wants* to have the long-festering secret in his breast removed by his interrogator as a tumor on the lung is excised by a surgeon, permitting the patient to breathe freely with at least one lung. Half a life is better than none. But he knows that this is a delusion. There is nothing waiting for him after the ordeal is over, not even half a life. This is his choice:

if he does not yield he will die; and if he yields, he will die. He is only valuable, and therefore alive, so long as he does not talk. The worst thing he can imagine is that the person who is asking him questions already knows the truth, and like the examining angel on the day of judgment, is adding up his evasions for no other purpose than to add to the weight of his punishment.

This was Butterfly's case. He may not have known what he had been asked or what he had answered while under the influence of drugs, but he knew that he had been under their influence. What had he done? What had he spilled? Why did he feel so guilty?

"Connect him to the lie detector," Yeho said into his microphone.

Wong did so, strapping the blood pressure cuff onto Butterfly's arm, the device that measures breathing onto his hairy chest, the part that detects sweating onto the palm of the hand. Yeho had no faith in the polygraph; too many categories of human beings were immune to it. Africans, Asians, and psychopaths laughed at it. As a practical matter it only worked on people who came from cultures that controlled human behavior by instilling guilt and mandating supernatural punishment. It had no power over those who were not possessed of a Western conscience. Yeho connected the polygraph to Butterfly because he was a Communist and probably also a vestigial Christian as nearly all Russians were, and therefore the creature of the two most implacably confessional faiths ever invented.

"Put the machine where the prisoner can see the needles," Yeho said into the microphone on his headset. The machine, autopens whispering over the graph paper without human intervention, would remind him of what he had to do in order to be saved. Or so Yeho hoped.

He began to ask questions at random. What was Butterfly's mother like? His father? Their names? The color of their hair? Eyes? Tall? Short? Humorous? Serious? What favorite food had his mother made him? What kind of a house had the family lived in? Where was it? Did he have sisters, brothers? What were their names? Did the children all sleep together? Had he ever fucked his sisters? What would his mother think if she knew he was a murderer? He asked the questions over and over again until he got answers. It did not matter whether the answers were correct; in fact it was better if Butterfly lied because each lie added a few grams to his burden of guilt. Yeho just wanted him to talk, to get into the habit of responding. Then he asked him questions about his recruitment into the RIS, his training, his assignments, his operations, repeating the same simple, even simple-minded questions over and over until he got some sort of answer—a lie, a joke, an insult, anything as long as Butterfly used his voice, as long as it took for him to begin to get the impression that he was smarter than his questioners.

Yeho kept up the drumbeat of stupid questions for fourteen hours while the ship's engines throbbed, driving it eastward through placid seas. Wong was replaced by a second Chinese, and that man by a third. To keep himself awake Yeho took amphetamines (his own, from his own pill box that he always carried with him). Butterfly was permitted no sleep, no food, no water, no opportunity to relieve himself. The box in which he was imprisoned was connected to an air conditioner—*America!*—and Yeho had the temperature turned as low as it would go. The interrogators put on jackets; on the TV monitor, Butterfly's half-naked image shivered.

Finally Yeho struck. He said (the young Chinese inside the box said for him), "Why do you call this cell of Arab terrorists 'the Eye of Gaza'?"

This was the first reference he had made to Butterfly's network.

"There is no cell."

"What did you say?"

"There is no such cell."

"Now you are lying. Look at the machine. It knows; the pens are going crazy. Do you think we don't know when you're lying? Do you think we don't remember what you told us after we gave you the drugs?"

Butterfly was silent.

Yeho said, "All we want is for you to tell us the truth while you're conscious. How else can we know that you're sincere? How else can we help you? Answer me. Why do you call this cell 'the Eye of Gaza'?"

"I don't know," Butterfly croaked, barely able to speak; he had had nothing to drink for all these hours. "The Arabs named it that."

"Which Arab?"

"All of them together."

"Which Arab?"

Yeho repeated this question many times. Finally Butterfly answered: "Hassan."

281

"Who is Hassan?"

Butterfly sighed; Yeho heard his expelled breath in his earphones. On the TV monitor he saw him close his eyes.

"Open your eyes," Yeho said. "You are not allowed to close your eyes. You know that."

Butterfly opened his eyes and looked down at the polygraph, the kilometers of tape covered with jagged peaks drawn by the automatic pen. The lines were flat now, three black squiggles across the snow bridge of the graph; the liar's vital signs were very weak.

Butterfly cleared his throat, long and convulsively.

"Give him water," Yeho said. "Not too much."

Butterfly drank. The dam broke. Butterfly could not spill enough. He told Yeho everything—all about Hassan, the leader of the cell. The details of this man's personality, of his skills, of his intentions, sent a cold shock, an actual icy sensation, along Yeho's spine.

"This man is a psychopath," he said.

"Yes, he is," said Butterfly in sober agreement. "In my opinion, a homicidal maniac."

"What are his future targets?"

"Not the Chinese. You needn't worry on that score. That was just training. I didn't choose the targets; I protested; I wanted to hit Americans, or at least West Germans. Never good Marxist-Leninists like our Chinese comrades. There was no malice on my part."

"We understand. If not us, then who is this Hassan going to kill?"

"Jews. They were always the real target. He would have done it anyway. We just made it possible for him to do what he would have done in any case."

"What Jews?"

"His goal is to kill all of them, complete the Final Solution; he's an Arab Heydrich. He even asked us for weapons to do that— poison gas."

"Why poison gas? Why not an atomic bomb?"

"He knows nobody would ever give him that. Gas, maybe—it could come from anywhere. It has certain historical associations."

Photographic images from Auschwitz and Treblinka flashed in Yeho's brain. He said, "Tell me names, times, places."

"Names I can give you; we gave them a shopping list. But there is no timetable. That's the beauty of the operation, it's absolutely random and completely unpredictable."

Butterfly reeled off a list. Yeho recognized all the names but one.

"The Ja'wabi?" he said. "Who are they?"

"I'm not sure. We'd never heard of them, either. It seems that they're some tribe of desert nomads who've been masquerading as Moslems even though they're really Jews. Some German Hassan met in East Berlin, a former member of the SS, told him all about them. The idea of these Jews touching the Holy Koran drove him wild; it was like a sexual reaction. That was when he asked for the gas."

"Did you give it to him?"

"No. But he'll find a way. Madmen are very resourceful."

TWO

1

WHEN CHRISTOPHER OPENED THE FRONT DOOR OF HIS HOUSE IN Washington and saw Zarah for the first time, he spoke to her in German: *"Lebst du noch?"*

"What? I don't understand," Zarah replied, looking straight into his eyes. She was a self-possessed young woman dressed for business: tailored suit, white blouse with one simple pin at the throat, low-heeled shoes, pink lips and fingernails, her mother's wedding ring on her right middle finger, a plain watch on her wrist.

This fashionable disguise could not conceal her intense physical attractiveness, but Christopher, even while he stared at her with something like hunger in his eyes, seemed oblivious to it. He was looking at, or for, something else in her face and body. Finally he said, "I'm sorry; forgive me. For a moment I mistook you for somebody else."

"My grandmother, I think. I'm told that I resemble her quite closely."

She spoke in Lori Christopher's incisive tones, but if Christopher heard what she said, he gave no sign. They looked at each other in silence. It was late morning in a neighborhood in which wives and husbands alike practiced one of the saprophytic Washington professions, law or journalism or politics, and a deep hush hung over the street of empty houses, as if everyone for miles around except Christopher had gone to a funeral.

She said, "May I come in?"

He stepped aside. Zarah came into the hall; it was even quieter inside than out. No radio or television played in another room, no household machines hummed in the kitchen or the cellar. Going inside was like crossing the threshold between imagination and reality. She thought, *That's exactly what I'm doing after all these years.* She looked around her. It was a high, narrow house, but filled with dappled sunlight that fell first through a very large oak tree growing on the curb and then through tall Palladian windows. Beyond the double door leading into the sitting room she saw Zaentz's drawing of Lori hanging on the wall and strode across the carpet to examine it. She had Lori's purposeful walk, and when she turned around after scrutinizing the picture, a process that took several minutes, Christopher saw that she had the same gravely inquisitive expression, the same wide-open unwavering gray eyes. He asked her no questions, expressed no surprise; standing politely in the doorway, he waited for her to explain herself.

"Yes, there *is* a close resemblance," she said. "This was made when your mother was what—nineteen?"

"About that age."

"Years younger than I am now." Zarah spoke English with a native American intonation, but with the faint hint of some other, more strongly aspirated language also present. She said, "Was that German you spoke to me on the doorstep?"

"Yes, it was German."

"What did the words mean?"

He hesitated for a moment, looking very intently at her face, and replied, "The English equivalent is, 'Are you still alive?' "

His voice was very soft; she had to strain to hear the words.

Zarah said, "Do you often speak German when you're surprised?"

"I haven't spoken it in twenty years. The words just came out."

Zarah stared at him, unblinking. "I've imagined your first words to me many times," she said. "But I never expected anything like that. Can we sit down? I don't think my legs will hold me up very much longer."

She sat on the bench of a piano beneath the picture of Lori. Christopher remained standing in the doorway. Framed photographs crowded the gleaming mahogany lid of the piano: sepia portraits of Christopher and his parents and relatives; a slim dark-haired woman with a nervous face, his second wife, holding a pretty female child who closely resembled her; the child by herself on a horse, on a boat, standing on the balustrade above the Place de la Concorde with Christopher's arm around her and the Arc de Triomphe in the far background at the end of the Champs-Elysées.

He was looking upward at the little girl with an expression of love on his face. Zarah looked away. The room ran the whole length of the house, like a gallery, and through the french windows at the back Zarah could see a garden with swings and slides and a doll-house. Both walls were hung with drawings, prints, and paintings. She had studied such things with one of her tutors, and she recognized a Pissarro, a Constable, a Munch, and a flame-filled shipping scene that seemed to be a Turner intermixed with two or three unrecognizable abstractions and one naive Douanier Rousseau-like picture showing lions and leopards lying down with farm animals and blond children dressed in gossamer togas.

"What is that picture?" she asked.

"It's by an American painter named Hicks," Christopher replied.

"I like it. I like them all."

"Most of them belong to my cousin. He lives abroad."

"Which cousin is that?"

"Horace Hubbard."

"Elliott's son?"

"That's right."

Just as Zarah had always been told, her father was, physically, a male version of herself, but far stiller. Framed like a portrait by the doorway, he was nearly as motionless as a figure in a painting—one of John Singer Sargent's would-be gentry posed on a platform above the artist except for the total absence of disdain and the rumpled clothes (old yellow corduroy pants, a checked shirt under a threadbare sweater). He seemed younger than she knew him to be. His hair was darker than she had pictured it, but it had not begun to turn gray. His well-made body had not thickened, no veins showed on his hands which hung quietly along the seams of his trousers. His face was weatherburned, like the face of a Ja'wabi of the same generation who had spent his youth in the saddle—but tan instead of olive.

"Do you want me to explain myself?" she asked.

Christopher smiled for the first time, faintly; he seemed to be amused by the question.

"Does that mean yes?" she asked.

"I'm a little curious."

"That's a relief. Can you sit down, too?"

He motioned to two facing sofas in front of a fireplace. They sat down opposite each other.

"I've rehearsed all this," she said, "but I don't think the performance is necessary. I think you can see who I am even if you can't quite believe it. I'm not sure I believe it, either, but here we are. I learned of your existence by accident when I was eight years old. I overheard my mother talking to Barney Wolkowicz . . ."

Christopher's eyes changed; the good humor went out of them.

" . . . who came to tell her that you were in prison in China. By that time you'd been a prisoner for years; it took him a long time to find us. I don't know how he did it. Or why. Nobody else ever did. He just rode over the mountains and knocked on the door one day. My mother was infuriated. She hadn't even told her own parents where we were, or that I existed."

"You're Cathy's child?"

"Yes. She went into hiding when she found out she was pregnant, to keep me a secret from you. I was born twenty-three years ago on April tenth, if you want to do the arithmetic. Do you find that too strange to believe?"

Christopher closed his eyes briefly. Opening them again he said, "No."

"You've thought about her, then?"

"Yes. Often. She was the most beautiful human being I ever knew."

"So everyone said. She hated it. Is that all you remember?"

"No. Far from it. I hope she's well."

"She's dead," Zarah said. "Otherwise I wouldn't betray her in this way."

2

ZARAH HAD BROUGHT SEBASTIAN LAUX ALONG AS A WITNESS. THEY had driven down from New York together in Sebastian's Bentley, and he had waited around the corner in the parked car while she made herself known to her father. He rang the doorbell at twelve-thirty precisely. His chauffeur stood behind him on the steps with a picnic hamper in one hand, a silver wine bucket in the other, and a plump old-fashioned briefcase, the kind with straps, under his arm.

"We left the city at five-thirty in the morning in order to get here in time for lunch," Sebastian said. To him, New York was "the city"; all other urban agglomerations were known by their proper names. Even more than most New Yorkers, Sebastian was uncomfortable in Washington. He could not be persuaded to spend a night there or eat the local food or drink the water. When he could not avoid a trip to the capital he had himself driven from Manhattan, a ten-hour round trip, in case the airlines and the trains failed or went on strike at the same time, trapping him in this strange disembodied metropolis of lethargic clerks and fried fish.

"Shall we eat in the garden?" Sebastian asked. "I think we have everything we need." He looked upward at the leafy canopy, which was just beginning to be touched by the first colors of fall. "It's a lovely day. The trees are wonderful in Washington, one always notices that."

On his way through the house he paused in the gallery to look at the pictures and the worn Afshāri carpets on the floor. He was on familiar ground here because he had bought and furnished the house for Christopher while the latter was in captivity. "Ah, Harvey Hubbard's Cappadocian fountain!" he said when he stepped outdoors into the garden. "Does it still work?"

Christopher turned a faucet; water gushed from a small Roman fountain that an archeologizing cousin had excavated in Caesarea Mazaca during the presidency of Theodore Roosevelt.

"Imagine tucking this beautiful thing away in an attic," Sebastian said. "But that's where we found it!"

While he examined its ancient dolphins anew, the chauffeur, an elderly, silent Cockney who also acted as Sebastian's butler and valet, changed into an apron, covered a small table with a checkered cloth from the hamper, and laid out the delicatessen luncheon that Sebastian had brought with him: smoked trout, chicken in aspic, string beans in vinaigrette, strawberries, *crème fraîche,* a liter of French mineral water, and a brown bottle of Alsatian Gewürztraminer. They sat down in the shade of an umbrella.

"Paul is not fond of wines that have German names," said Sebastian to Zarah, lifting his green-stemmed glass, "but this is exceptional even after five hours in the trunk of the car. It was your grandfather Christopher's favorite wine, my dear. He wrote a poem about it. 'Perfume of Bacchus, evaporating on the tongue of memory.' I think you'll like it."

For the remainder of the lunch they talked about the pictures and the rugs inside the house; Sebastian had definite opinions about such things. He did not like tribal carpets. He did not like abstractions, either; he himself had bought the Munch as a wedding present for Hubbard and Lori Christopher; he liked that, and not only because he had got it for a song. "Munch had potential, you could see that," he said. "In a hundred years no one will look at blobs and splotches. Faces and bodies, that's what pictures are all about." He was in his seventies now. None of his habits had changed, and as an old man he looked and behaved very much as he had done in Paris half a century before. He never mixed food and business, but as soon as the servant cleared the table and disappeared with the repacked hamper, Sebastian drew a gold watch from the breast pocket of his suit and put on his reading glasses.

"One-thirty. Time to get down to business if I'm going to miss the traffic on my way back to the city," he said. "I'm sure you're wondering, Paul, how all this came to pass, and if you can believe the evidence of your eyes. I don't blame you. The resemblance between this young lady and your mother at the same age is astonishing. Lori wasn't quite as tall or as fair-haired as Zarah, your mother's hair was almost auburn, but otherwise it was like being revisited by a ghost from the past when she came to see me for the first time."

"When was that?" Christopher asked.

"About a year ago, but of course the Bank has known about Zarah since before she was born."

"You *are* the Bank."

Sebastian returned his steady gaze. "D. & D. Laux & Co. has always handled her mother's account. And her parents' before her."

"You've never mentioned any of this to me, Sebastian."

"Catherine did not desire it. Obviously I am bound in these matters by the client's wishes. Now that Zarah has inherited she wants to make herself known to you. I am here at her request to assure you that in my opinion, based on all the information at my disposal, she is exactly what she represents herself to be—the daughter of your former wife."

"And mine."

"That certanly was Catherine's belief." Sebastian turned to Zarah. "Do you still wish to pursue this question in my presence?"

Zarah looked first at him, then at Christopher. "Yes," she said. "That's why you're here."

"Paul?"

"If that's why you're here, Sebastian, I guess you'd better get on with it."

"Very well. As you doubtless know, there now exist tests by which paternity can be proved or disproved with almost complete certainty. I believe they compare DNA samples. I have given Zarah the name of a specialist here in Washington who can help you if you wish. Now for the circumstantial case."

Sebastian unbuckled his briefcase, opened the lock with a tiny key attached to the watch-chain wound through the buttonhole in his lapel, and extracted a manila file tied with a cloth tape. From this he produced a number of documents and laid them neatly in a row on the table before him.

"There were reliable witnesses to Zarah Christopher's birth," he said. "In fact she was delivered personally by a woman in whom I have absolute trust. This is her affidavit, recorded a day or two after the event." He laid one of the documents in front of Christopher, who read it. It was a clinical description, written in lucid French, of Zarah's birth, which had taken place in a tent during a journey across the Idáren Dráren.

Christopher lifted his eyes. "This is signed 'M. Laux.' "

"My wife," Sebastian said.

"I didn't know you had a wife."

"You knew her well when you were a child in Berlin—Meryem."

"Meryem was your wife? Did my parents know that?"

"They were the only ones who did know."

"She's still living?"

"Yes. I haven't seen her since 1939."

"But you correspond."

"Meryem has her own ways of keeping in touch."

Sebastian gave Christopher another document. "There is room for doubt as to the date of conception inasmuch as you and Catherine, though still legally married, were no longer living as man and wife when it occurred. Here is an affidavit by Catherine as to time and place and certain other pertinent details."

Christopher had not seen Cathy's handwriting in more than twenty years, but he recognized it at once: the self-conscious backslanting letters climbing up the page, the circular dots over the "i's," the ornate capitals. She provided the date of her last menses, which had taken place fifteen days before conception. Letters attesting her pregnancy from the doctors she had visited in Geneva and Paris were attached.

"Does that accord with your recollection?" Sebastian asked.

"Yes. Completely."

Sebastian put a finger on Meryem's affidavit. "Meryem tells us that Zarah was a twin. As she wrote, the other child, a boy, was stillborn; he was buried near the place where he was born; apparently the grave still exists. She describes a very unusual complication in regard to the stillborn twin. The medical term is *fetus papyraceus*. Here is a passage from one of your father's novels, *The Small Rain*, published in 1928."

Sebastian handed Christopher the open book; the paragraph in question was marked with a paper clip:

> Still coated in blood and mucus the glorious boy opened his eyes and looked for the first time at his mother who said Dear God he spoke to me, he said where is my twin. But there was no twin except that there almost always was a twin in this family, but this time the other child was a *fetus papyraceus* with a girl's face as beautiful as the boy's own face, which was their mother's face in small, imprinted on the tissue of her body, and it had been pressed absolutely flat in the womb by the child that lived.

"This passage is a description of your own birth," Sebastian said. "Hubbard told me so himself when the book was published; also that this complication, in which one twin dies in the womb and is pressed flat by the other as it grows and develops, has occurred several times in the Christopher family. Your father's fiction, as I'm sure you realize, was really not fiction at all, but a sort of embellished diary, an imaginative rendering of the literal events of his life. He redecorated the scenery, he sometimes resorted to metaphor, but never departed from the essential facts. In that, as in so many other things, he was far ahead of his time."

Soon it was two-thirty, time for Sebastian to go. He closed his briefcase and rose to his feet.

"Paul will see me out," he said, holding out his hand to Zarah. "I'll say goodbye to you here, by this fountain. It would be wonderful to have one like it in Tifawt, in one of those garden courtyards, wouldn't it?"

"Different from what's there now, at any rate."

"So it would be. The Romans never got that far, did they? They would have had their work cut out for them building fountains in the Idáren Dráren."

The chauffeur waited by the Bentley. The window shades were pulled; through the open door Christopher noticed a pillow and blanket lying on the backseat. "What I do," Sebastian said, "is stretch out and take a nap; I'll be home in time for dinner."

"Have a safe journey, then," Christopher said.

"Wait."

Sebastian gripped his arm; there was quite a lot of strength in his hand, small as it was.

"I'm sorry about the surprise," he said. "It was what Zarah wanted and I didn't see how I could interfere. You're quite a romantic figure to her, you know. Catherine's responsible for that, rest in peace."

3

AS A CHILD, BEFORE SHE KNEW WHO HE WAS, ZARAH TOLD CHRISTOpher, she had invented him. In her reveries her father told her wonderful stories. He told her that the dinosaurs were the most beautiful creatures in the history of Creation, that they were not naked reptiles with scaly dull skins as scientists thought, but glorious animals covered with plumage, like their cousins the birds. Feathers of every conceivable hue and pattern kept them warm at night and cool in the daytime sun. In some cases these were attached to the triangular objects along their spines and tails that paleontologists had mistaken for armor plates. When they were pleased or excited, whole herds of dinosaurs opened their plumes in unison, like enormous peacocks, but with majestic slowness because of their great size, so that the emerald plain where they grazed was transformed into a vast tapestry of the loveliest colors ever seen on Earth.

After Wolkowicz came she began to gather facts. He gave her the book of Christopher's poems and other books describing conditions in Chinese prisons. She tried to live as she imagined Christopher was living. She slept on the floor, ate only rice and vegetables, wore the same clothes every day, spoke only when spoken to, imagined that the walled house in which she and her mother lived was a prison that she was not free to leave.

"Actually, it was a cloister," she said. "Mother lived the life of a nun after the two of you parted. She had a strongbox full of relics. Barney had taught me how to pick locks, so I was able to get into it."

"He taught you to pick locks?"

"Yes. And how to open letters, write in invisible ink, follow people, shoot his pistol. He knew everything, and everything he knew was interesting."

Cathy kept her papers under her bed in a heavy, old-fashioned, brass-bound strongbox. It opened with the key she had taped to the back of a drawer in her writing table—one of the spy's tricks that Wolkowicz had taught Zarah, who soon found it. The documentation of Cathy's life did not amount to much—two dozen photographs of herself, her parents, and various horses; her diplomas from school and college (because of her face and her music, she had graduated with honors from both places); a dozen letters from Christopher; their French marriage certificate, written in copperplate and sealed with a gob of red wax; bills from Salvator Mundi Hospital in Rome. In a cunningly concealed secret compartment in the lid, Zarah found some blurry photographs of Christopher which Cathy had made surreptitiously in the course of her detective work. They showed him talking to a woman on the Via Veneto, telephoning from a kiosk, sitting in a café with an Oriental who had two expensive cameras draped around his neck. There was more: a long dark hair from a woman's head, a cigarette smeared with lipstick sealed like criminal evidence in stiff brown envelopes.

Also Cathy's wedding ring and engagement ring, sealed inside a separate envelope. Zarah was wearing the former, a circlet of diamonds and rubies. She held up her hand, fingers outspread. "I'm sure you recognize this," she said. Christopher did not reply. "I liked your letters a lot," Zarah said. "They were written from all over the world, from places that don't even exist under the same names anymore—Leopoldville, Salisbury, Saigon. I wrote out my own copies and hid them under a rock in the desert, so I could read them over and over again. Even as a child, I saw that there was a lot you weren't telling Mother. I knew by then that she had left you because you didn't love her."

Christopher stopped walking. Zarah had to raise her voice to be heard above the sudden roar of traffic beneath their feet. They had arrived on the Dumbarton Bridge over Rock Creek Parkway, a whimsical structure designed by its architects to resemble a Roman aqueduct, but with four heroic sculptures of North American bison at the approaches. Annoyed by the noise, Zarah took Christopher's arm and led him off the bridge, back the way they had come, into the quiet shade of Q Street.

"I hated her for that," she said. "I still do. I had a right to be your daughter. What right did she have to take you away from me? Or me from you?"

"It may not have been as simple as it seemed when you were little," Christopher said. "All your mother wanted was love."

"That's all anybody wants. But most people don't go into hiding in the Sahara Desert for the rest of their lives if they don't get it on their own terms."

"Maybe she needed it more than other people do."

"More than you?"

"I don't know about that, but the blame wasn't all hers."

Zarah was still holding his arm. She dropped it and took a step backward. "It's very strange," she said, "that after all these years you're the one I'm talking to and she's the one who's dead. What's even stranger is, you're just as I imagined you and I can hardly remember her at all."

Christopher flinched at these words and turned his eyes away.

"You didn't like hearing that, did you?" Zarah said.

"No. Not at all."

"I didn't think you would; I didn't think you'd like some of the other things I've told you about myself. But I wanted you to know the worst about me from the first moment. I've held nothing back. That's as bad as it gets, but the demonstration's over. I won't do it again."

She was looking at him with the same frank intelligence that he had noticed in the first moment. It was very strange after so many years to be in the presence of someone else who looked and behaved so much like himself.

4

"YOU'RE PERSUADED THAT THIS STRANGE WOMAN IS YOUR NATURAL daughter?" Stephanie Christopher said.

"You make her sound like a Brontë character," Christopher said.

"*I* make her sound that way? There may be a vivid imagination mixed up in this situation, but it's not mine. What are we supposed to tell Lori? 'Oh, by the way, sweetheart, we've just discovered that you have this glamorous sister who's been hiding out in the Sahara Desert for twenty-three years, galloping Arabian horses across the sands. And do you know what? *She looks just like Daddy!*' "

They were in the kitchen at the back of the house. Even though they were alone behind a closed door, even though she was trying to provoke a quarrel, Stephanie spoke in a low voice. Zarah had declined to meet the brunette wife and child she had seen in the photographs on the piano until Christopher prepared the ground; the little girl, Lori, had gone to bed. Stephanie, who was herself young enough to be Christopher's daughter, was a professional psychotherapist who spent her days dealing with the havoc wrought on the educated classes by real or fancied parental lies, concealments, and betrayals. She was worried about the effect on Lori of Zarah's sudden appearance. So far, by following stringent rules of behavior based on prevailing theory, she and Christopher had avoided doing serious psychic harm to their child. But what would happen now?

"I don't like this situation at all," Stephanie said. "What right does Sebastian Laux have to bring this person into our house and vouch for her? How does he know, really know, that she's who she says she is? Why does he trust his information?"

"He describes the case as circumstantial. But it has the ring of truth."

"So you keep on saying. You're convinced by a physical resemblance, by the history of your family. You *want* to be convinced. Your mother has come back."

"Stephanie, that's mumbo-jumbo."

She smiled a patient professional smile. "If you say so. I can certainly understand why you'd give Sebastian the benefit of the doubt. Why not? All he did was conspire to keep the secret of your child's existence from you for almost a quarter of a century before showing up in his Bentley on a fine Indian summer day with a picnic lunch and this starlet on his arm. Look at you now."

"What do you see?"

"A changed man."

"I'm just the same."

She gave him a look filled with deep feminine skepticism. "Sure you are."

That morning when she kissed him goodbye he had had the look of a man who has come to terms with a troubled past and been cured of its disorders. She had seen love in his eyes, love for her, love for their pretty, brainy little girl, and she had thought, as she drove Lori to school, that she had made him happy where everyone else had failed. Now the past had come up the front steps and started to take him back.

"You look absolutely bewildered," she said.

"There's some reason for that, Stephanie."

"There sure is. What are you going to do about it?"

"We agreed to take the medical tests and abide by the result."

" 'We'? I notice you don't use her name. Why is that?"

"Maybe I think you don't want to hear it. It's a strange name for a Christopher. Anyway, Zarah and I will go to the doctor and have blood drawn tomorrow. According to Sebastian they can compare DNA and see if we're a match."

Stephanie, who held an undergraduate honors degree in microbiology as well as a Ph.D. in psychology, spoke with authority within the family on scientific matters. "Sebastian is right," she said. "Whose idea was it to take the blood test?"

"Zarah's. She wants all doubt removed."

"And a blood knot tied by science. How terribly Teutonic. And if you do match up, then what?"

"Then we tell Lori and everyone else the truth, accept Zarah as a member of the family, and go on with our lives."

"Go on or go back?"

"Go back? Where to?"

"To childhood, to Berlin. To the land of lost content. Wasn't it more interesting there?"

"It was interesting, all right. But Stephanie, I can't erase it."

"I know that. But you don't have to regress, either. Sane people live in the present."

Christopher smiled at her intensity. "I'll do my best to hang on to my sanity," he said.

"Good luck."

Stephanie feared the past as someone who has been revived after nearly drowning fears the ocean. She was the daughter of a spy, and as a student she had belonged to a secret group that played at

revolution; she had lived in a make-believe underground in
Dostoyevskian squalor and dementia; she had cut sugar cane in
Cuba as a member of the Venceremos Brigade. Like Cathy, she
hated secrets, but her reasons were different; because she had
overheard real ones while playing with dolls at the feet of her
father's agents and invented others while playing revolutionary, she
knew that secrets were usually fraudulent and almost always uninteresting. They withered when exposed to light. She had chosen
psychology as a profession because it made her an enemy of secrets. She pursued them relentlessly in her consulting room, identifying them, exposing them, robbing them of their power. In her life
with her husband and daughter she insisted on unvarnished truth,
on revelation, on the same fierce self-criticism that had been required of the members of her revolutionary cell. Christopher understood how she felt and what she wanted, and he tried to give it
to her. But after ten years of daily interrogation by earnest Chinese
inquisitors, he knew how utterly impossible it was to achieve a state
of understanding by relying on the confessions of human beings.

"The past is not a good place for anybody," Stephanie said.
"Especially you."

"I agree. But now I have this visitor from there. What am I
supposed to do about it?"

"You'll have to figure that out for yourself. What attracts you to
her? Apart from her facial features and the ties of blood and
family, I mean."

"She knows things I don't know."

"She does? What, for example?"

"She knows all about her own existence, to begin with. She may
know other things. I've been taken by surprise. I thought I knew
the whole truth about myself, and now I know I never did."

As a young woman Stephanie had worn the long lank hair of her
rebellious and distrustful generation, and now she shook her head
as if to fling these vanished tresses from her eyes, the better to peer
at Christopher.

"I see," she said. "And how do you feel about that?"

Her hands were folded on the table between them. Christopher
touched the hollow of her wrist and felt the tension coiled within it.

"I feel curious," he said. "Interested."

"How curious? How interested?"

"Like old times."

"I don't like the sound of that."

Stephanie rose to her feet and went upstairs. After a moment Christopher heard the shower running. Before following her he cleared the table and washed the dishes.

When Christopher joined Stephanie in bed half an hour later, she was wide awake, wearing her glasses. Usually they both read before going to sleep, but the book she was working on, a thick biography of Fidel Castro, lay unopened on her stomach.

"I wasn't being absolutely honest with you downstairs," she said. "I'd like to clear that up before we close our eyes."

No misunderstanding or resentment was permitted to survive past nightfall in Stephanie's house.

"All right."

"The fundamental fact is," Stephanie said. "I'm jealous because Zarah is a female and she's young and good-looking. If a prodigal son turned up from your past I'd feel different. I'm sorry, but I'm human, and there it is."

"So am I, and I don't intend to give her up or give in to your jealousy. It's ridiculous. She's my daughter."

"She may be your daughter, but remember that she's been dreaming about you all her life. There's risk involved, Paul. Be careful. This is a romantic young woman with an Oedipal fixation."

"Really?"

"Really. She's been fantasizing since childhood, but now she's in the presence of reality. Reality includes hormones. The incest taboo is a matter of conditioning and she's missed out on that. It will be amazing if she doesn't fall in love with you. Is that plain enough for you?"

"It will do. Even if everything you say is true, don't you think I'm a little old for her?"

"Are you? I'm only ten years older than she is."

"The cases are not quite the same. She seems to be a perfectly nice girl, Stephanie. You may even be friends after you get to know her."

"In spite of what my instincts tell me, that's my plan, assuming that she doesn't turn out to be an enemy, but it won't be easy. Does she really look just like your mother?"

"Yes. It's startling. When I first saw her I really thought that was who she was. I spoke to her in German."

"Good grief. But how could you think such a thing? She's a young woman."

"So was my mother the last time I saw her."

Stephanie turned off the bedside lamp. After a moment Christopher's eyes adjusted to the wavering light that shone in the window from the street, and he saw that his wife was near tears. This was a rare event.

"It's not your mother I'm jealous of," she said. "I want you to understand that."

"I do."

"Really?"

"Really."

She relaxed a little. He gathered her into the hollow of his body. Her hair was damp and her skin smelled faintly of hypo-allergenic soap from her bedtime shower. Stephanie never wore perfume or make-up; that much, together with her contempt for bourgeois reticence, remained of her radical convictions.

"I hate jealousy as much as you do," she said. "My mother used to laugh about Cathy's jealousy behind her back. I've never been jealous of *her*, God knows. You didn't love her, no matter how beautiful she was. Even as a kid I understood that. After I grew up I realized that she was a not-very-bright borderline personality who had no emotions of her own and attached herself to you so she could use yours."

"That's harsh," Christopher said.

"No, clinical. I just forgot about her; so did you. But now her daughter turns up, looking just like you even though you say she looks like your mother. It's a shock."

Christopher did not attempt to correct the errors in this analysis. Looking down into Stephanie's solemn face, he smiled in spite of himself. Her dogged searches through the cupboard of her own mind, and everybody else's, endeared her to him. Seeing the expression in his eyes, she began to kiss him; her anxieties nearly always turned into ardor after she had explained them to herself.

Later she said, "I'd just as soon wait to meet her until the blood tests come back. I don't want any shadow of doubt showing in my eyes."

"Who's going to tell Lori?"

"You are. After the tests come back. And then we'll have a party for her. The Patchens, my parents, the O. G. if he's up to

299

it—all the romantic figures from your world that she's heard so much about."

Except Wolkowicz, Christopher thought.

Stephanie always slept soundly after making love, and soon she was breathing contentedly in the half-dark beside Christopher. He lay awake for a long time, and when he woke from a dream of Germany at four o'clock in the morning he was not sure, for long moments, where he was. There was nothing unusual about that.

5

ON THE DAY THE BLOOD TESTS CAME BACK, AFFIRMING THAT THEY were father and daughter beyond any reasonable scientific doubt, Zarah and Paul Christopher went for a walk along the Mall. He arrived first at their meeting place, the Smithsonian station of the Metro. He and Zarah had already spoken on the telephone about the laboratory report, so they said nothing more about it as they rode up the escalator together. Still grinning in delight over the news, she was otherwise undemonstrative as they sauntered toward the dome of the Capitol. Other monumental buildings, pillared and porticoed or sheathed in glass, stood to right and left with American flags flying from the roofs; elms in their autumn colors glowed on every hand under a sky of cornflower blue. It was a day of surpassing beauty, and Christopher realized that Zarah was acutely conscious, as he was, that the two of them were figures in this captivating landscape.

Despite their physical resemblance, few would have taken them at this moment for father and daughter. The blood test had freed Zarah of all shyness, and as Cathy had feared and Stephanie had foreseen, she was behaving toward Christopher like a girl who had just become engaged to be married and therefore had a right to know the whole truth about his life before they met. She led Christopher to a bench and began to ask questions, beginning with the details of his imprisonment in China. He answered lamely. Zarah paused.

"Would you rather not be asked about this?" she asked. "Am I going too fast? Does it remind you too much of what you went through?"

"It's not that. I'm just out of the habit of answering questions."

This was the fact. By the time Zarah appeared on his doorstep Christopher had lived in inviolable privacy for nearly ten years, a period almost exactly equivalent to the time he had spent in prison. Ever since his return from China he had been treated like a man risen from the dead who knew things that no human being ought to know. No one asked him questions about himself. In early days Stephanie had satisfied her curiosity as Zarah was doing now, but no one else had trespassed onto this forbidden ground. Patchen had kept the Outfit snoops away, and in private life Christopher's friends, and even people who would ordinarily have been his enemies, seemed to think that he would somehow slip back into the nether world of his captivity if he described what had happened to him there.

"I don't really want to know everything," Zarah said. "Just some of the details, so I can compare what really happened to what I invented about you."

"From what you've told me already, the two are a lot alike," Christopher replied.

"That was because I didn't really invent these things. I had the book Barney gave me. And Lla Kahina saw you in the cards all the time. I just took it from there."

"She saw me in the cards?"

"You find that hard to believe?"

"Tell me what you mean."

"She *saw* you. For example, did you have a very large book with a blue cover that you read every night in your cell?"

"Yes. *The Shorter Oxford English Dictionary.*"

"Is that what it was? We thought it must be the Bible. When you were interrogated, did you write answers on a stone floor with chalk?"

"Yes. It's part of their technique."

"You've told me that your hard labor, day after day, consisted of digging a deep ditch that had no purpose. Did this ditch collapse in an earthquake, almost burying you alive?"

"Yes."

"And did someone in the hospital give you an orange to eat when you regained consciousness?"

"Yes."

"Lla Kahina saw all that. She said you were a very strong presence, always appearing when she got out the cards, always

301

insisting that she take notice of you. That was how she found my mother in the first place; you appeared in the cards and told her about me."

"But I didn't know about you."

"Not in real life, but she sees another world in which the dead and the living are all mixed up together. I think Lla Kahina believes that this person she called by your name is really your mother, speaking through you. She thinks your mother is in me, too; she never said so, but I know that's what she believed. Do you find *that* hard to accept?"

"That she would believe those things, no. She and your grandmother were very close."

"But you've just said that the things she saw happening to you in the cards actually happened in real life. How do you explain her knowing what was going on in a prison in Manchuria, ten thousand miles from where she was?"

"Unless she had spies among the guards, I can't explain it."

"No spies. But you still don't believe it."

"Why shouldn't I? It's all true. I only wish she had come to see me—in person. Then I might have known as much about you as you know about me."

They smiled at each other; Christopher's smile was in no way muscular, not brilliant like Zarah's, but a subtle change of facial expression, a more humorous light in the eyes.

"I see what you mean," Zarah said. "Maybe you should have had some cards of your own."

"Tell me what I would have seen."

"Not much; I led a very quiet life."

She told him the basic facts: Cathy had taught her to play the piano and ride; Lla Kahina had taught her Berber and Arabic and the history of the Ja'wabi; the Ja'wabi had taught her the ways of the desert. A long procession of tutors hired by D. & D. Laux & Co. had come to Tifawt and guided her through the core curriculums of the famous school and liberal arts college Cathy had attended, and well beyond.

"I think my schooling was based on what Mother read about Lori's education in Hubbard's novels," Zarah said. "God knows what she thought she was creating, or for what purpose. I sure didn't."

She knew European music of the eighteenth and nineteenth

302

centuries, English, American, and European history and literature, the Bible and the Koran, philosophy from Socrates to Heidegger, Western politics from Suetonius to Marx, mathematics through calculus, and five languages including the Mandarin she had learned at Wolkowicz's suggestion. Also the fundamentals of anatomy and internal medicine, subjects she had chosen for herself because they interested her.

"Why medicine?" Christopher asked.

"I thought I might have to nurse you after the Chinese let you go."

Because Zarah had never been inside a formal schoolroom, she had no diplomas or certificates; no memberships; no connections; no physical reminders of the process of learning; no identity in the terms of reference used by the modern world. Her tutors had known her under her mother's maiden name. Cathy had not even registered her birth, and one of the things Sebastian had done for her was to present the evidence of her existence and nationality to another of the Bank's clients, an official of the Consular Service, who issued an American passport in her true name.

"It's lucky Lla Kahina is an American citizen; they wouldn't have taken a foreigner's word for it," Zarah said. "According to Sebastian the man from the government said I was a perfect secret agent. A sleeper, Barney would have called me."

"You remember that word after all these years?"

"Yes, and lots of other things Barney taught me. If it hadn't been for him I might never have found you. Can we talk about him?"

"Another day, if you don't mind."

Christopher had said this before when she asked about Wolkowicz; she did not press the point.

Christopher said, "You don't think Meryem would have told you the truth even if there had been no Barney?"

"I'm not sure. My mother said she was hiding me from you because there's a curse on the Christophers. I think Lla Kahina may agree with her about that. Why else would she have taken us in and put up with my mother all those years?"

"Maybe she just liked your mother."

"I don't think that was the reason. You don't blame Cathy in the slightest degree for what she did to you and me, do you?"

"No. What would be the point?"

"Did you love her?"

"Yes." He smiled again in his quiet way. "I remember that part very well."

"Why did you love her? Was it because she was so beautiful?"

"That was part of it; most of it at first. Her looks affected everything. That was what troubled her. She wouldn't have put it this way, but I think she felt she was under an enchantment, that her beauty was some sort of cruel disguise imposed on her by the fates. She couldn't believe that anyone could see beyond it, or through it, and find within it the person she thought she really was."

"But you found the person inside the disguise."

"I don't know. Obviously she didn't think so."

"You seem to have no curiosity about her. Don't you wonder what her life was like after you said goodbye?"

"It's pretty obvious she didn't want me to know that."

"And you feel you have to respect her wishes even after she's dead?"

"Yes."

Zarah started to reply, but she was interrupted by a beggar. Zarah gave him a dollar; he shuffled away. She resumed her line of questioning.

"Sebastian's documents have made me wonder about the circumstances of my conception," she said. "You were already separated when it happened, apparently."

"Yes."

"Did you think about her at all afterward?"

"Of course I did. But I never suspected your existence."

"You never thought there might be a child?"

"I wondered. It was an unguarded moment."

"Wondered or feared?"

"Both. By then it was obvious that we couldn't stay together."

"You never thought she might have wanted to entrap you?"

"Entrap me? No. That was the farthest thing from her mind under the circumstances."

"What *were* the circumstances?"

Christopher compressed his lips, shook his head. Zarah thought that he might refuse to go on, but he answered the question.

"She had been badly hurt," he said. "What happened happened in the hospital, before she went in for surgery. She thought she might die. So did I. It was what she wanted."

"What did *you* want? Did you still love her when it happened?"

Christopher looked into her large gray eyes, the family eyes; they glistened with tears.

"How else could such a thing have happened at all?" he asked.

6

WHEN THE CHRISTOPHERS HAD GUESTS TO DINNER THEY SET UP THE table in the long gallery-like room in which the pictures hung and turned on the lights over the frames. For Zarah's party Stephanie had taken the plate out of its storage bags; a cold poached salmon and chicken breasts in aspic were displayed on glittering silver dishes arranged on a sideboard.

"No red meat is served in this house, ever; Stephanie is hell on cholesterol," said Sybille Webster, Stephanie's mother, joining Christopher and Zarah at the buffet. "Speaking of blood, I understand you and Paul passed your consanguinity tests with flying colors."

"Yes," Zarah said, opening her eyes a little wider in amusement as she listened. "A perfect match."

"Congratulations. I told Stephanie I didn't see how there could be any doubt about it. I knew your mother and you'd be lucky to look like her, but you don't. I've never seen two people who looked or acted more alike than you and your father."

Sybille was the first to call Christopher "your father" in speaking of him to Zarah.

"Thank you," Zarah said.

"Don't thank me," Sybille said, mistaking her meaning. "Thank your genes. Stephanie gets annoyed when I say so because it contradicts the intellectual fashion, but I've never believed in this nurture over nature nonsense. You can't turn a plow horse into a thoroughbred by buying it educational toys and reading it Dr. Seuss books. You're born as you always will be, a version of your ancestors. That's why I never gave up hope where Stephanie was concerned. Her father thought she might join the PLO, but I knew she'd be all right as soon as she found a husband, though I must say I never dreamed it would be Paul Christopher."

"The PLO?" Zarah said.

"Yes. She went through a revolutionary phase just before she married your father. It was a mystery to me. Yasir Arafat is such a

305

grotesque little gnome, with those whiskers and that checkered napkin on his head and that toy pistol sitting on his Santa Claus tummy. Of course, so is Menachem Begin on the other side; he started out as a mad bomber too, you know. One evening at somebody's house we met a man from the Smithsonian who told us about this forensic archeologist—that was the term, isn't it wonderful?—who could examine ancient human bones and tell you exactly what the person had looked like in life. All he needed was the skull and a leg bone or two and maybe a clavicle and he could make paintings of people who had been dead for hundreds of years. Imagine having a picture of Cleopatra or William Shakespeare. The Russians had just shot the pope in St. Peter's Square, so I said, 'Why don't you get the Vatican to let your man have a look at Saint Peter's bones? I'll bet he'd turn out to look like a combination of Arafat and Begin.' He said, 'No, he'd probably look like a centaur because there are horse and donkey bones mixed in with the saint's.' Can you imagine?"

Christopher asked Zarah what kind of wine she wanted.

"White, please," Zarah said.

"Ah, you drink wine," Sybille said. "I gather you're not a Moslem."

"No."

"Cathy didn't convert in all those years? Not that she was exactly born to wear the veil with that glorious face of hers."

"She did wear it sometimes. She liked it, in fact."

"She liked it? Honestly? Do *you*?"

"Yes; lots of women my age do. But my mother wasn't much interested in religion."

"Great beauties seldom are. I liked your mother. She played the piano very nicely. She wore the most wonderful clothes; I never saw shoes to compare to the ones she wore, they were absolutely perfect. I was very sorry to hear that she had passed away at such a young age. May I ask what happened to her?"

Christopher handed Zarah a glass of chardonnay; Sybille had not touched alcohol for years.

"Mrs. Webster was just asking me exactly what happened to my mother," Zarah said. Then she turned to Sybille and said, "She was shot to death by terrorists."

Sybille gasped. "*Arab* terrorists?"

"Among others."

"Oh, dear." Sybille put a hand on Zarah's arm. "Zarah, my child, I'm so sorry I made jokes about the PLO." Stephanie, seated beside the O. G., was watching them intently. "Here," Sybille said, handing Zarah the plate she had filled for herself. "Take this to the O. G.; I'll make myself another. There he is, with his napkin tucked into his vest. He's dying to talk to you; he knew your grandparents."

Sybille rushed out of the room with a clatter of high heels; Stephanie took in the scene with a glance, rose from her place, and followed her. Zarah put down her glass of wine and carried both plates to the table; the O. G. accepted his with a little bow.

"Salmon," he said. "The Washington standby. Did you know that it was against the law to feed indentured servants salmon more than twice a week in the Massachusetts Bay Colony? The rivers teemed with it."

"Would you rather have something else?"

"No; I like the stuff. I don't get as much of it as I did before my indenture expired. Sit beside me."

Christopher intervened, taking Zarah by the arm. "I'll bring her back in a moment," he said.

Outside in the garden, they sat down on a bench.

"I'm sorry," Christopher said.

Zarah was dry-eyed. "About what?" she asked. "Because my mother was shot full of holes by idiots or because I upset that foolish woman?"

"Sybille means no harm."

He laid his hand on her cheek; she remained as she had been, with her head lifted and her hands clasped in her lap. Over the mumbling of the party inside they heard the sound of high heels on stone. It was Stephanie, emerging from the house. She reached them in half a dozen strides.

"Zarah, I apologize for Mother. She had no idea what she was getting into."

"Thank you. There's no need to apologize. She asked an obvious question."

"A little too obvious. It's her style. She didn't mean to hurt you."

"I know that. It was a social occasion. I should have lied."

Stephanie sat down beside her and looked into her face for a long moment. Her manner was professional. "Do you want to talk about it?"

Zarah returned her gaze. "Not especially. Did *you* know my mother?"

"Not really. Whatever Mother may have said, none of us really knew Cathy; she came and went so quickly. I saw quite a lot of her in Paris when I was a child. She was always nice to me. We talked about horses. Once or twice she took me riding with her in the Bois de Boulogne; she rode like a dream."

"That sounds like Mother," Zarah said. She stood up, as if freeing herself of a restraining hand. "I think we should get back to the others."

"Not yet," Christopher said. "Tell us what happened."

Stephanie stood up, too. "Would you rather talk to your father alone?" she asked.

"No, stay," Zarah said. "Actually horses had something to do with what happened. We used to go on an ostrich chase every year. Mother loved it; she made everyone else go whether they wanted to or not. Ostriches run much faster than a horse, you know. The idea was to post a rider every mile or so, then get one started and chase it in relays."

Stephanie said, "It sounds cruel."

Zarah paused for a moment before replying. "It's not," she said. "It may have been in the old days, when they killed the animal for its plumes and its body fat—lots of Berbers and Arabs still believe that ostrich grease is a cure for practically everything. But all we did was run them, sometimes for fifty or sixty miles; it could go on for days with no harm to the bird. Distance means nothing to an ostrich."

In order to find ostriches, Cathy and Zarah and a party of about thirty Ja'wabi, almost evenly divided among mature people and the young, had caravaned several hundred miles through the Sahara and made camp in the Oën oasis. There they waited for a thunderstorm to appear in the distance, and rode toward it; ostriches instinctively run straight for lightning as soon as they see it, so as to graze on the green shoots produced by a cloudburst and the powerful sunshine that follows it. Soon after dawn a couple of days later Zarah and two other young people, riding in advance of the main party, sighted a troop of more than two dozen ostriches grazing on a low hilltop. A line of riders was established in the direction of the oasis. One large male ostrich was cut out of the troop, and the chase commenced. It began at noon because even ostriches are slowed down by the heat of the midday sun.

"Mother and some of the men her age were strung out nearest the oasis," Zarah told Christopher, "and when the chase was over they decided to go back to camp and spend the night there. We younger riders were nearest to the ostriches, so we stayed where we were, with the idea of having another chase in the morning. We did, in the opposite direction from the oasis, so we slept out a second night. When we got back to the oasis the camp had been attacked. They were gone."

"All of them?"

"Every one. The terrorists shot the horses and camels, too."

Stephanie had been listening with deep attention. "You're sure it was terrorists who did it?"

"Who else could it have been? Desert people don't massacre each other for no reason, and they certanly don't kill animals instead of stealing them. These scum train in that part of the Sahara sometimes. We found Land Rover tracks and hundreds of empty shells with Russian markings on them."

Stephanie recoiled slightly. "You used the word 'scum.' "

"I did? Do you think that's too harsh under the circumstances?"

"I understand why you feel the way you do."

Zarah looked at Christopher, who still said nothing, and then at Stephanie again. "Do you?" she said.

"On a certain level, yes; I think I do. I'm sorry that this happened; truly sorry. Your mother is buried over there? You didn't bring her home?"

"Bring her home?" Zarah looked into Stephanie's eyes with all the disconcerting candor that everyone had noticed in her from the first. "As I said, two nights passed before we got back to the oasis. The hyenas and jackals and vultures had been there before us. There was nothing to take home, not even bones. On the way home we saw some rags that might once have been their clothes blowing across the sand, a long way off. But that was all."

Inside the house again, Zarah sat down beside the O. G., who was now eating fruit salad for dessert. Christopher had remained in the garden with Stephanie, and from where she sat she could see the two of them talking earnestly.

"I hear that you grew up with the Ja'wabi," the O. G. said, resuming their conversation as if it had never been interrupted.

"You know about the Ja'wabi?"

"A little."

"Not many people do."

"I've been blessed with learned friends. Tell me about Meryem."

"She's called Lla Kahina now. Did you know her?"

"I was madly in love with her fifty years ago."

"You too? In Berlin?"

"Yes. Why do you say 'you too'?"

"In Hubbard's novels somebody is always falling in love with her."

"Ah, you've read the novels; that explains a lot. Hubbard was a very good reporter. But my love for Meryem was unrequited, alas, it was not to be. Meryem saw my future in the cards. She wasn't in it, but everything else that's happened to me was. It's uncanny, looking back, how often she was right on the button about the details of my fate. And everyone else's. Your father tells me she still does readings."

"Not so often anymore. She says her powers are getting weaker."

"I don't believe it. You should make Paul go see her. Back in the days when I knew her she was the talk of Berlin. The Nazis wanted to kidnap her and turn her into a secret weapon."

"They did? I'd never heard that."

"Well, it's perfectly true. That's why your grandparents smuggled her out of the country in '39. Thereby hangs a tale."

"I'd like to hear it."

The table was filling up with listeners. The O. G. looked them over benevolently, but stopped talking.

"Then come and see me," he said, leaning toward Zarah as if to murmur a confidence. "I'm in the phone book. Just call up and pop in any afternoon about four-thirty for a cup of tea. We'll swap yarns."

"It won't be much of a swap, I'm afraid."

"I'm not so sure about that," the O. G. said. "Why don't you make time for me tomorrow?"

7

THE O. G.'S HOUSE WAS LOCATED AT THE BOTTOM OF A NARROW cul-de-sac that ended in a bluff overlooking Rock Creek Park.

Zarah arrived there the next afternoon a few minutes early. Rain was falling; she put up the collapsible umbrella that she carried in her raincoat pocket and then, to kill time, studied the rocks and trees on the vertiginous slope below the balustrade.

When she turned around she saw a skewed figure dressed in black limping down the flagstone walk leading from the O. G.'s front door. It was David Patchen; she knew him at once. Their eyes met. Even at this distance she saw the light of recognition in his face. Or something more than that. But how after all could he mistake her for anyone else? He got into a car and drove away without looking at her again.

As she went up the walk the O. G. appeared in the doorway, a spaniel at his heels. "Come inside and sit by the fire!" he said. There really was a fire burning on the hearth in the library. The logs seethed and crackled, emitting showers of sparks. "Apple wood, straight from the Shenandoah Valley," the O. G. said. "The real stuff!" Tea had been arranged on a table before the fire. "Sit ye down," he said, drawing back a chair. "I'll be Mother. How do you take it?"

"Lots of sugar."

"Good girl. In my day young women made no bones about liking sweets."

While the O. G. poured, Zarah examined the room. The walls were lined with shelves of books, but there were also a large number of tables and pedestals on which were displayed dozens of objects, mostly deadly weapons and ritual masks from many different cultures. "Souvenirs of heathen countries," the O. G. said. "Brought back by friends." His thick pince-nez were slightly askew, and he took them off, opened the spring wide, and set them straight on the bridge of his nose.

"Learned friends?"

He grinned. "Not always, as you can see. A lot of the masks are from a fellow named Barney Wolkowicz. It was sort of a joke we had between us. I hear that Barney came over the mountains on a donkey and found you and your mother in the back of beyond. Is that so?"

"Yes. It was a great surprise."

"I'll bet it was. Barney was an amazing fellow."

"More amazing than I realized," Zarah replied. "While I was waiting for the lab report I read all about him in the newspaper files at the Library of Congress."

311

"*All* about Barney Wolkowicz? In the newspapers? That's a good one!"

"The papers all seemed to think he was some sort of monster."

"Barney had his moments. But speak only good of the dead."

"It's very hard to think of him as dead. Do you really believe he killed himself?"

The O. G. smiled with lively interest and handed her a cup of tea. "If he did, he did it up brown," he replied.

A few months after Christopher returned from China Wolkowicz's corpse had been found floating at the end of an anchor chain ten feet below the surface of Chesapeake Bay. The chain was wrapped around his corpulent body; the anchor had buried itself in the bottom mud. The autopsy showed that Wolkowicz's skull had been shattered by a large-caliber bullet fired into the back of his head. The weapon that killed him was never found, nor was the vessel from which he had presumably fallen or been thrown overboard. No suicide note was discovered. Although the victim was supposed to be an officer of the Outfit, even one of its heroes, the Outfit was silent, as usual. The press was bewildered when all other departments of the government turned out to be silent as well; even Congress was silent. Official discretion on this scale had not occurred in Washington since World War II. Despite these bizarre circumstances the local coroner had ruled the death a suicide, creating a sensation in the media.

"You said you read up on Barney while waiting for a lab report," the O. G. said. "What lab report?"

"The results of the test my father and I took to see if our DNA matched."

"Paul told me all about that; wonderful what they can do nowadays to take the mystery out of life. Fat chance of anything like that working on Barney." He took the lid off a sterling silver candy dish that bore the Euhemerian club seal. "I'm going to have one of these chocolates," he said, offering the dish. "Would you like one, too?"

"No thank you."

"Are you sure? They're straight from the source. David Patchen was over in Brussels last week; he smuggled them through customs. Have you met David?"

"Not yet. But I saw a man answering his description leaving your house just now."

"You've got a description of him?"

"From Barney."

"Then it wouldn't be very flattering. But David's the one who can fill you in on Barney—he and your father. The two of them knew him best and saw him last. Wolkowicz's later period—the breakdown and suicide and all that—was after my time."

"What breakdown?"

"He went a little funny in the head for a while. Lots of people do when they reach a certain age in life and realize that there's more behind than up ahead. These days they call it 'mid-life crisis.' Best sellers are written about it by people in New York."

"Is that what killed Barney, mid-life crisis?"

The O. G., chewing a second Belgian chocolate, regarded her with unshakable affability.

"I don't know about that," he said. "He was an anchorite among cenobites."

"A *what*?"

"Sebastian Laux didn't send you tutors in Latin and Greek?"

"No. Arabic and Mandarin."

"Then you may turn into a displaced anchorite too. It means he was a hermit monk in the midst of a religious community."

"So was my father. Surely that wasn't enough to drive a person like Barney to suicide."

"That wasn't all. If you've read the papers you know the hounds were after Barney; television cameras, newspaper reporters, the whole circus."

"Why were they after him?"

"Hounds have no reasons. They just follow the scent and tear the fox to pieces when they catch it." He offered the chocolates again. "The early Nazis used to wash these down with pink champagne. There's something about that in one of your grandfather's books—Lori playing Scarlatti on the piano while Heydrich gorges himself. Do you play the piano?"

"A little."

"It runs in the family. Your grandmother was a very good musician. So was your mother, of course, but they played in entirely different styles. The best amateur player I ever heard was Wolkowicz, but don't take that as an invitation to bring him up again."

"You mean ever again?"

"Not today anyway. We've gotten off the track."

THE O. G. BEGAN TO TALK ABOUT BERLIN AGAIN AND THE HABITUAL
cheerful note, almost a chuckle, that was his conversational trademark came back into his voice. He had not wanted to answer
Zarah's questions about Wolkowicz, but now that he was controlling the subject of the conversation again he was his old cordial,
avuncular self.

"The great thing about Hubbard and Lori Christopher, the thing
that made them so enviable," he said, "was that they had got
themselves right outside of the cage of the conventions. In the
1920s most poople were still prisoners of nineteenth-century codes
of behavior. But he had escaped from New England and all it stood
for in his mind, she had escaped from Prussia and all it symbolized
for her, and they made their own world in which they could do and
be anything they liked. It was an island they lived on, really, with a
population of two—later on three, counting Paul, then four when
Meryem arrived."

"I thought they had lots of friends," Zarah said. "The novels
certainly make it seem that way."

"They did, and they chose them for themselves. No one was as
happy as they were, of course; their friends were really just a bunch
of shipwrecked sailors who washed ashore at their dinner table.
They fed them and were kind to them and clapped when they did
the hornpipe. But at the end of the evening they put them all on a
raft and shoved them off."

"You make them sound very cold-hearted and selfish."

"No, no; you mustn't get that idea. They weren't either of those
things, not at all. Of course, people in love are selfish about each
other, and Lori and Hubbard were no exception, but they were
very good to their friends. Good gravy! They were willing to die for
them, as they proved more than once."

"It's true, then, that they smuggled people out of Germany
under the nose of the Gestapo?"

"Perfectly true. A dozen or more. And every one of them, with
one exception, was a Jew. This was treason; it was worse than
treason, worse than any crime in the Nazi law book; they were
poisoning the well of their own tribe, because Lori and Hubbard
were Aryans if anyone ever was. If they'd been caught not one
person in Germany would have stood up for them. And darn few

anywhere else. The fact is, most people in the western world thought that Hitler was onto a good idea where the Jews were concerned. Anti-Semitism was part of the air we breathed in those days; if you don't think so, read the novels others were writing. Hemingway, Fitzgerald and just about all the rest of them except your grandfather, who was never as famous as they were—funny coincidence—thought it was the most natural thing in the world to write the most disgusting tripe about the Jews . . . Sorry, I got carried away."

"You're not an anti-Semite?"

"No, thank you very much, I'm not. Far from it. But I darn well might have been if it hadn't been for your grandparents. Hubbard and Lori were the ones who made me see the light. Their house was the center of my universe in Berlin, and it was full of these amazing friends of theirs—brilliant people, good people, people who were capable of changing the world for the better with their work, and most of them were headed for the gas chamber and the ovens. Of course no one knew that at the time, with the single exception of Meryem. She saw it in her visions all the time."

"She told you that?"

"Hubbard did. It worried him because Lori believed it, dreamed about it, talked about it; he couldn't get her off the subject; he wanted to take her and Paul to America, get right away from the whole situation, but Lori wouldn't go. She was obsessed by it in the end, this vision of Hell on earth with Germans, *Germans,* people like herself, stoking the fires that Meryem kept seeing in the cards. You have to remember that your grandmother was a purebred Prussian who had been raised to believe that her menfolks were the most honorable creatures in the world; and of course, in their thick-headed medieval way, they were."

"Then how were they capable of doing what they did?"

"You haven't been paying attention to what I've been telling you. Any Christian nation was capable of slaughtering the Jews; believe me, there would have been no shortage of volunteers to run the death camps in Russia or France or England or even in the good old U. S. A. The truest sentence Hubbard ever wrote was the one that reads, 'Two thousand years of Christian teaching produced the SS.' It just happened to be the Germans who did the deed; it could have been anybody. Nobody wants to hear that, but you can take it from me it's true. That's why the whole world hates the

Germans so—they see their own secrets writ large in them. If the Nazis had won the war, as they darn near did, there wouldn't be a Jew left on earth, and sweet young women like yourself would be teaching little children what a wonderful thing the Holocaust was."

While the O. G. spoke Zarah watched him intently. It was a strange experience. The passions of the time and people he was describing did not register on his pallid face or in his genderless old contralto voice; he was as genial as ever in tone and expression. In describing these events seen with his own eyes, he might as well have been talking about historical incidents that occurred in the time of the Hittites, in a place that could not now be located with certainty upon a map. He seemed to sense her puzzlement, and paused for a moment to gaze at her with eyebrows lifted.

"Does all this disturb you?" he asked.

"No," Zarah said. "I'm just wondering how much of it my father knew and understood while it was happening."

"Oh, I think Paul understood what was happening, all right, at least the main points; he was a very clever boy. Very. But there were a lot of things he didn't necessarily *know,* and maybe still doesn't know, even after all these years."

"What things?"

"The things that made Hubbard stop writing his books."

"Is it something to do with the Experiment?"

The O. G. gave her a look of surprise. "That's right. But how did you know that?"

"I told you, I've read all Hubbard's books. There never was another one after *The Rose and the Lotus.* Did you know about the Experiment while it was going on?"

"No. Nobody did except the three of them. That's why there was so much gossip; naturally the Charlottenburg crowd suspected hanky-panky."

"But they were wrong?"

"Completely. A more virtuous couple never existed. Meryem, too; in spite of that wild air she had about her, the tattoo tears and all that, she was a very orthodox girl. I think the Experiment began as mockery, as a political joke, and then just got out of hand. Goodness knows there was a lot to mock in Berlin those days. The Nazis were the least of it—at first, anyhow. There was a famous story about the Christophers in Berlin. It was a moral hellhole in those days, musical beds, no such things as honor or fidelity, no idea that the Piper must be paid—something like America today. The Christophers took no part in all that. Hubbard was a Puritan Yankee at heart besides being in love with Lori, and Lori was a virtuous wife who thought her husband was a genius."

"Everyone says that. Why did she think he was a genius?"

"Because he was; if you've read his books you know that. You have to understand that he thought the Experiment was the cause of what happened to Lori, that he was responsible."

"Responsible? How?"

Evening shadows filled the room. In the flickering light from the fireplace the O. G. suddenly looked very tired. "Not now," he said.

" 'Not now'?" Zarah said. "How can you stop the story after making a statement like that?"

The O. G. lost his smile; he pointed a gnarled index finger at her chest; it was the color of a candle stub. "I can stop any time I want to, young lady," he said testily. "I've gone too far as it is."

Zarah's large eyes, fixed expectantly on the O. G., did not waver. Just then a log fell in the andirons with a shower of sparks, and behind the O. G.'s head this sputtering image was multiplied in the rain-streaked diamond panes of a bow window.

" 'Gone too far'?" Zarah said. "What do you mean by that?"

"You're a very good listener," the O. G. replied, "and I've let myself be carried away. You've come here in the shape of another being. Half the time I think I'm talking to your grandmother, telling you things you already know."

"Then what's the objection?"

"You're not Lori. You're the Lorelei, mesmerizing me into telling you things you have no need to know."

"No *need* to know? Nobody has ever had such a need to know as I do. Why won't you tell me the rest?"

"What makes you think I know the rest?"

"You're supposed to know everything."

"Am I? Who says so?"

"Everyone."

"Well, Everyone is wrong; Everyone almost always is. Remember that. I don't know everything, and what I do know I only know up to a point. I left Berlin before the play was over, remember. There was supposed to be a different ending. Then your father came back and upset the applecart."

"What applecart?"

"If Meryem has told you what she knows, you know more than I do."

"All I know is what I overheard her telling Barney, years ago."

The O. G. rose to his feet with a muffled groan, dismissing Zarah. "Did she mention a fellow named Dickie Shaw-Condon?" he asked, peering benevolently through the dusk at her. Zarah shook her head. "No?" he said. "Then you didn't overhear everything. Has Meryem or anybody told you about the last time Paul saw his mother?"

Zarah said, "No."

"Paul knew he was seeing her for the last time, that he was leaving her to her fate," the O. G. said. "She wouldn't let him cry, and she didn't cry herself. Her last words to him were, 'Control your face. They mustn't make you feel anything. No goodbyes.' Paul was fifteen years old. He never got over it. Not to this day."

9

CHRISTOPHER AND ZARAH MET THE NEXT MORNING UNDER THE MARBLE dome of the National Gallery of Art. Zarah entered through the door that faced the Mall, stepping through its little rectangle of light into the rotunda. She took off her sunglasses, and as she accustomed her eyes to the churchly dimness of the place, she looked around her, taking in the rotunda's enormous scale, its variety of stone and marble and granite, its central fountain surmounted by a bronze Mercury. She was precisely on time as usual. He was standing to her right, within the circle of mottled marble columns that support the dome, and she did not see him at once. She turned her head slowly from left to right, searching for him among the tourists in their bright vacation clothes, and when she caught sight of him a joyous expression of love rose to her face as if released from her very heart. In response Christopher's chest filled up with the same emotion, and he smiled at her across the vast, noisy, crowded space.

Zarah came toward him through the crowd, but she did not return the smile. After greeting Christopher she stood somewhat farther away from him than usual; her face, usually so calm and alert, was drawn and anxious. As they walked across the rotunda together, he began to tell her about a certan portrait by Ingres that had always reminded him of Meryem. "I thought we'd look at that first, then at a Gainsborough that looks something like your mother at your age," he said. "I wonder if you'll see the resemblance, too. Probably not. I've reached the age where everyone reminds me of somebody else."

He turned his head, meaning to say something else, but she interrupted him, something she had never done before.

"Can we sit down someplace?"she asked.

"Of course."

Christopher led her down the long nave of the museum to the garden court at the east end of the building. It was quieter in this space. The tinkling of another, smaller fountain accentuated the stillness. They sat down side by side in garden chairs.

Zarah took his hand. Once again this was something she had never done before. "I've been talking to the O. G."

Christopher, a little surprised by this abrupt change of subject, waited for her to go on.

"I like him," Zarah said.

"Most people do. Watch out he doesn't activate you."

"Why would he do that?"

"Because that's what he's been doing to people all his life. He can't break himself of the habit."

"All he seems to want to talk about is my Christopher grandparents. Lori especially."

Christopher waited again. He was like a priest in a novel by a convert, Zarah thought, relying on the power of one sin to remind the person in the confessional of another.

"He told me parts of the story I hadn't heard before." Knowing that Christopher, in his reluctance to interrogate, would not ask her to go on, she continued anyway, telling him everything she had overheard during Wolkowicz's visit to Tifawt, and everything the O. G. had told her.

"The O. G. mentioned a name—Dickie Shaw-Condon," she said, finally. "Do you know anyone by that name?"

"Yes," Christopher said. "He's an Englishman. He was a friend of my father's; he helped me out once. He must be very old now, if he's alive."

"I hope he *is* alive," Zarah said, "because the O. G. said you couldn't know the whole story about your mother unless you knew what this man knows."

"Did he?"

"Yes. He wouldn't say any more himself."

Christopher let go of her hand. It was an absent gesture; his thoughts were elsewhere. Where? Remembering what? Zarah did not ask. The two of them lapsed into a lengthy silence. The garden court, so called because ferns and other greenery grew in flower beds set into the marble floor, was a pleasant place to be; the fountain created the illusion that the dank refrigerated air was cooled by water running over stone instead of chemicals and machines. Zarah closed her eyes. Like her father, she was subject to rapid chains of thought that carried her in an instant through many years, many memories, and more than one language. In rapid succession she remembered everything that Lla Kahina and Wolkowicz and, only yesterday, the O. G., had told her about her grandmother.

"There are other things I haven't told you," Zarah said.

She opened her eyes. Christopher was looking at her; apparently he had been doing so for some time.

"You've told me enough for now," he said. "I think that you and I had better go and see Meryem."

10

STEPHANIE HAD A GROUP THERAPY SESSION THAT EVENING, AND AS soon as she came home she changed costumes and ran for two miles to relieve the stress that this induced. Consequently Christopher had no opportunity to describe his meeting with Zarah until Stephanie finished her shower and got into bed with him.

He had intended to leave any mention of the new clues to his mother's fate until last, but Stephanie interrupted before he got to that part of the story. "Are you telling me," she said, "that you're going to just take off for the Sahara Desert alone with that young woman?"

"Unless you want to join us," Christopher replied.

Stephanie snorted disdainfully. "You know perfectly well I can't leave my patients. Every hour of every working day is booked from now until February."

As a result of her long run in the emissions-saturated air of Georgetown and the sudden emotion that showed so plainly in her face, Stephanie's throat was dry. She had drunk all the water in the glass on her bedside table; she drank twelve eight-ounce glasses of water every day. Christopher offered her his own untouched glass of spring water, transported in plastic containers from an underground source in Maine. She waved it away and continued to clear her throat; there were tears in her eyes.

"Besides," she said, "What are we supposed to do about Lori?"

"She can go, too. She'd love it."

"She might, if she wasn't taken hostage by the people who shot Cathy. We can't just take her out of school for a month."

"It wouldn't be for a whole month. Anyway, what if it was? What would she miss?"

"A lot. She's in an intensive fast-track curriculum. She'd never catch up. Not everybody is as free as a bird to come and go as they please, you know. Some people in this society, even little girls who want to get into a good college, lead ordinary, regular lives according to a schedule and their obligations."

Coughing into her fist, Stephanie turned her eyes away, embarrassed that she had let these unkind words slip out. "I'm sorry," she muttered.

This was not the first time such a thing had happened. Stephanie insisted on paying exactly half of their household expenses, exclusive of wine and spirits, of which she did not approve; and books, on which Christopher spent far more than the whole family spent on food; and their child's tuition at a progressive private school, to which she could not afford to contribute and still buy all her own clothes. Although Stephanie insisted, as a matter of political conviction, that both partners in a marriage should have equal rights and responsibilities, another part of her nature caused her to resent the fact that she, the wife, went to work every day while Christopher, the husband, stayed at home. She knew that this was irrational, but there seemed to be nothing she could do about the anger it aroused in her. She understood, on the intellectual level, that this situation was not Christopher's fault. He was unemployable, even by the Outfit; fortunately, he had no need to earn a living. The Outfit paid him the modest pension that had accrued during his years of hazardous service under deep cover, but his main income came from elsewhere. Sebastian Laux, as the executor of Hubbard Christopher's will, had turned an estate of $78,000 into more than $1.5 million over a period of thirty years, including the decade that

Christopher spent in jail. This capital sum, invested by the Bank in tax-free bonds and U. S. Treasury notes, yielded more money than Christopher needed to live on. Thanks to Sebastian, who had bought it in his absence as an investment for the estate, he owned the house they lived in outright. He was not idle, in fact he worked hard—harder, perhaps, than Stephanie, who did little but listen to her patients all day and give them standardized advice according to the category of personality disorder into which they fell; she accepted no dangerous lunatics for treatment, only educated middle class people who did not understand why they were less happy and less successful than they deserved to be. Like his father before him, on the other hand, Christopher rose early every morning and wrote for several hours. Unlike Hubbard, however, he did not publish what he wrote. He delivered his manuscripts, instead, to D. & D. Laux & Co. for safekeeping; as his literary executor, Stephanie would have the right to publish, or not publish, what he had written after his death.

"I'm sorry," Stephanie said again. "I had no right to accuse you of being one of the idle rich." Christopher smiled gently, a humorous light in his glance. "Don't condescend," she said.

"All right," Christopher replied. "But getting back to Lori, ten seems a little young to be chained to a desk in the Ministry of Good Works."

"Please don't use Lori as a diversion. I want to discuss the real problem here, which is Zarah. It's only been two weeks since she showed up, and everything has changed."

"Stephanie, stop. Nothing has changed except that she's taken her rightful place in the family. You say yourself that this wouldn't be a factor if she were a male. She can't help it if she's a female; she can't help it if she happens to resemble certain members of her own family."

"Gender and resemblance are not the point. It's not her looks that bother me, although God knows she's every woman's nightmare. It's the way *you* look at *her,* as though a lover has come back to you from the grave. What are you remembering when she walks in?"

Christopher let several moments pass before he answered. Stephanie, who believed so strongly in the honest answer, and would settle for nothing less, did not always react to such answers happily. "Obviously she reminds me of my mother," he said at last. "But your intuition, if that's what it is, is correct—there's more to it than that. She's a lot like Molly. I don't know how that can be, there's no rhyme or reason to it. But it's true."

Stephanie gasped. "She's like Molly? She reminds you of *Molly*? How can you say such a thing to me?"

They had never in all the years of their marriage mentioned Molly's name. Everyone who remembered her, Stephanie's mother and father in particular, said that she was the woman Christopher had really loved. Christopher himself had never denied this. While in prison he had written an immensely long poem, filled with tenderness and lust and the deep amusement that always accompanies true love, that could only be about Molly. His enemies had killed her as a means of punishing Christopher, but he did not know this until the Chinese let him go. Stephanie had been waiting for him. She had married him, healed him, and borne his child, and now, after all these years and all that had happened between them, he thought that Molly had come back from the dead as his own flesh and blood, made young and beautiful again.

"That was really heartless," Stephanie said. "*Go* to Africa and be damned!"

She leaped out of bed, tumbling her unread biography of Castro onto the floor. Snatching up her pillow, she wrapped the light blanket from the foot of the bed around her naked body, as though she had just discovered that Christopher was not her husband, but someone who had been posing as her husband and had betrayed himself by falling disastrously out of character in the middle of the act of love. All this happened rapidly—Stephanie, lithe and mentally alert owing to her daily regimen of exercise and diet—was very quick in her movements, though a little clumsy. She knocked over the reading lamp as she ran out of the room, leaving Christopher by himself in the darkened room.

He fixed the lamp, then put on a robe and followed her downstairs. Still wrapped in her blanket, she was seated on a sofa in the long room. No lamps burned. He sat down beside her. In the faint wash of the streetlight coming through the front window she looked tousled and very young; Stephanie was a small woman, and in certain lights, while wearing certain clothes, and especially when she had been crying, she might have been mistaken for a schoolgirl. He touched her wet cheek. She turned her head away.

"I'm sorry to be behaving like this," she said. "But this situation is very threatening. I've spent our whole marriage trying to persuade you to put the past behind you and live in the present, and now this person shows up and all you want to do is go back with her to wherever she comes from. You can't change anything by going back, Paul."

"I don't imagine that I can, but at least I'll know the truth."

"Fuck the truth. On second thought, don't. I'll never get you back if you do."

"That's not very funny."

"Not if the DNA test didn't lie, it isn't."

She wouldn't meet his eyes. "Stephanie," he said. "Wouldn't it be better for everybody concerned if you stopped imagining that I'm going to fall in love with my own daughter?"

"I'm not the one who's imagining things. It would be better for you if you acknowledged your own fantasies."

They quarreled rarely; Christopher disliked it. He was seldom impatient with her, even more seldom outspoken because the consequences were so exhausting, but now he raised his voice.

"That's a lot of psychobabble bullshit, Stephanie," he said. "I don't fantasize about Zarah; the reality is enough. If even that is too much for you, then we'll find a way to work it out, but not at the expense of losing her again. I can't help the memories I have. I collected them before you came into the picture. I'm an old man."

"Like hell you are."

He paid no attention. "You have no rivals. Cathy is dead, Molly is dead. I loved Zarah at first sight because I recognized her as my child, and understood the feeling that gave me because I felt the same way the first time I saw Lori. But that's all there is to it. I can't hide my feelings to save your feelings. If I were your patient instead of your husband you'd call that healthy and wise."

"You're not my patient."

"No, but you're the one who taught me to accept my feelings. That's what I'm doing, and I'm grateful for the gift."

Stephanie inhaled and expelled half a dozen deep breaths; she believed in this exercise as a way to draw extra oxygen into the system and relieve emotional stress.

"All right," she said. "Have it your way. I'll say no more." Her voice was still husky. She had drawn a fresh tumbler of pure water from the plastic jug in the refrigerator, and she drank from the glass.

"You can say anything you like as long as I have the right of reply," Christopher said. "Now. Will you come to Africa with us?"

"No."

"Will you join us in London?"

"No. I can't just cancel people out on a whim. My patients depend on me. And you can't take Lori along as a chaperone. It's too dangerous. I won't have it . . . *Ostrich* chases. Jesus!"

"Are you interested in hearing why I want to make this trip?"

"Haven't you already told me? I assume it has to do with memories."

"It does. But you haven't given me a chance to tell you which ones."

Stephanie cut him off with a gesture. "Never mind." She stood up and gathered her blanket around her. "Don't tell me any more," she said. "I'll just bore you with psychobabble if you do."

She went upstairs, leaping up the treads for the exercise as she always did with a thudding of bare feet, and when Christopher joined her in bed a few minutes later, she pretended to be asleep.

The next morning when she woke, he was gone.

THREE

1

AFTER YET ANOTHER MEMBER OF THE OUTFIT WAS ABDUCTED, drugged, flushed clean, and returned unharmed to his employers, Patchen invited the O. G. to join him for supper at the Club. Patchen himself dined there almost every night, never at the Members' Table with the divorced, the widowed, the celibate, and the rest of the unwifed, but nearly always alone at a table with only one chair. He consumed half a bottle of wine from the private stock he kept in the Club cellar and swallowed the Club's soft college dining hall food—overcooked fish or baked macaroni or Salisbury steak—that could be eaten with a fork or spoon without the aid of a knife. The O. G. had put him up for membership twenty years before so that he would have a cheap place to eat during Martha's long sojourns in Guatemala, and Patchen had always used the Club primarily for that purpose. He liked the dull menu, the convenience of paying for his meals all at once when the bill came in at the end of the month, and, most of all, the freedom from tipping; giving money to waiters had irritated him ever since his honeymoon supper at Maxim's. At first the other members had tried to make him welcome, but he had shown no interest in playing bridge or attending round table discussions on foreign policy or joining the Friday night Bridge Group, and at length they had given up. Nobody bothered him now; he was left in peace to eat his supper and read his book—or, more lately, to listen to a recorded work over the button earphones of a Sony Walkman, a far more private way of doing things. They liked him in the Club even if they only knew him by sight, a scar-faced figure dressed in black who, like the unhappy bastard Mordred in the King Arthur stories, had

326

reasons for his mournful solitude only half-known even to himself; Patchen brought with him a certain shadowy panache, a hint that everyone who got in here could be trusted with the darkest secrets. They all knew what position he held, of course, and he was pointed out to guests: "That's David Patchen, the head spy, over there in the corner—looks the part, doesn't he?"

The O. G. was a different matter. He did not often eat at the Club. "If it wasn't for the honor of the thing," he said, "I'd just as soon go to McDonald's." But when he did come into the dining room he was overwhelmed by handshakes and greetings and by smiling old friends dropping by his table to swap yarns or introduce whomever they happened to be dining with. To avoid these interruptions, Patchen booked one of the small private dining rooms for their meeting. The O. G. arrived twenty minutes late, dressed in thick tweeds from the Outer Hebrides that smelled of spaniel and woodsmoke.

"Sorry to be behind time," he said, accepting a glass of sherry, "I got held up by some fellows on the way in; Old Boys." He mentioned a string of names and lifted his glass. "Absent friends."

Plates of Belon oysters had already been served by the impatient waiter and the ice beneath the shells was half-melted. Patchen poured white wine from a half-bottle that also dripped ice water.

"Bâtard-Montrachet," the O. G. said appreciatively; the Club wine list featured far less distinguished wines than this one. "You must have smuggled this in in your coat sleeve."

"I keep some here for sentimental occasions."

The O. G. ate a single oyster, then dropped his fork onto the ice. "These are those fake Nova Scotia Belons. Can't stomach 'em. I'll just drink the wine. Have you met Paul's prodigal daughter?"

"No, I just missed her. I was out of the country, and then she and Paul went away."

"Charming girl. Strange first name, but that's her mother's doing. She's the spitting image of Paul. Actually, of his mother. She's got the Christopher brain, too."

"That's a relief."

"Not everybody would say so. High I. Q.'s and loyal hearts have been a mixed blessing to that family. It's a pity you didn't meet; she's first-class material—speaks the languages, remembers the details. She says she spotted *you* coming out of my house the other day."

Patchen finished his oysters and rang the bell for the waiter. "I thought that might be her. How did she know who I was?"

"Barney furnished a description. He made quite an impression on her—got to her young; very jesuitical from the sound of it, but of course that was Barney's M. O."

"Then I'm lucky to be alive. Does she know what happened to Wolkowicz?"

"Just newspaper stuff. Or so she says. I don't think she suspects that you and her father were the ones who did poor Barney in. Best to leave that between her and Paul, I'd say. Anyway, they're off to the races in the Maghrib."

The upstairs waiter, elderly, black, and footsore, entered carrying a heavy tray bearing their next course. He set it down with a groan. Gazing over the O. G.'s shoulder at the five uneaten oysters on his plate, he nudged him sharply under the right shoulder blade with an index finger.

"Take 'em away, Albert," the O. G. said. "I don't like 'em."

"What's the matter with them?"

"Not salty enough; not chewy enough; not real oysters. Tell 'em downstairs to get the genuine article, will you?"

"I'll tell them. They won't listen."

Albert dropped the main dish onto the bare table and poured more wine, filling the glasses to the rim, then plunged the empty bottle upside down into the ice bucket. "No need to come back, Albert," Patchen said. "We'll ring before we leave." The old man shuffled away.

"We've lost another one," Patchen said, after the door closed.

The O. G. looked up with mild interest from his mushy swordfish steak. "Where from?"

"Headquarters."

"Headquarters." The O. G. spoke the word without inflection, but this was a startling turn of events. The other Beautiful Dreamers had been kidnapped on foreign soil, all in the Middle East or in European countries that followed a policy of appeasing Arab terrorists to protect their own citizens from murder and abduction. But Headquarters? That was a different kettle of fish. "Who was it this time?" the O. G. asked.

"A man named Walpole, from counter-intelligence."

The O. G.'s mental filing system clicked into operation. "I remember him," he said. "Tall fellow from Rhode Island with a bald

328

head and a Brigade of Guards mustache. Hearty laugh. Good mind for detail. Went to Wesleyan. What happened?"

"He went to the men's room at the movies last Saturday afternoon and didn't come back. He reappeared a week later, completely flushed out."

"Happy as a clam like all the others?"

"Yes. But there was a difference. This time there was no video tape."

"Then you don't know what he told them?"

"No, but that doesn't matter so much. We know what he knew."

"Which was what?"

"Anti-terrorist ops."

"Ah. It doesn't sound like they hit a random target."

"Why should they? They've got a lot of reliable information out of the others. What he told them is not the point."

"It's not? Then what is the point?"

"The video tape. They pinned a note to Walpole saying they're going to hand the tape over to Patrick Graham."

"Sugar!" said the O. G.

Patrick Graham was a famous television journalist, one of the new breed who were part leading man and part Grand Inquisitor. He had a long history of animosity toward the Outfit. This was partly political, because Graham in his youth had been a campus agitator and still believed that the United States of America was the chief enemy of the masses. But mostly it was personal. Even though he was wealthy and famous now, and married to the daughter of an English earl, his origins were humble, and as a scholarship student at Yale he had suffered rebuffs, real and fancied, from lesser men who had better pedigrees; in his heart he regarded the Outfit as the most exclusive fraternity in American history and he bitterly resented the fact that he had never been tapped for membership. He devoted a considerable share of his great talent and energy to discovering and exposing its secrets. It was Graham who broke the Wolkowicz story ten years before and he was still pursuing it long after the victim was in his grave. He had a particular hatred for Patchen because he believed that he had arranged Wolkowicz's murder and staged it as a suicide. He was not disturbed by the idea of official murder; it confirmed his dark view of the Outfit's real, though diabolically concealed, nature and methods.

Until now Patchen had dealt with Graham by ignoring him, a policy that turned him into an even more dangerous enemy.

"Have they actually given Patrick the tape?" the O. G. asked. He called Graham by his first name because, in his day, he had been polite to the announcer (as he called him), even accepting invitations to cocktail parties, though never to dinner, at his elegant house just down O Street from Christopher's.

"Not yet, as far as I know," Patchen replied.

"Patrick'll be in seventh heaven," the O. G. said, as if genuinely happy for him. "All the rest of them will have a fit because he's scooped them again. It will be a plague of locusts. It could be the end of the Outfit."

"No, that won't be enough to put it out of its misery," Patchen said. "I wish it were."

The O. G. frowned. "You do? You'll have to explain that to me. Why do you wish such a thing?"

"Because in my opinion," Patchen said, "we're going to have to destroy the village in order to save it."

The O. G. had always maintained that any good operation could be described in a single sentence. A single sentence was all Patchen needed to describe his plan, and when he had uttered it the O. G. reached across the table and gripped his forearm in such a way that the enthusiasm and admiration he felt for his protégé ran from one man to another like a current of electricity.

"Bless you," he said. "That's brilliant. But you can't tell anybody who works for you what you're up to. It would destroy the whole purpose."

"Exactly," Patchen said. "But I can't do it alone."

"Don't worry, son," the O. G. said. "You won't be alone." He gave Patchen's forearm, the dead one, another squeeze. "I'm proud of you."

2

THE SENTENCE THAT PATCHEN MURMURED TO THE O. G. OVER THEIR inedible supper at the Club was this: *If I were the next Beautiful Dreamer we could start all over again.*

There was no need for him to explain his idea. The O. G. grasped its perfection and its simplicity as soon as the words were spoken. If Patchen's memory was emptied by an enemy like those of the others who had been kidnapped, the Outfit could not con-

tinue to exist. There could be no going back to what had existed
before; something new would have to be created to take the Outfit's place—something that would recapture the energy, the patriotism, the audacity, the sheer fun of the Outfit in its youth.

Both Patchen and the O. G. had believed for a long time that a
way must be found for American espionage to start over again. The
Cold War was over. Marxism-Leninism-Stalinism (always, as the
O. G. liked to say, "a lie wrapped up in a sham surrounded by a
delusion") had collapsed under the weight of its own pathology.
The old secret alliances against the Russian Communists, built up
over half a century by the O. G. and Patchen and their operatives,
had outlived their usefulness. A new world was in the making. A
new intelligence service was required to study it, to understand it,
to discover America's real enemies and to help her real friends.

The Outfit in its present form could not do the job. Its methods
were outdated, its purposes irrelevant. Its best people, the brilliant,
intrepid eccentrics recruited by the O. G., were gone, having
grown old in the service or been driven out of it by wave after wave
of exposés in the press, investigations in Congress, reforms by the
Executive, and mutilating internal reorganizations imposed from
above. The combined effect of these assaults on the Outfit over
many years had been to render it almost incapable of operating as a
secret intelligence service. Its agents in the field could no longer
behave as spies must behave—with duplicity, ruthlessness, cold
logic, and utter unquestioning devotion to their cause (that is to
say, like idealists)—without fearing that they might be called home,
frog-marched through the media, and indicted on felony charges.

This state of affairs was a triumph for the Outfit's foes, foreign
and domestic. Some of the Outfit's own former officials had gone
so far as to testify before Congress or talk to the press about
"legalizing" the Outfit's activities. This was an absurd notion on
the face of it—the very purpose of a secret intelligence service is to
carry out illegal actions with the unacknowledged blessing of its
government—but it was eagerly taken up by goodhearted, patriotic
people as well as by others, like Patrick Graham, who instinctively
loved their country's enemies better than they loved their country.
Little by little the Outfit had been robbed of its reputation and its
élan, and of all but a few of the tools it needed to carry out its
mission. Now, according to the same people who had reduced the
Outfit to this feeble condition, even the mission had disappeared.

Patchen and the O. G. did not agree that this was true. The three great ideologies of their lifetime had been capitalism, Communism, and anti-Americanism. Communism had been defeated but the other two remained, and in the years ahead the United States would be faced with far more powerful and intelligent adversaries than totalitarian Russia and China had ever been, peoples who were possessed of a far stronger reason than the Communists had ever had for hating her: she had defeated them utterly in war, compelling their unconditional surrender, and then lifted them up and healed them and given them back their nationhood and their place in history. How could such magnanimity ever be forgiven? How could people laboring under such an unbearable moral debt ever be trusted?

However right they were about this, they knew that there was no point in struggling against the conventional wisdom. In its great, early days under the O. G., the Outfit, manned by the flower of American youth, had been something almost entirely new in history, a secret intelligence service that was dedicated to doing good in the world by stealth. "If we said that out loud we'd be laughed out of town," the O. G. had told Patchen soon after he took him into his confidence. "But by George, I know it can be done!"

With the help of Patchen and thousands of others, he had done it. He knew it could be done again—but this time in a way that would put it out of the reach of fools. The Patrick Grahams of this world, who had been tormenting the Outfit for so long, were dying to administer the coup de grâce. Well, let them, as long as the Outfit chose the time and place and put the pistol into their hands.

3

PATRICK GRAHAM NEVER BELIEVED OR SAID OR ATE OR DRANK OR wore or displayed anything for any other purpose than to be admired by the best people. By this he meant conscientious objectors to capitalism and liberal democracy like himself who had been made rich by a system they despised. He loved the common people but lived in Georgetown in an imposing Federal house filled with the works of fashionable artists living and dead and owned a weatherbeaten twenty-room summer "cottage" on Chipmunk Island, off the coast of Maine. He played tennis on the White House courts, always using a Head Genesis racquet, and golf at Burning Tree with Ping Eye II clubs. He owned two of the largest and most powerful German automobiles that U. S. dollars could buy, dressed (when not on camera) in three-thousand-dollar suits tailored in Savile Row, ate only organically raised vegetables and meat from animals that had been fed natural fodder and humanely slaughtered, and now that California wines were admired by connoisseurs, drank nothing but undiluted chardonnays and cabernets sauvignons from small coastal vineyards, open to the Pacific winds, whose appellations were known only to the cognoscenti. He liked to see Republicans lose elections and Communist insurgents win wars of liberation; he gave all leftists the benefit of every possible doubt and greeted each new Soviet dictator as a possible messiah. Broadcasting from Moscow after the death of Leonid Brezhnev, he had described his successor, Yuri V. Andropov, the sometime head of the KGB who had been the Kremlin's ambassador to Hungary during the popular uprising against Communist rule, as "the savior of Budapest." During the Vietnam War he had escaped the draft by pursuing a graduate degree in political science at Yale University. He joined the antiwar movement, waved a Vietcong flag in marches for peace, and hoped in his heart that the enemy would win and thus demonstrate the hollowness of American ideas and life. He made a name for himself early as a journalist by tracking down the semi-literate black amputee who had been drafted in his place (and blown up by a mine in the Mekong delta) and interviewed him on national television as an example of the injustice imposed upon the wretched by a heartless Establishment. He spent eleven days in Vietnam preparing this broadcast and afterward hung photographs of himself in full war correspondent costume, Army fatigues and Australian bush hat, on the wall of his office; for a year or so after his return from the war zone he habitually shook hands with his left hand and smiled enigmatically when asked what was wrong with his right. Now that the Vietnam War was over he had the same sentimental admiration for terrorists as he had formerly had for Vietcong guerrillas. As intellectual fashion made it desirable to become an "anti-Zionist," he believed as a matter of faith that Palestinians were helpless in the grip of their history but Jews had no right to mention theirs.

David Patchen thought that Patrick Graham was a fool and an enemy of mankind, a disgusting hypocrite who had volunteered to believe and merchandise the lies the Russian totalitarians told the world about themselves, and was therefore an accessory to millions of political murders and other crimes against humanity. Nevertheless he invited him to his house for supper on the night after he dined at the Club with the O. G.

The invitation came at the last minute. In order to accept it, Graham and his wife, Charlotte, begged off a previous engagement to dine with a member of the Supreme Court. They were surprised to discover, when they arrived, that there were no other guests besides themselves. There was hardly room for any. Patchen and his wife, a mousy little woman with graying hair, lived in a tiny house like a packing box facing an alley off P Street. Graham had never been inside this house before, and he was so surprised by its extreme modesty that he did not, at first, notice the remarkable paintings and antiques that Patchen had collected over the years; his tastes had been formed in New Haven by Europhile professors, and he had no eye for American works of art and craftsmanship. After one glass of very dry manzanilla sherry, drunk in puckered silence in the cramped living room, Patchen led the party into the tiny dining room where they were all seated at a small round table set with plain white china.

A tuxedoed footman from a catering firm poured the wine; Graham knew the man and greeted him by name in Spanish ("¿Cómo estás, Miguel?"); they had met many times before in other Washington houses.

"I haven't tasted a drinkable Château Margaux in years," Graham said, reading the label on the bottle in the waiter's hand. "It was Tom Jefferson's favorite Bordeaux, as you no doubt know."

"I didn't know," Patchen replied.

"No? He bought some of the 1784 vintage—the best since 1779, Tom said—and wrote home about it from Paris when he was ambassador." Graham had read this interesting fact a few days before in a popular book on wine and stored it away for conversational use. "The Margaux Jefferson drank was altogether different, of course," he said. "You can taste the merlot in this. Funny how drinking unblended wine spoils you for these French concoctions."

Charlotte Graham uttered a one-syllable laugh, "*Ha!* How about the Petit Verdot and the Cabernet Franc, Patrick? Can your palate detect those, too? Really! Why don't you hit him over the head with the bottle, Mr. Patchen? That's what my father would have done in a case like this . . . What is this, a '78?"

"Yes," Patchen replied, impressed.

"Is it good?" Martha Patchen asked. She was dressed as usual in somber homemade clothes. There was no wineglass in front of her, and her plate was heaped with vegetables; everyone else had been given the caterer's trademark medium-rare beef filet with béarnaise sauce.

"It's delicious," Patrick said. "I see you don't drink alcohol yourself. Very wise; I wish I could kick the habit. And we'd all be better off if we stuck to vegetables for good measure, the way you do. Do you feel better since you gave up meat?"

"I have never eaten the flesh of my fellow creatures," Martha said.

"Never? Good for you. Why not?"

Martha gave Graham a long faraway look, but did not speak. She never watched television or read newspapers and had no idea who Patrick Graham was. He waited attentively for her reply. None came. Instead, a faint, fond smile spread over Martha's plain face. Graham watched her in bafflement. She had just got back from Guatemala. Patchen knew that she was thinking of her Indians and very probably had not heard Graham's question. After a long pause he answered for her.

"My wife is a Quaker," he said.

"Really?" Graham said. "I didn't know the Friends were vegetarians. Are you one, too?"

"A Quaker? By birth and upbringing, yes."

"Amazing."

"Why is it amazing?"

Graham smiled tolerantly. "Well, you drink wine and eat meat. And throw babies out of helicopters, of course." This remark was meant, Patchen realized, as a pleasantry; Graham was demonstrating his sophistication, even a kind of wry sympathy, as if to say that he knew exactly what employees of the Outfit were paid to do, and while he could never do that sort of thing himself, he understood that somebody had to, given the nature of the imperialistic state for which Patchen worked.

Charlotte Graham changed the subject. "My, what a lovely lot of pictures you have, Mrs. Patchen," she said.

Martha had come back to the present and she answered at once. "My name is Martha, please. Yes, aren't they nice? I like the ones with fruit in them especially. They're David's hobby."

"It must be a very expensive hobby. Isn't that still life a Raphaelle Peale, and that portrait over there a Thomas Eakins?"

"I'm not sure. Does thee know the painters' names, David?"

Charlotte did not wait for Patchen's answer. "You're not *sure*?" she said. "That's wonderful." She beamed at Martha as if she were a kindred soul. Since coming to Washington she had learned to discuss her hosts' possessions—the Americans seemed to think it polite to do so—but she had never got used to it. The hired servant left the dining room. "Perhaps you could help me with another question, Martha," Charlotte said. "Why do menservants in this country always wear dinner jackets? It's a great puzzlement to me."

"Do they always? This one is the first one we've ever had in the house. I thought he looked nice. Maybe it's because those suits last such a long time. David has had his for years and years. He got it on sale at Brooks Brothers, so it was a good one, I guess."

Graham hid a smile. Charlotte avoided his glance. "It would be, coming from there, of course," she said. "Isn't Brooks Brothers the shop where President Lincoln bought his Inaugural overcoat, Patrick?"

"Yes," Graham replied. "I believe Richard Nixon bought his clothes there, too."

At almost any other table frequented by the Grahams, this sally would have provoked laughter. Here it produced silence.

Graham said, "Are you an acquaintance of Dick Nixon's, Martha? He was a Quaker, too, wasn't he?"

"Yes, poor man."

"You sympathize with him?"

"Yes, of course, they have tormented him so. But I feel even more sorry for his enemies."

Sorry for his enemies? What was this? Both Grahams were fully alert now.

"You do?" Charlotte said. "Why is that?"

"Because they hate him so that they put their own souls in jeopardy."

"My dear Martha, what an original way to look at it. I'm not sure I understand what you're saying."

"They have made Mr. Nixon stand for evil and they think that all it takes to be virtuous is to hate him. It is the sin of pride. My husband calls it 'the politics of self-congratulation.' Nixon arouses something primitive in people. David says Nixon is a Neanderthal among Cro-Magnons; they thought their ancestors had killed them all, and when they saw him and heard him speak they wanted to kill him without knowing why. It was an instinct, a voice from prehistory; he made them remember their own suppressed guilt. If Nixon had looked and sounded like a Kennedy and committed exactly the same crimes, my husband says, the people who hate him would all love him instead. I don't know about that, but it's very sad to hate someone so much that it makes you love all the wrong things."

Patrick Graham, who had never before been in the same room with someone who was willing to defend Richard Nixon, was visibly shocked and offended by Martha's words. He turned to Patchen. "Is that what you say?"

"It sounds like me," Patchen replied, smiling fondly across the table at Martha, who had innocently gone back to her plate of vegetables.

"It's a good thing you only sound like that in the privacy of your own home," Graham said. "Unfortunately, you seem to have married a female Candide. I can sympathize."

His voice was clipped, cold, different from the mellow one Patchen knew from his broadcasts. Off-camera, Graham spoke with a faint upper-class English accent that simulated his wife's. He had adopted her two-fisted table manners, too, and the overbearing tone of voice in which she asked rude questions of strangers. She was famous for asking such questions, questions that Graham lacked the breeding to put to a guest when he was not looking into a camera. Like his other acquisitions, his titled wife was an asset to him—"the jewel in the crown," as a witty writer called her in the "Style" section of the *Post*. Everyone knew she had come down in the world by marrying Graham, but like many before her, had done so at a price she regarded as satisfactory. Although some of the most famous blood in England flowed in her veins (through ancestors bastard and legitimate she was related to four English monarchs in three different dynasties), Lady Charlotte was penniless, the only surviving descendant of an ancient but now extinct line of improvident earls. The Grahams' marriage was not a romantic one; Charlotte was not so déclassée as that. She and her husband were friends and partners in his career; that was all. It was enough for Graham. She gave honest value in return for his money, tutoring him in the politics of friendship, running an efficient house and filling it with important people who almost invariably went home happy. Sexually they lived their own lives. According to the Outfit's files, she had conducted at least six brief love affairs in the five years of her marriage to Graham, all with elderly senators and Cabinet members entrusted with sensitive national secrets. Her regular lover was a member of the British secret intelligence service, well known to the Outfit, with whom she had been sleeping since her teens. It was assumed that her Washington adulteries were in aid of her husband's career. They were always followed by a sensational broadcast embarrassing to the Administration. Graham's own infidelities were numerous but fleeting, and nearly always involved very small women with long black hair—"spinners," as one of Patchen's sources called them. This, Patchen knew, was because Graham, while at Yale, had fallen hopelessly in love with a petite, spirited, dark-haired Viet Cong sympathizer who had later married Horace Hubbard's younger half-brother, Christopher's cousin.

All this, and more, passed through Patchen's mind as he nodded politely at Graham's last insult. He knew a lot about his guests—not, as Graham suspected and feared, because the Outfit had ever gone to the trouble of investigating either one of them, but because he and his wife kept turning up in cameo roles in the lives of people who *were* of interest to the many other government security agencies that shared gossip and information with the Outfit as a matter of routine. Graham, of course, had his own files, very like the government's, filled with gossip, innuendo, meaningless detail, malicious invention by disaffected friends, and the occasional kernel of truth that was most likely of all the items in the dossier to be discounted or overlooked. That was why he was here tonight.

After the exchange about Nixon, Graham fell into a hostile silence. This suited Patchen, who did not want to make small talk with him anyway. Charlotte, having struck gold once, spent the rest of the dinner plying Martha with questions. Martha was glad to answer them, and Charlotte learned about her Indians, the *guaro* cult, Maximón, and Martha's hope of rescuing at least some of the children from a life of alcoholism.

"How dreadful," Charlotte said, on hearing a description of the drinking hut and the ceaseless beat of the marimba.

"I wouldn't use that word," Martha said. "Their religion makes them quite happy."

"I should think it might." Charlotte's eyes danced with what Martha mistook for a sympathetic light. "Do they do anything else whilst performing their religious duties besides gargle the *guaro*?"

"They copulate."

"Copulate? You mean all together?"

"No. They just crawl over to one another as the spirit moves them. No one knows who the children belong to; after they're born the mothers hand them back and forth to be nursed, so after a while they don't remember which is theirs and which is somebody else's. I've finally realized that that's the way they want it to be; it's part of the cult to obliterate personal identity."

"It sounds like they're on to something. If they don't claim the kids as their own, though, I shouldn't think they'd mind your taking them away."

"But they do mind, terribly. Last summer the Maoists came and took some of the boys and girls."

"Maoists?" Charlotte said. "In Guatemala?"

"That's what they call themselves. It means they kill more than the other guerrillas do."

"How dreadful. How did the grown-up Indians feel about the Maoists?"

Graham broke in. "Why would they tell a middle-class American woman that?" he asked.

Martha turned to him. "They don't tell me anything, but they cried for days. They knew they'd never come back, that the girls would be raped and the boys would be turned into slaves."

"Is that the Nixonian line this week?" Graham asked. "Have you ever seen the Guatemalan army operate in an Indian village?"

Charlotte said, "Patrick, hush. Go on, Martha."

"If the children go, the cult dies," Martha said. "They understand that."

"What could be sadder?" Charlotte asked. "How many of these sad little creatures have you rescued?"

"None, so far."

"None? None at all? Haven't you ever asked if they'd let you take them?"

"There's nobody to give permission because nobody knows their own child. Besides, what difference does it make if you take them away by force or by lying?"

"And how long have you been working with these people?"

"Well, I'm taking care of the children of the first children I knew."

"And the originals are in the drinking hut? Blimey, what a book you have!"

"A book?"

"You've never thought of writing a book about all this?"

"A book? No, I haven't. How could I? They trust me."

"What?" What did trust have to do with anything? Charlotte gave Martha a searching look and saw that she meant what she said. "Never mind. I wonder why you keep on. How long *have* you been going down there, exactly?"

"Since before David and I were married."

"And how long is that exactly?"

Martha was beginning to blush under this interrogation. Patchen intervened. "There's coffee in the other room if anyone wants it," he said, standing up.

Charlotte said, "I don't drink the stuff, it keeps me awake, and I can't think that Martha does, either. Do you, Martha?"

"No."

"I thought not. You two go away and drink your coffee and tell each other boring stories. Martha and I are quite happy as we are. Aren't we, Martha?"

As Patchen led him into the living room, Patrick Graham, like a fundamentalist after an argument with a freethinker about the existence of Satan, was still seething. Graham had, in fact, been raised in a strict Christian home in Ohio, and in his mind (though he fought against the imagery) Karl Marx closely resembled Moses, V. I. Lenin played the part of Jesus, and Joseph Stalin and his cohort were the Disciples. Graham believed in some deep recess of his being that the Soviet state was a kind of Kingdom of Heaven made visible on earth. There the secrets of every heart were known to the examining angels, the whole truth about past and future, called "History," stood revealed, and those who perversely refused to believe in History were remorselessly sent to Purgatory (the Gulag) or Hell (the cellar of Lubiyanka Prison).

To conceal his anger and disgust, Graham examined another still life hanging on Patchen's wall; it was badly framed in the kind of dark wood that had not been used for such purposes for years. He suddenly remembered that a painting by one of the Peale brothers

had recently been auctioned off for a couple of million dollars at
Sotheby's or Christie's. "Is this a Raphaelle Peale, too?" he asked.
Patchen nodded. Graham walked—or, rather, as he later told Charlotte, the room was so small that he *leaned* closer to the picture, an
eerily lifelike rendering of a plate of lemons and a speckled trout.
"How," he asked, with his face very close to the painting, "do you
afford these museum pieces on a civil servant's salary?"

"I bought them a long time ago, when they were cheap and
unfashionable."

"How much did you pay for this one?"

"Four thousand dollars, I think."

"Jesus!" The word came out of Graham's mouth as a little yelp
of envy. "It must be nice to have inside dope."

"I'd never heard of the artist. I just liked his pictures."

Graham, who bought everything on the basis of fashion, did
not believe that anyone would invest in a work of art merely for the
pleasure of looking at it. He shot a quick skeptical glance toward
Patchen and uttered an even quicker snort of laughter. "I see," he
said. "If you say so." He looked around him at the walls and
ceiling. "I don't suppose you have to worry very much about
anyone stealing them, with the kind of electronic security you must
have in this place. Are we on camera now?"

In fact Patchen did not even own a burglar alarm, but because he
did not want to do anything to erode Graham's bottomless suspicion of the Outfit and himself, he smiled and said, "It's always wise
to make that assumption."

Miguel entered with a tray. Graham refused the weak Maxwell
House coffee he offered, but accepted a glass of port from a
decanter. Patchen sat down on a straight chair. Graham settled
onto a sofa opposite him and sat back, crossing one leg over the
other, the picture of relaxed self-confidence.

"All right, my friend," he said. "What is all this in aid of?"

Patchen placed his own glass on the low table between them. "I
asked you here to call upon your patriotism," he said.

"That sounds ominous. You and I have somewhat different ideas
of what constitutes patriotism, you know."

"True. And we've certainly had our differences in the past."

"Like who killed Wolkowicz."

"Oh, Patrick, that again. Barney Wolkowicz shot himself. Why
can't you accept the simple truth?"

"The answer to that is simple. Because you *say* it's the simple truth. Therefore it cannot possibly be the truth."

"I thought that might have something to do with it. But I asked you here tonight to talk about something else. It involves the most important questions of national security."

"I can well believe it," Graham said. "You must be talking about a certain video tape of one of the Outfit's finest babbling on about your totally illegal operations against the freedom fighters of the world."

"Ah," Patchen said, calmly returning Graham's agitated stare. "Then you've already received the package. Was there a return address?"

"Of course there wasn't."

"A letter signed by anyone or any organization?"

"Tune in tomorrow. And thanks for confirming the tape's authenticity."

"I didn't realize that I'd done that."

"You're denying it?"

"How can I? I haven't seen or heard what's on the tape you've received, and even if I did you wouldn't believe me. But if it's anything like the ones *we've* been receiving through the mail I can understand why you'd be taken in."

"Taken in? What are you talking about?"

"Well, for openers we don't have a Harvey P. Walpole on the rolls of the Outfit."

This was literally true; Walpole was a pseudonym to begin with, and only that morning Patchen had signed an order separating the man known by that false name from the Outfit and transferring him, along with the other Beautiful Dreamers, to cover organizations operated by the Outfit in Papua New Guinea, Saudi Arabia, Korea, and Taiwan. There they would live with their families in American compounds, go to work every day, receive full salary and benefits, and retire in due course on pensions equivalent to the ones they would have received if they had gone on working on the inside. This collective transfer had left a broad paper trail, but Patchen had taken that into account.

"I didn't mention anyone named Walpole," Graham said.

"Do they call him by some other name in your copy of the tape?"

Graham's face registered impatience. "What point are you trying to make, exactly?"

"After what you said a moment ago about your opinion of my truthfulness, I'm not sure that it's worth making."

"Cut the crap, Patchen. What's your point?" Graham's accent was perfectly American now.

Patchen gave him a sardonic smile. "I'm trying to plant the idea that you may be dealing with a hoax."

"Like hell I am. Everything Walpole says on that tape checks out."

"Did you say 'Walpole'? How interesting. How did you check it out, may I ask?"

"We used the network's files and my personal files."

"Which are based on what?"

"All kinds of things."

"Old broadcasts? Transcripts of interviews? Correspondents' reports? Newspaper clippings?"

"Among other things."

"Of which how much—eighty percent? ninety percent?—is in the public domain and available to anyone?"

"We don't compile those percentages."

"But you know what they are. I think you should consider the possibility that anyone who knows his way around a public library could have come up with the basic facts in that tape—names of terrorist organizations, names of their leaders, dates and circumstances of all the sudden deaths and other misfortunes that are blamed on the Outfit. Inventing the rest—the parts you *can't* check out—would be child's play."

An expression of stubborn skepticism fixed Graham's handsome features in place, like a television freeze-frame. "Why exactly would anyone do that?" he asked.

"I don't know, exactly. But the possibilities are obvious—a fraternity house prank arising from youthful high spirits, dementia arising from political conviction, a black operation by a foreign intelligence service designed to embarrass and discredit the U. S. government."

"So what are you telling me?"

"That you should consider all the possibilities before you go on the air with this tape that fell into your lap."

"In other words, you're asking me to kill the story."

"I haven't asked you to do anything. Please remember that. I've tried to make you aware, in the friendliest possible way, that there's a high potential for embarrassment in this situation."

343

"For the Outfit."

"Obviously. Also for the President and the committees on the Hill. They don't know anything about all this."

"You haven't told them?"

"Why would I tell them?"

"Why the hell wouldn't you? I wish *I* had a camera running right now."

"I think the answer to that question is implicit in what I've been saying to you."

Graham was on the attack now. "What the hell *have* you been saying to me? Just tell me in plain English."

"I thought that was what I had been doing."

"Then you've got a funny idea of what constitutes plain English. I'll tell you what I think all this double-talk means. I think you're trying to get me to kill this story."

"So you've already said, but you misunderstand. I hope you *will* broadcast the tape."

"What?"

"You heard me. I hope you go ahead. If you have no interest in covering your own ass, so much the better. I just wanted you to be aware of the pitfalls."

Graham stood up, a sudden and, as it seemed to Patchen, involuntary movement. The two men could hear the women's voices in the other room; they were laughing delightedly.

"What are you up to?" Graham said.

"Why do I have to be up to anything? Why are you so paranoid, Patrick?"

"Ha!"

Graham had never before been so close to Patchen in such strong light, and he saw for himself that the stories were true—Patchen's left eye *was* made of glass. It was a nearly perfect prosthesis which moved with his other eye and was precisely the same color. But it had no expression, and this created the uncanny illusion that Patchen's real eye was somehow not natural, either; it crossed Graham's mind that the false eye might be a demonic, privacy-destroying device—a camera? a listening device? something even worse? —fabricated in the Outfit's secret laboratories. Nevertheless, he did not flinch or look away.

"Look at it rationally, if such a thing is possible for a man of your convictions," Patchen said.

"What's that supposed to mean?"

"It means that you're predisposed to hear, see, and expose evil where the Outfit and the U. S. government are concerned and give our enemies the benefit of every doubt. The whole world knows that, including the person or persons who sent you that tape. You're eager to be used if the cause is right."

"Is that so? And what cause is that, exactly?"

"Come off it, Patrick. What I'm saying to you is, 'Broadcast and be damned.' You'll probably get away with it—you've gotten away with worse—and it may turn out to be a very good thing for the Outfit and the country."

"You're crazy. People believe what they see and hear on my show."

"That's why it will be a good thing. If we didn't do the awful things you say Walpole says we did on that videotape, then we have nothing to lose. No secrets are betrayed and we get credit for dirty tricks and dastardly deeds that will scare the bejesus out of every little Marxist rodent cowering in a hole anywhere in the world."

Patchen, who had chosen these last, unforgivable words very carefully, winked at Graham. This was a laborious process that slowly covered and uncovered his eerie artificial eye with a lid that was cross-hatched by scar tissue like the scales on a serpent's skin. "And now I think we should say goodnight," he said, getting to his feet. "Time flies when you're enjoying yourself."

In the next room, Martha and Charlotte were still laughing like schoolgirls.

4

YEHO STERN WAS RETIRED NOW, A POLITE WAY OF SAYING THAT HE had outlived his era and been replaced by a younger man who was not burdened by his memories or obligated by his debts. Yeho had always known that this would happen sooner or later—after all, he himself had climbed over an old man to get to the top—and when it did, he accepted it with a shrug and retired to the Negev to grow tangerines.

"The tangerine business is a good business, very interesting," he told the O. G. "You have to run operations against nature all the time."

"Is that tea all right?" the O. G. asked.

Yeho had just taken two cubes of sugar out of his pocket and popped them into his mouth; he was now filtering green Japanese tea through them. He made a face, but nodded. "Very bitter," he said, "but stimulating."

They were sitting around a marquetry table in Sebastian Laux's office at D. & D. Laux & Co. Yeho was almost as comfortable here as in a bubble, but he was restless. The room, furnished in the style of Louis XIV, was too luxurious for him. He knew the decor was a kind of cover, that people expected the back offices of private banks to look like this, but he did not like it.

"You're not really supposed to take sugar with this tea," Sebastian Laux said. "It comes from Kyushu, and the plant is fertilized with the night soil of people whose diet, apart from rice and a few vegetables, consists entirely of oily fish, such as mackerel. That's what imparts that bitter tang you noticed. You kill that taste, which is the whole point of the tea, when you put sugar in it. Or right on top of your taste buds, like Yeho's doing."

"How can they be sure these people eat only fish and rice?" Yeho asked

"By tasting the tea," Sebastian answered. "The tea grower provides the fish. After that it's the honor system, though of course he can tell if he's got the real thing. Anyway, the Japanese are pretty scrupulous about keeping a bargain, among themselves at least."

"The stuff makes my ears buzz," said the O. G. "Have you ever had it analyzed for dope?"

Sebastian, who was a tea snob in the way that the O. G. was a wine snob, paid no attention to the teasing; he was used to it. He lifted a Temmoku tea bowl to his lips and took in a noisy mouthful of air along with the liquid, in the Japanese manner. No other noise intruded, although they could see the glass towers and teeming traffic of New York's financial district through the windows of one-way glass.

Yeho hoped that the O. G. would come to the point of this meeting soon. Sebastian, not the O. G. or Patchen, had asked him to come to New York for this meeting, and he had flown from Tel Aviv on twenty-four hours' notice to be present, but the arrangements made him wonder. If Patchen and the O. G. were using a cut-out, even if the man in between was Sebastian Laux, then they must intend to ask him to do them a serious favor. That did not trouble him; he would do for them whatever he could, as they would do for him. That had always been the arrangement. But his power to do favors was greatly diminished. The new boys didn't like it when he paid visits to his past. New boys didn't like Old Boys; it was a fact of nature.

Finally Sebastian finished his tea. The O. G. had been holding a plain manila envelope, sealed with Scotch tape, on his lap. He now handed this over to Yeho. "Here," he said. "Skim this and tell me what you think."

Yeho, throwing back his head and holding the papers at arm's length, read through the file Patchen had handed to him. It was a digest of the Beautiful Dreamers case, badly typed (by the O. G. himself, Yeho assumed) on drugstore foolscap. When he had finished reading, Sebastian switched on a television set and they watched the tape of Harvey P. Walpole's drugged confession.

"Beautiful," Yeho said, as the screen went black. "If I didn't know better, if the target was different, I'd say it had to be us."

"*Do* you know better?" the O. G. asked.

"Only on principle; nobody talks to me anymore. But it cannot be. We all know that. So who *can* it be?"

"David has his suspicions. You remember the Eye of Gaza."

"Butterfly's Arabs. Yes, certainly. You suspect the dead?"

"Did you kill them all?"

Yeho paused; this was not the sort of question the Americans usually asked him. "No, not every single one," he said. "The number one asset, Hassan Abdallah, as Butterfly called him, was very good, very slippery. He got away from us, with two others."

"You never told us that," the O. G. said.

"We thought we could deal with him before you knew he was gone, and then it was too late to tell you. He's never been heard of since."

"That could mean he's been sleeping and someone has woken him."

"I agree. So what do you want me to say?"

"At this late date, what is there to say?" The O. G. went imperturbably on. "One of the things this fellow Harvey P. Walpole was working on before he was kidnapped was the Eye of Gaza. Walpole was a very good man. And just a week or two before they grabbed him, he made Hassan Abdallah."

"Made him?"

"Identified him. Got him cold. True name Soubhi El-Nazal, born in Jordan of Palestinian parents. He went to Berkeley under a scholarship fund set up by good-hearted citizens for deserving young Palestinians. Got a Ph.D. in chemistry with honors. Brilliant student. When Butterfly picked him up, he was working for Kelch und Kuhns, A. G., a research laboratory in Munich. He specialized in pharmacodynamics, which is the experimental study of the action and fate of drugs in animals. What works with animals, of course, usually works with people."

Applied research in drugs? Yeho was very interested now. "Did Walpole tell his kidnappers this?"

"If he did, it's not on the tape. 'Gee,' we said to ourselves, '*That's* funny. Everything else Walpole told them is on this tape. Only the part about Hassan Abdallah is missing.' That tickled our funny bone."

"Maybe he didn't tell them. Under drugs people don't remember everything, or sometimes even remember what's true and what isn't."

"That's a possibility. But it was the freshest thing in Walpole's mind. He'd made the discovery only days before. If he was right, and he knew he was, he'd solved the case. He was elated. It was the breakthrough of a lifetime. It was the first thing he would have talked about."

"You've got a point, I admit it," Yeho said. "So why am I here?"

"I don't want to embarrass you, Yeho," Patchen said. "But you questioned Butterfly before you handed him over to the Chinese. As I understand it, you know everything he told us; Horace gave you the transcript of our interrogations. But your methods are sometimes a little more effective than ours. The question is, did Butterfly tell you anything he didn't tell us?"

Yeho said, "Let me think." He was not evading the question. He had dealt with hundreds of cases, conducted dozens of interrogations, since the Butterfly operation; the details of this particular case were stored somewhere in his memory, but it would take a moment to search them out. Seated in one of Sebastian's three-hundred-year-old J. Lepautre armchairs, his sandals dangling a few inches above the magnificent rashan rug that meant nothing to him, he closed his eyes and concentrated.

After a moment he opened them again. "Only one thing that

might have been important," he said. "Butterfly said this man Hassan Abdallah was not a political, even though he said he was. What he was was a true Jew hater, a psychopath, a fellow who carried a picture of Hitler in his wallet. He wanted to finish what the Nazis had started—kill us all. He was particularly obsessed with a tribe of Jews in the Maghrib called the Ja'wabi. He wanted to exterminate them most of all."

"The Ja'wabi?" Sebastian said, starting a little in his chair.

Yeho noted the involuntary movement. What was this? he wondered, but asked no questions. "The Ja'wabi are *anusim,* which means that they're Jews who practice their own religion in secret after a forced conversion to another religion," he said. "In this case the Ja'wabi have been pretending to be Moslems for more than a thousand years, ever since the Arab conquest of the western Sahara."

"A thousand years?" the O. G. said.

"There's nothing so unbelievable about that," Yeho replied, happy to enlighten these Americans. "At least a hundred thousand Spanish Jews were baptized as Christians in the 1390s. Over the next three centuries the Holy Inquisition burned more than thirty thousand of these converts at the stake on suspicion of insincerity, and tortured another thirty or forty thousand. Nevertheless, secret prayer houses that had been in constant use by Jews since the days of the Inquisition were discovered in Spain as recently as the nineteenth century, and groups of secret Jews, the descendants of these false converts, or 'Marranos'—the Spanish word means 'swine' —were found even later in Portugal and as far away as Mexico."

"If these people have been doing what they do in secret," Sebastian asked, "how did Hassan Abdallah find out about them?" His voice was thin and piping; it was even more obvious than before that he was shaken by what Yeho had told them. Still Yeho betrayed no curiosity. He went on with his story.

"The Russians trained the Eye of Gaza in Libya, out in the desert," he said. "According to Butterfly, one of the trainers was an East German, a former SS man. He and Hassan were kindred spirits, of course. One day the German was telling dirty Jew stories around the campfire, and the subject of the Ja'wabi came up. Hassan was hooked."

"The SS knew about the Ja'wabi?" Sebastian said.

"Evidently they had a file from before the war. Don't ask me how—German thoroughness. From the moment he heard the story, the Ja'wabi gave Hassan Abdallah a purpose in life—Jews defiling Allah's mosque, touching the Holy Koran with infidel fingers. They had to be exterminated. That very night he asked Butterfly for poison gas to do the job."

"Poison gas?"

"He even specified the kind he wanted. I don't remember the name, but it produces vomiting, shitting, burning of the eyes, boils on every inch of skin, maximum agony. If he was a chemist, as you say, that explains how he knew what to ask for. Butterfly says he told him he had more important things to do with his time."

"You let it go at that?"

"No," Yeho said. "But it wasn't easy to follow up. Nobody in Israel had ever heard of these people. Finally we found a scrap of information in an old file. In the eyes of the rabbis they weren't even Jews. The Ja'wabi believe they're the descendants of Joab, the commander of King David's army, and that they left Judah in the first year that Solomon was king—that's 965 B. C., approximately. They're educated people in most ways, but they're very primitive Jews, right out of the Torah. They don't even have the Torah; to them the first five books of the Old Testament are family stories; their ancestors were *there* when everything happened. They know nothing of synagogues or rabbis or Talmudic law. They live in the mountains because when the Ja'wabi got there three thousand years ago they thought they had found the highest place in the world. In the time of David we talked to God and burned sacrifices to him from the hilltops, which the Torah calls 'high places'; temples came later, with Solomon. The Ja'wabi still do it the old way, but secretly. To the outside world they pretend to be Moslems, calling the faithful to prayers five times a day, going to the mosque, performing ablutions, making the *haj* to Mecca, the whole business. Living their cover. And they've gotten away with it right under the noses of their Moslem neighbors for ten centuries. No wonder this Hassan Abdallah wanted to gas them. The experts said forget these people, they're not Jews anymore; after all this time pretending to be Moslems they *are* Moslems."

"Did you agree?"

"No. Who listens to experts? I sent a couple of agents, a man and wife, very good people, anthropologists, to visit the Ja'wabi. We offered to transport them to Israel. They said no thank you; it sounded to them like Solomon had ruined the country with temples and idols just as Joab said he would. So we explained the danger from the Eye of Gaza, gave them some weapons and equipment, and helped them train a defense force. They already had one, called the Ibal Iden, made up of teen-age boys. To them it was a strike force; they had no tradition of passive defense. Ever since the time of Joab, if they had an enemy, they sent the Ibal Iden to wipe them out."

"I see," the O. G. said. "Most enlightening."

Sebastian gazed at an invisible object in the middle distance. Yeho looked from one old man's face to the other. Finally he asked the question. "I'm under the impression," he said, "that all this about the Ja'wabi means something to you. Am I wrong?"

"No, you're not wrong," the O. G. replied. "Paul Christopher and his daughter are with the Ja'wabi at this very moment. And thereby hangs a tale. With Sebastian's permission, I'll fill you in. Is it all right, Sebastian?"

"Go ahead."

In a few sentences, he told Yeho the stories of Sebastian and Meryem, of Cathy and Lla Kahina, of Christopher and Zarah.

"You're telling me that Sebastian has a wife, and that she's a Ja'wabi, and that she knew *Heydrich?*"

"Yes. So did Hubbard Christopher and his wife. You knew Hubbard, of course."

"And owe him, as you know," Yeho said. "But Christophers again." He clutched his head. "Trouble, trouble."

The O. G. smiled sympathetically. "Three generations of them this time. Plus the Ja'wabi. Which brings us to the point."

"That makes me glad," Yeho said. "But also a little nervous."

"The point is not Christopher or the Ja'wabi. It's David and the Outfit. He has a situation on his hands that can't be handled by conventional assets. But Old Boys might be able to do it. Of course nobody in the government except David could be told. It might embarrass them."

"Old Boys? What Old Boys?"

"Us'ns," the O. G. said.

Yeho thought for a long moment. "What's the objective?"

"Flush out this Hassan Abdallah and his wretched crowd. Clean 'em up once and for all. Save the Ja'wabi."

"Save the Outfit, you mean."

The O. G. nodded sagely. "That too," he said. "As a beneficial side-effect. Will you join the club?"

"What you're talking about would be expensive," Yeho said. "Where is the money coming from?"

The O. G. gave Yeho Stern one of his merry schoolboy smiles transported across a lifetime from the sunny playing fields of the Old Hundred. "That was why Sebastian asked you to come over. David has sold one of his paintings, got a big price for it from a private buyer. He's always wanted to invest in the tangerine business."

"Then he should have his head examined," Yeho said. "But who am I to say no?"

5

THE HIGHWAY THROUGH THE MOUNTAINS HAD BEEN IMPROVED SINCE Cathy's day, and it was possible now to go all the way to Tifawt by car, but Zarah wanted Christopher to see the same sights her pregnant mother had seen when she ran away from him a quarter of a century before, and she had arranged for them to cross the Idáren Dráren on horseback. They were met at the airport by a young female dressed in the hooded, all-enveloping chador of a fundamentalist Moslem woman. She and Zarah embraced, then spoke to each other in rapid Berber.

"This is Kbira," said Zarah to Christopher in English. "She's going with us over the mountains."

Kbira peered at Christopher with animated brown eyes through a slit in the headpiece of her costume, but said nothing. She led them outside to a Peugeot, and despite the chador, took the wheel. As they left the airport she pointed at a range of snow-capped russet mountains beyond the pink city.

"The Idáren Dráren."

Then, resuming her silence, she weaved adroitly through chaotic traffic in which cars, trucks, horse-drawn wagons, camels, and donkeys all moved at their respective maximum speeds. They had arrived at midday, and even at this altitude it was very hot. Everything—vehicles, houses, trees, animals, people in their flowing Islamic robes—was powdered with red dust; a man beating a camel by the side of the road raised little clouds of it every time he struck the animal with his whip. The temperature became noticeably cooler as the car moved higher into the hills, tires shrieking on the switchbacks as Kbira worked the clutch and changed gears, knees pumping inside the chador. Finally she turned into an unpaved road that climbed for several miles through a forest of stunted pines and oaks. At the end of this track, Kbira stopped the car, leaped out, and stripped off her chador. Beneath it she wore faded jeans, scuffed Reebok running shoes, and a burgundy T-shirt that read, in a lighter shade of red, "I ♥ ♥." She peeled the sweat-soaked fabric away from her breasts and stomach, then plunged her hands into a mop of curly dark hair that had been crushed flat by the chador, and shook it loose. Unveiled, she was a merry, sweet-faced girl, somewhat younger than Zarah. She grinned at Christopher and shook his hand with a firm grip.

"I'm glad to meet you at last," she said in English. "You *do* look a lot like Zarah."

She folded the chador and threw it into the trunk of the car, then picked up a hand-held radio and spoke into it in Berber. It crackled in reply. "They'll be right down," she said. "Want a Coke?" She opened a cooler and extracted three bottles of soda. Inside the cooler, sealed in transparent plastic bags, Christopher saw an Uzi submachine gun and two heavy semi-automatic pistols. Kbira, without a trace of self-consciousness, removed the bags from the ice and, while continuing to drink her bottle of pop with one hand, wiped them dry on the folds of her discarded chador. She kept the Uzi for herself and handed the pistols to Zarah and Christopher, with two extra clips of ammunition.

"You know how to use this?" she asked.

"Yes," Christopher said. "But I'd rather not have it."

Kbira smiled again and closed her fingers over the butt. "Better keep it."

The radio crackled again. A couple of minutes later four very young men wearing khaki shorts and maroon T-shirts like Kbira's came into sight on the steep trail above them. They, too, were armed with diminutive Uzi machine pistols slung under their right armpits. One after the other they embraced Zarah, kissing her on both cheeks and gazing into her eyes. Two of them were nearly as fair as Zarah. One of the darker ones had Meryem's intense green eyes, and these were even more startling in a young face than in an older one. This youth and Kbira were kissing each other fondly and murmuring in dialect. They were about the same size, just over five feet tall, but muscular and quick in their movements. Zarah, a woman of ordinary size for an American, towered above them. She answered the question in Christopher's mind.

"They're all quite small," she said. "No one except Lla Kahina has married outside the tribe for a long time. Maybe it was Sebastian's size that appealed to her."

"Is that fellow related to her?" Christopher asked.

"Yes, but I don't know exactly how. They're all cousins. Why?"

"He has her eyes."

"You're right. So do a lot of the other Ja'wabi."

She beckoned the green-eyed man closer and introduced him.

"This is Ja'wab, the leader of the Ibal Iden," Zarah said; Christopher already knew who and what the Ibal Iden were.

Ja'wab shook hands with Christopher. When he spoke, in English, he did so in Zarah's faint Kentucky accent mingled with echoes of Semitic triple consonants. "Welcome to the Idáren Dráren," he said.

Without another word, he picked up Christopher's bag, balanced it on his shoulder, and led the way up the mountain.

"Your friends are well-armed," Christopher said.

"Yes," Zarah said. "Ever since the ostrich hunt. I should have warned you."

"How does it happen that they all speak English with a Bluegrass accent?"

"Mother taught them, so they could understand the tutors."

"They studied with the tutors, too?"

"We all went to school together and studied the same things."

"Your mother paid for all that?"

"Ostensibly."

"Ostensibly?"

"I think the Ja'wabi may have slipped the tutors something extra. She loved to do things for them, but they don't like charity."

On the trail above them, Kbira and Ja'wab turned around and watched them. Kbira now carried two Uzis slung around her neck—her own and Ja'wab's. Christopher said, "Your friend is called Ja'wab, as in Ja'wabi?"

"That's right," Zarah said.

"Is that a common name among the Ja'wabi?"

"No. There's only one man by that name in every generation. He's the seventy-sixth Ja'wab."

"Like the Dalai Lama?"

She laughed. "Ja'wab would like that idea. No. It's just a name that's handed down. Like Kahina, for females. You aren't born with the name; it's given to you if you have some special quality."

"Like what?"

"In Ja'wab's case, bravery."

"In what context?"

"In the context of finding and killing the people who killed our people," Zarah said. "All of them."

She broke into a trot, leaving Christopher behind. They had almost reached the top. Christopher smelled smoke and the aroma of roasting meat. Around the next bend in the trail the camp came into view, half a dozen khaki tents pitched in a meadow near a waterfall. The cascade, flowing over henna sandstone, was a shade of red, like nearly everything else in this landscape. Across the rusty brook a dozen horses, neatly made Barbs with large liquid eyes, grazed among sheep and donkeys.

Zarah awaited him. "Our transportation and food," she said. "Five days on the trail, five sheep. I hope you like roast mutton."

There were two other women in the party, one middle-aged and the other still a girl, introduced by Zarah as Aziza and her daughter Dimya. They gave the newcomers glasses of sweet mint tea, then went back to tend the cooking fire. The young men, except for Ja'wab, went into separate tents. A silence settled over the camp.

"I'm going to change clothes and help Aziza with the food," Zarah said. "Do you want a nap? That's what the others are doing. Ja'wab is on sentry duty."

"No thanks," Christopher said. "I think I'll hang out with the Dalai Lama."

By now it was late afternoon. A chilly shadow crept across the meadow. Ja'wab had been searching the surrounding heights with binoculars. Now he crossed the brook with a running jump and inspected the horses' hobbles. Christopher followed him, stepping from stone to stone across the rushing water, and waited quietly for him to finish what he was doing.

Ja'wab approached him. He had exchanged his Uzi for an American M-16 rifle. "Do you like horses?"

"These are very good-looking."

"The best. Your late wife bred them. If she saw a beautiful horse, no matter where it was or what it cost, she bought it and brought it back to Tifawt."

Christopher said, "You knew Zarah's mother well?"

"Nobody knew her well. She never learned to speak Ja'wabi. Only a few words, nearly all nouns."

"That's funny, because you all seem to speak English with her accent."

"She was the one who taught us. We played in English two days a week; Zarah insisted on it, so we'd all speak English when we grew up. Your daughter is a very systematic person."

"You know *her* well."

"Oh, yes. As well as myself."

"I should thank you for avenging her mother's death."

"Is that what Zarah told you?"

"She said you killed the people responsible."

"Single-handed?"

"I got that impression?"

Ja'wab grinned. "Zarah," he said. "Look, I'm going to climb up the mountain a little way, where I can see the camp better. Would you like to come with me?"

"Yes."

"Then I'll get another rifle for you."

They took up a position on a hilltop that commanded a view of the camp and its perimeter. Ja'wab was well equipped; in addition to his American automatic rifle and his Japanese binoculars he carried a hand-held radio. Only a few miles below them in the valley, crops and orchards grew in orderly patterns and sunlight flashed on windshields.

"Is it really so dangerous, this close to civilization?" Christopher asked.

"Civilization has always been the main problem for the Ja'wabi," Ja'wab replied. He stood up and began pointing out landmarks. Nearly all had to do with the death of Ja'wabi: by this misshapen rock, in the time of the Romans, two of them had killed seventeen legionaries before dying themselves; in that defile, in the time of Oqba ben Nafi, who conquered the Maghrib for Islam, fifty Ja'wabi had fought to the death rather than accept conversion; in the rubble of yonder brick fort a Ja'wabi force had died to the last man against a French detachment equipped with mountain howitzers and Gatling guns.

The Ja'wabi have always been here," Ja'wab said, "and the others had no right to be. But they kept coming anyway. So it's best to watch. Think of Zarah's mother."

When they returned to the camp, after being relieved just before twilight, they found the women working by the cook fire, all four of them dressed in bright Ja'wabi clothes, purple tassels swinging from the hems. With her bright hair covered by a scarf and a gold piece resting on her forehead, Zarah was all but indistinguishable from the others. Her skin, like Christopher's, contained a good deal of yellow pigment and she was deeply tanned, but it was not her complexion that created the resemblance; it was the way she moved and spoke. Yet she was a different creature here. Her voice was deeper and somehow more womanly when she spoke the Ja'wabi dialect. The young men had changed into Ja'wabi costumes also; it was clear that there was going to be a feast.

The women placed a platter on which the whole roast mutton was displayed on the ground. The whole party sat down together in a circle on a carpet, men on one side of the platter, women on the other, eating with their fingers. After the mutton came chicken cooked with dates and figs, then a stew with more lamb and hard-boiled duck's eggs, then a couscous with carrots, turnips, and other root vegetables.

They ate by the light of the full moon. The meal lasted a long time. Around midnight two or three of the young men got out musical instruments—a drum, a flute, and a stringed instrument Christopher did not recognize—and began to play. After a few moments Kbira and Dimya, carrying tambourines, came out of a tent into the moonlight and danced, clapping their hands and singing in a high treble falsetto, one voice singing a long phrase and the other replying, then the two of them singing a refrain in unison. There was no harmony, just the chanted minor-key melody and the counterpoint of clapping hands.

The young men laughed at the songs and looked at Zarah out of the corners of their eyes. She covered her smile with the end of a scarf. Christopher, who had never before observed her in the company of males her own age, broke the silence with a question.

"What are they saying?" he asked.

"They're singing a song about negotiating a marriage contract," Zarah said. "They make up the words as they go along, but it's an old joke about Ja'wab and me. Kbira just sang, 'She is worth a hundred black she-camels and one bay *faâl* because of her beautiful silver eyes,' and Dimya sang back, 'By the time I dye two hundred camels black I won't love her anymore and the *faâl* won't love the she-camels.' "

"What's a *faâl*?"

"A stud camel, very valuable, very disagreeable."

"Who are you supposed to be marrying? Ja'wab?"

"That's the whole point of the song," Zarah replied. "Our marriage has been prophesied, but they don't think he needs a new wife."

"Why not?"

"Because they're both married to him already."

"In the song?"

Zarah unveiled her face and grinned with unconcealed amusement. "No," she said. "In real life."

Three nights later they arrived on the slope of Tinzár. "The highest place in the world," Zarah said, smiling. Leading him among the rocks, she showed him the place where the birthing tent had been pitched, then pulled up the sleeve of her blouse to show him the red thread tied around her wrist.

"Kbira tied this on me this morning," she said. "She always does when we come to Tinzár."

"She knows the story?"

"Everyone does. You mustn't laugh or think that I'm making this up. The Ja'wabi really think that Mother and I and my twin were the same people as the ones in Genesis, born into another age. According to the way they look at the world, things happen over and over again, with people sort of leapfrogging through history to relive their lives in different times and different places."

"Then they must know exactly what's going to happen to you in this life."

"Lla Kahina knows. I don't know about the others." She glanced quickly at Christopher, as if to catch the slightest glint of skepticism in his eye. "Don't," she said, "form an opinion about what Lla Kahina knows until you've met her again."

She pointed out the cairn under which her stillborn brother was buried. "Mother made me memorize the location," she said.

"She visited this place?"

"Every year on our birthday. It nearly always snowed; we'd bring flowers and put them on the grave. Lla Kahina always cleared them away before we left to preserve the secret. It bothered Mother that the grave wasn't marked. But if she had put up a cross as she wanted to, the poor little fellow would have been dug up and thrown over the cliff. Christians are really hated in this part of the world; worse than Jews, even."

"Do the Ja'wabi hate them?"

"Christians? They hardly know they exist. The French were their only experience of them, apart from Mother, who didn't count, and now she and the French have come and gone."

"What about you?"

She slipped her arm through his and walked with him a few steps before answering. They could hear the wind howling among the red crags and the river brawling through the gorge at the bottom of the precipice. She smiled at him; since leaving America she had a beautiful smile, filled with good-hearted innocence. "I'm a different case," she said at last.

That evening, in the last light of the day, the whole party climbed to the summit of Tinzár and slept under the shelter of a ledge that had obviously been much used by campers in the past. Tonight there was no singing or merriment or even any food; immediately on arrival the Ibal Iden crawled into sleeping bags and went to sleep.

Christopher was awakened before dawn by the smell and crackle of a huge fire. The Ibal Iden had brought the smallest of the lambs with them, carrying it over rocks that it could not negotiate on its own and tethering it outside the shelter overnight. By the time Christopher woke up it had been slaughtered and bled, but left unskinned. At the moment that the sun came up, Ja'wab, reached into the flames and laid the dismembered carcass on a platform of rocks blackened by many previous fires. The oily wool burned off in moments, sending up an acrid unmistakable stink, and then the flesh began to cook, creating a more familiar and agreeable aroma. Another man threw what looked like a ball of oiled bread dough onto the platform; it was consumed almost at once, after burning with a surprisingly strong, sweetish odor.

All this took place without conversation, much less with prayers. It was obvious, nevertheless, that the burning of the lamb was a solemn ceremony and the Ibal Iden were deeply moved by it. Ja'wab watched the flames with his arms around his wives, the other boys sat close together in a row. By the time the fire died, about three hours later, the lamb was cooked through, and the Ja'wabi ate it. They used no knives or other implements to carve it, but tore bits of it from the bone with their fingers and passed it to each other, eating it under the shelter of the rock with flat bread that the women had baked the day before.

Zarah was included in all this as an equal. So was Christopher. He was not surprised. Zarah had told him what to expect, and why, and in the small Bible that he carried among his books he had looked up the relevant passage in the Book of Numbers: *"Yahweh spoke to Moses and said, 'Whenever [offering] food burnt as a smell pleasing to Yahweh . . . there will be one law for you, members of the community, and the . . . alien alike, a law binding your descendants for ever: before Yahweh you and the alien are no different.'"*

"Yes," Zarah said when he showed her the passage. "That's what the Ja'wabi say. That's how they live."

6

CHRISTOPHER AND ZARAH AND THE IBAL IDEN ARRIVED AT TIFAWT IN darkness—the village had never been electrified—and went to bed immediately. The old woman, Aziza, who had been with them in the mountains, lighted Christopher with a candle down a gloomy corridor to his bedroom. He found it impossible to sleep. Seeing the place on Tinzár where Zarah had been born in secrecy and her twin buried in stealth had made him visualize Cathy again as she had appeared to him during their conception, battered and desperate and afraid to die. Against all odds, she had gotten what she wanted, and it seemed to him that Cathy was still present in this house where she had hidden herself and their children away for almost exactly half her lifetime—not present as a complete ghost, but lingering in some partial form, as if her poor numb heart had escaped from the ectoplasm at the last moment and stayed behind, too difficult a case even for death to cure.

When, at the crack of dawn, Christopher heard the muezzin calling the *salat as-subh,* he went out into the courtyard, intending to write in his notebook. A dwarfish figure crouched by the fountain and groped in the water. Because the sun was only just beginning to rise, the garden was still filled with shadows, and for an instant Christopher mistook him for a servant performing his ablutions. Then Yeho Stern stood up and spoke to him in German.

"Good morning," he said, holding up two dripping hands for Christopher to see. "I've been playing with the fish; I was told that your daughter Zarah taught them to eat bread crumbs out of a human hand. It's true. They do." He wiped his palms on his trousers and shook hands. "Yeho Stern."

They had never met, but Christopher knew him by reputation and recognized him even before he heard the name. He said, "You've been waiting for me?"

"Yes, but you're an early riser, so not for long," Yeho replied. "Here—this is for you."

He handed Christopher an envelope. The letter inside, scribbled in the O. G.'s Palmer Method hand on both sides of a sheet of drugstore paper, was written in German—but in the Greek cipher. This presented certain problems with diphthongs and umlauts, but Christopher read it easily enough. It was a terse but essentially complete account of the latest developments in the Beautiful Dreamers case, omitting any reference to the Eye of Gaza. All proper names were omitted also. The last line read, "Your friend from Okinawa days needs you; the bearer will explain."

"Are you instructed to wait for a reply?" Christopher asked.

Yeho ignored the other man's sardonic tone of voice. "I'm here to tell you what the plan is," he said. "Then if you want to reply, I'll listen and pass on what you say."

Christopher handed back the O. G.'s letter. "I don't need to know any more," he said, speaking English. "I'm out. Forever. Old times are gone and forgotten. Tell the O. G. that."

"You don't want to help David?"

"David has a cast of thousands to help him."

"But nobody like you anymore, according to him. He thinks you're the only one who can do the job. You and your daughter."

Christopher had begun to turn away. He stopped. "My daughter?" he said. "What does she have to do with it?"

"A lot. There's a connection."

"A connection to Zarah? Like hell there is. Look around you."

"Listen," Yeho said.

"*This* is where she comes from," Christopher said. "This is where she's spent her life. There's no possible connection."

Yeho took Christopher's arm and repeated, "Listen," he said, "I'm trying to tell you something." He was standing quite close now, so that the two of them could speak in very low voices. Barely moving his lips, speaking German again, he told Christopher about Hassan Abdallah. Christopher, rigid and cold in manner, but listening at last, stared down at him, eyes glittering. Yeho had seldom seen a trained agent show so much anger. He was surprised by the display. How could Christopher have been as good as everyone said he was if this was how he behaved before strangers? Well, who knew? Maybe he had changed. And if he had changed once, he could change again and go back to being the operator he used to be. Yeho described Hassan Abdallah's obsession with the Ja'wabi.

"You understand what I'm saying to you?" he said. "This man wants to wipe out the Ja'wabi to the last fetus."

"Including Zarah," Christopher said. "Is that the point you're making?"

"That's it. She may not look like a Jew, but she thinks like a Jew, feels like a Jew, talks like a Jew, and hangs around with Jews. To this psychopath who wants to kill her, she's a Jew."

Christopher said, "Is that all you came here to tell me?"

"Unless it's not enough," Yeho replied. "Maybe you have questions."

"Like what?"

"Like who was this Russian named Butterfly, and why was he talking to us. Does that make you wonder?"

"Not especially."

In the strengthening light—no more than five minutes had passed—Christopher's anger was still visible, but he was beginning to control it better. Yeho understood. This was a man who had lost almost everything, and then got some of it back, more than he ever expected. And now he was being asked to gamble it all. No wonder he looked like he might kill Yeho with his bare hands before he remembered that Yeho was not the enemy. Yeho stood his ground; Christopher was not the first man he had ever seen in this condition. Or the first he had cured of it.

"I'm going to tell you, like it or not. Butterfly was the man David gave to the Chinese to get you back. It was a very big price to pay. At the time I thought he was crazy. Why did I think so? Because I knew something like what's now happening was bound to happen if he traded this Russian before we rolled up his networks. David knew that, too, but he did it anyway. Why? To get you, his friend, out of China. It was a stupid thing to do. They tell me you were a great operator in your day, so maybe you wouldn't have made the same mistake if you'd been him and he had been the one in chains. But David did it, and I was the go-between because I knew how much value he placed on getting you out. Now this bad deal is coming back to haunt us, even here in this place where your daughter grew up in peace and innocence. So don't tell me there are no connections, Paul. There are plenty of connections."

Until this moment Christopher had known nothing about the details of his release from prison; Patchen had never mentioned the negotiations, except to tell him that he owed no debt to the Outfit. On hearing the truth he felt slightly nauseated and lightheaded; turning his back to Yeho, he took several deep breaths to draw oxygen into his lungs and bloodstream—Stephanie's trick. Because of the altitude, it did not work too well, and when he turned around again, the same lifetime of bad memories that Yeho had detected a moment before still came and went in his eyes. Then his expression changed.

"All right," Christopher said calmly. "But not with Zarah, and not right now. I need a few days to myself."

"Zarah may have her own ideas about all this," Yeho said. "But one thing at a time. Lla Kahina told me what you're after. I wish you luck. Where I come from, your parents are remembered. One more connection."

7

THE MYSTERIOUS GREEN EYES AND THE TATTOOED TEARS BENEATH them were the same, but otherwise little was left of the Meryem Christopher had known half a century before in Berlin. As an old woman seated in her garden in Tifawt she was paler, smaller, stiller—a bundle of dark clothes deposited in a wicker chair. The bony hand she held out to him was webbed with blue veins under its desiccated skin. When to his own surprise he kissed it (a Prussian gesture he had not made since boyhood) the hand had no more scent or taste than an object made of wax. Holding it to his lips he understood the reality: his mother, if still alive, would be as old as Lla Kahina; older. In Christopher's memory Lori had remained as she was when he last saw her in the hands of the Gestapo, a woman of thirty-five who still looked very much like the girl of nineteen captured in Zaentz's drawing. If Zaentz could paint these two friends together now, would he still suggest they were somehow the same woman inhabiting two bodies?

363

"Well," Lla Kahina said. "Paul. At last."

"It's been a long time, all right," Christopher said. "But I understand you've been keeping in touch."

Affection and amusement mingled in her smile. "The same Paul," she said. "Sit down beside me."

They talked for three days, always in the cool of the garden. It was October now; the days were mild and bright. It snowed on the mountain peaks almost every night, and during the daylight hours flocks of alabaster birds passed overhead. At night they roosted in the orchards above the village and when Christopher woke up and looked outside at the moonlit panorama of valley and mountains, it seemed that snow had fallen on the trees as well. These birds always flew over Tifawt at this time of the year, Lla Kahina said; she did not know their names. "What would be the point?" she said. "Naturally the French gave them all Latin names. Cataloguing is one of their passions, but no one else was interested."

"Not even Zarah?"

"No. She's like her mother in that respect. Cathy never knew the name for anything, or where she was on the surface of the earth. She was quite a young soul, I think. Language was a mystery to her. Do you hear that?" The muezzin was calling the late afternoon prayer. "That was her favorite sound. She could understand it because it's a kind of music. But she never guessed, even though she lived among the Ja'wabi for twenty-two years, that we weren't Moslems. Right up to the end she asked me questions about Islam."

"That's a tribute to your tradecraft, I guess. But there are other things that could be said about it. Why didn't you tell her the truth?"

"Because I wasn't free to do so. Any more than I was free to tell Zarah about you against her mother's wishes."

"Is that the only reason?"

"What other reason did I need? Also, she wasn't Ja'wabi."

"Neither was Barney Wolkowicz."

"He found out everything for himself. In a single day."

"What about Zarah?"

"She took in the truth with the milk she drank."

"Not Cathy's milk."

"No. Ja'wabi milk."

"Did that make her Ja'wabi?"

"It satisfied a custom that everybody understands. But even before she was born she was already what she was."

All this was said in a light, even playful tone of voice, as if Lla Kahina believed that she was telling Christopher things that he had long known but may have forgotten—stories about a remote, poor, but interesting branch of the family. He was not diverted from his real line of thought.

"And what was it, exactly, that Zarah already was?" he asked.

"Exactly? No one can say exactly because not everything has happened yet," she replied. "But she belongs here. She is going to do some great thing in this lifetime."

"What great thing?"

"She will show us when the time comes. Zarah is not a young soul. I think she may be living her last life. She has some debt to pay the Ja'wabi. That's why she's here. Every Ja'wabi feels it. That's because of the story of her birth. I knew she was someone like that even before she reached out of the womb and touched me."

"She touched you?"

"Yes. She held on to my finger while I tied the red thread around her wrist, then let go. It was the grip of a person who knew me."

"But you say you knew even before that she was . . . whatever you think she is. How long before?"

"Since the first time I saw her in the cards. In Otto Rothchild's house on the lake of Geneva on the day I met Cathy."

"What did you see?"

"Will you be able to believe what I tell you?"

"Believe it or understand it?"

"No one can understand it, not even me. I saw her as she is now, but, at the same time, as she was in the past. This often happens. At first I thought I was seeing your mother as she had been in another life a long time ago, but then I realized it was only a resemblance. It was your child I saw."

Christopher did not ask her how she had known this. He said, "Do you often see my mother in the cards?"

Before answering, Lla Kahina looked up at the patch of cloudless sky above her garden.

"Always," she said, and when she lowered her eyes to look directly into his face, he saw that she was weeping.

He said, "Tell me about Heydrich."

"About Heydrich? How much do you know already?"

"What's in *The Rose and the Lotus*. And what Zarah overheard you telling Wolkowicz."

"Then you know almost everything."

8

SHE TOLD HIM THE REST, AS FAR AS SHE KNEW IT. ONE MORNING IN August 1939, after they had finished their pastries and coffee and Meryem had read the cards, Heydrich suddenly decided that he would keep Meryem.

"Keep her?" Lori said. "What do you mean, 'keep her'?"

"It is a necessity," Heydrich replied. "I foresaw that this might occur, so I have arranged to have a special room prepared upstairs."

He himself marched Meryem upstairs and locked her in a room. It looked like an ordinary bedroom, with dresser, wardrobe, and narrow bed with a gray army blanket folded in regulation manner at the foot. A loaf of black bread, a jug of water, and a pack of cards had been placed on the table. But there was a judas hole in the door and bars on the window; geraniums grew in a flower box.

"She will be treated well, as a prisoner of the Reich," Heydrich said to Lori, as if Meryem, who stood impassively beside the bed, had been transformed into one of the trophy heads that gazed down upon them with lacquer eyes.

Once outside, he locked the door with a bar and padlock and pocketed the key. "She will be quite comfortable here," he said, inviting Lori to look through the judas hole. She drew back. "You won't look?" he said. "Well, tomorrow, perhaps. You can see her through the inspection window every day when you come. That is an irrevocable privilege. But you mustn't speak to her, and I really can't permit her to join us for coffee until further notice."

By now Lori understood the situation. A madman who had the power to do anything he liked was madly in love with her. She no longer treated him like a lunatic; it was too dangerous. She spoke calmly to him now as if imprisoning Meryem in a bedroom decorated with stuffed boar's heads and the antlers of stags was something that no ignorant woman could understand unless a man explained it.

"Why is this necessary?" she asked.

Heydrich smiled indulgently. "To save Meryem from something far, far worse," he said. "You must take it from me that every reading of the cards is filled with secrets of the Reich."

"Really? That part of it escapes me entirely."

"Of course it would, darling girl. You are perfectly innocent."

"But I want to understand. What secrets did she reveal this morning, for example?"

That morning in the cards Meryem had seen Heydrich sitting in the dark in an open car, between two stone walls that led to a half-timbered farmhouse with a thatched roof. It was early morning; the darkness around him was filled with soldiers. He was waiting for something to happen. He looked at his watch; it said 4:40. At that moment, just as dawn broke, swarms of airplanes appeared overhead, and all around Heydrich in the lifting darkness thousands of engines stuttered to life.

"She described something that I know is going to happen," Heydrich said. "More than that I cannot say, even to you. But the detail is so precise that anyone but me who heard it would believe she must be a spy, and a very dangerous one at that. Luckily I know better; I believe in her powers. But what if she blurted this out in the presence of an enemy of the Reich—one of those Jew Communists your husband brings home? The result would be disastrous. No, she must be protected. We will keep her here, in this place that has so many happy memories for all three of us."

Then, as usual, Heydrich drove Lori into Berlin, gazing worshipfully at her profile while the car rolled through the streets of the northern suburbs. When the driver opened the door to let her out at the end of Goethestrasse, Heydrich put his gloved hand over hers and detained her for a moment. "How much more enjoyable it was to be alone in the car—don't you agree?" he said. Lori was silent as usual. He kissed her hand. "Until tomorrow!"

This happened on a Monday. Apart from the fact that Meryem was locked in a room in the forest, nothing changed. In the days that followed Lori was "arrested" as usual every morning in the Tiergarten and driven to the hunting lodge. Heydrich insisted that she gaze through the judas hole at Meryem, who was always in the same position, seated at the table, facing the door, with the cards spread out on the polished tabletop. If she had not moved, and sometimes even spoken, Lori would have thought that she was

367

looking not at her living friend, but at some sort of mannikin Heydrich had placed in the room to deceive her.

Their mornings together went on as before, cakes and coffee, music and gallant compliments, except that Meryem was locked away upstairs so there were no readings of the cards. Then, on the Friday, Lori arrived to find Meryem downstairs again. She read the cards as before, this time predicting that Heydrich was going to be decorated by the Führer himself. "Describe the medal," he said. Meryem did so. "The Knight's Cross of the Iron Cross with Swords and Diamonds," Heydrich said, wagging an admonishing finger. "No! Really, you little nigger scamp, this time you've gone too far!" But it was obvious that he was very pleased. Lori played a Lehár medley on the piano, which had just been tuned, Heydrich said, by the best expert in Berlin and a party member since beer hall days.

"I have never heard the music sound more glorious," Heydrich told Lori. "And now I have a little surprise for you. Something has happened that makes it possible for Meryem to leave Germany, and I think she should do so at once, this weekend at the latest. But with the utmost discretion."

"If you advise it, it shall be done," Lori said. "But tell us your opinion. By what means should she travel?"

"Oh, no!" said Heydrich playfully. "None of your guessing games! I am not a travel agent. I myself am going sailing this weekend. You're such a wonderful sailor, I wish we were going out on the water together, but that cannot be. It may be the last chance any of us have to enjoy the Baltic in our innocent little pleasure boats. More than that I cannot say."

As soon as Heydrich let them out of the car, the two women collected Hubbard, interrupting him at his writing. The three of them took the first train to Rügen, and at midnight that night they sailed for the coast of Denmark in the Christophers' yawl *Mahican*. At dawn they put Meryem ashore on the Danish island of Falster.

On the beach, Meryem embraced Lori convulsively. They had swum ashore through the frigid water, and both were shivering.

"Don't go back," Meryem said in a shaking voice.

"I must," Lori replied.

"For God's sake, why?"

"I feel it. Very strongly. But if you tell me that I'm wrong, that there's no reason to go back, I'll believe you."

They looked at each other for the last time, gray eyes and green. Meryem, knowing that her friend saw the same future for herself as she did, said nothing more. Suddenly Lori began to cry, wildly. She pushed Meryem away, a violent shove into which she put all the strength of her body, then plunged into the water and swam back to the *Mahican*. The tide was running out, so she covered the distance between the shore and the boat very quickly.

Nine days later, at 4:40 in the morning as Meryem had foretold, the mechanized German army started its motors and invaded Poland under a canopy of hundreds of warplanes.

"What was it that you knew?" Christopher asked Lla Kahina. "What was going to happen that made it impossible for my mother to stay in Denmark?"

"It would be wrong to tell you that," Lla Kahina said. "Maybe what I saw in the cards never happened. I wasn't there, so I don't know."

"I was."

"I know you were."

"Let me judge the right and wrong."

She held up a wrinkled palm. "No," she said. "I can't. Go to England. Talk to Dickie Shaw-Condon. He was there, too."

9

AT ROSSENARRA HALL, THE DRAUGHTY SEVENTEENTH-CENTURY HOUSE in the extreme north of England that was the seat of his family, Sir Richard Shaw-Condon, ninth baronet, explained the etymology and history of his title to Paul Christopher.

" 'Baronet' seems originally to have meant 'young' or 'little baron,' and for a long time it was used in England as a title by the sons of barons," he said, punctuating his sentences with a phlegmy barking laugh. "Then, in 1611, King James, bless his Scotch soul, needed money to send Protestants to settle in Ulster and keep the papists down, so he created the baronets of England; people *bought* the dignity, you see. Not that it was much of a bargain, ha-ha. One gets to walk ahead of all the knights except Knights of the Garter on ceremonial occasions. Baronets are commoners, you know. Rank without privilege, that was the royal idea."

Although a drizzle was falling, the two men were seated outdoors in a gazebo because it was warmer in the open air than in the dank interior of the house. Indoors, Sir Richard had worn a long woolen scarf from his public school, Worksop College, in addition to several layers of sweaters, a greenish tweed jacket thick enough to stand up in the corner by itself, and a French fisherman's cap. "Do come, always happy to see you," he had shouted into the telephone when Christopher called from London. "Can't ask you to stay, though. My American guests always go away with chilblains." In fact Sir Richard never invited foreigners, especially not Americans, to stay at Rossenarra Hall. He had had enough of them during his long career in the secret service. Like the rabbits and cats and tortoises in *Alice in Wonderland* dressed up in English clothes and speaking a demented sort of English, people from abroad were dotty impostors. This perception had given him certain advantages in his dealings with British agents of other, expendable nationalities.

Now, unwinding his Worksop scarf and doffing his jacket under the roof of the gazebo, Sir Richard said, "Always used to keep a flat in London in the winter when I was gainfully employed. Can't manage it now." As a much younger man he had had flaxen eyebrows that flowed like mustaches and a pink, disdainful face; in those bygone days he had looked fashionably steamed in an upper-class way, as if he had just stepped out of a hot tub. The eyebrows were gray-white now, and so was the petulant face. There were few hot baths at Rossenarra Hall; the water had to be heated in the kitchen and carried upstairs in buckets, and even if Sir Richard had been able to afford the wages, few in Britain would do such work nowadays. He produced a hunting flask and offered it to Christopher.

"Brandy? It's Spanish, I'm afraid."

"No thank you."

"I will, if you don't mind," Sir Richard said, tipping the flask. "They say it's good for the heart. I've heard it said that Winston drank a pint of this stuff every day, besides buckets of champagne, when he was running the war. He had the heart of a lion. Do you think there was any connection?"

"I don't know. What kept you going?"

"During the late war? Not brandy; you never saw spirits unless you happened to be prime minister. Dreams of glory kept me going, I suppose; I was younger in those days. It was all such a long time ago. One hardly remembers. Sorry I can't offer you luncheon here. But they do a rather good mixed grill at the pub in the village, if you're up to the local cookery."

"I don't think I am, honestly."

"Oh." Sir Richard's tone was resentful. He had hoped for lunch in the village; he lived without servants or wife and ate very little cooked food.

"The last time we met, as I remember," he said, "I gave you luncheon at my club. We shared a bottle of the '71 Riesling. It's all drunk up now. You were just out of the jug and were looking for the bastard that got you put inside."

"That's right. You were very helpful to me."

"I hope you haven't told anyone that. It was the hell of a scandal you stirred up afterwards over that man Darby."

"That was long before."

"Was it? Well, one bad 'un is much like another. I suppose you're on the trail of some new mystery. What do you want this time?"

"Something a bit more personal. I've recently learned that you knew my mother in Berlin before the war."

"Did you indeed? May one ask from what source?"

"From two separate and usually reliable sources, actually—the O. G. and Meryem."

"Oh, dear," Sir Richard said.

10

IT DID NOT TAKE UP VERY MUCH OF SIR RICHARD'S MORNING TO report the essentials of Lori Christopher's fate. Nettled as he was by missing out on lunch, he came straight to the point.

"There's not much to tell," he said. "In the summer of 1939 I was sent to Germany under deep cover to meet Nazis and recruit as many of them as possible. Awful job. They were true believers as well as being frightened out of their wits by the Party police, worse than the Russians in your day because the Nazis really *were* believers, so I got nowhere for weeks. Finally I was reduced to trolling in the nightclubs, and one night I ran into this disgusting Hun in a low dive called Kaminskys Telephonbar. It was just the sort of place the Brownshirts liked. Every table had a telephone, you see, and if one of the tarts, *Knabe oder Mädel*—they had both sexes—took your fancy you could ring up him or her and arrange the price. Blind drunk this Hun of mine was, ringing up the girls and suggesting the most appalling acts to them, all the while pawing the ones sitting at the bar. He kept on buying me drinks and talking to me between fondlings about Heine; fortunately I'd read German at Oxford so I had the old Jew-baiter by heart. I quoted *Die Lorelei* and *Romanzero* by the yard, making a tremendous hit."

Christopher interrupted. "But Heine was a Jew."

"A Catholic Jew who despised Jews," Sir Richard said. "My Hun adored that. It tickled him so that I began to wonder if he didn't have a Jewish grandmother himself. Anyway, he seemed to have a lot of money and the barmen and the tarts were sucking up to him; I thought the money was why.

"Well, to make a long story short, just as the dawn was breaking he left off kneading one of the tarts, and with lipstick all over his face, turned to me and said, 'I suppose you think I'm enjoying this.' He made this woeful Hun Pagliacci face, so of course I said, 'Certainly not. One can see at once that you're not enjoying it at all, old boy. Obviously you're used to the company of a much finer type of woman.' 'How right you are,' the Hun said. 'Come along and I'll show you.' All this was a bit off-putting, as you might imagine, but against my better judgment I went along with him, up the steps of Kaminskys Telephonbar, out into the open air and into this great black Hun motor car awaiting him with purring motor at the curb. It came equipped with a couple of obvious Gestapo thugs—leather coats, gangster hats, stupid eyes, the whole kit. What's this? I thought, and then I took a closer look at the Hun himself and realized who he was—none other than Reinhard Heydrich, head of the Nazi secret police, first deputy to Himmler, homicidal maniac, the lot, exactly the sort of target I was instructed to attack. It was like winning the sweeps. I've often used this episode to illustrate to younger men the importance of seizing the main chance. Serendipity—wonderful Yank word, that—is all. One never knows who anyone is going to turn out to be, don't you agree?"

"Completely," Christopher said.

"I knew you would, old boy; so do we all who know the feel of pavement beneath our feet, ha-ha. Not many of us old parties left in the great game."

"You're right. Please go on."

"Yes, of course, mustn't lose the thread. Well, inside his staff car, Heydrich chatted away as if we'd been at the dear old SS Academy together. It seems he'd found the ideal German woman and fallen madly in love with her. She was beautiful, the blood of Prussian nobility flowed in her veins, she rode like a Valkyrie and played the piano like Clara Schumann used to do. Unfortunately she was married and she was as virtuous as a vestal virgin. Not only that, she loved her husband. None of this discouraged Heydrich. 'I could take her by force, or have her husband killed, of course,' he said . . . those were his exact words, I've never forgotten them . . . 'but *she* must make the choice. She must sooner or later realize that my love cannot be denied and come to me of her own free will.' Calm as you please, old Reinhard was. He was quite mad, you see, born that way probably, and as your father wrote about him, he saw things with the joyful clarity of the incurably insane. In the meantime, he said, he was having this woman arrested by his men two or three times a week and brought to his hunting lodge.

" 'My aim is to relieve her of the burden of her scruples by taking the matter right out of her hands,' he said. 'She can hardly blame herself for anything if she's under arrest. Not that she has any reason to do so up to now. I assure you our friendship is perfectly innocent, she always brings along this Gypsy girlfriend of hers as a chaperone and to divert suspicion I pretend to flirt with the friend and have her tell my fortune. Actually the woman disgusts me; she's as dark as a nigger and I think she may even be a Jew. She's hinted as much to me. We have coffee together, discuss music and poetry and painting, all the finer things; sometimes I persuade my love to play something restful for me on the piano, and then we go our separate ways—I to my work, she back to her dreary world. These moments are the bright spots of my life. Of hers, too, but of course she's not yet ready to admit that to me.' "

Sir Richard had a reputation among his own kind as a storyteller; he had lived as a bachelor in a society that placed considerable value on the extra man's ability to keep a dinner party interested. He surpassed himself in his description of how he sat with Heydrich in the backseat of his Mercedes and watched through the bullet-proof window while the Gestapo thugs arrested Lori and Meryem and loaded them into another car. The women were on horseback and Heydrich instructed his men to let them finish their ride, so that he could watch them canter by for his pleasure, black hair and blond hair flying like the pennons (as Heydrich put it) of Aryan and barbarian womanhood.

"I need hardly tell you," Sir Richard said, "that the blonde was your mother. Puppy love was written all over Heydrich's face. I mean to say, if he hadn't been who he was it would have been quite pathetic. As it was, I knew that I had him, one way or another, if only I could stay in touch with him and get in touch with his lady love."

It did not take him long to accomplish the latter. One of the first people Sir Richard met after his arrival in Berlin was Otto Rothchild.

"Amazing chap, Otto, the perfect slippery exile, knew absolutely everybody in Berlin, that was his stock in trade," Sir Richard said. "That included your parents, of course. For a fee of only two hundred American dollars he introduced me to your mother. For obvious reasons I didn't want to meet your father just yet, so we called at that flat in Charlottenburg with all those marvelous pictures one morning whilst he was writing. Of course I was taking the hell of a chance going there because Heydrich had the place wired and watched round the clock, but there was no means of seeing your mother without being seen by Heydrich's men in any case, so it had to be done. I went straight to the point, knowing quite well that I might never have another chance. Before coming I had typed out a note; I can still quote it by heart: 'I AM AN AGENT OF BRITISH INTELLIGENCE. IF YOU WILL HELP ME TO KILL REINHARD HEYDRICH PLEASE SAY THE WORDS "GOD SAVE THE KING". HIS DEMISE WOULD BE A BLESSING TO YOUR COUNTRY AS WELL AS MY OWN. MY COMPANION KNOWS NOTHING OF THIS AND NEITHER MUST ANYONE ELSE. YOU UNDERSTAND THAT I HAVE PUT MY LIFE IN YOUR HANDS ALONG WITH THIS LETTER. IF YOUR ANSWER IS YES YOU WILL FIND FURTHER LETTERS HIDDEN IN YOUR SADDLE IN TIERGARTEN STABLES.' Your mother was a natural agent. She sent Otto into the kitchen to fetch a glass of water, read the note, handed it back to me, and said, cool as you please, 'God save the King.' By the time Otto came back, the deal was done and old Reinhard was a dead man."

"What deal, precisely?" Christopher asked.

"Well, as I just said, the assassination of Heydrich."

"What was the point of killing him?"

"The *point*? The point was that your mother made it possible. Obviously this lunatic couldn't be recruited. What could we offer him? He thought Germany was going to win the coming war and he was going to be the second Führer after Hitler retired full of honors and much beloved. So did a lot of other people. The only thing to do with him, if we were going to do anything at all, was to kill him and hope for happy results. The trouble was, the war came much sooner than anyone expected. I handed Mrs. Christopher my *billet-doux* on August tenth. On August twenty-third the Hitler-Stalin Pact was signed. On September first Germany invaded Poland. There was no time to lay on the operation.''

"So you abandoned it?"

"Delayed it. It goes without saying that your mother was the key to success. She wanted to get your father and herself out of Germany, having already got you out, and of course she had her opportunities. Heydrich in his loony way encouraged her to sail off to Denmark, smuggling Jews and other enemies of the Reich in that famous sailboat your parents kept in Rügen. Each time she returned he regarded it as a sign of her love for him. He would get quite emotional about it. I'm truly sorry to tell you these sick-making things in such plain language. After all, this woman was your mother, and one can imagine how you feel even after all these years, but these were the facts. Of course he kept a jolly close eye on the *Last of the Mohicans* . . . have I got the name right?"

"It was just *Mahican,* spelled with an 'a'."

"Really? Well, I was rather close. Odd how one remembers every detail of the long ago at my age and forgets to button one's trousers," Sir Richard said with a smile. "Anyway, Heydrich took the precaution of shadowing the *Mahican* with a Gestapo E-boat out of Rügen, and I suppose the crew would have intervened in certain circumstances. You may recall that you were always stopped and searched *after* you came back into harbor; that was Heydrich's way of saying cheerio. In any case, your mother and father got Meryem out, and I was quite sure that they'd try to do a bolt, too. But Heydrich was much more sure that they wouldn't. Very serene about it, he was."

"He talked to you often about my mother?"

"My dear fellow, he talked to me about nothing else. We kept on meeting in the fleshpots. Heydrich would have two or three or four tarts a night; I've never known a man with such an enormous appetite for female companionship. He never touched Lori, of course. In his mind she was far above all that; you can be quite at peace on that point. In any case, he wasn't a bit worried about her

375

coming back from the sail with Meryem. He'd set the whole thing up as a test of her fidelity. The details were appalling."

"In what way?"

"In what way?"

"I'd really rather not go into it. It's enough to say he locked Meryem up in a room as a means of tightening his hold on your mother. He was crude, you see. That was why he was so effective. One simply can't deal with the unthinkable unless one is as mad as Heydrich was. But he knew he held all the aces."

"Which were what?"

Sir Richard coughed, a sign, Christopher thought, of mild embarrassment, or of the wish to feign it. He pressed him to continue.

"Well, of course he was head of the entire German police apparatus," Sir Richard said. "So he knew all sorts of things. Things that might influence your mother."

"What, specifically?"

"Specifically?" Sir Richard said. "I'm awfully sorry to tell you this, my dear fellow, but since you ask, Heydrich knew, on the morning that he let Meryem go, that you yourself had landed in Hamburg on that very day and taken the train for Rügen. Your parents had sent you off to America with the O. G.—or the Y. G. as he then was, ha-ha—but I gather you turned right around and came back on the next ship. Isn't that so?"

"Yes," Christopher said. "It's so."

Two days after the O. G. delivered him to Elliott Hubbard on the pier in Manhattan, Christopher had used a letter of authorization given to him by his father to draw money from his parents' account at D. & D. Laux & Co. Then he had bought a third-class ticket on the *Bremen* and sailed back to Germany. His mother and father were in danger; he wanted to be with them.

"When your parents got back from smuggling Meryem out of the country," Sir Richard said, "there you were, waiting for them. That changed everything, of course, because it gave Heydrich a rather valuable hostage, your parents' only son, the last of the line on both sides of the family; Heydrich researched matters of that kind. He still managed the odd charade, of course, just to touch up the parental anxiety—I believe you went along on the last voyage of the *Mahican* when Otto Rothchild was the only passenger. The E-boat tagged along on that one, too. Heydrich was taking no chances. All the same, he was pleased as punch when your mother turned up back in Rügen. By then it was all over. Whatever arrangements she made for you and your father, your mother had to remain in Germany. Heydrich had won. She knew that quite well. She got you out on the last possible day, of course."

"Stop," Christopher said. "Are you telling me that her arrest at the frontier was pre-arranged, that Heydrich let my father and me go in order to keep her? That she *agreed* to that?"

Sir Richard sighed. "I'm afraid so. But in the end, remember, we *did* kill the bastard after he became the führer of Czechoslovakia. He took your mother with him to his kingdom in the east, of course, and it was she who made it all possible because she knew what his every move was going to be. She died at the hands of the Gestapo, of course, like all the others who played a part in the operation. I won't burden you with the details. Of course we hadn't a hope of getting her out, but she knew that from the start. She was a very, very gallant lady, and I'm glad you know the full particulars at last."

He looked into Christopher's ravaged face, then reached out a hand in genuine sympathy. After all, even though Christopher and his people were not English and could never be English no matter how hard they tried, he had known the family for fifty years.

"My dear boy," he said. "My dear, dear boy."

11

CHRISTOPHER TREATED SIR RICHARD SHAW-CONDON TO LUNCH AT the local pub after all. To the Englishman's relief his visitor had quickly regained control of himself—outwardly, at least. He did not touch the food that the waitress, an unkempt trollop who scratched her itching scalp with a ballpoint pen, dropped onto the table before him. While Sir Richard ate his gummy smoked salmon followed by a leathery mixed grill and drank the better part of a bottle of Romanian merlot, they discussed the twentieth-century novel, remembering the names of characters and plot details for each other. Christopher was not saying much, so Sir Richard did most of the talking. He had always been a great reader, he said, passing the time with novels purchased from operational funds while waiting in hotel rooms or train compartments or on windswept park benches for agents to turn up. Spending his service's money on books had never troubled his conscience. They were very useful as recognition signals: "I shall be reading a novel called *Nile Shadows;* if the coast is clear I shall close the book and put it into my pocket of my mackintosh. Follow me into the lavatory." Lately he had been reading these works all over again, revisiting the scenes of his youth, as it were, because he had known most of the originals of the characters. The English novelists of his generation had in many cases spent the whole of their adult lives writing about the adolescents they had met at Oxford. "I seldom bother with books written by Cantabrigians," he said. "They're always by and about boring Communists who call themselves Catholics or vice-versa. Not that it matters any longer. I mean to say, it's all over."

"What's all over?" Christopher asked.

"The age of political delusion. Communism, Socialism, Fascism, Gandhism, Nkrumahism, the lot."

"You think the gods are dying?"

"They're in their boxes, my dear fellow. Except for the eternal Tories, of course. *In their boxes.* Seems odd to have one's own century almost over with and all passions spent and near-forgotten, doesn't it?"

"A relief," Christopher said, very softly, even for him.

Sir Richard looked up warily, wondering if this American, if that's what he was, was actually going to reopen the subject of his mother in the midst of the gang of provincial solicitors and bank clerks who were crowded into what used to be the saloon bar, eating their midday sausages. Well, he was welcome, if that's what he wanted. Sir Richard fixed Christopher with a bulldog look. He made no apologies for having sent Lori Christopher to her death half a century before; unless he was actually telling the story, he could barely sort out her demise from all the other heroic sacrifices he had made possible during his long career as a handler of agents. But Christopher uttered no reproaches. If he knew anything, he knew that secret agents, like all other members of the human race, did what they wanted in their hearts to do; they were only coerced into destroying themselves in the kind of novels that Sir Richard refused to buy, even with other people's money.

"What time is your train?" Sir Richard asked.

"One forty-five."

"Then you'd better be hopping."

Christopher paid the bill, and as he waited for his change, Sir

Richard slid a book across the tabletop. It was a copy of the British first edition of *The Rose and the Lotus.*

"I bought this long before I knew either of your parents," he said. "Saw it in Hatchard's as I was stocking up on reading matter for Germany. On first reading I thought for a few pages that the author must be an Englishman. He certanly wrote like one. But then I realized that he couldn't be because I didn't recognize anybody in the book. Wanted to meet them all the same."

He was an admirer of Hubbard's work. On his last meeting with Christopher, when the '71 Riesling was poured, he had quoted a line of Hubbard's poetry comparing the taste of hock to hyacinths and honey. Now, with a rueful glance at the empty bottle of Iron Curtain claret before him, he quoted it again. "I'm sure you read all your father's books as a younger man," he said. "But if you haven't read this one for some time, then you ought to try it again in the light of the new knowledge that's just come your way. Another thing you might like to know. Your father and I used it for a book code when he went into Germany for us in '40."

"Did you tell him about your connection to his wife?"

Sir Richard looked shocked. "Good heavens! No. Nor would you have done. What if the Gestapo had got him?"

On the long train ride from Northumberland to London, Christopher read the book, with its description of the Experiment and its portraits of Lori and Meryem that were more vivid than Zaentz's painting. It was the first time he had looked into its pages for many, many years, and by the time he reached his destination, he had decided what he was going to do.

379

BEAUTIFUL DREAMERS

"I UNDERSTAND YOU AND YEHO HAD A TALK IN THE DESERT," SAID Patchen to Christopher.

"Yes," Christopher said.

"I'm sorry I couldn't tell you all that myself, but you left town before I had the chance."

"That's all right. The story had a certain added force, coming from him."

Patchen coughed, as if covering some other sign of emotion. "I'll bet it did," he said, "but that wasn't the reason the messenger was chosen. It's nice of you to help us out, all things considered."

"There were other considerations. Yeho explained the situation very clearly."

They walked on through the autumn night with the Doberman scouting ahead along the murky tow path. In spite of the kidnapping of the third Beautiful Dreamer in Washington itself, the dog remained Patchen's only visible protection from his enemies. A bolt of lightning rent the black sky far to the west, over the Appalachians.

"Rain in the suburbs late tonight, high pollen count tomorrow," Patchen said. "Have you ever noticed how much people in this town talk about the weather?"

In Christopher's experience they spoke of little else. He said, "I've noticed. Do you have a theory about that?"

"Funny you should ask. Yes, I do. It even has a metaphorical dimension. Shall I go on?"

Patchen was in a caustic mood.

"Go on," Christopher said.

"It has to do with the fundamental nature of the place," Patchen

380

said. "You remember Sebastian's eightieth birthday party up in New York—all those friends of his, stock market wheeler dealers, big-time lawyers, publishers, Hollywood producers, that man who owned a baseball team, captains of industry, doctors who were curing diseases by replacing people's genes?"

"I remember. The baseball man told the O. G. he always wanted to be a spy."

"What did the O. G. say?"

"His eyes lit up. *Baseball!* He said, 'It's never too late. Let us know if you want to start up a team in some interesting place and need a silent partner.' The fellow thought he was kidding. Go on with your theory."

"Well, looking around the table at all those New York faces," Patchen said, "I realized that I was surrounded by people who lived by their wits, whose whole purpose in life was to make things happen. Whereas in Washington the entire purpose of being, the real function of government, is to *prevent* things from happening—war being the supreme example."

Christopher chuckled. "The moral being that the weather is interesting because it can't be prevented?"

"No, that's the metaphor," Patchen said. "The moral is more interesting. The Outfit's purpose is to make things happen in an organism in which nothing is permitted to happen. That's why it's always being attacked by white corpuscles like Patrick Graham and White House assistants."

"It's a virus?" Christopher said.

"Worse, a conscience. 'Out of darkness, truth.' Well, let there be darkness."

The thought seemed to cheer him tremendously; he had not spent a lifetime at the O. G.'s elbow without learning to love a joke on the opposition.

Christopher put a comradely hand on his friend's paralyzed shoulder and felt him chuckling within himself. Even the Doberman, cocking its head and uttering a questioning whimper, seemed to detect the change in his master's mood. Patchen thought the animal was merely bothered by the distant electrical storm.

"See?" he said. "In Weimar, even the dogs talk about the weather."

V

OLD BOYS

ONE

1

TWO DAYS AFTER HIS DINNER AT THE PATCHENS', PATRICK GRAHAM received another mysterious communication. A man with a Middle East accent called him on his unlisted number at home and identified himself as a member of the group that had kidnapped Harvey Walpole and sent Graham the tape of his interrogation.

"What may I call you?" Graham said, with flawless underground etiquette. "What is the name of your commando?"

The caller answered the second question.

"I've never heard of any freedom fighters operating under that name."

"There are many things you have never heard about, Mister Graham."

"What, for example?"

"Be patient. Walpole is not the only one. Perhaps you will be told who the others were. Perhaps you will be sent other tapes."

"Some say that Walpole doesn't exist."

"Doesn't exist? You believe this?"

"I can't discount it. What proof do you have that this man is who you say he is?"

"You will have proof," the voice said, before disconnecting.

Graham was breaking in a new secretary, a young woman who had just graduated with honors from Dartmouth (he hired Ivy Leaguers and graduates of the Five Sisters only), where she had been a marathon runner. She ran to work every morning in the dark because she had to report to Graham's house on O Street at five o'clock in order to tape the satellite network news feeds that he watched while he did his exercises, an hour later.

As she crossed the P Street bridge on the morning following the phone call, another runner, also a woman, overtook her in the half-darkness and thrust a plastic Safeway shopping bag into her arms. The lower half of this woman's face was concealed by a surgical mask, but the secretary had an impression of intense Oriental eyes and black hair. "For Mister Graham," said the masked woman. "Very important." Then she accelerated, turned left into the ramp leading to Rock Creek Parkway, and got into a car that sped away in the direction of the Kennedy Center.

"Did you see her face? Did you get the license number of the car?" Graham asked.

"No. I told you, she had this mask on. She may have been Japanese."

"Japanese? Why do you say that?"

"The surgical mask. They wear them when they have a cold."

"Did she have a cold?"

"I don't know. She was short like a Japanese."

"Did she have Japanese legs?"

"Japanese *legs*?"

"Short, thick, bowed—Japanese legs. Did you look at her legs?"

"No."

"I'm not surprised. What was her accent like? Was it a Japanese accent?"

"I didn't notice. She only spoke five words. She just spoke English."

"Goddamnit, Dorcas! What *did* you notice?"

"Only what I said. I was startled. I mean, she just ran up to me and slammed this thing up against my chest. And I don't wear my glasses when I run."

"Then get some contacts. And don't give me any more excuses. You're paid to keep your eyes open. Remember that."

He was shouting at the top of his powerful voice. The girl was stricken to the heart by his displeasure. She was blushing. Her voice trembled. Tears spilled from her sleepy eyes. Graham observed these symptoms with satisfaction; he was merely testing her to see how she responded to negative reinforcement. All the signs were excellent: Criticism frightened her, gave her a feeling of failure. She was consumed by guilt; she belonged to a class to whom failure was the worst of the sins.

He was pleased by what she had brought him, too. Inside the supermarket bag he found a large brown envelope, and inside the envelope was a glossy photograph of Walpole, an ordinary-looking, unsuspecting suburbanite walking away from a car on which the Virginia license plate was clearly visible. His expression was less euphoric than on the tape, but it could not be anyone else. Pasted to the back of the picture was a brief message in dot-matrix characters generated by a cheap computer printer: "CHECK OUT THE LICENSE NUMBER. GO TO THE OWNER'S ADDRESS. ASK THE NEIGHBORS IF THEY KNOW THIS MAN."

The neighbors did know him, as Garth T. Robertson, the name under which the car was registered. He worked, as an accountant, perhaps (no one was sure), for one of those acronymic Beltway Corporations—TEBAK? BATEK? He and his family had recently been transferred overseas. No, they didn't know where they had gone, exactly. The Robertsons hadn't been very outgoing people.

The fact that Walpole had lived under a different name, and had suddenly vanished, was all the proof Graham needed that Walpole, or Robertson, was an employee of the Outfit. He decided to broadcast the tape.

The man with the Middle East accent called again that evening. "Have you identified Mister Garth T. Robertson?" he asked.

"We found the house he used to live in. Where is he now?"

"Patience, Mister Graham. We will be watching your show."

2

IN LATE TWENTIETH-CENTURY WASHINGTON, DAVID PATCHEN SAID blandly to Patrick Graham, a certain politicized segment of the news media exercised many of the functions belonging to the secret police in totalitarian countries. They maintained hidden networks of informers, carried out clandestine investigations, conducted interrogations on the basis of accusations made by anonymous witnesses and agents provocateurs, and staged dramatic show trials in which the guilt of the accused was assumed and no effective defense was allowed. They had far greater powers of investigation than the government. The authority of the state to persecute the individual was defined and limited by the Constitution, whereas the media were restrained by nothing more than the rules of theater. Because their targets were usually thought by the best people to deserve the punishment they might otherwise have eluded, the media had no need to worry about the quality of its evidence; journalists were not concerned with truth in any case, only with "accuracy." That consisted of verifying the existence of their sources and confirming that they had actually spoken the words quoted, or something close to those words; nothing beyond that was required. If one person denounced another, even if anonymously, that was reason enough to publish the charge. There was no requirement to question the evidence or the accuser's motives, or even to identify the accuser; in fact the accuser usually spoke on the understanding that his anonymity would be preserved under all circumstances. Verdicts of "innocent" based on these rules of evidence were almost unknown. The sentence was degradation, shame, exile, and, usually, a lifetime of impoverishment resulting from the attempt to pay lawyers' fees incurred in the vain hope of self-defense. Conviction in the media was sometimes followed by conviction in the courts, but the punishment handed down by judges, a mere prison sentence or fine or condemnation to a stated number of hours of good works among the underclass, was regarded as the lesser penalty.

Hearing these outrageous statements, Patrick Graham stared dumbfounded at Patchen—or rather, stared into the pitch darkness through which they were walking. He could not actually see Patchen, only his silhouette and the dull reflection of the neon corona of the city in his eyeglasses. After trying all day to get Patchen on the telephone, he had accosted him as he and his Doberman began their regular nighttime walk along the tow path of the C & O Canal. Graham had hoped to conclude their business on the spot in a matter of minutes, but Patchen had plunged off into the shadows. Graham had no choice but to follow. The threatening surroundings, thickets on one side, deep stagnant water on the other, made him nervous. He felt vulnerable, exposed, hunted by stronger beasts; he was usually accompanied by a bodyguard when he went out at night but he had left the man behind tonight so as not to arouse Patchen's anxieties.

He didn't seem to have any. He seemed to have no protection besides the dog. This astonished Graham, but Patchen gave him no chance to raise this or any other subject. He immediately launched into this crackpot diatribe about investigative journalism. Crackpot or no, Graham was deeply offended. Who was this blackshirt to criticize the press? (Graham still called the media "the press," though he himself had never worked a day in print journalism after resigning from the staff of the *Yale Daily News* in protest over the undergraduate paper's refusal to print a story he had written about the death of Che Guevara in which Graham remarked that the martyr's waxen corpse, photographed in a morgue in Bolivia, had "assumed the authentic expression of Christ." The managing editor, later a fighter-bomber pilot in Vietnam, had called this phrase, and Graham's whole report, which had been inspired by Radio Havana's obituary notice of the fallen Fidelista, "counterculture gibberish.")

In the years since then Graham had learned not to let his anger show in the presence of ideological enemies. Instead, he put a question to Patchen that he had always found to be an effective weapon against McCarthyites. "Do you," he asked with a knowing smile, "think that the entire press is involved in this conspiracy?"

"No, I don't think there's a conspiracy," Patchen replied. "It's worse than that. I think that you and your fellow true believers are in the grip of a collective dementia that makes it impossible for you to perceive reality."

"I see. But whatever is going on involves every reporter and editor in town."

"I didn't say that and what's more I don't believe it. Most reporters are perfectly sane and highly competent. If life were baseball, I'd gladly swap every agent the Outfit now has in the field for the editorial staff of the *Washington Post* and throw in a hundred future draft choices from Yale and Princeton. No, I'm talking about the few ideologues to whom the many owe so much."

"Including me."

"Yes, of course. You're the star. Everybody in town is terrified of you, Patrick."

They were entirely alone now, strolling farther and farther into the darkness—if they really *were* alone; Graham could not bring himself to believe that the woods along the canal were not, in fact, full of heavily armed Outfit men, dressed in black and drifting from tree to tree.

"I don't know whether it's occurred to you," Patchen continued cheerfully, "but there's a paradox in all this."

"In all what?"

"In the media giving birth to this Cheka."

" 'Cheka'? *Cheka?* That's insulting."

"Then what is the word? Thought Police? Night Riders?"

"Try 'defenders of the First Amendment.' "

"Ah," Patchen said, "that has a ring to it, and English words have been distorted to mean stranger things than that. The point is that even in a democracy like ours, it is the government, not the press, that controls information, for the obvious reason that the government manufactures it. All you people do is call at the back door and cart it away and sell it. And because your information comes from anonymous sources inside the government that you protect with your lives, your fortunes, and your sacred honor, it's possible you're not quite the swashbucklers you think you are."

"Swashbucklers? What a weird vocabulary you have. Nobody I know in this business thinks that way."

"Okay, but think about something. But what if the government, or certain elements within the government, are using the media as a supernumerary ideological police force? What if you're just assets in somebody else's covert action operations?"

" 'Assets'? 'Covert action'?" Graham's voice broke; Patchen might as well have flung human feces into his face as these hated words describing abominable practices. "That's a lot of Outfit bullshit," he snapped. "We do what we have to do."

"Of course you do. And let me tell you something: Finding somebody who wants to do a thing, and then making it possible for him to do it in what he believes to be his own interest, is the definition of covert action."

Dark as it was, Graham could see, or feel, that the other man was smiling at his own sarcasm. Graham was being goaded, ridiculed. He knew this, but he could not control the waves of anger that rose from his entrails. It had been years since he had been forced to listen to someone he disagreed with; since his first semester at New Haven, when he discovered his true beliefs with the assistance of a sympathetic professor and his circle of like-minded friends, he had selected his company so as to isolate himself from heresy. Even when traveling he took the necessary precautions, moving from one pious counterculture household to another, as an incorruptible Dominican might have traveled during the Thirty Years War from monastery to monastery of his own order, avoiding any possibility of meeting the Devil by shunning not only Protestants but Franciscans and Jesuits, too.

Without warning, Patchen stopped in his tracks. "Let's go back the other way," he said. As the two men turned around, the Doberman watched Graham's every move, keeping himself between Graham and his master. The dog was so well trained that it seemed less an animal than a machine—or was the air of menace that it radiated related to the fact that it was Patchen's dog? In spite of himself, in spite of his loathing for the work Patchen did, Graham was in awe of the other man's power, or what he imagined to be his power. Presidential assistants seemed larger and fiercer in the White House than otherwise; they shrank back into their former, uninteresting selves when their man left office and the mystique hissed out of them like gas from a toy balloon. Why wouldn't Dobermans who guarded people like Patchen seem bigger to a common man like Graham than they really were? Graham made a mental note of this thought; it was something he could use while broadcasting, disguised as an idea that had popped into his mind the instant before it was spoken.

Patchen continued to talk in his maddeningly reasonable tone of voice. It was his habit at bedtime, he told Graham, to read authors who were no longer read by the intelligentsia. This enabled him to escape, for a few minutes at least, from the orthodox opinions of his own time. Graham had always heard that this man was blessed with a photographic memory, and now Patchen confirmed this by quoting examples from history to show that the ordeals by slander so common in their own time and place were nothing new.

"Do you ever read Macaulay?" Patchen asked.

"Not since Yale," Graham replied. "He's a bad habit." In fact he had never read Lord Macaulay at all; the sympathetic professor, who had told him what not to read, had equipped him with an opinion of the essayist.

"I was reading his essay 'England in 1685' just the other night," Patchen said, unperturbed. "Macaulay has some interesting things to say on the connection between entertainment and political revenge. One passage in particular struck me as very apt. In fact it's what got me started thinking along the lines we've been discussing. I think I can quote it more or less verbatim: 'The spirit by which Dryden and several of his compeers were at this time animated against the Whigs deserves to be called fiendish. The servile judges and sheriffs of those days could not shed blood so fast as poets cried out for it. Calls for more victims, hideous jests on hanging, bitter taunts . . . were publicly recited on the stage, and, that nothing might be wanting to the guilt and the shame, were recited by women, who, having long been taught to discard all modesty, were now taught to discard all compassion.' "

Graham said, "You don't seem to have a very high opinion of women."

"I don't?" Patchen said. "What makes you think that?"

"Those were hardly feminist sentiments you just quoted so approvingly."

"No? Then you should read Macaulay. He was talking about the bawdiness of the Restoration period and how men exploited women by corrupting their virtue for what they called political truth but was in fact simple lust. Licentiousness of speech and deed was a reaction to Puritan repression under Cromwell, something like the sexual revolution of your own generation after Eisenhower. The same things happened to the girls. How did you put it in the Movement—'Chicks up front'? 'The correct position of women in the Movement is prone'? Of course, Macaulay was a Whig propagandist. And I'm not for a moment comparing the Patrick Grahams of this world to Dryden and his compeers. But you see the point."

"No," Graham said. "I *don't* see the point. You *have* no point. But I don't have time to argue with you. I came here to tell you something important."

"Oh, my," Patchen said. "And here I am babbling on about Macaulay. I'll shut up now."

Up ahead, the humming sodium lamp under which they had met half an hour before cast a pool of welcoming light. Graham picked up the pace so as to reach it as quickly as possible, and this change in behavior made the Doberman nervous again. Bleached by the incandescent glare, the dog's eyes seemed even more robotic than before. Graham had never in his life been in any real danger, and he knew that he was in none now, unless a gang of muggers burst out of the undergrowth. But it was chilling to realize that this animal could and would kill him. All that was required was for Patchen to give the command and he would tear out Graham's throat. Graham was in no doubt that Patchen had given similar commands to scarcely more human assassins many times in his life.

"Will you listen to me?" he said.

"Certainly," Patchen replied.

"Two things. First, I'm going on the air with the tape tomorrow night."

"You are?"

"I'm going to tell the audience everything I know. Everything. Including everything you told me at your house the other night. If that upsets you, I'm sorry. But you knew who I was when you talked to me, and you know the rules that apply in this town."

"I'm glad I made myself understood. But why are you telling me all this?"

"In case there's anything else you want to tell me. If it's meaningful I'll work it in. You have my word on that."

"It has to be meaningful? Thanks. But no thanks. What made you decide to go ahead?"

"That's the second thing. We found out who sent us the tape. It's a small underground group of freedom fighters called the Eye of Gaza."

" 'Freedom fighters'? Is that what you call them?"

"You know about this group? Nobody else has ever heard of it."

"Then how can you be sure it exists?"

"Well, does it or doesn't it?"

"You know we never answer questions about what we know."

"A wise policy," Graham said. "If you did, people would realize how much you don't know."

Patchen smiled in cordial acknowledgment of a point well taken. "That's the operating principle, all right."

"Whatever you say or don't say, David, I have reason to believe that the Eye of Gaza exists and that it kidnapped a real person named Harvey Walpole. And that Walpole, or, if you prefer, Garth Robertson, worked for the Outfit."

Graham watched Patchen for a reaction to the link-up of identities. There was none.

"We're following up on what we know," Graham said. "That's all I can say about the matter. Unless you have something to add."

"What is there to say?" Patchen said, still affable. "If you believe in the existence of this Eye of . . . what?"

"Gaza."

". . . Gaza. As I started to say, if you believe in it, then I suppose it exists," Patchen said. "Did they teach you anything about solipsism at Brown?"

"*Yale*," Graham said. "What does that have to do with anything?"

"A solipsist is someone who believes only in himself and his own perceptions. Nothing else has any reality, and the world is a dream that would vanish if he did not exist to imagine it."

"Now I'm a solipsist? What's that supposed to mean? What's all this shit you've been handing me all night supposed to mean?"

"It's all part of a diabolical plot to save the Outfit with your help," Patchen said. In the weird and shadowless lamplight, he looked more than ever like Mephistopheles. "We couldn't possibly do it without you."

This was the unvarnished truth. As Patchen had expected, Graham did not believe it.

"You're crazy," he said, and hurried away.

3

AS SOON AS GRAHAM BROKE THE BEAUTIFUL DREAMERS STORY, Patchen was besieged by a large crowd of journalists. This had happened before, notably when Wolkowicz's anchored corpse was discovered ten years before by a fisherman in Chesapeake Bay, but never while Martha was at home. On all other such occasions she had been with her Indians in Guatemala, and by the time she returned the incident was over, all memory of it obliterated by the hundreds of tiny, routine electronic shocks that had been administered by the media to Washington's brain in the intervening months. Patchen never mentioned these episodes to her; sometimes others did, at dinner parties, but they quickly changed the subject, mistaking the look of bewilderment that came into her eyes for the humiliation they themselves would have felt if they had been married to a man like Patchen.

It was widely assumed among Washington hostesses (their husbands tended to like her) that Martha, who had graduated from Radcliffe College summa cum laude, was simple-minded—the homely, foolishly dressed, pathetically unsuitable wife Patchen had had to settle for because of his grotesque appearance. She was certainly nothing like the wives of other men of his rank and celebrity. Her table talk consisted almost entirely of non sequiturs and unfunny witticisms derived (though nobody guessed this) from her Indians' dreamlike view of existence; these remarks drifted over the heads of her dinner parners like fluttering reed arrows launched from a Stone Age bow. Martha had no small talk, no gossip. She had no interest in politics, fashion, the rise and fall of Presidential favorites, the adulteries and other follies of the renowned. This waste of opportunity was maddening to the few career hostesses who knew her. Here she was, married to the one man in America who knew everything about everybody, and she did not even understand that to be in the know was to be alive, and vice-versa.

Martha was only dimly aware that her husband was a famous man—or as Patrick Graham described him on national television, an infamous one, in command of the darkest, most satanic powers of the American government. "The Man on the Dinosaur," Graham called Patchen, the dinosaur being the Outfit and all the atavistic horrors that it stood for. Martha knew what Patchen's position in the government was, of course, and in a vague way, what the Outfit did. She knew perfectly well that its employees did not commit the awful crimes of which they were always being accused by Graham and even by some of the politicized Quakers and Jesuits she encountered in Central America. The O. G.? David? Paul? Horace Hubbard? Murderers? Enemies of the people? The idea was ludicrous; at least one of them, Paul, might even be a saint. She knew that her husband saw the President often, testified before Congress, knew nearly all the famous personages in Washington by their first names, and supervised thousands of employees who worked in secret ways in every country on earth, "doing good by stealth," as the O. G. had described it to her the first time she met him. She liked the phrase; it also perfectly described what Martha had been trying to do among her Indians all these years.

Nevertheless, she worried about her husband's soul. What did fame and position matter if Patchen had not yet found the Inward Light? She knew in her heart that he would find it one day, even if he had not yet done so; even if he was as unhappy now, and as lonely, and as skeptical of her love, and as angry about his affliction, as he had been when he came home, ruined in body and sore in spirit, from the war.

"Have you looked outside?" Patchen asked her on the first morning of the media siege.

Martha opened her eyes and saw him standing by the window, already dressed in one of his dark Brooks Brothers suits. "No," she replied. "Are the leaves on the maple turning?" That was the last thing they had talked about the night before, the autumn foliage and the order in which the trees changed color; they could never agree whether their sugar maple, transplanted from the woods at the Harbor, was among the first or the last to turn because it was growing in the wrong climate. The bed was warm and filled with the fragrance of marriage; she had awakened David and been a wife to him in the night. Her voice was drowsy and happy.

"Come look," Patchen said.

Martha got up, put on her glasses, and, modestly using his clothed body to shield her naked one from peering eyes, looked outside. It was just after five o'clock, but a large crowd of media people had already gathered in the darkness at the gate; she was able to see them in the dazzling camera lights that went on and off as the television reporters practiced stand-ups.

"Who are they?" she asked. "What are they doing?"

Patchen explained, tersely: "Some of our people were kidnapped by terrorist guerrillas and the media have got hold of the story."

"*Guerrillas?*"

She pronounced it with dread, as a Spanish word; she had told him over and over how the Maoists had come into the village to collect "taxes" from her Indians, how they had offered the armed strangers the only thing they had, *guaro,* how the guerrillas had beaten the people in the drinking hut and taken the boys and girls away. Martha, following their trail the next day, found two corpses, both girls, and buried them where they lay. One of them was the child who, long before, had sewn her finger to the cloth.

Patchen knew what her memories were. "Everybody's all right," he said, touching her. "The terrorists let them go after they questioned them. If you want to read about it, there's a story in this morning's *Post.*"

"Thee knows I never read the newspaper."

Standing behind Patchen with her arms wrapped around his waist, she gazed on the scene below. Because she was so recently awake, it seemed even stranger to her than it was. It was a chilly morning. The news people hunched their shoulders against the cold as they sipped coffee from Styrofoam cups, gazing vacantly into space like her Indians in the moment following the bicycle accident—as though, having witnessed that strange event, they never wanted to see anything interesting again.

Just then Patchen's car arrived, not his usual nondescript Chevrolet but a long black-windowed limousine bristling with antennas. The news crews sprang to life, all staring hungrily at the front door of the house. They seemed to do everything in unison.

Patchen kissed Martha goodbye and went downstairs. When he emerged from the house the journalists surged forward, shouting and brandishing their cameras, tape recorders, and microphones. Strobe lights sparkled in the darkness like the feverish impulses of a mob, and then the floodlights came on and absorbed the flashes into a single glaring entity. The people reminded her again of Indians, as when they danced, or when an entire village rushed menacingly toward a visitor to see if he could be frightened away. This had happened to her more than once, and she had learned that such behavior was a sign that the Indians themselves were frightened and uncertain. All you had to do was smile and stand your ground and make no threatening gesture that might cause some drunk or fool or frightened boy among them to shed your blood.

Patchen never spoke to the media; he did not even smile at them. Now he simply walked through them as if they did not exist, saying nothing in response to a babble of questions, lurching from side to side because of his limp. There was something threatening about this behavior; Martha could see it in the faces of the crowd. Tears came to her eyes. How alien he always seemed among normal people, she thought, how like a man from another world or time who did not bother to listen to people's voices because he could read their thoughts. How unfair it was that he should seem to be like this when his heart was so good; how much she loved him because others seemed to be unable to do so.

Patchen got into the backseat of his car and was driven away, followed by a motley convoy of vehicles with the names of news organizations painted on the sides.

A few blocks away in the exercise room of his house on O Street, Patrick Graham watched live coverage of this scene on a bank of television monitors while he took his usual brisk morning walk on a treadmill.

"The night of the living dead! Great shot!" he said to Dorcas, his secretary. She laughed more heartily than the joke deserved, but she was glad that he was speaking to her at all. He had ignored her for two days after she had failed to give him a description of the runner in the surgical mask. Graham had hired her because he liked the look of her, and now he liked the chastised look on her face. Because she had overslept and arrived five minutes late that morning, she still wore running shorts and sweat-soaked T-shirt. Graham stopped exercising. "Take off that sweatband," he said. She did as he ordered, shaking out her long dark hair. "Come here," he said. The girl looked questioningly at the door leading into the master bedroom; behind it, Charlotte was still abed. "Do as I say," Graham said. "She knows better than to open that door."

4

"PATRICK GRAHAM LIVE" WAS BROADCAST AT SEVEN O'CLOCK ON Saturday evenings. This was an advantageous time slot because it gave the Sunday newspapers and the other television networks plenty of time to pick up and repeat Graham's revelations, but made it difficult for anyone he happened to attack on the air to get out his side of the story until Monday morning. By that time, unless the material was unusually sensational, the evening news and the front pages had gone on to something else and had no room or time for rebuttals. Although this was no direct concern of Graham's (he never even looked at the commercials on the studio monitor), the network's commercial billings for his half-hour of prime time averaged just over a million dollars a show, or about $40 million a season. These numbers did not include the millions collected by television stations across the country for the local commercials sandwiched between network advertising messages. Nor did Graham's own earnings from the show, just over three million dollars a year, constitute his total income. He took in almost as much again from books, lectures, and other appearances. After ten years as a media celebrity of the first rank, he was one of the richest men in Washington—not merely one of the best paid, one of the *richest*, because he had invested much and invested well in real estate (but only in buildings with acknowledged architectural merit), works of art, rare books, an extremely profitable health food and recycling enterprise, and other politically clean possessions. He did not own a single share of stock or a single bond.

Graham was explaining to Dorcas why he refused, as a matter of principle, to invest in capitalistic enterprises that supported an imperialist foreign policy, when the telephone rang. This was not the business phone with its many blinking Lucite buttons, but his personal instrument. No one had its number unless Graham provided it; he called it his "black number," and it was the only telephone he ever answered himself. No one else was permitted to touch it. If he wasn't there, it rang until the caller hung up. All this had been explained to Dorcas. Nevertheless, when it rang she started to answer, crawling across the mat on which she and Graham were lying. He slapped her hard on her upraised bare bottom before she could touch the phone. She squealed in pain and surprise; they had become lovers only fifteen minutes before. She had never before been physically hurt so soon after making love, or in a part of her body so close to the seat of pleasure. Still gasping in pain, still disconcerted by the stinging blow, she rolled helplessly over onto her back, so that when Graham reached across her supine body to pick up the receiver he found himself looking down into a tear-stained face in which feelings of betrayal and reawakening lust transparently mingled. It was an exciting combination. The phone rang for the third time. Graham kissed Dorcas on the lips and lifted her head to arrange her hair in a fan around her face. She sniffled like a child and smiled tentatively. He took her breasts, very nice ones but a bit larger than he liked, into his hands and manipulated the nipples with his thumbs. On the fourth ring he pushed her legs apart with his knee and mounted her, all in one practiced seignorial movement. Then he picked up the phone.

"Patrick Graham here."

The voice on the line was male and Middle Eastern. But it did not sound exactly like the voice Graham had heard the last time. As he listened, he pumped rhythmically; beneath him, Dorcas responded, her bland face thickening slightly as her passion mounted.

The man on the line said, "You have betrayed us, Mister Graham. We require an explanation."

"Betrayed you?" Graham said. Obviously this call was a joke—someone in the White House or Hollywood putting on an accent before asking him to lunch to discuss his last show. How could a terrorist have obtained this number? Dorcas twined her legs around his waist and moaned. He lifted a threatening hand at the sound.

She shut up immediately. She liked power; they were going to get along just fine.

"Who the hell is this?" he said into the telephone, controlling his impulse to laugh with great difficulty. If this was a joke, the joke was on the joker.

"This is the Eye of Gaza."

Graham barely registered the name; he had not thought about the Eye of Gaza since leaving the studio. "Is it really?" he said. "How'd you like the show?" He changed position, rearranging Dorcas's body into the position called "the yawning position" in the *Kama Sutra;* in the terminology of the Hindu classic (which Graham *had* read), Dorcas was a mare, possessed of the middling of the three sizes of *yoni.* Wild-eyed and gasping, she achieved orgasm. He cupped her face in his hand; she covered it with kisses. He put his hand over the mouthpiece. "It's the Eye of Gaza," he said. He withdrew and rolled over onto his back.

The voice said, "We require to know the source of your information concerning the identity of our commando."

Something in the caller's tone made Graham pay closer attention.

"You require to know the source of my information?" he said. "What are you talking about?"

"How did you know who we were?"

"Come off it. You told me. On the telephone."

"That is impossible. This is our first call to you."

Was this a joke? Graham pushed Dorcas's sweaty body aside and leaped to his feet. He said, "How did you get this number?"

"We know a great deal about you, Mister Graham. We know who you have dinner with. We know you go for midnight walks in very strange company. Afterwards you broadcast our name to the world without our permission."

"Bullshit. That's a lot of bullshit."

"Bullshit? I don't understand 'bullshit.' "

"It means filthy lies."

"Be careful, Mister Graham. You knew something you had no right to know. We did not tell you. How, then, did you know? You betrayed us, put us in danger. Why should we believe anything you say?"

Suddenly Graham was confident that this was no prank. But how had they got this number? Was one of his closest friends mixed up with these killers? "Who is this?" he said, placatingly. "What's your name? Give me a number where I can reach you." He snapped his fingers at Dorcas and mouthed the word "pad." She said, "What, darling?" He covered the mouthpiece and hissed, "Pad, pad, pad. Get your fucking pad and write down this number."

But the man from the Eye of Gaza did not give him a number. He said, "We think you are a tool of the Outfit, Mister Graham. You are very clever, but we are not deceived. You are a friend of our enemies."

"Wait a minute!" Graham said. "Just a goddamn minute! I won't take that from anybody!"

"You will not take? We shall see, Mister Graham, what you will take. You have put us in danger. You owe us a debt. It will be collected. The Eye of Gaza does not forgive or forget. Goodbye."

"Just a minute," Graham said. "I need a telephone number."

But the line was dead. He stood for a long moment with the buzzing receiver at his ear, looking at himself in the long mirror across the room and seeing the lean body of a man years younger than he really was, and a face blank with terror. Dorcas was looking up at him. As soon as he noticed this, he changed his expression at once from panic to nonchalance, but waves of nausea continued to surge through his body, and at the back of his throat he tasted the sour contents of his stomach.

Around eleven o'clock Graham's producer called from New York. It came in on one of the regular lines and Dorcas answered; the producer was not one of the people who knew Graham's black number. When Graham came on the line, he said, "The lawyers just had a call from Garth Robertson's attorney. He says that Robertson is a devout Mormon who has always worked for the Church of Latter-day Saints except for a hitch in the Army. He had an arm blown off in Vietnam. He's just been transferred to Vietnam, to work with the GI orphans."

"A likely story."

"Well, we checked with Salt Lake City. They say Robertson's legit. And they are not amused by having one of their people identified as an Outfit thug."

"You believe this crap?"

"I'm telling you what's been said."

"It's the Outfit fucking us around."

"Could be," the producer said. "But Robertson is suing you and the network for a hundred million dollars. If he wins, he says he's going to give the money to the orphans. The papers are already on the story. So stand by for inquiring reporters."

"*Me?* Inquiring reporters?" Graham said. "What am I? One of the bad guys already?"

5

MARTHA WAS SURPRISED TO RECEIVE AN INVITATION TO LUNCHEON from Charlotte Graham. She accepted without hesitation, then called Patchen at the office. She did this so rarely that there was anxiety in his voice when it came on the line, and she could sense his relief when she told him what had happened.

"It sounds like fun," he said. "Enjoy yourself."

"Does thee object?"

"Why should I object? What does she say she wants?"

"She says she wants to talk about my Indians some more. She has some ideas."

"Indians, eh? Keep your knees together."

"What does thee mean by that?"

"I mean listen to what she has to say, but don't promise any favors."

"Thee isn't angry with her husband?"

"No. You might as well be angry with an alley cat. You can say that's what I said in case she asks."

"Thee *should* be angry. I'll tell her that."

"Okay. Have a nice lunch. Just don't ride in the Grahams' car."

"All right. But why not?"

"Just promise me you won't."

The women met at the Age of Enlightenment, a fashionable restaurant in a little street off Wisconsin Avenue. Martha arrived first, and as she came through the door the greeter looked her up and down and hesitated; they didn't get many customers dressed up as Salvation Army maidens in this place. Martha was used to this sort of scrutiny, and in order to put the doubtful young woman at ease, she said, "I'm joining Mrs. Graham."

The greeter smiled with sudden charm, thinking, *Old money; maybe even English.* "This way, please," she said. "Lady Charlotte should be along any minute now."

As Martha made her way to a front table, the other customers gazed at her with open curiosity. Like the greeter, they were slender well-barbered people in their thirties and forties who retained the self-absorbed, discomposed air and the vacant faces of adolescents. Male and female dressed alike in drab pinstripe suits with pink or yellow neck cloths and costly slip-on shoes. When they lifted their drinks (mostly iced tea or mineral water, Martha noted with approval), gold Rolex watches flashed on their wrists. Their demeanor was somber and wary, like that of actors playing idealistic conspirators in a Costa Gavras movie. Many wore wire-rimmed spectacles with tiny round lenses hardly larger than the eyes they covered, like those in old photographs of Leon Trotsky and Jean-Paul Sartre.

Charlotte arrived, dressed in a Chanel suit and Gucci pumps, with a small crocodile bag slung over her shoulder by a long gold chain. (She did not share Patrick's anxious concern for endangered species. "Crocodiles are better off dead," she had told Martha during their chat after dinner at the Patchens'. "So are tigers; they ate two relations of mine on their honeymoon in India—just came into the tent and trotted off with them clamped in their jaws. It's enough to make one vengeful. Of course, to my husband and his friends, one live croc is worth any number of starved natives.") Her clothes reminded Martha, who could not tell one couturier from another, of the expensive things Cathy Christopher used to wear, but Charlotte herself was not nearly so beautiful. She had a face like a cat's, absent-minded and bored by the daylight world, and a long-waisted feline body. She "kissed" Martha, a cool efficient touch of powdered cheek, before she sat down.

"I hope you haven't been waiting long," she said.

"Only a few minutes," Martha replied. "It was very nice just looking at everyone. What pretty people they have here."

"Yes, isn't it wonderful, they all strive to look as though Jack Kennedy banged their mothers on his way through Milwaukee," Charlotte replied. "The menu here is nouvelle American cuisine. They're quite snobby about it, but they don't mind if you don't order fish or fowl; the prices take that into account. I recommend you to try the watercress, arugula, radicchio, and walnut salad with walnut oil and raspberry vinaigrette."

"That sounds very healthy. And a cup of tea, please."

Charlotte gave the order to the hovering waiter, who had set an

Old Fashioned glass filled with milk before her almost as soon as she sat down. "I'll have another of these with my salad," she said, drinking half the milk at a single swallow.

Martha watched curiously. "That milk has a brown tint," she said.

"That's because it's got Scotch whisky in it," Charlotte said. "Would you like to try one?"

"No, thank you."

"You can have it without the whisky if you like. Or without the milk. No? I think you'll like the salad as much as you like the clientele. I have luncheon here quite often, but I can't get Patrick to touch this kind of food. He lives on protein."

"I don't think David would like it, either."

"No, I shouldn't think so. Toads and spiders would be more his thing."

"What?" Martha's brows knitted.

"Joke," Charlotte said. "My husband thinks your husband is the Wicked Witch of the West. Men can be witches, did you know that?"

"Not David. He's a very good person."

"I'm sure he is," Charlotte said. Martha's hand lay on the table. She squeezed it affectionately. In actual fact, she had taken a liking to Martha; she was rather like the sort of girl, plain and earnest and middle class, she had chosen as friends at school. They had made excellent chums. Charlotte still wrote to them all; mostly they had ended up in African countries whose names began with "Z," trying to make up for the overweening pride and arrogance of the British Empire by performing demeaning services for indifferent blacks. The food came. Martha ate her salad with good appetite. Charlotte left her own greens untouched while she drank her second Scotch and milk.

"I enjoyed our talk at your house tremendously," Charlotte said. "Especially the part about the tiddly Indians. Can't I do something to help?" Martha was chewing her salad and could not answer at once. "I mean to say," Charlotte continued, "why not simply rescue a few of the little chaps, educate them in America, then send them back to save the rest? They could set up some sort of Mayan Alcoholics Anonymous."

"Rescue the children?" Martha said. "How would you do that?"

"Just abduct them, that's my idea. It's done all the time for

404

immoral purposes. Evil white men are always buying little girls in Thailand and little boys in the Philippines and posting them off to Europe and America and Japan like tins of biscuits. Why not do it for a moral purpose?"

"How could it be moral if it began by doing a wrong?"

Charlotte picked up a sprig of watercress in her fingers and nibbled it. "Quite right," she said. "It couldn't possibly be. I must tell Patrick what you've said and see if he thinks it applies to his terrorists. He's been trying to ring up David on that subject, but his calls are not returned."

"I don't think the children would be able to help the others even if they did go somewhere else to grow up," Martha said. "They'd be very homesick, and when they got back to the village they'd be so glad to be home that they'd go straight into the drinking hut."

Charlotte let a moment go by before answering. "I see what you mean—the jungle claiming its own," she said at last.

"It's funny," Martha said, "but somebody else had almost the same idea as you years and years ago."

"Really? Who?"

"You wouldn't have known her."

"Ah, a spy. What a dilemma it must be, having all these secret friends."

Martha, smiling angelically, ate the last of her salad.

"Look here, Martha," Charlotte said. "I'm in something of a dilemma myself. I want to ask you a question I can't really ask anyone else. But I wonder if I should. I do like you so much."

It was clear to Martha that Charlotte meant what she said. "Thank you," she replied. "I enjoy our time together, too." The look of goodness on her face intensified slightly. "Why shouldn't you ask, Charlotte?" she said.

"It's rather difficult because it involves our husbands, and they don't like each other at all."

"Maybe that's because Patrick used to be a toad before you turned him into a Patrick."

Charlotte shouted with laughter. A dozen glossy interchangeable heads turned curiously in her direction, toy eyeglasses glittering. No one else in the restaurant had laughed in all the time Martha had been there; judging by the snatches of conversation she had overheard, they had all spent the entire hour and a half talking to one another about fractured relationships, personal or professional, and trying to discover the reasons for these puzzling little divorces. However, they seemed prepared to laugh now, if only they could find out what Lady Charlotte considered funny and repeat it; you could see the curiosity in their studious faces.

"What is the question, Charlotte?" Martha asked.

"Will your husband meet Patrick and talk to him?"

"I really don't think so. He never talks to journalists."

"Then why did you have us for dinner?"

"Oh, that was just one of David's evenings. He likes to have people taste his wine."

"Oh, dear. Well, perhaps you could persuade him to forgive and forget about the Margaux and return Patrick's calls. The poor man is quite shaken up about this Eye of Gaza business. He's not used to being sued by Mormons and threatened by bloodthirsty terrorists over the telephone."

"Is he being threatened?"

"He thinks so. Perhaps even with death; it's not entirely clear what the Eye of Gaza has in mind for him but I assure you he fears the worst. It's so unfair when he's been such a champion to the wretched. He thinks your husband is behind it all."

Martha was taken aback. "How could he be?"

"That's his job, my dear, laying traps. He's famous for it."

"You don't know my husband," Martha said.

Charlotte looked into her serene face with dismay. She was beginning to think that this woman was no fool. What a mistake it was to let oneself think that someone else was stupid. Patrick did it all the time; that was why he was so often at a disadvantage. Usually it did not matter; he just went on to the next broadcast, leaving the field littered with the sadder but wiser. This time, it seemed, it *did* matter. Charlotte was now quite sure of that.

She said, "Tell David that Patrick is through with this story. No matter what happens, he's going to let it die."

Martha nodded, but said nothing.

"If he *can* let it die, that is," Charlotte added. "He's not so sure that they'll let him. The phone calls really are quite theatrical."

Martha smiled luminously. It resembled, Charlotte thought, the transforming smile of one of those flat-faced peasant madonnas in an Italian painting made before the discovery of perspective. Behind Martha, the restaurant crowd babbled and preened. She had lost interest in it, you could see it in her eyes. The racy post-modern world that meant so much to Patrick and Charlotte, and even to David Patchen, had no more reality for Martha than some jumbled medieval village teetering on a cliff beyond Mary's halo in a gaudy pietà by some thirteenth-century monk.

Charlotte called for the bill and paid it by scribbling her name and a not very generous tip across the bottom with a square Cartier pen provided by the waiter. "This has been very enjoyable," she said to Martha. "Can I drop you anywhere?"

"Thanks, but David made me promise not to ride in your car."

"*Did* he?" Charlotte said, her eyebrows rising in alarm. This time it was Martha who touched Charlotte's hand in womanly sympathy.

6

AFTER THE NETWORK LAWYERS REVIEWED THE VIDEO TAPE, THERE was no question whatever that Harvey Walpole had two normal hands. In the course of the interrogation he had gesticulated freely, showing first the left, then the right. "Four fingers and a thumb and lots of hair on each one," Graham's producer reported. "Garth Robertson wears a hook." His voice was jaunty. He was one of the new breed who had picked up all the right opinions in college but had no commitment to ideals. He did not seem to be altogether unhappy about the lawsuit; Patrick Graham would remember that.

By the end of the day, Graham had looked at an edited tape that showed nothing but freeze frames in which Walpole's hands were visible. The producer was right: there was no mistaking them for artificial ones. As he sat slumped in the ergonomic chair in front of the huge back-projection screen in his study, he fought against depression. How had this happened? Whose fault was it? His people, beginning with the producer, were supposed to protect him from things like this. "I'm very disappointed," he said in his booming voice, rehearsing the tongue-lashing the producer was going to get. Just then Dorcas brought him the tall glass of yoghurt, ice cubes made from Evian water, honey, and wheat bran, all beaten together in an electric blender, that he ordinarily drank at six o'clock. She jumped a little at the sound of his voice, but he did not seem to realize that he had spoken. He waved the drink away.

"Get me David Patchen on the telephone," he said. "Call his

office, his car, and his home, in that order. Don't take 'no' for an answer, and don't come back in here until you have him on the line."

To his surprise, she succeeded on the first try.

"David!" Graham said. "You're a hard man to catch up to. I wanted to tell you that I found a couple of bottles of '61 Château Margaux downcellar and I'm sending them over to you."

"That's nice of you, Patrick," Patchen replied, "but I couldn't accept such a handsome gift without breaking the law."

"They're not poisoned, I assure you."

Patchen laughed appreciatively at this meager joke. Why was he being so agreeable? There was clicking on the line; his voice sounded distorted and far away. Graham said, "Where are you? In the car, or what? You sound like you're talking from a vault."

"I'm at my desk," Patchen replied. "A lot of people complain about this phone. Was the wine all you called about?"

"No. I was wondering why you wouldn't let your wife ride in my car."

"It's a Mercedes, isn't it?"

"Yes. What does that have to do with it?"

"People like Martha shouldn't ride in cars that run on human hair. Not that I think there's anything strange about your owning one if you can afford it."

Graham did not understand the full import of this outrageous remark—was Patchen suggesting he was some kind of Nazi because of his anti-Zionism?—until he, Graham, was halfway through his next sentence. When the realization that he had been insulted struck him, he was saying, in a casual tone, that he had received an interesting phone call that morning from the Eye of Gaza. His voice faltered. Patchen interrupted.

"As a matter of fact," he said, "I'm glad you called, Patrick. Our conversation about the exploitation of women by radical political movements got me thinking about the similarities between the Hitler Youth and the American counterculture of the sixties."

"*What* similarities?" Graham cried, sitting bolt upright in his chair. What was going on here? *He,* not Patchen, occupied the moral high ground. "Wait just a goddamn minute."

But Patchen merely raised his voice slightly and talked over Graham's interruption. "The counterculture was clearly totalitarian in its impulses and methods," he continued.

"Totalitarian?"

"Shocking thought, isn't it? The sixties always puzzled me, that army of foul-mouthed runaways, all dressed up like the proletariat, squirting urine on the cops and waving marijuana lollipops at the TV cameras. Why did you bourgeois kids who had everything decide to hate everything you might ordinarily be expected to love—freedom, country, family, school? It couldn't just be puerile self-hatred; that was far too simple an explanation for a movement of this magnitude. I kept wondering where this mass temper tantrum came from. And then I stumbled onto the most amazing book about the *Wandervögel,* the pre-Nazi German youth movement. This was the precursor to the Hitler Youth, of course, but it began before the First World War as a reaction to post-Bismarckian industrialization. A schoolteacher named Karl Fischer got it started as a sort of back-to-nature thing in 1896. *Wandervögel* means 'birds of passage.' Very apt. Here, let me read from the book."

"What book?"

"This one is called *Young Germany,* by Anne Merriman Peck, published in this country in 1931. It's a sort of primer on the subject, a bit gushy, but very revealing."

"I don't have time to listen to this crap, Patchen."

"That's all right. I'll compress as I go along. Here we go: 'The German people became very materialistic. Cities grew big, noisy and driving, and factory work made life unhappy. The school system was so rigid and severe that there was no room for young ideas to grow. But boys and girls, idealistic and romantic, as German youth have always been, rebelled against this kind of a world. They spent their free time in the country, making friends with the peasants and learning from them the old folk songs and dances which had been almost forgotten. They had a great longing to get away from this harsh civilization. They adopted a costume which represented the repudiation of confining city life, velveteen suits and peasant dresses [because they] wanted to be different from their world even in their clothes. They revolted also against the strict conventional rules for the relations between boys and girls. They tramped and swam together, slept side by side in all sorts of shelters or in the open fields. They held high-hearted discussions around their camp fires about the meaning of life, what they would do with it, and how they would make it beautiful.' . . .Sound familiar?"

"No," Graham said. "It doesn't. David, I have to talk to you about something important. It affects both of us."

"Let me finish," Patchen said. "It will only take another minute. This is damn interesting—how the German youth movement became the Hitler Youth. This is from *Nazi Youth in the Weimar Republic,* by Peter D. Stachura: 'The NSDAP,' . . .that's the Nazi Party, Patrick . . . 'portraying the movement as one of youth and for youth, judiciously sensed the latent tensions between the generations in German society, played the young and new against the old and decayed with consummate skill, and denigrated 'the system' as the vile creation of a declining, older generation. The alternative was the destruction of the republic by the dynamism of national socialism and its replacement by the Third Reich of Adolf Hitler. The goal of the Hitler Youth was to rouse youth and direct their resentments against the state.' "

"So?" Graham said.

"So change a couple of proper names—Peoples Republic for Third Reich, for example—and think about it. Of course you had no Adolf Hitler to look up to, and your enemies had Richard Nixon. The question is, who benefitted? You were upset the other night when I mentioned covert action, but maybe being covert action assets is the fate of idealistic, romantic folks like yourself, Patrick. You seem to have been weaned on it."

Graham gritted his teeth. "I don't know what your purposes are in hammering away at me with these stupid lies and false comparisons," he said. "But it's not going to work. I know exactly who I am and what the Sixties Movement was all about, and I don't have any trouble looking at myself in the mirror when I shave every morning. Now, damn it, *you* listen to me."

"I'll have all this-Xeroxed and sent over to you so you can read it for yourself," Patchen said.

"Don't bother. David . . ."

"No trouble at all."

The line went dead, and when Dorcas called back a stern, grandmotherly voice told her that the Director had left for the day. When she called the Patchens' home number she reached an answering service.

"Shall I keep trying?" she asked.

"Of course you should keep trying. Every ten minutes. In between, get me two bottles of 1961 Château Margaux—write that

410

down: 1961, Château M-a-r-g-a-u-x—and have them delivered with my card to Patchen's house."

"Where do I get it?"

Graham threw up his arms with a roar of exasperation. "From a plumbers supply store! Where do you think you buy wine? Call the fucking wine shops here and in New York until you find one that has it!"

He stormed out of the room. Dorcas had always heard that this was the way geniuses behaved, and she was glad to find out that it was true. At college she had conducted brief affairs with a couple of disagreeable associate professors, but even before meeting Graham she had guessed that they were imitations of the ideal. All that was behind her. More had happened to her in this one week at Graham's side than in all her previous life, and she realized with a pang of joy that she had escaped at last from the busy emptiness of the suburbs and the university into the real world.

7

THAT EVENING MARTHA COOKED ONE OF HER VEGETARIAN DINNERS for Patchen. Afterward they talked about her Indians and all the years she had spent among them with so little sign that her presence had made any difference.

"Have you ever regretted it?" Patchen asked.

"How could I regret my work?" she asked.

"You mean the Indians are your purpose on earth? The reason for your being here?"

"What is is what was meant to be. But thee is my purpose on earth."

"Then why do you go away for half of every year to be with the Indians?"

"It is part of the purpose."

"But you're invisible to them."

"The Inward Light is invisible to thee. But it exists, and one day thee will see it."

"Will the Indians see thee in the same instant?"

"Thee called me thee."

"I always do, in my mind. What is the answer?"

"Thee laughs at miracles. But when thee sees at last, thee will see what has always been real, and so will my Indians."

She smiled with such particular sweetness and happiness that he remembered, as if it were happening to them now, the first time she had been a wife to him in Paris. They went upstairs with their arms around each other, and in the morning Martha went back to Guatemala.

8

YEARS BEFORE, WHEN THE O. G. HAD BEEN ORDERED BY ONE OF THE half-dozen Presidents who had come and gone during his long tenure as Director to build a new headquarters for the Outfit in the suburbs of Washington, he demurred. There were any number of reasons for a master spy of the old school to dislike centralization; to name only three, it encouraged the pesky weeds of bureaucracy, it made it easy for anyone to compile a roster of headquarters personnel merely by reading the license numbers of cars taking the Outfit exit off the main highway during rush hour, and it threatened to turn a broad natural savannah filled with exotic specimens into a rabbit warren where the ground trembled with the thump of the President's big rubber boots on the sod overhead. "Dying institutions build monuments to themselves," the O. G. argued, paraphrasing one of Parkinson's propositions. "Let's use all those millions of dollars this skyscraper would cost to raise hell with the opposition." But his protests fell on deaf ears. The President laid a cornerstone containing an encrypted letter to future generations of spies ("intelligence specialists"), and in due course the imposing new glass-and-granite building went up on a densely wooded site, complete with a motto (*"Out of darkness, light"*) coined for the occasion by the O. G. himself. This inscription was rendered into English from the original Latin at the insistence of a different President, a fretful man who sensed a pun on the name 'Caligula' in the O. G.'s use of the noun *caligo* for 'darkness' instead of the more usual *obscuritas*. As the O. G. had feared and the two Presidents had intended, the new headquarters made the Outfit less adventurous by rendering it more visible.

New construction provided certan opportunities, however, and one of the ways in which the O. G. took advantage of these was by having a team of Seabees construct a tunnel leading from the shaft of the Director's private elevator to a safe house some two miles away. No one knew about the existence of the tunnel except the Director and the retired Navy chief petty officer who maintained the ventilating system and the golf carts used to travel through the tunnel; the chief lived in the safe house. It was there, in the oversize garage into which the tunnel debouched, that Patchen rendezvoused with the O. G. after midnight of the day of his telephone conversation with Patrick Graham. Meeting openly for the purposes they had in mind was out of the question. Although the media crowd assigned to Patchen had thinned to a twenty-four-hour pool of half a dozen reporters and cameramen as the Beautiful Dreamers story cooled, he still found it difficult to move about freely.

Patchen and the O. G. did not speak to each other while they were inside the garage; the safe house was equipped with listening devices and other gear that only the chief petty officer fully understood. Instead they got into the four-wheel-drive Cherokee (registered in the name of a male child who had died in Catlettsburg, Kentucky, two days after his premature birth in July 1930) and drove southward into Virginia. Their destination was Camp Panchaea, named for the mythical island where, according to Euhemerus, the gods had lived as men before ascending Mount Olympus. It was a hunting and fishing reserve formerly located at the center of a five-thousand-acre private forest. The O. G.'s Uncle Snowden, a keen hunter and angler, bought this property when the Society of Euhemerus disbanded, and in his will gave the O. G. its exclusive enjoyment during his lifetime. When he died it would go to the Panchaea Foundation, a tax-exempt institution devoted to the rediscovery and propagation of original North American species of plants and animals, in whose name the deed was already registered.

It was a long drive, especially since the O.G., who was at the wheel, took only rural roads. Patchen, exhausted by eighteen uninterrupted hours of meetings, telephone conversations, and deep thought, fell asleep almost immediately. He did not wake up until the O. G. slammed on the brakes as the car was traveling along the rutted woodland road that led to the camp. He opened his eyes and saw a herd of whitetail deer bounding like rubber-band toys through the beams of the headlights.

"These woods are full of game," the O. G. said. "The eastern cougar, thought to be extinct for two hundred years, has come back. So have black bear, wild turkey, egrets, otter, even coyotes. Wouldn't surprise me if I saw a woodland bison crossing the road one of these times. The wild, wild East! Nature is a lot more resilient than these environmentalists who grew up in the suburbs think.''

The O. G. had spent his boyhood summers on his grandfather's farm in the state of New York, milking cows by hand, making hay with scythe, hand rake, and pitchfork, and chopping down brush in an unceasing and ultimately hopeless attempt to keep the surrounding forest from taking over cultivated fields. He had a low regard for nature lovers who had never chopped down chokecherry bushes or had a chicken coop cleaned out by a weasel that killed a whole flock of Barred Rock pullets just for the merry hell of it. He often said so.

Patchen looked at his watch. It was four-thirty. "How close are we getting?" he asked.

"Should be there to see the sun rise over the lake," the O. G. replied. "Speaking of weasels, do you think your man is spooked?"

"Graham? Yes. Which of those phone calls was genuine and which were Yeho's?"

"You have no need to know that." The O. G. grinned happily. He was back in the saddle, the case officer for this operation. Nobody before him had ever had the Director of the Outfit as an agent under discipline. The thought tickled him, but he resisted giving voice to it. He changed the subject back to Patrick Graham. "Is he sufficiently angry at you?"

"You could say that, I think. I may even have gone too far. I had no idea that baiting pinkos was so much fun."

The O. G. laughed. "There's nothing you can do while standing upright that's more pleasurable," he said. "Same thing applied to crypto-Nazis in their day. Used to kid the pants off them in Hitler's Berlin. They were the same class of people as Graham—telling themselves they were doing good in the world by doing well by themselves and closing their eyes to horrors done unto others in the name of the cause. But you have to be careful. These make-believe revolutionaries are like virgin aunts—they've got all the standard equipment under their petticoats, but they've never had them lifted except in dreams. They live in their fevered imaginations, and if you tease 'em too much about the real thing they go all to pieces."

414

They arrived at the camp in the moment before sunrise. Patchen had never been here before and he was surprised by the size of it and its well-kept appearance. The log buildings—a large lodge and several smaller cabins distributed along the shore of a small lake—shone with varnish, and the network of white gravel walks that connected them were weeded and freshly raked. Mallard ducks and Canada geese bobbed in water dimpled by feeding fish. They were standing on the highest point for miles around, but to the west, beyond the lake, a range of blue mountains was visible. The O. G. sniffed the air.

"Somebody's having a barbecue," he said.

Footsteps crunched on the gravel behind them. "Welcome to paradise," Yeho Stern said. Despite the weather—it was the first of November and the camp was fifteen hundred feet above sea level—he wore his usual khaki shorts, but with hiking shoes and an old canvas hunting jacket, stained with the blood of duck and pheasant, that was several sizes too large for him.

"What's that aroma?" the O. G. asked.

"The Ibal Iden are burning a lamb," Yeho said. "Zarah bought them a flock of sheep."

"A flock of sheep? Isn't that a little insecure?"

"Maybe. But they won't eat anything they haven't killed themselves."

"Just the same, buying a whole flock of sheep."

"Relax," Yeho said. "She went a long way away to buy them—all the way to North Carolina. A very smart girl. You're going to love her, David."

9

ZARAH ATTENDED YEHO'S BRIEFING IN THE LODGE. EVERY SQUARE foot of wall space in the gathering room was hung with memorabilia contributed over many years by the Members: battle flags and school pennants, Revolutionary War muskets, Civil War cavalry sabers, spiked helmets and bayonets taken in Belleau Wood, footballs and baseball bats, yellowed posters of broad-hipped Floradora and Ziegfeld girls, mottoes ("LEAVE SWELLED HEADS BEHIND, ALL YE WHO ENTER HERE"; "YALE 6 VASSAR 0"), and two whole walls of photographs of good fellows holding up strings of smallmouth bass or gazing at large dead bears. In its exuberant clutter it resembled an enormous boy's bedroom into which no mother had ever been permitted to intrude.

"You must be the first member of your sex ever to set foot in here, my dear," the O. G. said, sliding a stack of hot flapjacks onto Zarah's plate. He was the cook for breakfast and he wore the red, white, and blue-striped apron and the tall chef's hat required by Club rules.

"What happens if I'm caught trespassing?" Zarah asked.

"No chance of that." The O. G. indicated the photographs with a wave of his spatula. "They've all gone West. Every one."

But Zarah was looking down at her plate as if avoiding somebody's eyes. Not the O. G.'s; she looked directly at him when he finished speaking and smiled. He gave her a quizzical look. She was nervous and spoke in a slightly tremulous voice. The reason was Patchen, who sat directly across the table from her. But why? They had not met before, but it had been clear from the moment the O. G. introduced them that Paul Christopher's daughter had some reason to dislike and distrust his best friend. *Wolkowicz's work,* the O. G. thought. *He* hadn't gone West in the minds of those who had known him. Would he ever?

Yeho ate his pancakes and scrambled eggs smothered with onions and ketchup with great rapidity, then waited impatiently for the others to finish. He knew that the O. G., whose hearing was failing, could not hear while he was chewing his food. At last the O. G. cleared the dishes and took off his cook's regalia. Yeho began.

"All right," he said. "First, security. This is a private enterprise in which neither the Outfit nor any other service is or will be involved. They are not even aware of it. As agreed, all field work has been done with retired people. Will they be quiet when they see their old friends? Who knows? I've explained we are doing something that headquarters will not want to know about, so maybe they'll spare people who are still inside the embarrassment. Anyway, they don't know why they're doing what they're doing, or who they're doing it for, so let them gossip after it's over. Now, the target. They've reported some results."

Yeho had activated a surveillance team of decommissioned agents in Switzerland. By methods he did not describe, they had located Hassan Abdallah. He now worked in his old specialty for a drug research laboratory in Geneva, where he was very highly regarded. He was married to a Swiss woman whose surname, Balmont, he had adopted, along with the forename Marcel. There was nothing unusual among Europeans in a man adopting his wife's name if it was a better one than his own, and clearly it was more advantageous to have a Gallic name in French Switzerland than an Arab one. "In the next generation," Yeho said, "no doubt it will be *de* Balmont." Before he met his wife Hassan Abdallah's appearance had been altered by plastic surgery, eliminating the more pronounced Semitic facial features. In Western clothes, with Western manners, accompanied by a Swiss wife, he could pass for a Mediterranean Frenchman; looking at him in a café, you might think that he was a *métis,* half French and half something else, but that was all. According to his identity card he was thirty-six years old, born in Damascus, formerly the center of French civilization in the Middle East, so he could very well have had one French parent. Monsieur and Madame Balmont, who had no children, attended a Calvinist church in Plainpalais, and were active in one of Geneva's innumerable patriotic organizations. He had marched in medieval costume in parades commemorating the Night of the Escalade.

"Ah-ha!" said the O. G. "Mère Royaume!"

Yeho looked annoyed. "What?"

"The heroine of Genevese history. Around 1600 she dropped a kettle of hot soup onto the head of a soldier of the Duke of Savoy who was about to scale the walls of Geneva and saved the city from sneak attack."

"Very picturesque," Yeho said. He sighed and went on. Although Balmont/Abdallah was not accepted in his own right as a Genevese, and never could be, his wife came from a long-established Huguenot family, and owing to his marriage to her he enjoyed all of the legal rights of a Swiss national and citizen of the Canton of Geneva. In the twelve years that had passed since he led the team of assassins that machine-gunned a Chinese intelligence officer in the Parc Mon Repos, he had managed to build a nearly perfect cover as a hardworking, frugal, punctual citizen. No suspicion of political activity, much less of terrorism, attached to him.

"You're sure of that?" Patchen said.

"Ninety-nine percent sure. I realize it seems impossible, knowing the Swiss police, but it seems to be the case. This man is a born deceiver. He met his wife on a beach in Yugoslavia one August, took her skiing in February, and re-entered Switzerland as her husband in April. We think she has no knowledge whatsoever of his other life. He has a mistress, a Frenchwoman who was an auxiliary of the original Butterfly team, living in the countryside a short drive into France. This female is his only known link to the old Eye of Gaza. He never goes to the house where she lives. She works as a nurse in a surgical clinic in Annecy; they meet every second Thursday in the same small hotel at Aix-les-Bains, on the other end of the lake, *pour faire l'amour,* always in the same room. This cuckoo clock adultery is part of the cover. The innkeepers are quite fond of them; they're like an old married couple, they play Scrabble afterward and always stay for dinner. They drink no alcohol. This is what we found under the floor of the bathroom of her house in the country while they were having their biweekly orgasm and game of Scrabble two Thursdays ago."

Yeho handed Patchen an enlarged photograph of a cache of arms and ammunition and other supplies, including apparatus for intravenous administration of fluids.

"The handguns are nine-millimeter Jerichos, made by Israel Military Industries, and of course you recognize the Uzi machine pistols. They use the same ammunition. The clips shown here are loaded with unmodified production rounds. Very interesting that they'd choose Israeli equipment, but as you know, these weapons are available over the counter in the United States, and as we also know, they've been here recently. The serial numbers have been defaced with acid. There are three of each kind of weapon, which may mean that there are three members of the cell, or six, or some number in between. Obviously, it may not be the only cell."

"What is this?" Zarah asked, pointing to a small pistol-like device attached to a length of tubing.

"I was getting to that," Yeho said. "That is a device used to force fluids through the skin. They use it on children because it doesn't hurt as much as a needle. The tube attaches to a small container of compressed air, like this one." He pointed to a metal object about the size of a flashlight.

"Let me see that," said the O. G. "By golly, that's how they've been knocking our people out in the toilets!"

Yeho produced a plastic bag containing a tiny amount of white powder shaken down into one corner. "We also found this," he said. "We had no secure laboratory facilities, so we couldn't test it scientifically, but one of my friends gave a small dose to his poodle, and judging by the way the dog behaved, I think it may be the stuff you've been looking for. If you can have it analyzed, David, presumably we can come up with an antidote."

Yeho himself was too old a dog to suggest by word or gesture that there was anything out of the ordinary in the work his team had done. He distributed more photographs: many shots of Marcel Balmont/Hassan Abdallah and his mistress, a scrawny blonde with the hostile face of a political zealot; several candid views of his wife, also a dehydrated Nordic type, and a number of contact prints showing exteriors of the target's office and apartment in Geneva, his mistress's country house, and the cheap hotel used by the lovers in Aix-les-Bains.

"One question," Patchen said. "If his habits are so regular, how does he account for the absences necessitated by the kidnappings?"

Clearly Yeho had been waiting for this question. "Under the law, and because of his seniority," he said, "good burgher Balmont is entitled to seven weeks' vacation a year. For sentimental reasons, presumably, he and his wife take a week at Megève for skiing in February and four weeks in Yugoslavia on the beach in August. Madame is entitled to only five weeks. As a good Swiss, however, she insists that he take all the time he is entitled to. That leaves him with two weeks', or ten days', extra vacation time all to himself. When he wants to snatch somebody from the Outfit, he takes off a Friday and a Monday, which gives him four days in which to operate. Does that fit with what you know?"

"The Beautiful Dreamers have all disappeared for four days— back on the morning of the fifth, which was always a Tuesday. How do you know this?"

"Luckily there was someone inside the laboratory," Yeho said, "who was willing to help us." There was always someone inside any given target in any city in the world who was willing to help Yeho when called upon for the right reasons; that was why he and Patchen had run such amazing operations in Russia without the traitors embedded in the British intelligence service finding out about them; that was why the Ibal Iden were in Virginia. "This person inside looked up our man's leave records," Yeho said. "His short holidays coincide exactly with the dates on which the Beautiful Dreamers were taken."

"He *is* a good Swiss," the O. G. said.

Yeho said, "Speak, David. How many has he kidnapped so far?"
"Three."

"So he's only got six days' vacation left this year and it's November already. If you want him to kidnap the person you have in mind, you'd better dangle the bait pretty soon."

"What person do you have in mind?" Zarah said.

"The Big Cheese," Yeho said, pointing at Patchen. "Who else?"

The O. G. smiled at Zarah. "That's where we hope you will be able to help us, my dear."

10

CHRISTOPHER ARRIVED AT CAMP PANCHAEA AT TWILIGHT, AFTER A flight from London and a drive from the airport in a rented car. Zarah awaited him on the veranda of the lodge. As she walked toward him across the gravel, the muffled POP-POP-POP of small arms fire sounded in the woods, and the pet waterfowl on the lake took wing half-heartedly before settling back onto its still surface.

"The Ibal Iden," she explained. "Yeho is showing them how to use a new kind of pistol on the firing range."

"The Ibal Iden are here?"

"Yes. We all arrived the day before yesterday—Ja'wab and Kbira and Dimya besides Ibrahim, Yussef, and Tammuz. And myself, of course. Yeho arranged everything after you left Tifawt."

"For what purpose?"

"To go after the Eye of Gaza, to capture this man Hassan Abdallah."

"Are you going after him, too?"

"Where they go, I go." She pointed a thumb in the direction of the gunfire. "They hope to go soon. Except for testing the weapons they don't like it here very much. It's the trees; they're used to seeing for miles, so they feel hemmed in."

"What made them agree to Yeho's arrangements?"

"It wasn't a matter of agreeing. They cast the dice and got *thummim.*"

"I see." Except for the noise of firing there was no sign of life in the camp. Christopher said, "Where are the others?"

"The O. G. is taking a nap; he was up all night. Patchen went back to Washington right after breakfast. I want to talk to you about him. But not now. What did you find out in England?"

"Let's go out on the lake."

They put one of the canoes into the calm water. Christopher paddled to the center of the lake, then let the canoe drift. It hardly moved; there was no wind at all. The surface of the water, silvered by the twilight, reflected unrippled images of oaks and maples in autumn foliage. In his muted voice, he told her what Sir Richard Shaw-Condon had told him at Rossenarra Hall. Zarah listened in silence, and even after the story was over, remained very still. Finally she said, "Do you think he's telling the truth?"

"As much as he's capable of doing so after the life he's led. I think he did the things he said he did and heard the things he said he heard, more or less. What your grandmother was thinking and doing only she, and maybe Meryem, knew."

"She did die?"

"Dickie Shaw-Condon seems to think so. That doesn't make it a fact. He wasn't there himself and none of his people got out."

"But how could the Nazis have let her live after what she did?"

"I don't know. I've spent my whole life keeping the question open. It's hard to change."

Zarah was sitting backward in the canoe, facing Christopher, so that she was only a foot or two away. He closed his eyes. It was startling, after only a few days of separation, to see how much like Lori she looked.

"Father."

Zarah had never called him by that name before. Christopher opened his eyes.

Zarah said, "She *is* dead." Another string of muffled detonations sounded in the woods. "Lla Kahina has always said so."

"She has? How does she know?"

"She knows," Zarah said. "Didn't she tell you? She thinks that's the reason I'm on earth."

11

AT SIX O'CLOCK EVERYONE SAT DOWN AT THE ROUND CLUB TABLE to a meal consisting of the Ibal Iden's barbecued lamb, served with heaping platters of raw-fried potatoes and onions doused with vinegar and black pepper, the O. G.'s specialty. The Americans drank pewter tankards of ale. For dessert the O. G. served peach ice cream with fresh peaches, in soup bowls. "Can't eat like this in the city," the O. G. said. "Your heart would stop."

The O. G. offered inky coffee—"destroyer coffee," he called it. Zarah and the Ibal Iden declined and left for the firing range. Yeho gestured to Christopher. "Come with me while the Directors do the dishes," he said. "Bring your coffee." In the billiards room, he delivered a condensed version of the briefing he had given the others at breakfast.

"You're absolutely sure this is the same man?" Christopher said.

"If you believe in fingerprints and voiceprints, yes," Yeho said. "We've compared everything but blood. It all matches. Why do you ask?"

"The profiles are very different. As I understand it, the Hassan Abdallah you knew twelve years ago was a psychopath."

"He thought he was the reincarnation of Hitler."

Christopher said, "Yet this man Balmont seems to be in perfect control of himself. How can that be?"

"He's older and wiser. As you go along you learn."

"Even if you're crazy to begin with? There has to be another element, something new in his life."

"You think so? All right. We'll consider the idea. What is the new element?"

"The obvious answer is drugs. He works with drugs, invents new ones. Maybe he's concocted something to control his insanity."

Yeho nodded admiringly. Patchen and the O. G. were right. This fellow *was* a thinker. "That's possible. You're right—he could have invented some kind of tranquilizer for himself. Nobody would know he was taking it. I like it. It explains a lot—if true. Of course he'd have to know that he was crazy, and crazy people usually don't. And he still goes crazy on long weekends."

"Then what is the explanation? David thinks he's dealing with some kind of mastermind. Would Hassan Abdallah have been able to design an operation like Beautiful Dreamers? According to David it's so subtle nobody can figure out its purpose."

"I don't know if he could. He pulled off some pretty good ones twelve years ago."

"And got caught."

"The Russian who was running him got caught. Some of the

others got themselves killed. Not him. He was smart enough to get away from us, change identities, and fool the Swiss police for ten years."

"Maybe he had good advice."

"A new case officer? No. The Russians dropped the whole operation after Butterfly disappeared."

"Why does it have to be a Russian who's running him?"

"Why should anybody be running him?" Yeho said. "Why can't he be doing this on his own?"

"Because his behavior is not consistent with what Stephanie would call his personality disorder. Someone has made him listen to reason—cured him. Who? Why?"

All his life Yeho had realized that he was smarter than taller and handsomer people, but he had been forced to suppress this knowledge in order to get what he wanted from them. As a result, exasperation was never far below the surface of his outward manner, and now he raised his hands in mock surrender and looked heavenward. He said, "We're checking, we're checking. Believe me."

Christopher persisted. "Are you checking Yugoslavia? There must be some reason besides sentiment why he goes there every year."

"Paul, my friend, yes. Believe me, we're checking Yugoslavia." He uttered an exaggerated sigh.

Christopher said, "Are you offended by my questions?"

"No. Why should I be offended? All questions are welcome. That's why you're here, to question. According to the O. G. and David, nobody's better at it than you. I'm beginning to see what they mean. You want to know about Yugoslavia? I'll tell you something about Yugoslavia. The beach the good Swiss couple goes to on the Dalmatian coast every August? It's a nudist beach."

Christopher said, "Germans."

"Yes, Germans. Lots of Germans with no clothes on. They go into the shops stark naked, they walk down the street eating ice cream cones that way."

"May I make a suggestion?"

"Speak."

"Find out which photographers covered this resort last summer. Then look at all the pictures they took, good and bad. They shoot thousands to get a dozen good enough to sell."

Yeho nodded. "It shall be done. We'll invent a nudist magazine. If we see a familiar face, or whatever, you'll be the first to know."

He made a gesture closing the discussion. "Now I want to show you the equipment."

He pulled the cover off the billiards table. Arranged on a clear plastic sheet laid over the green felt surface were six identical sets of equipment: six nine-millimeter semi-automatic pistols with silencers; six stun guns; six small aerosol tubes of Mace; six blackjacks; six hanks of insulated electrical wire; six bricks of plastic explosive, each about the size of a pound of butter, with electronic detonators; six short-bladed Buck sheath knives; six small but powerful flashlights, six hand-held radios. There were also, unaccountably, six toy wooden noisemakers.

Yeho picked up one of the noisemakers and twirled it on its handle so that the wooden gears fluttered a thin strip of wood, creating a subdued but unmistakable sound. "This is a grager, used by the children at Purim—a modified model to make it less noisy," he said. "It's better for signaling than a radio—even fancy Outfit-type encrypted radios like these. The Ja'wabi don't know about Purim, which is the festival of the Jews escaping from Persia in the time of Xerxes, because they'd already left the Land of Israel four hundred years before then. You know what *purim* means in Hebrew?" Christopher shook his head no. Yeho said, "It means 'lots' or 'dice' because the King of Persia cast lots to see whether or not he should massacre the Jews. We did the same in the old days. That's how the Ja'wabi make up their minds about everything to this day—did Zarah tell you about that?"

"Yes."

He wagged a finger. " '*Un coup de dés jamais n'abolira le hasard.*' That means 'a throw of the dice will never eliminate the unexpected.' "

Christopher said, "What does Mallarmé have to do with it?"

"Mallarmé! You're very well read. You remember the poem?"

"Not really. I used to know someone in Vietnam who read that book day and night. Or pretended to."

"Did he take the title seriously?"

"He didn't take anything seriously."

"He must have been a happy man."

Christopher looked at the display of equipment. "This seems like a lot of stuff," he said.

"Just enough," Yeho said. "Watch." He thrust one of the pistols into the waistband of his shorts and stowed everything else in the pockets of his oversize hunting jacket in a matter of seconds. "Everything can easily be carried on the person," Yeho said. "There is also a collapsible sniper's rifle with a laser sight and a silencer, but right now the boys and girls are trying it out on the range at night. That's where they were going. Ja'wab had the rifle broken down inside his shirt and pants legs during dinner. Did you suspect?"

"No."

"They're all very good shots, you might even say amazing. Their hands absolutely do not shake because they don't drink or smoke or use coffee." He lifted his eyebrows. "And, most of all, because they trust the *purim.*"

He handed Christopher one of the pistols. "You know this gun?"

"No."

"It's something new called a Glock—Austrian. The whole thing, almost, is made of plastic. The safety is tricky, so if you're not careful you can shoot yourself in the foot. But it has a special thirty-three round magazine and it takes a very good metal detector to find the gun itself. There are two types of special ammunition. Have a look."

He thumbed two cartridges out of extra-long clips and handed them to Christopher. "The one that looks something like a regular round fires a pure copper bullet weighing ninety grains at just over half a kilometer a second. Copper is a very soft metal, so the bullet has a nylon tip to help it penetrate the target. When this round gets inside the human body the nylon tip peels off and the copper bullet expands to nine times its original caliber, making an internal wound in the shape of an eggplant three inches in diameter and six inches long."

"What's the point of that?"

"Very simple. After this soft copper bullet makes the eggplant, it stops, still inside the body, instead of going right on through and killing a couple of bystanders like a normal Parabellum round."

"Always?"

"Always, unless you're shooting a very skinny person. The copper bullet stays inside, like the stem on the eggplant. This other round—see it?—looks like a brass shotgun shell because that's what it is. It's filled with number eight birdshot. Very small pellets, you'd shoot larks with this shot. When fired from a distance of three meters or more it will lacerate, stun, and shock, but probably not kill."

"What happens if the target is closer than that?"

"Then the shot stays bunched like a bullet with its molecules very far apart, and a direct hit in the heart or a big artery may kill the target. But if you're too close you can aim at the point of the shoulder and usually the target will lose the use of his arm and get a face full of pellets—but survive, if what you want is a disabled enemy instead of a dead one. I hear that used to be your preference."

"It still is, if the idea is to capture these people alive and question them."

"That's the idea. We hope we won't have to use these things. But the other side is armed, and the Ibal Iden are in this to kill their enemies so they themselves can go on living. Hassan is the only one they need to bring back alive."

"And David, presumably."

"They've been told not to shoot at David."

Yeho started to cover up the equipment. Christopher said, "Wait. There's gear for six people here. I count seven Ibal Iden."

Yeho looked up. "You're counting Zarah?"

"Yes."

"Zarah's not part of the assault team," he said.

"I'm glad to hear that."

"She wasn't. Neither were the Ibal Iden. They wanted her with them, and I sympathize. Did she tell you what happened in the desert after her mother and the others were massacred?"

"No."

"She and Ja'wab, just the two of them, tracked the terrorists' vehicles on horseback. They killed the sentries, cut off their heads, threw them into the tent where the others were sleeping, and shot them with the sentries' Kalashnikovs when they came out screaming. Nine altogether. That's how Ja'wab got his name."

While Yeho spoke, the O. G. came into the billiards room.

"This time she's got another job," Yeho said. "Your friend will explain."

12

AFTER LISTENING TO THE O. G., CHRISTOPHER WOKE ZARAH AND asked her a question.

"Yes, that's what they want me to do," she said. "Go to France with David Patchen. That's why I wanted to talk to you."

"I'll tell you whatever you want to know about him," Christopher said. "If I know it myself. But I want you to say no to the O. G. and Yeho about this."

"I've already said yes. They're right. No one but me can do it."

"Then it can be left undone. It's too dangerous."

"The whole thing is dangerous. We knew that from the start. But not as dangerous as letting Hassan Abdallah do what he wants to do."

"All right. I'll use another word. It's foolhardy. If you're with David they won't just grab him. They'll take you, too. They can't do anything else."

"I understand that."

"Understand what?"

"That I may be in captivity for a while."

"With no certainty that you'll ever be released and the knowledge that the people who are holding you can kill you any time they like. Or not kill you. They'll assume that you're from the Outfit and nothing will make them believe otherwise. That means that you're not human in their eyes. That you're less than a Jew. Let me tell you something. You *don't* understand what that's like."

Moonlight shone through the window, but there was no electric light. She groped for his hand. The bed she lay in, with the scratchy covers pulled up to her chin, was a low army cot. The floor and walls were made of splintery unplaned lumber; Spartan accommodations were part of the fun at Camp Panchaea. He leaned over slightly to give her his hand. She pressed it against her cheek for a moment, then released it.

"Turn off the flashlight for a moment," she said. "I want to get dressed."

Christopher went out into the hallway and waited. He was already wearing outdoor clothes because he had gone for a long walk after his conversation with the O. G. In a surprisingly short time Zarah emerged, carrying a jacket and a flashlight of her own.

They went outside. Walking on the grass beside the gravel path, rather than on the noise-making stones, Zarah led him along the trail to the firing range. The target silhouettes at which the Ibal Iden had been firing their Glocks were still in place, a rank of bullet-riddled cartoons with the faces of Bambi and Yogi Bear and Elmer Fudd grinning in the moonlight. They sat down on a sapling bench.

"Was tonight the first you heard about Patchen and me?" Zarah asked.

"Yes," Christopher said. "You mean they told you before you got here?"

"No. I thought I'd be with the others. But I had the impression, when they told me what they wanted me to do, that you knew all about it."

"They said that?"

"No. They didn't even suggest it. It was a feeling."

"And that's why you said yes without talking to me first?"

"No, that's not the reason. But why should I have to talk to you first?"

"Because I'm your father."

"True. But I've only known you in the flesh for a month. I've known the Ja'wabi all my life—longer, according to Lla Kahina. I said yes for them."

"Is that the only reason?"

"I am the enemy of their enemies. What other reason do I need?"

Christopher shrugged and turned away. Zarah gripped his arm.

"Are you thinking that there's some kind of Cathy game going on here?" she asked in a harder tone of voice. "That I'm trying to be like you, trying to duplicate what's happened to you in the past?"

"Are you? I'm not a mind-reader."

"And I'm not my mother."

"I know that. But I remember my own mistakes. And if I'd told your mother how I felt twenty-five years ago—yelled at her, shook her, forbidden her to do some of the things she did—she might be alive today."

"Is that what you think?" Zarah lifted her arm and turned toward him. Her coat, swinging with the movement, thumped against the bench. Christopher realized that she was carrying a pistol in the pocket. She completed the gesture, laying a surprisingly

428

rough palm on his cheek. "Nothing you could have done would have made a bit of difference," she said. "Mother got the life she thought she was destined to live and she lived it. It was the life she wanted. It made her happy. You must know that."

"You're very hard on her."

"You've pointed that out before. But you haven't said I'm wrong." She tossed her head to shake her hair out of her eyes. "And it won't do you any good to yell at me or forbid me to live my life, either," she said. "I'm your daughter, but I'm a lot of other things too. And I'll say it again—I'm not my mother."

"Which part of you wants to go to the Riviera and get itself kidnapped by the Eye of Gaza?"

"That's obvious. The Ja'wabi part. I want to help get Hassan Abdallah."

"And kill him and the rest of the enemies of the Ja'wabi?"

"Yes," Zarah said. "That's right. All of them. Even if we are ten against ten thousand."

"They may kill you instead," Christopher said.

"I know that."

"Are you at all afraid?"

She shook her head. "No."

Christopher believed her; he had believed her grandmother before her.

The plan that the O. G., Patchen, and Yeho had agreed upon was one of the oldest of all ruses, and therefore one of the best. Patchen and Zarah, a beautiful girl many years younger than he was, would be seen together in Washington. Patrick Graham would be led to believe they were lovers, that Patchen had lost his head over her. Then they would go to the Riviera together. If Graham took the bait they were going to offer, he would get word of their whereabouts to the Eye of Gaza, and one or both of them would be kidnapped. The Ibal Iden would follow them, and before drugs could be administered or questioning take place, they would rescue them and seize the kidnappers. There were many other elements of the plan, but these were the essentials.

"You understand," Christopher said to Zarah, "that plans almost never work as they're supposed to, that even Yeho and the O. G. make mistakes, that you're dealing with professionals and the Ibal Iden may not be able to follow you or rescue you, that you may disappear forever. That you may not die for a long time. That under the drug you will tell them what you and Ja'wab did in the desert. That they will go insane when they hear it."

"I understand. And I hear what you're saying to me. Except for the part about the Ibal Iden. Whatever may be wrong with anybody else, they won't fail. Now, please. Enough."

"All right," Christopher said. "What do you want to know about Patchen?"

"Only one thing, really. Why do you trust him?"

"Because he is the only completely sane person I have ever known."

"Sane? With those wounds?"

"Sane because of them, maybe. I didn't know him before it happened."

"Is it true you saved his life on Okinawa?"

Christopher was taken by surprise. "Who told you that?"

"Wolkowicz. He said somebody in Vietnam told him that you carried two wounded Marines back to your own lines under fire. And that one of them was Patchen."

"It's possible that he was one of them," Christopher said. "I've never been sure. We were in the middle of a fire fight. It was dark. His face was blown away. He was delirious from shock and loss of blood. So was I; I'd been hit a couple of times. And then when I got to our perimeter one of our own sentries fired his M1 right into the man I was carrying in my arms. I don't know to this day which one I was carrying when the sentry opened fire, because he shot me, too—the rounds went through the other man's body and hit me. Then Patchen turned up in the next bed in Hawaii with his face in bandages. It seemed impossible, too much of a coincidence, that he could be the same man."

"But you know he was."

"Sometimes I think so. I don't know for sure. Evidently Patchen thinks he was the one. I think he's thought so from the start."

"Then why, if you saved his life, did he hand you over to the Chinese?"

"Who told you that?"

"Barney."

Christopher laughed, explosively. In the moonlight Zarah's face was intense, solemn, filled with suspicion—but plainly not suspicion of Wolkowicz. "He said that Patchen handed you over to the

Chinese to save your life," she said. "He said both sides wanted to kill you because of what you had found out, and a Chinese prison was the one place on earth where the Americans, the Russians, and the Vietnamese couldn't touch you."

"Barney told you that?" Christopher laughed, the loud ha-ha and chortle that was so surprising coming out of a man of such composure.

"Yes, he told me that. Why is it so funny?"

"It's funny," Christopher said, "because it was Barney who did it, and those were his reasons. He was trying to save my life. And, of course, he succeeded."

"Barney *said* that was Patchen's reason. He said that Patchen thought he was saving your life by having you put into prison for life. He kept repeating the sentence: 'Death with twenty years suspension of the execution at solitary forced labor with observation of the results.' I thought it was the most horrible thing I'd ever heard of one person doing to another. Barney said, 'Don't blame him; he did it for love. It's okay to hate him, but you can't blame him.' He *sympathized*. Why would Barney tell me that Patchen did it if he was the one who did it?"

"Barney was never one to take credit for good works," Christopher said. "Whatever you may have thought then, whatever you may still suspect, what Barney told you was a lie. Not about the motive; that was the truth. But it was Barney's motive. He was the one who crashed my plane in China, not Patchen. He was the one who gave me to the Chinese for safekeeping. That's how he knew what he knew about how the traitor felt and why he did what he did. Barney's lies were always versions of the truth. That's why he was so good at what he did, and why he got away with it for such a long time."

"Are you absolutely sure of this?"

"Of the basic facts, yes. No one was ever absolutely sure of anything beyond the facts where Wolkowicz was concerned. He had his own reasons for everything. No wonder you liked him so much as a little girl. So did Stephanie. She says he was the King of the Fibs." Christopher grinned again, shaking his head in a gesture that could easily have been mistaken for affection.

"Are you going to be with me in France?" Zarah asked.

Christopher opened his eyes and looked at her. All resemblance to Lori and Cathy had vanished from her face and body. She was herself and no one else he had ever known.

"Yes," he said. "I'll be there."

On their way back to the lodge, father and daughter stopped for a moment to look at the glassy lake, in which the gibbous moon and some of the brighter stars were now reflected.

"Does this lake have a name?" Zarah asked.

"Can't you guess?" Christopher said. "Mirror Lake. As a boy I swam across it one night with your Grandfather Christopher and the O. G."

"Why?"

"It was something everybody was expected to do. It was a bright night like tonight. All of a sudden a moose swam past us, I suppose Uncle Snowden or one of the other Euhemerians had it shipped down from Maine, and when it got out of the water it stood on the shore looking at us. You could see its reflection in the water, dripping wet, antlers and all, like a photograph of a painting."

"Hubbard was a Euhemerian?"

"Your great-great-grandfather was a charter member—I don't know how, because the first Christophers didn't appear in North America until around 1700. Membership was by inheritance."

"So you're a member?"

"I guess I would be if the club still existed. Hubbard used to bring me deer-stalking in these woods."

"You shot deer?"

"No. I've never killed an animal. We stalked them with bow and arrow. The idea was to get close enough to hit a buck with a blunt arrow."

"Did you ever do that?"

"Once or twice. You have to be able to do it with your eyes closed and think the arrow to the target because the deer will see the movement of your eyelids and run away if you blink."

"Like shooting a pistol. Fire and look."

"Not quite. But almost."

"Did Barney ever swim across the lake?"

Christopher shook his head. "I doubt it. He hated to swim. But he swam across a river in Taiwan once. It was full of crocodiles."

"Crocodiles?" Zarah said. "Tell me."

"Another time."

"No. Now, please."

"All right," Christopher said. "Barney didn't learn to swim until he joined the Army. A connection of ours named Waddy Jessup taught him how during the war, but Waddy had a sense of humor, so instead of teaching Barney the crawl, he taught him an old stroke called the trudgeon that nobody had used since the Spanish-American War. After the war Wolkowicz found himself in Taiwan on an exercise for trainees, fellows who had just joined the Outfit—mostly Ivy Leaguers. One of them was a Waddy type. He'd been on the swimming team at Yale just like Waddy, and when he saw Barney thrashing across the pool with his head way up out of the water it tickled him—the trudgeon looks just like the word sounds. The kidding went on for weeks, and on the last night in camp, when there was a farewell party and a lot of drinking, it came to a head. So Barney said, 'I'll tell you what, Bulldog, if you're such a great fucking swimmer, how about racing me across the river and back for a hundred bucks?' The Yalie accepted the bet. The others were all too drunk to remember the crocodiles, or maybe they thought Barney wouldn't actually do it, but when they got to the river bank Barney jumped right in with all his clothes on and started swimming. There was a very strong current; the water was muddy. The kid stripped and jumped in after him, possibly with the idea of rescuing him, and just as he caught up to Barney, about halfway across, a crocodile pulled him under. Wolkowicz swam on, doing his trudgeon, turned around, and swam back. He'd been so busy pounding the water that he had no idea of what had happened. The others told him."

"What did Barney do?"

"He said, 'Okay, which one of you is holding his wallet?' "

T W O

1

WHEN CHARLOTTE GRAHAM SPOTTED DAVID PATCHEN AND THE LOVELY
young blonde having lunch together at the Age of Enlightenment,
it did not occur to her that it was anything but an innocent
encounter—Patchen obliging some old war horse of the Outfit's
(probably a European, judging by the clothes and manners of the
glorious being who sat next to him on the banquette) by taking his
daughter to a trendy restaurant and paying the bill with secret
funds. How, she wondered, had Patchen even known about this
place? Had Martha told him? Was this tête à tête between beauty
and beast her reward? Charlotte's eyes met the blonde's; they
exchanged brief strangers' smiles. She decided to stop by Patchen's
table on her way out; it never did any harm to have a warm little
chat on the fly with the head of the secret service in full view of a
room filled with Washington climbers.

"She knows we're here," Zarah said to Patchen. "We'd better
look like we're in love."

"Don't you think she'll guess we're acting?" Patchen said.

"Not if our faces register emotion."

"Which one?"

"They all look alike from a distance." She leaned against him
and took his hand. "Tell me, why do you believe that my father
saved your life in the war?"

Patchen's arctic face seemed to break up into a number of floes
and then reassemble itself into a slightly different surface—refrozen
but subtly fretted and fractured beneath the surface.

"Who told you about that?"

"Barney. Father says he's never been sure whether you were the one he rescued or not," Zarah said. "What about you? This is our chance to clear up the mystery. I'll be the detective."

Charlotte watched while Patchen talked and the beauty listened. It was clear from the expressions on both their faces that this was no casual meeting of strangers. Once or twice Patchen seemed to be on the point of tears. The girl took his hand, the useless one, and warmed it between both of hers. Then she whispered something into his ear and they left, arm in arm, before Charlotte could approach them.

"I must say it was very odd, seeing that creature being fondled by a girl like that," Charlotte told Patrick Graham that evening as they changed for dinner. "It was altogether too Frankenstein-meets-Snow White. D'you suppose old David is having a bit of that delicious stuff on the side? It must be very dear."

Patrick boomed out his reply; they were conversing across the length of the bedroom through the open doors of their dressing rooms. "You think he'd cheat on that sweet little wife of his? Come on."

"He's quite alone and fancy-free, you know. Martha's gone back to Guatemala or wherever it is to rejoin her drunken Indians. She called me to say goodbye; I thought that was rather sweet."

"Who is this sexy girl?"

"I have no idea. They'd never seen her before at the Age, and I'm quite sure they would have remembered if they had. To give you an idea of the type, the waiters all thought she was the ghost of Madeleine Carroll; they're old movie fans, it's part of their customer chat."

Patrick Graham appeared in the doorway of his wife's dressing room, tying the silk polka-dot tie from Sulka that was his trademark. "I'll cause inquiries to be made," he said.

They dined that night at Ristorante Cerruti, an unfashionable little place in Alexandria, because the people they were entertaining, a propagandist for the Sendero Luminoso ("Shining Path") guerrilla movement in Peru and her live-in collaborator, an unkempt *National Geographic* staff writer, were not interesting enough to invite home. Also, Graham adored the many kinds of peppery sausages that were the specialty of the chef, his old friend Giacomo Pazzo. He preferred soft food; early in his television career one of his capped teeth had broken off as he chewed a steak sandwich an hour before going on the air, and he had been cautious ever since.

To their surprise, Patchen and the blonde arrived soon after the Grahams were seated and were shown to a corner table.

"I see what you mean," Graham said.

Charlotte's eyes sparkled with the joy of the born gossip. The couple's behavior was as she had described it. They were utterly absorbed in each other. The Grahams could not, of course, hear what Patchen and Zarah were saying on the other side of the babbling crowd, but in fact they were discussing the way in which Ja'wab and Zarah had slaughtered the terrorists.

"Why did just the two of you go?" Patchen asked.

"The rest were needed to defend Tifawt in case it was attacked."

"Yeho says you decapitated the guards after you killed them."

"Not really. Ja'wab used a strangling wire. It cuts through everything but the bone. Even that if you saw a little."

"How did he manage to get behind them?"

"It was a problem because the moon was full. We used a pincers movement. I went in front, he went behind. Then I rose up out of the desert, practically at their feet, and while they were distracted, he attacked."

"Why didn't they shoot you?"

"I think it was the element of surprise. When the Ibal Iden enter an enemy camp at night they always take off all their clothes. They used to believe that a naked person was invisible to his enemies."

"Is that true, on the basis of your experience?"

"No."

Graham watched them closely while avoiding the eyes of the chattering Peruvian, who had renounced her Spanish names because they had originally belonged to imperialist rapists and insisted on simply being called "La Senderista"; her boyfriend called her "Sendy."

"The ultimate objective of the Shining Path movement is to eradicate all stains of the colonial experience, including the existing bourgeoisie, thus restoring Peru's original and unique culture and people," La Senderista said.

Graham did not hear her.

"Sounds rather like what the Khmers Rouges did in Cambodia," Charlotte said.

"Except that we will steadfastly carry out our program to the logical end," said La Senderista.

"You mean you plan to kill *everybody*?" Charlotte said. "I bope you're in touch with the IRA; it sounds just the thing for Ireland."

No one thought that she was joking. The *National Geographic* man, stirring his third Negroni with a stiff forefinger, nodded judiciously. La Senderista, eyes blazing with conviction, drew breath and continued with the indoctrination. Graham continued to stare across the room like a man hypnotized. It seemed to him that Patchen's blonde emitted a post-coital glow; it reminded him of the sensuous, half-contemptuous, half-inviting look of an expensive cat after stretching.

"She looks like somebody we know," Graham said to his wife. "But it's not Madeleine Carroll."

He sent a bottle of fifteen-year-old Vino Nobile de Montepulciano, the most expensive Italian wine on the list, to Patchen's table. On the way out, quite soon afterward, he stopped to chat, sending La Senderista and her slow-witted boyfriend ("Who's that?" he had asked when Graham and Patchen lifted their glasses to each other, causing La Senderista to snarl like a jaguar) outside under Charlotte's care.

"Patrick Graham," he said heartily, extending his hand, as if the wholly superfluous gesture of identifying himself were proof of his democratic modesty.

"Hello, Patrick," Patchen replied.

The girl said nothing and Patchen made no move to introduce her.

"I didn't quite catch your name," Graham said.

Patchen remained silent. Zarah said, "Zarah Christopher."

"*That's* who you look like—Paul Christopher. My wife and I have been racking our brains. What's the relationship?"

"He's my father."

"You're Christopher's daughter?" Graham was genuinely surprised and let it show. "I didn't know you existed."

Zarah smiled up at him with Paul Christopher's aloof, well-bred smile, as if, Graham thought, she were being polite to the Invisible Man.

"Well, now that you do know, I do exist, obviously," she said.

2

DORCAS HAD SOME DIFFICULTY IN ARRANGING AN APPOINTMENT between Patrick Graham and Stephanie Christopher. Finally, after refusing invitations to breakfast at the Hay-Adams Hotel and luncheon at the Lion d'Or, Stephanie agreed to drinks after work at Joe and Mo's. They sat in a front corner, beneath the framed and autographed dust jackets of Graham's books. He and Stephanie had known each other before he was famous; he had recruited her for his Maoist cell in the East Village after the original small black-haired girl, the one he had loved, defected from it in order to marry Julian Hubbard. He admired Stephanie. Of all the look-alike diminutive brunettes Graham had collected over the years to service his obsession, Stephanie was the only one he had been unable to get into bed. She was also the brightest and toughest and most skeptical. In the Maoist cell he had believed that she refused him because she was a lesbian, but he subsequently learned that she had known Emily at school, where they were sometimes mistaken for sisters, and understood what he was up to. Now, however, it was his secret opinion that she had never slept with anyone except Christopher, that she had been waiting for him even then. It was certainly true that she had pounced on Christopher, despite the difference in their ages and political sentiments, almost as soon as he stepped off the plane from China.

They both ordered carbonated mineral water. Graham lifted his glass, and said, "Power to the people," their toast from the old days. Then, after swallowing, he came directly to the point. "I didn't know that your husband had a grown-up daughter," he said.

"Really?"

"Really. She looks just like him. What's the story?"

"The usual, Patrick. Her mother got pregnant and nine months later out came Zarah."

"Who was her mother?"

"Someone Paul married and divorced when I was a child. She's dead."

"Did you know her?"

"Very slightly."

"Was she a German, too?"

"She was a Southern belle. I'm in a hurry, Patrick. What's this all about?"

"So is her daughter. *Belle,* I mean." Graham smiled and batted his eyes in mocking imitation of the flirtatious unliberated females of a bygone age. "Unless I'm reading you wrong, old friend, and I don't think I am, you didn't like wifey *número uno* one little bit. Or is this retroactive jealousy? What was her name?"

"What difference does it make? What are you up to, Patrick?"

"Why should I be up to anything? I'm sure Paul has forgotten all about this kid's mother even if she was as big a knockout as the daughter. I would if I were in his shoes. The greatest regret of my life is that you and I never . . ."

Stephanie started to slide along the banquette. Graham seized the strap of her shoulder bag to stop her from leaving.

"Don't go yet," he said. "Stay and talk. You of all people know how good it is for the lovelorn to get it all out. Come on, tell the nice doctor—what *was* she like?"

"Cathy was just a normal, old-fashioned American girl," Stephanie said. "All she wanted was twenty-one orgasms a week, a hundred thousand dollars a year in spending money, and total and unquestioned control over the actions, speech, and thoughts of the lucky man who was providing these things for her."

"Sounds like a pretty good deal. Which part of it did Christopher fail to live up to?"

"Goodbye, Patrick."

He let go of her purse. "You're really pissed off about something, aren't you?" he said. "It can't be me you're mad at because I've never done anything to you. Literally. So it must be Zarah. Let me tell you what I think. I think your stepdaughter is fucking David Patchen."

By now Stephanie was standing up. "I'm practically sure of it," Graham continued in a voice audible in every corner of the restaurant. "What does it all mean? *That* is the question."

Stephanie tossed her hair from her face and stared at him with withering contempt. Graham, smiling amiably in return, felt a pang of nostalgia. She didn't look a day older than she had looked as a Movement chick. She still wore her hair in a mop, she still dressed with no regard to bourgeois style, she still peered through her tresses with those burning hostile eyes. Sixties eyes. And she was sleeping her life away with an old spy. *What a waste.* Well, her life wasn't yet over and neither was his. Graham lifted his glass of sparkling water in a toast.

"Here's to dangerous liaisons," he said.

"Patrick," she said. "You really are an asshole, do you know that?"

STEPHANIE, SITTING CROSS-LEGGED ON THE RUMPLED SHEETS, SWITCHED
on the bedside lamp and looked down into Christopher's face. She
was naked; nudity seemed somehow to complete the atmosphere of
total frankness she strove for. Her face was troubled and angry.

"Something's happened to you," she said. "You're not the same."

Christopher said, "Yes, we've just got through discussing that."

They had just made love, but before that they had talked for
hours. She knew every detail of Christopher's conversations with
Lla Kahina and Sir Richard Shaw-Condon. Their revelations had
horrified Stephanie, not in and of themselves, because descriptions
of human behavior never shocked her out of her clinical detachment, but because of what she feared they might do to Christopher.
She had always thought that he needed professional help to come
to terms with the disappearance of his mother; he had always
refused to talk about it to anyone but her.

"I'm not talking about your mother," Stephanie said. "This has
to do with you and me. You've changed. You were like a stranger
when we were making love just now. You were *evading* me; I could
feel it. Something is going on with you. I know it."

She was right. Christopher did not know how to explain it to her.
In the middle of the act he had suddenly realized that his wife's
body was not the one he had imagined himself making love to. The
feeling was so strong that he drew back to look at her. He had
expected to see Cathy, or Molly, or even Lê—anyone but the
familiar woman whose face he recognized on the pillow. Stephanie,
the physical Stephanie, was an intruder in this fantasy, and he
forced himself to remember who she was and where in time he was.
This strange, faintly pornographic trick of the mind surprised him
as much as it distressed Stephanie. Only once before, shortly after
his return from China, had anything like it happened to him. The
first time he made love to Stephanie (or, more accurately, the first
time she had made love to him; he had done little more than
acquiesce in what she obviously regarded as an act of healing),
Molly had hidden in Stephanie's body and he had believed—only
for a moment, but with every nerve in his own body—that she was
with him again even though she had been dead for more than ten
years. But always after that he had kept her ghost at bay.

Stephanie had been watching Christopher's face as it registered these thoughts. "Is there someone else?" she said. "If there is, tell me. We can deal with it."

"It's not as simple as that," Christopher said. "It's a whole roomful of others."

"What?"

He told her what had been in his mind. Relief, then sympathy, then reassurance flooded into her face.

"There's nothing so bizarre about that," she said. "People fantasize all the time."

"I wouldn't call this a fantasy. It was involuntary."

"Whatever you want to call it, you suppressed it. Why?"

"Because thinking about one woman while making love to another is a betrayal of both."

Stephanie raised her eyebrows. "Double infidelity?"

"You could call it that."

"Oh, Paul!" Stephanie smiled for the first time that evening, wagging her tousled head. "Who but you would invent a scruple like that?" Now she did giggle. "Is fighting off the memory of all these ex-wives and lovers a constant struggle for you?"

"No. No more so than any other form of fidelity is a struggle. You just put temptation out of your mind."

"It's impossible to put *anything* out of your mind, as you've just found out. All you do is repress it."

It was Christopher's turn to be amused; psychology was a religion to Stephanie, and her certitude always entertained him. He said, "And then one night when you open the closet door, there it is among the clothes-hangers, grinning at you out of horrible empty eye sockets."

"Exactly," Stephanie said. "Go ahead and make fun—that's just another form of repression. The question is, why is this happening to you? Do you have any idea?"

"I think I do, yes. But let me hear what you think."

"All right," Stephanie said. "I'll tell you what I think. You haven't left me, you've left the man you are now and gone in search of the one you used to be. You've gone back to the past, to a time when I wasn't in your life. That's why you didn't know who I was just now."

She was right. Christopher knew it. He said, "Go on."

"Prison was like the grave for you. You died in China because you were sure they were going to kill you, and then David Patchen brought you back to life. And now the past has come for you again—first Zarah, materializing out of thin air, then these revelations about your mother. It's no wonder you're disoriented."

Christopher was amused again. "Doctor Webster-Christopher explains it all."

"Go ahead and scoff," Stephanie said. "But this is not the next world, Paul, even if you have found more happiness in it than you think you have coming to you. I'll tell you something else I suspect: You've gotten yourself mixed up with the Outfit again. True or false?"

"True."

He told her everything he knew about the Beautiful Dreamers operation. She understood each nuance of the plan. Stephanie had been born into the Outfit. She knew how the game was played, and what motivated the players.

"Why, for God's sake?" Stephanie asked.

"Old debts," Christopher replied.

"Bullshit. You don't owe David or the O. G. or the Outfit anything. Remember what happened to you; the Outfit did that. Remember the facts of the case."

"I do remember. This is something else."

"How can you say that? It's always the same. It's always crazy. David will be tortured and killed. So will all the rest of them, probably. They'll never get away with it."

"Probably not," Christopher said.

"Then why are you helping them?"

"You know why."

"Because you think you can take care of Zarah?"

"In a word, yes."

Stephanie snorted. "You actually think she needs you? I'd say that anybody who goes around cutting off people's heads in the Sahara Desert doesn't need her daddy's protection."

"I'm going to be there anyway."

"Why, for God's sake? Isn't knowing what these psychopaths did to your mother and you and your father enough for you?"

"You think that Zarah is a psychopath?"

"I'm not even going to respond to that," Stephanie said. "If you want to behave like a father, then forbid Zarah to go on this mad expedition. Lock her in her room. But don't give her the keys to the car and then drive off the cliff with her." Stephanie's tone was reasonable, even conversational. She was no longer angry. She said, "You won't be able to control what happens to Zarah any more than you could control what happened to your mother."

"Maybe not," Christopher said. "But this time at least I'll be with her to the end."

"*Be* with her or die with her? Are you sure which you mean? Which you want?"

"Come on, Stephanie."

"Then what *do* you want? What about me? What about your other child? Is knowing the dead all that matters to you?"

"Not the dead. The truth."

"You think there's a difference in your case? It *is* all that matters to you. It always has been."

Christopher was smiling no longer. "You're entitled to your theories. But what if it were Lori? Would you say the same things then as you say to me now about Zarah?"

It was not like Stephanie to cry, but when Christopher spoke these words, first one tear and then another coursed down her cheek.

"That's not fair," she said.

"I know," Christopher replied. "But let me tell you something. You say I died in some symbolic way in China, but China came twenty years too late."

"You mean your life stopped when the Gestapo led your mother away. I know that. That's why you can't admit she's dead forty years later."

"Longer," Christopher said.

"Because if she's dead," Stephanie said, "then you are too."

Christopher was so silent that Stephanie was not sure that he had heard what she said. Finally he said, "Molly used to say that the dead know everything. All I can say is, I hope not."

4

TO ANALYZE THE DRUG SAMPLE COLLECTED BY YEHO'S TEAM, PATCHEN called on a retired Outfit scientist who now worked in a private medical laboratory in the suburbs.

"It appears to be a drug called Versed," he told Patchen.

" 'Appears to be' or is?" Patchen said.

"Is. Chemical name, midazolam hydrochloride. It's a benzo-diazepine from the same family of tranquilizers as Valium, but much more powerful."

"What are the effects?"

"It depresses the central nervous system. When administered in sufficiently large doses it induces euphoria, suggestibility, and a tremendous sense of cooperativeness. The subject will do anything. Anything. The beauty part is, it's hangover free. The subject doesn't remember a thing that he did or said afterward or have the slightest feelings of guilt or remorse."

"Is there an antidote?"

"In an unscientific manner of speaking, Versed in big doses *is* an antidote to the natural responses of the brain. It turns off the conscience."

"Can it be overcome with another drug?"

"In theory, yes. Amphetamines might work. But no sane person would administer them for that purpose."

"Why?"

"Because you'd probably kill the patient. Or worse. You could stop the heart or damage the brain and turn the patient into a vegetable."

"But if you accept the risk, how would you do it?"

"Ideally, by intravenous drip, being super-careful to balance the two drugs against each other in minute, scrupulously measured doses."

"That's impossible if you're trying to conceal what you're doing from the people who are administering the Versed. How else?" Patchen had already been considering this problem. "What about an implant," he said, "one of those things they put under the skin of diabetics to release timed doses of insulin?"

"If, as I say, you're willing to take the chance of killing the subject, it might work," the scientist replied. "But it would be imprecise—and I say again, very, very dangerous."

"How is the dosage of Versed decided?"

"Like everything else. By body weight and the effects desired."

"Then you could calculate that dosage and balance it with an anti-dosage of amphetamine in the implant."

"In theory, yes. But as far as I know, no one has ever tried anything resembling this on a human subject."

"That's not a problem," Patchen said. "We're dealing with a

volunteer. How long would it take to run a test on an animal and prepare an implant on the basis of the results?"

"Not long. But I wouldn't do it, David. Really I wouldn't."

"The subject weighs a hundred and seventy-three pounds," Patchen said. "I need the implant, fully loaded, by this time tomorrow."

Patchen went to New York and took the elevator to the top floor of a building on Park Avenue. It was Saturday morning, and most of the offices were closed. He walked down the corridor until he found the number he was looking for on a door marked PRIVATE, then knocked. Red Conaghan opened the door at once. He was white-haired now and fleshier than he had been as a Navy surgeon. He was dressed for golf in bright pastels.

"Cary Grant," he said. "I'd have known you anywhere."

"You haven't changed all that much, either, Doc," Patchen replied.

They sat down, Conaghan behind a desk crowded with photographs of his many children and grandchildren, Patchen in the patient's chair. The office was brilliantly lighted—an aid, Patchen supposed, to Conaghan's first impression of candidates for cosmetic surgery. According to Patchen's research, he specialized in breasts, backsides, and bellies. They had made him rich.

"I've read about you in the papers over the years," Conaghan said. "Christopher, too. Even I was young in those days. *'That is no country for old men. The young/In one another's arms, birds in the trees . . .'* Christopher knew his Yeats. Does he still read poetry?"

"Writes it, even."

"I suspected him of something like that way back in Hawaii. However, I didn't foresee the exciting careers the two of you have had. You never can tell about the future. What can I do for you?"

"Some minor surgery."

Patchen told him what he wanted, displaying the implant as he spoke. It was designed to dispense medication on a timed basis, and could be activated by breaking a glass ampule.

"What are you going to do, bang yourself on the chest, *mea culpa*?" Conaghan asked.

Patchen explained; Conaghan listened without expression. When Patchen was through he asked a question.

"How's your health? As a kid you had an amazing heart. It just wouldn't stop. Otherwise you'd be dead and buried on Okinawa. Is it still pumping away like old times?"

"Yes."

"Good. You're going to need it if you go through with this."

Patchen handed him an envelope. "I've brought you this. It's a complete medical history."

Conaghan put on reading glasses and scanned it. It was many pages long. "I'll tell you what," he said. "Go through that door. Take off your shirt and lie down on the table. I'll be in as soon as I finish reading."

In the examining room, he looked Patchen over at length, listening to his heart, taking his blood pressure, fingering his scars. No one had touched them since the last time Conaghan himself had done so, more than thirty years before.

"Funny, I remember the whole topography," Conaghan said. "I wish you'd come to see me after the war. We could have done something about this. You say you want the squirter in your chest about there?" He touched Patchen.

"That's right," Patchen said. "Can you hide it under an old scar?"

"In your case, that's no problem."

"Do you have any other problem with all this?"

"No. It's your body. But don't you guys have your own secret doctors?"

"I'd rather have this done by an outsider. Will you do it?"

Conaghan looked down at Patchen's ruined face and torso. "Sure," he said. "Why not? It's the least I can do, considering what I wasn't able to do for you forty years ago in Hawaii."

"You understand that lives depend on your taking this secret to the grave with you?"

"To the grave?" Conaghan, filling a hypodermic needle, glanced toward Patchen and grinned delightedly. "Jesus, is that the way you guys talk?" he said. "This is better than the movies." He jabbed Patchen with the needle. "The answer is, you don't exist," he said, in Jimmy Cagney accents. "You never come here; I never seen you. Relax, copper. You won't feel a thing."

The procedure took only a few minutes. Patchen, wide awake and lucid, watched in a mirror.

"I've never seen anything like this rig before," Conaghan said, examining the implant. His eyes danced behind the goggles. "Diabolically clever," he said, slipping the device through a tiny incision.

5

ON THAT SAME SATURDAY MORNING, LESS THAN EIGHT HOURS BE-
fore air time for his show, Patrick Graham received another Beautiful Dreamers tape. The network refused to let him use it on the
air.

"Why the hell not?" he asked the vice president in charge of the
news division.

"Because we've been burned once."

"That's Outfit disinformation and you know it."

"I know we've got a hundred million dollar lawsuit to settle with
a one-armed Mormon war hero. Besides, it's boring."

"Boring? It's a trip through the belly of the beast."

"Beast? What beast?"

"The Outfit. The whole rotten Establishment."

The vice president sighed theatrically over the car phone. They
were talking Mercedes to Mercedes while Graham raced to the
studio on the outskirts of Washington and the vice president drove
to his tennis game in Westport, Connecticut. "Patrick," he said,
'the Cold War is over; it's yesterday's news."

"You may think so. I don't."

"I know you don't. The audience knows it, too. Once in a while
you should ask yourself if that's good."

"Until a minute ago nobody ever said it was bad."

"They pay me to be impolite. Even your audience doesn't *like*
terrorists who kidnap Americans. Neither do sponsors. This is not
ratings-positive material. The answer is 'no.' No more mysterious
tapes. No more one-armed Mormons. No more heroic Arabs. No.
No. Do you hear what I'm saying to you?"

"Clear as a bell. You're saying you're afraid of the popularity of
that dim-witted Republican in the White House. You're asking me
to sell out. I won't do it. Do you hear what I'm saying to *you?"*

"Oh, Patrick, spare me. You'll do what you're told. Have a nice
day."

The vice president broke the connection. Dorcas, who had been
listening in and making notes, said, "What will you do?"

"Say 'too bad' and bide my time," Graham said. "Like the
Russian general in *For Whom the Bell Tolls. La guerre n'est pas
finie* until *we* say so."

THE O.G. CAUSED DISCREET INQUIRIES TO BE MADE UNTIL HE DISCOV-
ered someone who had invited the Grahams to a cocktail party on
Sunday afternoon. The hostess was happy to invite the O. G., too,
when a mutual friend called and asked for the favor.

At the party, held in a plywood-and-stone-veneer facsimile of a
French manor house in McLean, Virginia, the O. G. sipped his
usual plain tomato juice and chatted easily with any number of
strangers while confidently waiting for Patrick Graham to approach
him.

"Patrick Graham." The firm handshake.

"By golly, so it is," said the O. G. "I thought that looked like
you talking to Justice Corash over in the corner. Splendid fellow,
Corash; fine American."

Corash was a conservative member of the Supreme Court who
consistently voted against Graham's beliefs.

"If you like pterodactyls," Graham said.

The O. G. went on as if he had not heard this witticism. "How
are you?" he asked. "How is your lady wife?"

"Charlotte will be disappointed to have missed you," Graham
replied." She's got a touch of the flu tonight."

"Bad luck. What does an announcer do when he gets flu? How
do you keep from coughing and sneezing on the air?"

"The network has vets who fix us up with shots before we go on,
like race horses or professional football players."

" 'Vets?' That's a bitter one, my lad."

"It's a bitter world when it comes to bosses and workers,"
Graham said. "Loyalty up and loyalty down are things of the past.
Even your man David Patchen was telling me that he'd swap the
crew he has for the staff of the *Washington Post* anytime."

"Did he? Jehoshaphat! That's quite a statement."

"I don't think he'd have too many takers. What about you?
Would you have made a trade like that if life were baseball?"

"In my day? No, I don't think so. Back then, of course, we were
getting most of the bright-eyed and bushy-tailed types out of the
best schools that now apply to places like the *Post.* As you say,
times change."

"So do perceptions of what constitutes honorable employment."

"How true. When did you last catch sight of David?"

"Not long ago. Right after I broke the story about the Outfit kidnappings. There's been more than one. Did you know that?"

"More than one of those tapes? By George, I hope not. One was enough. David was pretty upset, but I suppose he told you that."

"Upset? Really? He didn't say anything to me about that."

"He didn't?" the O. G. said. "That's funny. You drove him right out of town with that broadcast of yours."

"I did?"

"Yes. Poor fellow went on vacation. Shocked them out of their socks over at the Outfit. It's the first time he's taken a day of annual leave since he came to work more than thirty years ago."

"Good Lord, I had no idea. Where did he go?"

"What? I have a hard time hearing at these things with everybody chattering in the background. Can't smell or taste or feel a pretty knee at full power anymore, either. That's what they mean when they say you're losing your senses. Don't grow old, Patrick, that's my advice. But I guess you don't have to worry. One of those vets can fix you up with an elixir. Nice to see you."

The O. G. started to turn away. Graham caught at his sleeve. "I said, 'Where did he go?' "

"Who?"

"David Patchen."

"Oh, David. He went to the south of France. Borrowed a house up in the hills near Grasse. Lovely country. The French eat larks in country restaurants at this time of year."

"Do you know where, exactly? Clive Wilmot has a place in that neck of the woods, in a great little *village perché* called Spéracèdes. Did he borrow Clive's place?"

"*Clive's* place? No, I don't think he'd do that."

Graham looked to left and right to make sure others weren't listening; there were other journalists in the room.

He leaned closer to the O. G. "Did he take Christopher's daughter with him?"

The O. G., visibly shocked by the question, took a step backward.

"Well," Graham said. "Did he or didn't he?"

The O. G. shook his head. "You're a rum fellow, Patrick," he said. "Very rum. Got to go. It's been a treat talking to you."

7

GRAHAM, KNOWING THAT HE HAD HIT HOME WITH THESE UNANSWERED questions, left the party, too. He called Dorcas on the car phone.

"It says on your resumé that you speak French," he said. "Do you?"

"Sort of."

"Do you or don't you?"

"Yes, but not like a native. I took four years of it at Dartmouth and spent half my junior year in Grenoble."

"Good. Pack a bag for a week. Bring your passport. Bring them with you to the house. We've got work to do. And then you're going traveling."

Four days later, after many frustrating interviews with locals who spoke French with what sounded to Dorcas like an impenetrable Italian accent, she wandered by chance into the market place in Grasse and saw David Patchen and Zarah Christopher shopping. They bought twelve *spéciales de portugaises* oysters, a small sea bass, string beans, strawberries, a whole goat cheese, and half a dozen bottles of ordinary Provençal wine. They behaved like lovers, holding hands and making jokes.

Dorcas, while pretending to take pictures of the market scene, recorded their every action with the small video camera Graham had given her. She then followed their car over winding country roads to a secluded house below a town called Saint Vallier. Dorcas could see Zarah kissing Patchen through the rear window, and when the two of them got out of the car, they kissed again, passionately, with the groceries crushed between them. Dorcas taped this, too, panning to the sign on the driveway, "LA CADÈN-IÈRE," to the house itself, and all around the horizon to show the magnificent view of the Mediterranean below and the quaint hilltop village above; she even photographed the red-and-white milestone showing the rural route number and the number of kilometers to Grasse.

All this took some time. While she photographed, Dorcas blocked the narrow road with her car, but the people in the car behind her, a handsome man about her own age accompanied by two girls, all of them small and dark and exotic looking, did not seem to mind. She waved an apology; the others smiled forgivingly as if to say, "How charming! A pretty American madcap with a video camera, recording the beauties of Provence!" She almost photographed *them*: the man had the most startling green eyes set in a hawk's face.

Two nights later Patrick Graham ran Dorcas's footage, edited and enhanced, on his Saturday show. It was, he said, taken by a tourist with a home video camera who happened to recognize Patchen in the market of this small French city named for the counts and marquises of Grasse-Tilly, one of whom had commanded the French fleet at the Battle of Yorktown. (This historical reference, he thought, provided an almost subliminal patriotic note, in case the vice president for news had anything to say on that subject.) In order to explain who Zarah was Graham had to rerun some film from an old show about the Christophers. With excerpts from the Beautiful Dreamers tape spliced in, a couple of interviews with academics who specialized in intelligence matters, and a chat with a former Outfit clerk who had written an exposé of his old organization and then taken up residence in a Scandinavian country that Graham did not identify, it made an interesting twelve-minute segment.

That night Graham brought a magnum of Dom Perignon champagne with him when he got into bed with Dorcas. They replayed the show on tape while they drank the wine.

"How do you like being a spy of the people?" Graham asked. He poured a full glass of Dom Perignon, which cost a hundred dollars a magnum, between her breasts.

"It's not boring," Dorcas replied. "*Definitely* not boring."

8

BECAUSE THE CLOCK WAS SIX HOURS LATER IN THE MARITIME ALPS than in Washington, "Patrick Graham Live" came on the satellite at two o'clock in the morning. Christopher taped the show in the farmhouse in the Préalpes de Grasse that he was using as a command post. Half a mile down the mountain, Zarah and Patchen were asleep inside another farmhouse. Chistopher stepped onto the terrace and whirled the child's noisemaker that Yeho had provided; the Ibal Iden who were guarding the house replied in the same manner. The others were deployed in cars along the Route Napoléon to watch the highway approaches. He went back inside, leaving the door open, and waited in the dark. Patchen's Doberman slept contentedly at Christopher's feet. He knew the animal, and in the last week it had been trained to obey him—up to a point. It would come, stay, find, sit, and lie down at his command, but it would only attack on Patchen's orders, or to protect Patchen if he was unconscious. After a moment it lifted its head and growled. Ja'wab, smiling as usual, stepped through the open door.

"They should have no trouble finding us," he said, after watching the tape.

"No," Christopher said. "I want to talk to Patchen and Zarah tomorrow morning in Nice. Keep up your watch on the house until morning. Then get everybody in the cars and string them out to cover their car. Make sure everybody has a full tank and ten liters extra in a can. You know the rules."

The cars, six of them, were changed every other day at rental agencies in Cannes, Nice, and Monte Carlo. On the following morning, Monday, Christopher drove to the Nice Airport and turned in his car, then took the bus along the beachfront and rented another with one of the false driver's licenses and national identity cards Yeho had provided; one of his Geneva retirees was a forger. A mile from the rental agency, Christopher parked the car at a meter, walked through narrow streets for fifteen minutes, and, finally, dialed a number in Annecy from a pay phone on the street. Yeho answered on the first ring, speaking German. They exchanged the false names and the meaningless phrases which were that day's recognition code. Christopher had not gone through these motions in more than twenty years, and like a victim of seasickness stepping aboard a docked vessel, he tasted the acid memory of other voyages.

"I'm in a terrible mood," Yeho said. "Last night the man in the next apartment was watching television so I couldn't sleep. You could hear it through the wall."

"What a pity," Christopher said, knowing that one of Yeho's team in Geneva had managed to plant a listening device in Hassan Abdallah's apartment, a tiny transmitter that slipped into one of the holes in an electrical outlet but was powerful enough to pick up conversations two rooms away. Yeho's collaborator inside the laboratory had been induced to plant another transmitter in the wall plug in Hassan's office.

"So," Yeho said. "How would it be if I come down for the weekend?"

"We can accommodate you easily. Just you, or will you bring friends?"

"My friends are still making up their minds, but I'll keep you informed of their plans. Oh, I almost forgot. I'll bring the pictures from the beach. Some of them came out very well."

They repeated the code words to signal that all was well:

"*Wunderschön!*"

"*Lebe wohl!*"

9

BEFORE LUNCH, CHRISTOPHER MET PATCHEN AND ZARAH IN THE archeological museum at Cimiez, the site of a Roman settlement at Nice. As he arrived Christopher saw Ja'wab and Dimya drive by in opposite directions; another pair of Ibal Iden, too far away to identify, wandered through the ruins of a Roman arena. Inside the museum, at this hour and season, the three Americans were quite alone with a single elderly guard and the dusty displays of Roman pottery, coins, and jewelry. They paused before a marble statue said to be that of Antonia, a niece of Augustus.

Christopher told them about "Patrick Graham Live" and his telephone conversation with Yeho Stern.

"Where is Hassan Abdallah?"

"According to Yeho, still in Geneva. Of course he may have helpers, coming from someplace else, that we don't know about."

"When is Yeho estimating contact?"

"He isn't. Not yet. But if the pattern holds it will happen Thursday or Friday."

"Do you think the pattern will hold?"

"No. I think it will happen very soon, and very suddenly."

"Why do you think that?"

"I have a feeling."

"*A feeling?*" Patchen said. "This does seem like old times." He had always made fun of Christopher's intuition.

Christopher shrugged. "Be logical, then. They won't want to take a chance on missing you. If you know what was on the Graham show, you'll leave the country immediately. That's what any sane man in your position would do. And then there are the French. If they saw the show, with that shot of the milestone at the

453

end of your driveway, they're going to flood the neighborhood with cops. That means they can't afford to wait."

"You don't think they're going to spot Zarah's schoolmates and suspect a trap?"

"That won't stop them."

"You have the Ibal Iden scattered one to a car. They're vulnerable."

"That's true. On the other hand, if the opposition decides to attack they'll have to catch them and kill them one at a time, and I doubt that they've got the manpower or the time for that. They'll snatch and run. We have to observe the snatch, follow you to your destination, watch the place where they take you, and wait for Hassan to show up. Then all we have to do is get you back."

"Good summation," Patchen said. "Good luck." He uttered a short laugh and walked to the other side of the room, leaving Zarah and Christopher in privacy.

Zarah linked arms with her father. He could feel the life in her body. They could see their reflections in the glass of the showcase, and Patchen's charcoal figure in the background.

"How strong is this feeling of yours?" she asked.

"Very strong," Christopher said, tasting nausea again. "I don't like it."

"I think we'd better trust it anyway," she said. "Don't worry. Everything will be all right."

"You're sure of that?"

She looked directly into his eyes and smiled. "Absolutely," she said. "As sure as if I'd seen it all happen before."

She kissed him, something she had never done before in real life.

10

THE EYE OF GAZA TOOK PATCHEN AND ZARAH THIRTY MINUTES LATER just beyond Vence, where the road descends through the gorges of the River Loup in a series of sharp switchbacks. It was very professionally done, with one car pulling out in front of Patchen, causing him to brake, and another, proceeding in the opposite direction, swerving wildly to avoid a collision and ending up crosswise to the road so that Patchen was blocked front and rear. The drivers of the other two cars leaped out, shouting excitedly in the fashion of outraged French motorists. As they approached, Patchen punched himself in the chest, breaking the ampule of amphetamine inside the implant. Less than a second later the terrorists smashed the windows and injected them, painlessly, at the base of the skull with what they knew must be Versed. The terrorists stepped back and smiled, waiting for the drugs to take effect. Patchen and Zarah, awash in chemical happiness, smiled back cheerfully and opened the doors themselves.

Christopher, in position behind Patchen's car, observed all this from the next higher switchback. By the time he reached the scene, Patchen and Zarah were already in the other cars and one of the terrorists was driving off in their car. Both wore the same look of wonder and delight as all the other Beautiful Dreamers. The road was still half-blocked; Christopher blew his horm impatiently while glaring at the terrorists from behind his rolled-up window. Above them, Kbira took advantage of the diversion to photograph the scene with a miniature Japanese video camera identical to the one Dorcas had used. Christopher drove on.

The Ibal Iden, strung out along ten kilometers of mountain road at all the key intersections, had no difficulty in following the kidnappers through the Clues Haute de Provence and the gorges along the River Var to a stone *mas* built into a mountainside at the end of a gravel track far back in the Maritime Alps. As soon as it was dark Ja'wab and the other males drifted down the mountain and surrounded the house, keeping watch while Kbira and Dimya rigged radio-controlled bombs and homing devices on each of the terrorists' cars. Then the girls sank into the ground, too. They had no trouble operating in this steep, parched country with its snowcooled winds. It reminded them of the Idáren Dráren.

THREE

1

AS HE RECEDED INTO HIS OWN PAST ON THE WINGS OF THE DRUG,
Patchen grew younger and younger and smaller and smaller. He
felt that this rewinding of his life must end at the moment of
conception, when sperm penetrated egg and created the micro-
scopic Patchen. This event and its meaning were blindingly clear to
him. He had been unwounded then, perfect, the receptacle of all
information about himself, an infinitesimal being that was all mind.

This marvelous speck of pure intelligence, traveling down the
Fallopian tube, possessed the secret of its own unique genetic
nature and fate. Because it was already Patchen and could not be
anything but what it was designed to be, it immediately set about
transforming itself into his body. Patchen's rudimentary heart appeared by the fourteenth day; his spine, brain, eyes, ears, alimen-
tary canal, and the buds of his limbs by the twenty-first, and then,
day by day and organ by organ, all the rest of his parts sprang into
being. Floating in the fragrant amniotic fluid, Patchen heard voices
from outside, saw light filtered through membranes, heard the
beating of an enormous heart above his head, felt his mother's
emotions coursing through his own body and so learned that there
were others like himself.

Was it possible to go farther back than this, beyond the muted
rosy light inside the womb, was it possible to break in two again
and rise up through the blood vessels and cells of his parents'
bodies, to swim into their very brains and find the storage places of
their own original memories of themselves, in which, surely, he
himself was already present along with all his ancestors and all his
descendants that he would never have? Was it possible to go

farther back, even, than that, possible to know *everything* by crossing the brilliant constellation of these innumerable generations of tiny minds like stepping-stones to their source, the Original Mind? Was knowing what Patchen had known in the first microsecond of physical being, before he set about manufacturing himself and forgot the secret of life in the travail of breaking its code, the same as knowing everything? Was this knowedge the bliss of Samadhi, satori, salvation, Martha's Inward Light? Was he on the threshold of understanding the infinite?

Even under the influence of the Versed that was dripping into his arm and the amphetamine that was being released into his bloodstream by the implant in his chest, Patchen could not bring himself to think so. If he was traveling through the infinite, how was it that he remembered things about the nature of the infinite that the speck-mind of the fertilized egg could not possibly have known and had no need to know? His bedtime reading flooded his memory with what he now recognized as false data—verses from the Upanishads, the arithmetical formula based on the Ceylon Chronicles for computing the dates of Gautama Buddha's birth and death, passage after passage from Genesis and Aquinas's *Summa Theologica,* a poem about ghosts written in Vietnam by Paul Christopher. He fought to bring his brain back to equilibrium. His conscious mind began to function again. A brilliant light shone into his eyes. No longer deceived, he knew it was a camera light. He saw strange figures moving through the glare and knew they were his captors. But what had happened to him before he began to think again? Where had he been? Had he gone farther back than he knew? Was he not where he thought he was now, but somewhere else? Where was his dog? Where were the Marines of his patrol, Corporal Bobby Poole and all the others? Where was Zarah? Where was Christopher? *Where?*

"You're home," a kindly voice said. "You're among friends. Everything is already known about everyone here; that's why we're so close. Nobody has any secrets. You can talk about anything to us. Anything."

It was an Outfit voice, female. Patchen thought he recognized it, but he could not place it. He hadn't heard it in years. To whom did it belong? He tried hard to visualize the face that went with the voice, but it was like a forgotten name.

"Don't try to remember anything in particular," the voice said.

"Particulars are not important. Relax. You can talk about anything. Anything at all. Start with a name. Any name. Tell me someone's name."

Patchen's head cleared as one drug momentarily overcame the other, and in this moment of lucidity he recognized his questioner. He was astonished. It was a face from the far past. How could this be? Was he hallucinating? He knew that he was not, that the face he saw before his eyes, though much older and more disappointed than the one he remembered, was the face he thought it was.

He said, "Joshua."

"Joshua?" the voice said. "Joshua who?"

"Joshua Josephson," Patchen replied. The amphetamine was helping at last. He was no longer dreaming. The heart he had heard beating was his own, accelerated by the drug. It pounded in his ears and temples. A thrill of pure energy coursed through his whole body, so strong that he had the brief illusion that he could use his left arm and leg or see out of his left eye if he wished to do so. His glass eye was still in place; he could feel it, or, rather, not feel the toothachey movement of air on the empty socket.

"Tell us about Joshua Josephson," the familiar voice said. "Is that a funny name or a real name?" The enunciation was not quite flawless, as happens with people who live too long abroad. He remembered that, too. He now remembered everything about this person in a long string of memories.

"Joshua was an unwitting asset," Patchen said. "We were having trouble with the priests."

"Where?"

"In Joshua's country. They were a threat to our authority. We wanted to put them under an obligation, make them easier to handle. So we sent in an agent to recruit this Joshua and run him against them. It was a political action operation. The objective was to put a thorn in their side, make them come to us for help getting rid of him."

"What was your agent's name?"

"Judas."

"I mean his true name. Please don't use cryptonyms."

"That was his true name. His father had been executed by the imperialists for underground activity; the son belonged to the same secret underground his father had, twenty years earlier. He built a cell around Joshua, eleven assets besides himself. They weren't much as revolutionaries go. It was low-grade agit-prop—street-corner speeches about bribery and corruption in high places, demonstrations and rabble-rousing, nothing serious. But it was enough to alarm the priests. Joshua was beginning to have a following. So they came to us for help. We set Joshua up, asked the local police to arrest him. Judas was supposed to finger him for the cops, who didn't even know who he was, but he had the case officer's disease, he loved his agent more than he loved the operation. He tried to warn him. Joshua wouldn't listen; he *wanted* to be arrested, he wanted to be a martyr to the cause; it happens. He got his wish, and after he was arrested and executed, Judas hanged himself. We planted some money on the corpse to make it look like he had been bribed by the police to turn in his leader. Everybody bought it; he was branded a traitor, a police spy. Nobody suspected us. The op was a success. We had the priests where we wanted them, they owed us. And we had ten assets under discipline for future reference. But the problem was, what might Judas have written to give the game away before he died? He was twice as smart as any of the others, and he was the only one who knew we were involved. We had to discredit his version before it was published, assuming it even existed. So we got the others to write reports of the operation making Judas the villain. That was the end of it."

"Very funny, David," the voice said to him, patting him maternally on the cheek. "But it won't work." And then to somebody else who was concealed behind the lights, the voice said, "He's resisting the drug."

"But he's talking."

"Yes. And telling us the story of Jesus Christ as a Roman spy thriller. Step up the dosage. I'll go talk to the girl."

2

NEARBY, YEHO SAID, "WE LOST HASSAN ABDALLAH."

"*Lost* him?" Christopher said. "How can you lose somebody on a road that has no crossroads?"

It was well after midnight. They were standing in a light snowfall on an unpaved road in the Alpes de Haute Provence. The ground was beginning to be dusted, and the dark coat of Patchen's Doberman, quivering at Christopher's knee, was also turning white.

"We should get into the car," Yeho said. "Otherwise we'll leave tracks."

Inside the automobile, Yeho continued his narrative. Abdallah and three companions had vanished. Yeho's team, who had followed their car all the way from Geneva, had bracketed it with vehicles of their own, two in front and two behind. Because of the switchbacks it was impossible to stay completely out of sight and still maintain contact, but they had maintained a considerable distance so as to allay suspicion. After all, where could they go? There was not so much as a gravel pit into which to turn, much less hide. But when the lead car reached the bottom of the mountain just after dark and pulled off the road to let the next vehicle to take its place, it was observed that the terrorists' car was empty except for the driver, Hassan Abdallah's French girlfriend. She continued on, under surveillance, and checked in, alone, at a mountain hotel a few kilometers away on the Italian side of the Lombard Pass.

Christopher said, "That means Hassan and two others got out of the car and continued on foot."

"But which way?" Yeho said. He began to unfold a large-scale topographical map of the area.

"Did anyone try to follow them?"

"What was the point? They were already gone. Besides, the tag team were not Ibal Iden. Like you and me, they're too old to go scrambling over Alps. They did the correct thing—continued on their way and reported. So we can assume Hassan Abdallah doesn't know he was being followed." Yeho shone a flashlight on the map. "The Nazi and his friends got out somewhere in here," he said, drawing a circle with the beam. "They could either go east to Italy, where they have absolutely no reason to go, or they could go over the top of this hill to the *mas,* which is here." He switched off the torch. "They can't get inside without being seen by the Ibal Iden, so what have we lost?"

"Certainty," Christopher said. "That's all."

The *mas,* a stone farmhouse, was built into a steep hillside. From the top it looked like a shepherd's hut of uncut stone, but seen from the bottom it was a three-story structure cut into the living rock and finished with stone and mortar. From the military point of view it was an almost impregnable position, because the tall side of the house commanded a clear field of fire along its entire front, and there was no other visible way in except through the back, which could be defended by one armed man, or even sealed with a small explosive charge if the defenders were willing to die inside.

"I've told the boys and girls to let Hassan and his men go inside in peace," Yeho said.

"*You've* told them?"

"I know you're in charge of them, but there was no time to go through channels."

"How long ago was that?"

"Over two hours. One of them is supposed to report here at fifty-five minutes after midnight."

It was now 12:50. Exactly five minutes later Ja'wab appeared, his parka covered with snow. The road was white with it. Yeho rolled down his window.

"They haven't approached the house," Ja'wab said. "I think we should start hunting them. We can take Hassan before he goes in, then go into the house and get the others."

"No," Christopher said.

"No?" Ja'wab said. "How long do you think Zarah will last after she starts talking under the drug?"

Christopher, who had got out of the car, looked down on Ja'wab, surprised again at how small he was, and by the worry in his face. He said, "If you didn't see them, Ja'wab, they're inside by now."

"Inside?" Yeho said. "How can they be inside?"

"If you lived in a house built into the side of a mountain," Christopher said, "and you used it as a place to interrogate people you had kidnapped, and it had a front door and a back door that everyone could see, what would you do?"

"I'd make a hidden door, a secret way to get out."

"Or in," Christopher said. "A tunnel. Ja'wab, I want to talk to you again an hour after sunrise. Go back now. Yeho and I are going to get up higher, where we can see the house and wait for the sun to come up."

3

CHRISTOPHER CHOSE A LOOKOUT POINT A MILE OR TWO UP THE ROAD. It commanded a view of the back of the villa. The snow squall was slackening; Christopher put the Doberman outside and told it to guard the car.

Yeho unzipped an airline bag and handed Christopher a Glock pistol. "Take this," he said. Christopher made no move to accept the weapon. "*Take* it," Yeho repeated. Christopher did so, and worked the action to make certain it was unloaded. Yeho handed him two clips of ammunition, one of ordinary size and the other twice as long. "In the regular clip are all copper rounds, the ones that expand after hitting the target. I know you hate guns even though you're such a good shot, but do me a favor and load it. I want to be able to sleep without worry."

Christopher shoved the shorter clip into the pistol, worked the slide and the safety, and placed it on the passenger seat beside him.

"You can sleep first," he said.

"Okay. Here," Yeho said, handing over a large buff envelope. "It's the sunbathers."

There wasn't enough light to look at photographs and Christopher did not want to use the flashlight, so he dropped the envelope on top of the pistol. Yeho stretched on the backseat—he could do so without discomfort—and began to snore.

At dawn Christopher got out of the car and located the *mas* on the lower horizon. This was no easy task even with nine-power binoculars. Like the rest of the landscape, the house was floured with last night's snow, and from Christopher's vantage point, two miles distant or more, the part that could be seen against the low horizon looked like a heap of rubble left by an avalanche. Using Yeho's map to measure distances, he located and memorized a dozen landmarks in a semicircle around the *mas*. As the sun, rising to his left so that it threw visible shadows, grew stronger, he watched the snow melt. After about twenty minutes he saw what he was looking for—a dark, unnaturally square spot where the snow melted faster than elsewhere because there was air beneath it rather than earth and rock. This was the entrance to the tunnel. A clearly discernible track led to it from the road.

Something moved at the edge of Christopher's field of vision. He put the glasses on the object. It was Tammuz, one of the Ibal Iden, rising up out of the scrub where he had lain hidden throughout the night. Hassan Abdallah and the others had virtually stepped over him on their way inside.

Yeho drove. As the car moved slowly down the steep road, shocks jittering on the washboard surface of the road, Christopher opened the envelope and began to look at the thick sheaf of large photographic prints inside.

"You were right about something else," Yeho said. "It's truly amazing how many pictures these photographers take. They shoot everyone. Out of maybe ten thousand slides we found twenty-five shots of our friend and his wife. In about a dozen of those they're talking to other people, or just in proximity to them. We didn't know any of them. How about you?"

Christopher shuffled the prints. Beach scenes: umbrellas, blankets, soft drink bottles, sand castles. All the human subjects were nude. The photographs, taken mostly through long lenses, were slightly distorted, but faces and bodies were sharp enough: Hassan Abdallah, hairy and stringy, and his Genevese wife talking in a beach café to a bloated man with his arm around a stout woman; chatting to a slimmer couple by a beach umbrella; playing volleyball with flaccid breasts and penises flying. There were also a dozen candid shots of what seemed to be an intense conversation with a well-preserved woman in her fifties. It was obvious that she had possessed a lovely figure when young; even now it photographed beautifully, which was why the photographer had kept the camera on her for such a long sequence. In one particularly artistic frame, the woman had thrown her head back in order to inhale deeply from a cigarette, inflating, as it seemed, her large, girlishly uptilted breasts.

It was Maria Rothchild.

"You dwell on that one," Yeho said, watching out of the corner of his eye. "Are you admiring the cantaloupes, or do you see something else?"

"I know this woman," Christopher said.

Through the windshield, he saw Ja'wab waiting at the appointed spot beside the road ahead, and got out of the car before it stopped moving.

4

THE DARK, WINDOWLESS ROOM INSIDE THE *MAS* WHERE ZARAH WAS being held had walls of unplastered rock and a concrete floor. She knew this much from having explored the space around her with her bare feet. She was naked, handcuffed to the head of the iron cot on which she was lying. Her cell was so cold and damp, and such a good place for the rats she thought she heard scampering in the darkness, that she supposed that she was in a cellar.

A bosomy middle-aged woman in a thick sweater and a tartan skirt opened the plank door and turned on the feeble French light bulb that dangled from the ceiling. She checked Zarah's handcuffs to make sure they were still locked, then leaned against the rough wall and looked her up and down.

"Are you all right?" she asked in brisk Oxbridge English.

"I have to go to the toilet," Zarah said.

"Of course you do, you poor thing. It's been *hours*."

The woman's tone was filled with womanly solidarity, as if she herself had often been handcuffed naked to a bed in a frigid dungeon while longing to urinate, and only the two of them could understand the feeling. She freed Zarah's left wrist, snapping the empty cuff back on to the frame of the bed, and set a galvanized bucket closer.

"It's more comfortable if you don't sit all the way down," she said.

Zarah, crouching over the bucket, tried to turn her back, but this was impossible.

"Don't be embarrassed," the woman said. "I took care of an invalid husband for many years. I am beyond disgust."

"Lucky you."

The woman smiled, very brightly. "You sound like your mother."

"You knew my mother?"

"We were at school together."

"What school was that?"

"Miss Porter's in Farmington, Connecticut."

"Is that where you learned to talk like that?"

"This is a very strange conversation, Zarah. Do you always try to catch people you've just met in lies?"

"It depends on the circumstances. What name did my mother know you by?"

"Maria," the woman said. "Maria Custer."

"I'm sorry," Zarah said. "Mother never mentioned that name."

She pushed the bucket away but remained crouched by the head of the bed. It was that or lie down on the bare straw mattress; the cuffs were too short to permit standing up. She was clear-headed,

even exhilarated. The effects of the Versed that had been injected
into her neck at the moment of capture had worn off.

"You don't *look* like your mother," her jailer said in a conversational tone. "But then, who ever did? Paul Christopher is your
father?"

"That's right."

"You resemble him. He'd do anything for old men when he was
young. But you can't really be in love with a freak like David
Patchen, can you?"

Zarah said, "You don't really sound like a friend of the family,
you know."

The woman laughed again, evidently delighted by Zarah's spunk.
"Oh, but I'm not; I never was more than a useful acquaintance."
She reached into the pocket of her cardigan and produced a pack of
French cigarettes. She lighted one with a match, inhaled so deeply
that the paper crackled, and blew the acrid smoke out through her
nose. After this one prodigious drag she flicked the long stub of the
caporal into the bucket.

"Anyway I'm glad to meet *you*," she said. "You may think,
considering the circumstances, that it would have been better if we
never met." She lifted an eyebrow, waiting for Zarah to say something, but she did not. The woman shrugged and continued. "All I
can tell you is, I did my best to prevent it when you were still a
tadpole. But Cathy wouldn't listen."

She handed Zarah her clothes. "Now you'd better get dressed.
I'm sorry about the enforced immodesty, but we had to check out
your garments. Your father once caught a Russian spy, who just
happened to be his best friend, by loaning him his raincoat—an
Aquascutum, of course; Paul would never have been so uncouth as
to wear a Burberry. It had a bug sewn into the hem. Did anyone
ever tell you that story?"

"No."

"Well, now you know. There are so many stories about your
father. He was the best ever at what he did, a member of the
all-time Outfit backfield. I'm sure David has told you that. Question is, are you really your father's daughter?"

Zarah said, "Can I get dressed now? It's cold in here."

"I know. And the stones make it seem colder than it is. Sorry. It
was the men who undressed you. I would have done it myself, but I

was totally occupied with David. He's a very difficult man. Were you insulted in any way?"

"I was searched."

"But not harmed?"

"It's hard to remember. My head was swimming."

"Allah is merciful."

"Does Allah have something to do with this situation?"

The woman laughed at this new defiance. "No." She smiled broadly. "All appearances to the contrary notwithstanding, nothing. Much older gods than him are at the bottom of this. Now turn your back, please, while I unlock the handcuffs."

Zarah felt the muzzle of a pistol pressed against the base of her skull, on the exact spot where the Versed had been injected. She got into her underwear, skirt and sweater. The pistol remained pressed against her head, following her every move. She expected to feel the sting of another injection at any moment, but this did not happen. When she was fully dressed the woman cuffed her ankles together, then turned her around. She had put the pistol away, probably in the back of her tartan skirt because Zarah could not see its outline from the front. She grasped Zarah's jaw and gently turned her face this way and that.

"Do you know what I think, Zarah?" she said. "I think we're going to be great friends. We have a lot more in common than you may realize."

Zarah did not speak or make a gesture. Her hands were free now; she knew that she could overpower this woman, kneel on her back, break her neck, take her weapon. It was the wrong time.

"Do you?" Zarah said. "Do we?"

"Oh, yes. You're going to be astonished at what a long way we go back, you and I. I may have been the first person to know that you were coming into the world. And that's not all. Give me your hand."

Zarah complied. The woman pressed something into her palm, a piece of paper folded into a very small square. Zarah unfolded it. It was the other half of the hundred dollar bill that Barney Wolkowicz had given her ten years before when he said goodbye to her under the Ja'wabi date tree, on the road to Tinzár.

"IT CAN'T BE DONE IN THE DARK," YEHO SAID. "YOU SHOULD WAIT until dawn tomorrow. It has to work the first time. There'll be no second chance."

He had just heard Christopher's plan for attacking the *mas* at nightfall and rescuing the prisoners.

"Dawn tomorrow is almost twenty-four hours from now," Ja'wab said. "If what Paul says about this woman is true, if she's out for revenge, they may both be dead by then. We have to go in as soon as it's dark."

"People like Hassan Abdallah get away in the dark," Yeho said. "If he runs away through his tunnel you'll lose him."

"Then we'll go in now, in daylight."

"If you do that you'll lose your people," Yeho said. "All of them, maybe. Hassan is not alone. He has lookouts, weapons, hostages. I know you want to save Zarah because to you she's one of the Ja'wabi. But if you save her life and let Hassan get away, all the Ja'wabi may die a year from now or ten years from now. She will have died for nothing. Your people will have died because you didn't think about them. Remember what this operation is all about. The objective is to capture Hassan Abdallah. He's your enemy, not some hysterical female with an old grudge against Patchen and Christopher. She's irrelevant; shoot her and forget her. He's a lunatic, a Nazi, a carrier of disease. Paul, remind him."

"Ja'wab remembers all that," Christopher said. "It isn't just the woman and what she might do. You should remember who Patchen is. If we don't go in now we may be brushed aside. The Director of the Outfit has disappeared in France. What if *that's* on television this evening? What if the French police come in? What if the Outfit decides to send in an assault team to rescue him? Then everybody inside the house *will* die, and we'll never see Hassan Abdallah again."

"You're a thinker," Yeho said. "A real thinker. I admire that. I understand all the risks, maybe better than you. But wait for the right time. What difference can a few hours make?"

Christopher was kneeling on the wet road beside Patchen's Doberman, examining the battery pack and radio receiver riveted to the leather strap around the dog's neck.

"My friend, forget about fancy dog collars," Yeho said. "This is no time for bright ideas. Don't put into the soup kettle something new and complicated at this late hour. Just go inside when it's dark and kill them all. Except Hassan."

Christopher stood up with the collar in his hands. ' 'I hear you, Yeho," he said.

"Hearing is not enough," Yeho said. "I hope you're *listening* to me. Forget gimmicks. This is a cave we're dealing with, and the mentality of the cave. We're in the Stone Age with this murderer, so fight him with stones."

6

PATCHEN KEPT HEARING MARIA ROTHCHILD'S VOICE AND SMELLING the smoke from her stinking Gauloises Bleues cigarettes, but he knew these sensations were only a dream. In reality he was floating in a sampan on the River of Perfumes, listening to a tinny phonograph record of a girl singing in Vietnamese. Vo Rau translated the lyrics: "She says that God is the smallest thing in the universe, so small that he cannot be imagined; he does not wish to be imagined, so he fills the sky with the stars that are his uncountable thoughts and we look not at the place where he is, but at the places where he has never been." Patchen nodded sagaciously; this much of the truth he had already perceived. How beautifully the girl sang, how the river smelled of the flowers that turned its torpid waters into perfume, how much like his own mind and voice were the mind and voice of Vo Rau! It was uncanny.

Someone seized Patchen's lower lip and twisted. The pain changed his idea of where he was. Maria Rothchild said, "Wake up, David." His right eye focused, briefly, and he glimpsed Maria's face. A second later he was back in Vietnam; evidently it was midday, because the sun was almost unbearably bright. The phonograph started up again. Vo Rau murmured, "Now she is singing about war." Someone twisted Patchen's lip again. Maria's voice said, "What is your name?" Patchen replied, "Patchen, David S., 041167, second lieutenant, USMCR." His vision cleared completely this time. The woman before his eyes *was* Maria Rothchild, no longer young and speaking with a different accent, as though like one of Gertrude Stein's characters she had come to Europe to cultivate her voice. She had the angry face of someone who has made herself ill with politics. Beyond her looming figure Patchen saw a television camera with its blinding lights, and beyond that, Zarah Christopher in shackles. "David, listen," Maria said. "David, where are you?" She twisted his lip again. "Judging by the personnel," he replied, "Hell." Maria went on talking to Patchen in an urgent British voice. He didn't bother to listen because he was straining to hear what Vo Rau, who had been joined in the sampan by Christopher, was saying. They were speaking a language he did not understand. It did not sound like Vietnamese.

Hassan Abdallah, wearing a Palestinian shawl drawn across his face in the presence of his prisoners, took Patchen's blood pressure and listened to his heart through a stethoscope. He shined a flashlight into his right eye. "He's telling us nothing," he said in Arabic. "Something is wrong."

He aimed the beam of the flashlight into Patchen's other eye and recoiled. "What is this?" he cried, ripping the false eye from its socket and throwing it to the floor. He smashed it with his heel and found among the shards a tiny transmitter and the battery, no larger than a fish scale, that operated it. "Why wasn't this found before he was brought here?" he cried. "Put it in water at once! I want four men outside immediately to sweep the area for surveillance. If you find anyone, bring them to me for questioning. Bring two if you can."

Zarah had been given no more Versed, or any other drug, since Maria came for her. She knew that this meant that her captors intended to kill her, because she saw, heard, and understood everything and they did not seem to care. Hassan slapped Patchen's face. Maria put a comforting arm around Zarah's shoulders. Patchen was counting in German, *"Eins, zwei, drei, VIER!"* Maria said, "Why is he doing that? He doesn't speak German." Zarah shrugged. Maria had been questioning her about Patchen's every word and movement for more than an hour now. It was obvious that Patchen was not reacting to Versed as they had expected. He displayed the euphoria that was one of the drug's effects but not the usual cooperativeness and urge to confess. When he talked at all he babbled nonsense, quoting long passages from books, reciting lists of wines, conversing with unseen companions about baseball, but saying nothing useful.

"Can you give him more?" Maria asked.

"Only if you want to kill him."

"Not yet," Maria said.

Zarah understood them with difficulty because they spoke Palestinian Arabic which was so different from the Maghrib pronunciation.

"I'm going to stop the drip," Hassan said. He ripped the needle from Patchen's arm. "When he wakes up we'll talk man to man." He began to feel Patchen's naked body, inch by inch, as if searching for something under the skin.

Maria turned to Zarah. "I know this is painful to watch," she said in English. "Just remember: This is mild compared to what Patchen did to Barney Wolkowicz after he framed him—drugged him, put him into a cell, took away everything, even his clothes, tortured his body, manipulated his mind and his emotions, threatened to have his wife committed to an insane asylum. Barney wrote it all down. Here, read it."

She handed Zarah an envelope. Inside, written in Wolkowicz's unmistakable hand, was a letter providing details of his captivity in a secret Outfit installation after he had been seized by Patchen's men. Zarah read it; the first two pages were missing.

"It's as clear as clear can be," Maria said. "Patchen charged Barney with the crime he had committed himself, delivering your father into a Chinese prison, and got away with it. Even your father believed him. Paul Christopher was the one who caught Barney. Patchen couldn't have done it without him, he's never been able to do anything without Paul. He always lived on your father's talent like a snake sucking milk. I told you about the bugged raincoat; typical Christopher. Here, read for yourself."

She handed over the missing pages from the letter. It described Paul Christopher's homecoming, his investigation of his own case, the trap he and Patchen laid to capture Wolkowicz and brand him a traitor. Maria, anxious and maternal, waited until Zarah was through reading.

"Barney Wolkowicz wasn't the first good person the two of them destroyed," Maria said. "Far from it. Patchen did the same to my husband with your father's help, and to me because I loved my husband and believed in your father's honesty. There were others, a lot of them, before and after us. Remember your mother. She was a victim. Patchen used your father to do his dirty work for him, to win people's trust, because everyone always loved Paul Christopher. No one has ever loved Patchen . . . Zarah, I want you to tell me why Patchen isn't affected by the drug. Did he take something?"

Zarah did not answer. Maria rearranged her tangled hair for her with a few deft movements and gazed lovingly into her eyes. "Please tell me," she said. "Because if you don't, that man will ask you the same question."

Hassan was cutting into Patchen's chest with a small Swiss Army knife, delicately, feeling for something with a finger inserted beneath the skin. Suddenly he uttered a triumphant grunt and ripped out the implant. "Clever bastard!" he said, holding it aloft. A trickle of blood, surprisingly dark, meandered among the purple contours of Patchen's scars.

Hassan took a stun gun out of his pocket and pressed it against the reopened incision. Zarah saw Patchen's body leap convulsively under the electric shock; he appeared to stop breathing for a moment but then uttered a strangled scream. Hassan jammed the intravenous needle into another vein in Patchen's arm. *"Now* we'll see," he said.

"Don't be upset," Maria whispered. "He can feel it now but he won't remember it later. It will be like the pain never existed."

Hassan used the stun gun on Patchen again, this time on his face. Patchen saw the Japanese grenade explode and heard himself screaming for a corpsman. Christopher appeared out of the smoke of battle in helmet and denims, carrying another Marine in his arms like a child. A naked Japanese soldier, gibbering in terror and missing a hand, rose up in front of him. His stump spurted blood. Christopher stopped in his tracks, immediately understanding what was happening, and waited for the man to finish bleeding to death; he did not seem to be afraid or compassionate or even curious; he did not touch a weapon, he simply watched. Then he laid the American he was carrying on the ground and gave Patchen an injection of morphine. Patchen's vision cleared momentarily and he saw Christopher's face quite distinctly in the blue-white flash of exploding naval ordnance. In a confidential murmur, Christopher said, "I'm going to carry you for a few yards, put you down, then come back for the other fellow. Then I'll come back for you. I won't leave you. You'll be taking turns. Do you understand?" Patchen opened his mouth to reply but instead of the civil "yes" he had intended to utter, he shouted hysterically for the corpsman; Christopher gave him more morphine, his own syrette. The Vietnamese girl began to sing again. Christopher carried Patchen and the other Marine across the mud; Christopher himself was wounded and paused to bandage his injury. Because he could no longer walk he dragged first Patchen then the other man toward the American lines, counting softly in German. A mortar shell exploded nearby. The Vietnamese girl, dancing in her white *ao dai* on the sun-drenched River of Perfumes, continued to sing. With grave Oriental courtesy Vo Rau said, "I'm very sorry, I don't understand German, but *she* is singing that when God decides to make himself visible to us he approaches not in fire and majesty from the immensity of the heavens but shyly and intelligently, as a buddha, out of the body of a woman." On hearing these words, Patchen saw the Inward Light. It was immensely small though it contained innumerable collapsed universes with all their indescribable luminosity; inside, as from inside his mother, the light was rosy, but vast. The rescue complete, Christopher laid him down in the sampan and went back for the other wounded Marine. One of the troops fired eight rapid shots from an M1 rifle which ejected the empty clip with the familiar SPANG! Martha stood in the bow of the sampan with gossamer sails billowing around her beautiful young body. "O David, I am so happy for thee," she said. Patchen opened his lips to thank her for her patience and understanding, and once he began to speak he could not stop. He told her over and over again that he loved her. He had never been so happy as he was now, even though he heard mortar shells exploding all around him and he knew that he was dying of his wounds at last.

7

HASSAN ABDALLAH HAD THROWN HIS RED-CHECKERED *KAFFIYEH* aside, baring his face. He looked, Zarah thought, like a disgruntled clerk who had never been given the promotions he knew he deserved. While Patchen made his intoxicated confession, Hassan operated the television camera himself, as a means of showing his displeasure at the inefficient way in which Patchen had been searched. There were three of his people in the room, but he ignored them. The four he had sent outside to take prisoners had not come back. The others stood idly by, shamefaced, with their weapons in their hands.

Hassan was peering through the camera lens at Patchen's smiling features when the charges set by the Ibal Iden went off, blowing off the doors of the *mas*. These first two explosions were muffled and far away, but there was a louder bang as the trap door to the tunnel that led into the room blew inward. The pressure wave knocked Patchen off his chair and staggered the guards who stood beside him.

All this Hassan saw through the lens of the camera. Then he, too, was knocked off his feet—not by the explosion but by an assailant who came out of the hole in the floor and struck him from behind with terrific force, jamming the camera against his face and starting a nosebleed. Using the camera as a weapon, Hassan struck hard at his attacker, thinking to smash his face, but the blow struck only empty air. He felt an excruciating pain in his leg, and looking downward, saw that he was being bitten by an enormous black dog. He smashed the camera against the animal's skull with one hand in a series of frantic but ineffectual blows while reaching for his pistol with the other.

Ja'wab and Tammuz came into the room shooting. All three of Hassan's men died in less than three seconds. Hassan had reached his own pistol by this time and holding off the dog with his other hand, he shot Tammuz through the forehead. Tammuz's pistol, fitted with an elongated ammunition clip that protruded from the butt, spun from his hand. Maria picked up the weapon, and with her eyes fixed on Ja'wab, began to raise it expertly into the firing position. Ja'wab's pistol was pointed straight at Hassan's head, but Hassan knew that he had no intention of killing him. Ja'wab shouted something in incomprehensible Arabic, then saw Maria out of the corner of his eye and leaped backward through the door just as she fired the first round at him; it slammed into the rocks. Maria charged the door and fired half a dozen rounds into the darkness. Hassan jabbed the muzzle of his weapon into the dog's rumbling chest, pressed the trigger three times, and saw the Parabellum bullets, trailed by streamers of blood, strike the wall on the other side of the room. He rolled free of the dead animal and leaped into the tunnel.

Zarah, her ankles still shackled, had floundered across the floor to the place where Patchen lay. Just as she reached him Patchen got to his feet. He was smiling joyously, oblivious to the hail of bullets ricocheting off the masonry walls. Zarah saw Maria pointing her captured Glock, loaded with Yeho's copper bullets, at the two of them. Zarah, fighting her shackles, stood up and threw her arms around Patchen, intending to pull him back to the floor, but Patchen saw Maria, too, and with his one incredibly strong arm whirled Zarah off her feet, placing his body between hers and the gun. Maria fired two shots, Outfit-style, into Patchen's thorax. The soft copper bullets opened within him just as Yeho had said they would, then stopped before they reached Zarah. Ja'wab stepped back into the room and killed her, too late.

Patchen grunted loudly and said, "I remembered." It seemed to Zarah, then and for the rest of her life, that he spoke these words with his last breath, after he had stopped the expanding bullet with his body. He was talking to Christopher, who had climbed out of the tunnel carrying the splayed, unconscious person of Hassan Abdallah in his arms. Patchen's weight pulled Zarah to her knees when she tried to keep his smiling corpse from falling.

THANKSGIVING

LLA KAHINA AND SEBASTIAN LAUX STOOD BY A STONE WALL WITH the O. G., a little apart from the other mourners among the tilted headstones in the graveyard at the Harbor. It was very early in the morning on Thanksgiving Day, and a wind that smelled of winter howled in the surrounding forest. The moss beneath their feet was brittle with frost. The gravestones of the Hubbards and Christophers had been planted in rings, one for each generation. Christopher and Martha stood in the center among the elongated shadows thrown by the barely risen northern sun, holding the funeral urn between them. Christopher removed the lid and the wind stirrred David Patchen's ashes. There were no prayers, no stone engraved with his favorite verse from Housman, no eulogy by the O. G.; everyone knew that the deceased hated ceremony.

"It's very strange," Lla Kahina said, "but I never saw this man, never."

"In life, you mean, or in the cards?" Sebastian asked.

"Not in either. What did he look like?"

Stephanie gave them a surprised look. They were not whispering. Sebastian, taking Meryem's arm in his, drew her closer. "The truthful answer," he said, "is 'like a corpse.' Tall, thin, limping, mournful, with a scarred face and a crippled arm. He was wounded in the war, almost mortally."

Martha and Christopher tipped the urn and shook it. At first Patchen's ashes were a little too heavy for the wind, but after a short delay they ascended in a fluttering cloud before breaking apart, as it seemed, molecule by molecule, and disappearing into swirling air.

"You say he was almost killed in the war?" Lla Kahina said.

"That explains it. Sometimes people die before they die. He must have had some debt to pay and remained in this life to pay it."

Although he had not seen her since the summer of 1939, Sebastian knew from the tone of her voice that she thought that Patchen's long-ago escape from death explained everything. Maybe it did; he was willing to think so. The beaky, shrunken Meryem standing beside him now was the same Meryem who had been able to see through mountains and across the deeps of time when he first loved her; she knew things that were too simple for others to understand. As if she had read Sebastian's thoughts, Zarah smiled at him across the concentric, weatherworn headstones.

The O. G. thought Zarah was smiling at him. "Lovely young woman," he said in a hearty voice, grinning back with his healthy square old teeth. "David did right to do what he did for her."

Lla Kahina gave him a questioning look. "What was that?"

"Died to save her life," the O. G. said. "You didn't know?"

"No. I told you, he was invisible to me."

"You weren't the only one," the O. G. said. "Anyway, it was about time somebody died for a Christopher instead of the other way around." He sighed, lost in his own memories. "Circles within circles," he said. "I first laid eyes on David right here, on this very spot, when we buried Hubbard Christopher. That must have been forty years ago, wasn't it, Sebastian?"

"Nineteen hundred and forty-eight," said Sebastian, who never forgot a number.

They turned to go, each old man holding one of Meryem's arms to assist her over the rough path that led down through the overgrown pasture to the Harbor, which lay with smoking chimneys in the vale below.

At Thanksgiving breakfast the O. G. made a toast in ale that included Patchen: "Absent friends." Nothing more than that was said about him. Under the rules of marriage and friendship and the laws of the United States of America, no one present, not even the O. G., was free to discuss in the presence of others secrets they knew about the deceased. In his last operation Patchen had achieved what he wanted. The White House had already announced that the Outfit had been irreparably compromised by the capture of its last Director, and that it must be replaced by a new intelligence service that could operate in a world in which there would be no deadly enemies, only the disappointed, the disillusioned, and the deluded. This string of evocative words beginning with "d" was Patrick

Graham's invention; Graham had coined the phrase while announcing not just the death of the Outfit but the dawn of a new
era. He suggested in his wrap-up remarks from the White House
(at the O. G.'s confidential suggestion, the President had given him
an exclusive interview in which he had revealed his thoughts about
the future of American espionage and intelligence) that the future
might see a world without secrets in which Americans and Russians, Israelis and Arabs, Hindus and Moslems, Christians and
Communists worked hand in hand on earth as they were already
doing in outer space. Both activities, after all, were intelligence
missions, searches for pure knowledge as opposed to the patho-
logical appetite for secrets that had driven the Outfit throughout its
short, anti-democratic, maddeningly obscure history. ("Jeepers Ned!"
responded the O. G., watching at home, among his souvenirs.)

After breakfast Martha said goodbye; she had to catch a plane
for Guatemala.

"Will you be back?" Christopher asked.

"Oh, quite soon," Martha said. "I'm only going to say goodbye
to my Indians."

"After all these years?"

"There's no reason to go back. The children will all be gone
soon; the guerrillas keep coming back for more. Maybe they've got
a Zarah of their own. David would be so happy that our Zarah did
the great thing for the Ja'wabi that she was born to do."

"Do you think he believed in such things?"

"Everyone does, inwardly. Doesn't thee?"

Her unwavering eyes looked deep into Christopher's. He kissed
her, gently, on both cheeks.

"Of course I do," he said.

Soon after Martha departed Christopher got out the treasure map
and marked the square to be searched this year. There were very
few left. Only he and Zarah and Lori went on the treasure hunt;
everyone else except Stephanie was too old, and she did not believe
that the treasure existed.

It was Lori who found the ledge with the letter "T" carved on it. It
was only a few paces from the fallen maple that had concealed the
Mahican burial ground. Christopher had walked past it many times
without seeing it, and Lori had only noticed it because the angle of the
light was exactly right. The "T" was not printed but carved in script,
like a note of music, so it mimicked the natural cracks in the granite.

Christopher took a compass sighting while Zarah and Lori stretched a cord thirty-five paces straight north from the ledge. Kneeling in a circle, they dug into the soft forest floor with their hands and sharp stones. They uncovered a rusted log chain about eighteen inches below the surface. "That's from the apple tree split by lightning," said Lori, who knew her Harbor lore. "The treasure chest will be more than three feet down, below the frost level."

They found it at four feet, a tin box inside another tin box. Within the second box were mad Eleazer Stickles's treasures: a handful of gold pieces, a locket containing a picture of his wife, a letter to posterity confessing the murder of her lover and of the innocent man who hanged for the crime.

There was something else in the box, something that did not belong there: a title page torn from a rag-paper copy of *The Adventures of Tom Sawyer,* a novel published forty years after Stickles died. A row of numbers was written across it in pencil with the date abbreviated below in the European style, 27.XI.47—the day that Wolkowicz found the Mahican burial ground.

"What is it?" Lori asked.

"A book code," Christopher said. "Go down to the house and tell them the news, and bring back *Tom Sawyer* from the library. We'll meet you in the graveyard."

It was the right book; the title page was missing. Sitting on the stone wall, Christopher looked up the pages and the letters of the alphabet corresponding to the scribbled numerals and decoded Wolkowicz's message: KILROY WUZ HERE.

Christopher laughed out loud. Tears rose in Zarah's eyes. The wind roared inside the forest. A wedge of Canada geese, wintering against nature on some Berkshire pond where city people gave them food, flew overhead. Lori pressed her cheek against her father's and gestured for her sister to do the same. All three joined hands, and in the rapturous, slightly hoarse voice that filled Christopher's heart with love and his mind with memories, the little girl recited the lines he had taught her in the only language that lions understand:

> Lion, Lion, burning bright
> In the forests of the night,
> What immortal hand or eye
> Dare frame thy fearful symmetry?

To the Reader

On one occasion Matisse was showing a lady a picture of his in which he had painted a naked woman, and the lady exclaimed, "But a woman isn't like that": to which he answered, "It isn't a woman, madam, it's a picture."

—W. SOMERSET MAUGHAM
Points of View

Second Sight is the seventh and final volume of the long episodic novel about Paul Christopher and his family that I have been writing over the past eighteen years. Like the six earlier freestanding volumes in the series, this one is a work of fiction in which characters and their actions and the institution called "the Outfit" are imaginary. Where historical detail falling outside the mechanism of the story is concerned, however, I have, as before, tried to avoid departures from the accepted facts. Thus, although the Ja'wabi and their history are invented, the existence of tribes of Jews among the Berbers before the Arab conquest and the legend of Joab's pursuit of the Philistines into North Africa are firmly established; Punic, the language spoken and written in Carthage and elsewhere in the far Maghrib, is thought by scholars to have been similar to the Hebrew spoken in Canaan in the Late Bronze Age and the Early Iron Age. I have devised a fate for Joab that differs from the one recorded in the Bible, but my account of his relations with King David and King Solomon is meant to be consistent with

2 Samuel and 1 Kings. Kahina, the seer-leader of the Jerawa Berbers, is a historical personage mentioned by Ibn Khaldūn, among many others, and I have made no attempt to embellish her life or character. Reinhard Heydrich's encounters with the Christophers and Meryem are notional, but his personality, habits, physical appearance, and real-life crimes are taken from the archives. Patchen's quotations regarding the *Wandervögel* and the Hitler Youth are from the actual books cited. I have mined the works of writers from the authors of Genesis onward for details to support my story, but I owe a particular debt to General Melchior Joseph Eugène Daumas's wonderful account of nomad life in the French Maghrib in the nineteenth century, *Les chevaux du Sahara et les moeurs du désert,* from which I have borrowed Meryem's name, the poem on 177, and more than a little of the desert lore attributed to the Ja'wabi. Scriptural quotations are from The New Jerusalem Bible and (usually) from Arthur J. Arberry's translation of the Koran. Martha Patchen's Indians have their origins in a story told to me more than thirty years ago by Alfonso Crespo of La Paz, Bolivia. Aamir Ali, who has climbed many of the peaks in the main range of the Alps, refreshed my memory as to their nomenclature. Bruce M. Cowan, M. D., provided advice on medical matters, as he has done with previous volumes, but it should be mentioned that I disregarded Dr. Cowan's warning of mortal consequences when I permitted Patchen to inject himself with an amphetamine as an antidote to Versed. Professor Tran Van Dinh reviewed the sections dealing with Vietnamese culture and mythology; references to the latter owe much to the admirable *Village in Vietnam* by Gerald Cannon Hickey. Marjorie E. Rynas searched many libraries for source material and Nancy Stanford McCarry checked the manuscript for accuracy. Any remaining errors are the result of my own carelessness or the requirements of the plot.

—C. McC.